MW00791222

HOME FIRES

W.L. RIPLEY

WOLFPACK
PUBLISHING
— EST 2013 —

Copyright © 2020 (as revised) W.L. Ripley
Paperback Edition

This book is a work of fiction. Any references to historical
events, real people or real places are used fictitiously. Other
names, characters, places and events are products of the
author's imagination, and any resemblance to actual events,
places or persons, living or dead, is entirely coincidental.

Published in the United States by Wolfpack Publishing, Las
Vegas

Wolfpack Publishing
6032 Wheat Penny Avenue
Las Vegas, NV 89122

wolfpackpublishing.com

Paperback ISBN: 978-1-64734-879-3
eBook ISBN: 978-1-64734-692-8

HOME FIRES

People sleep peaceably in their beds...because rough men stand ready to do violence on their behalf.
– George Orwell

Godlike the man who sits at her side, who watches and catches
that laughter which softly tears me to tatters:
nothing is left of me, each time I see her.
– Catullus

1

Jake Morgan's first day home in a decade, four thirty in the afternoon, on his first beer in two weeks, he runs into trouble with a couple of guys he remembered from high school.

And now they were waiting for him, just outside.

He poured beer from the bottle into a short glass and nodded at the bartender, Hank, who brought him another long neck. There was a mist this morning and now a smoky cast to the murky late afternoon atmosphere through the bar's windows.

Administrative leave. That's what they called it. Guess they couldn't call it 'what the hell did you do; get out of Texas'. Jake chose to think of it as a 'vacation'. The complainant called it 'Excessive use of force'. Jake thought of it as something else. The guy, full of Old Crow and Lone Star Beer, was working over his wife with a leather belt, really giving it some extra when Jake intervened.

The rub was it was the second time he had been called in because a different wife-beater complained. Domestics. They were tough. Some guy weighing 250 pounds liquored up wailing away on a woman who weighed less than half that. He tried to be professional, but the guy wouldn't stop slapping the woman around.

"You broke the man's jaw and two of his ribs, Morgan," said his supervisor, Captain Parmalee.

The guy came at him with a baseball bat. What was he supposed to do, unfriend him on Facebook? Unfortunately, he said it, not just thought it, unable to hold back. Worse, the woman wouldn't file charges on her husband. Mark Twain was right. No good deed goes unpunished.

So, Jake packed a bag and headed back to his hometown to wait it out. Home. Thinking of it as home. That was something. 800 miles away from Texas and 13 years apart. Driving into town Eric Clapton was singing, Someday After Awhile.

Was it someday yet?

Life in the bloodstream of his hometown. Paradise was a nice kind of Norman Rockwell town, with third generation homes on the main drag and a red brick courthouse with a WWII memorial and a World War II soldier standing on a pedestal in front of the courthouse.

Same hometown but the melody was missing.

This time the melody was a dirge because his longtime friend, Gage Burnell, was dead. He would be too late for the funeral but needed to tidy up affairs for Gage. Gage had been operating as his proxy on the family farm since the death of Jake's Father, Alfred Morgan. Another funeral Jake had missed. It wasn't going to be a fun homecoming.

Thomas Wolfe might be right. Maybe you couldn't go home.

And now the two guys waiting outside.

Sometimes, huh? He hadn't liked the way the guys, Noah Haller, who they nicknamed 'Fat Boy', back at Paradise High School 13 years ago and smaller guy, Tommy Mitchell, a shithead bully, was treating the server, nice young girl. So Jake expressed his objection to their less-than-stellar manners.

He drank off half the beer straight from the bottle, sat the bottle down. Right through those doors lay a new obstacle.

What could you do?

Jake got off the barstool and heard the girl say, "Don't go out there. I'm okay."

Hank said, "She's right. You're in town five minutes and this? Use your head, Jake."

"Hate to disappoint when they're all worked up."

He walked outside and there they were. They were bulled up and getting ready, confident the two of them would be enough.

He turned his baseball cap backwards on his head and said, "Well, kids, let's get things started. And remember, you dealt it."

***

The dispatcher, young guy named Franklin only on the force six months, said to Chief Deputy Buddy Johnson, a tall black man wearing shoulder patches that said 'Paradise County Sheriff', "you're not going to believe this one."

Johnson gave him a look, being patient, knowing Franklin loved to relay information and said, "I give up."

"Got three guys out front. A fight. Two of them pretty beat up."

Johnson said, "Well, tell me about it, I'm busy."

"The one guy, Morgan, says it was because the other guys were rude."

"Rude?"

"Said they were hassling the waitress down at Hank's, you know that bar..."

"I know the place. Wait a minute. You say the name was Morgan?"

"Yeah."

"Jake Morgan? You're kidding me."

"No. Trust me. It's him."

Deputy Johnson smiled thinking about Jake getting arrested. His old friend back in town and picking up right where he left off. The boy was incurable.

Franklin said, "The best part is who he beat up."

"Beat up? You said it was a fight."

"Not much of one. Morgan knocked their dicks in the dirt."

"Your language. So colorful. Are you telling me Jake whipped two men?" Two against one he came out ahead. Jake had picked up some skill compatible with his attitude. "Is he injured?"

"Said his hand is sore."

"Franklin, is there some reason you want to build suspense? Who was it he beat up you think will interest me?"

"Tommy Mitchell and his buddy, Fat Boy Haller."

That did get Johnson's attention. Interesting. Tommy Mitchell and Fat Boy had been in rows before where the victims would backtrack and withdraw their complaint or Tommy's dad would bail him out and sure to happen again. They'd found a guy didn't play that game. They should've remembered Jake Morgan. Sometimes people forget.

"Beautiful ain't it?"

Johnson had to admit it was but knew others, wouldn't think that way.

"So, what did Jake say for himself?"

"Asked if we could put them in the same lock-up. Said he wasn't done."

***

Call Sue for bail money. Sue was a forensic artist, that's what the rangers called the position, rather than lab tech, was someone Jake had been seeing off and on, a loose friendship bordering something bigger but never getting there. Sue was cool, like she expected it, when Jake called her from a police station. Asked did he remember he was suspended and what did he expect from her?

"Sympathy," he said. "Also, wire money for bail. Otherwise I spend the night and the room service here is unacceptable."

She laughed. "You drive hundreds of miles and locate trouble like there wasn't enough for you back here in Texas. Problem is you think it's all cowboys and assholes. Get a cowboy hat so we'll know who you are."

"I don't wear hats."

"Not literally, anyway," she said. She agreed to wire the money and hung up.

Good thing she liked him. Good thing she was 800 miles away. Jake sipped his coffee and thought about his situation. The server thanked him for intervening with the two creeps. Her name was April. April Armstrong. He knew her family from years ago. Good people. Said she remembered him.

"Good to be remembered," Jake told her.

She'd smiled and said, "Well, for the most part."

Then, a familiar face. A very large black man in a Deputy Sheriff's uniform.

"Well, well, well," Buddy Johnson said, flashing a smile reminding Jake why he liked Buddy. "If it ain't the Jake Morgan, biggest pussy I ever knew."

Jake closed one eye and looked at Buddy Johnson, all six and a half feet of him. Jake ran a hand threw his hair.

Jake said, "What's up, Buddy?"

"I see you're still allergic to this town."

"How's that?

"You broke out in handcuffs."

Jake shook his head, then looked up at Buddy. "Enjoying this are you?"

"Most fun I've had this week. What brings you back to Paradise?"

"Gage's death, among other things." Hedging on the administrative suspension issued by the Texas Department of Public Safety. "Also there seems to be a land dispute."

"Land dispute?"

"Yeah. Some old stuff came up when Alfred died."

"Alfred, meaning your dad."

Jake gave an affirmative grunt.

"What's the dispute?"

"Complicated."

"Well, you're now part of the criminal element. Heard you engaged in fisticuffs with a couple of our leading citizens. Tsk, tsk."

"Wasn't much of a fight."

Buddy saying, "Guess you couldn't wait to stir up the biggest snake hole around here."

"Trying to keep things lively."

"Didn't you have some sort of contretemps with Fatty back in high school?"

"Contretemps, huh?" Jake said, smiling. "Look at the guy paid attention in Language Arts."

Jake did have some problem with Haller back in high school. Fat Boy decided he needed to 'borrow' a dollar from Jake when Jake was a freshman and Haller was a junior. Said he wanted a soda, Jake asking why he would give Fat Boy, using the nickname, a dollar since he didn't like him, and he could do without the empty calories anyway. Haller called him a runt and grabbed Jake's shirt, Jake kneed the larger boy in the balls and Haller went down puking on the cafeteria floor. Jake spent three days in detention doing his homework and smiling a lot. Worth it.

"There was something," Jake said. "Don't remember much about it."

"So, what happened with Tommy and Fatty?"

Jake told him. Told him about arriving in town and the first thing was wanting to have a beer at Hank's and abuse Hank, the town curmudgeon and owner of the only bar left in town that wasn't a chain or a franchise and still located on what used to pass for the main drag; pavement and sidewalks crumbling like a bittersweet memory. Tommy Mitchell and Fat Boy Haller began harassing the server, April. Grabbing at her skirt and making rude suggestions to her. He requested that they discontinue bothering the girl.

"What's it to you?" is what Tommy Mitchell had said.

"I came in to have a beer and enjoy the afternoon. Annoying shitheads wasn't on the menu. Least I didn't see it. Is annoying shitheads on the menu, Hank?"

Hank shook his head.

"You saying something?" Tommy said.

"You know, you talk like you're something special, but the problem is you think I'd be interested in anything you say."

And, that's when it escalated.

"And so," Buddy said, "you rode to the rescue. Guns blazing." Smiling now and shaking his head. "You never learn, do you?"

"Aw," Jake said, rubbing an eye with the back of his hand, "you wouldn't like me if I did."

Buddy took a sip from his coffee, sat it down and said, "What makes you think I like you?"

"Figure you don't have many options."

"Good to have you back," Buddy said. "Surprised to see you since, you know, you didn't come back for your old man's funeral."

"No, I didn't." He gave attention to some lint on his shirt. "Missed Gage's funeral too. Nobody told me about it, so I missed it." Leaving out he found out when he tried to call Gage and didn't get an answer back until he checked with Leo Lyons.

"You know your old girlfriend, Pam Kellogg, married a Mitchell? The brother of one of the guy's you roughed up."

Pam Kellogg. Pam had a face and body allowed her to get away with things, the girl most likely. The relationship shifted into high gear teen love for a year. After she graduated, Pam went off to college and they drifted apart.

He missed her for a long time during a short period.

What would she be like now?

Buddy saying now, "Married Tommy's older brother, Alex, everybody calls him Alex, even though he is Vernon Alexander, Junior named after his dad. Call him "Junior" you want to piss him off. Remember him?"

"How could I forget?"

Buddy smiled. "Whole thing's kinda ironic. Humorous even."

"If you're easily amused."

"Whatever happened with you and Pam?"

"One of those things. She went one way and I went another." Which was the abridged version.

"That girl, for whatever reason, always had something for you. Probably still does. You whistle and she'll run from Alex."

"Those days are over."

Buddy laughed. "Think so? The one thing I remember was Pam Kellogg always got her way. She decides she wants you she'll be around to claim what she thinks is hers."

"Delusional fantasies the way you cope with your basic ignorance?"

"You think things changed and you call me delusional?"

"Leo still around?" Leo was Leo Lyon, Buddy and Jake's running buddy from high school

"Leo the Lion? Oh yeah, Leo? He'll never leave. My wife and I get together with him and his wife from time to time." Buddy looked away, then back at Jake. Buddy leaned forward, his elbows on his knees, serious now. "Not the same with Gage gone."

Jake nodded.

Gage gone. There it was. Like a symbiotic mosaic missing a piece. Gage looking at the world with his sideways point of view and goofy smile. Gage assailed the walls of normalcy on a daily basis. Leo the Lion was the brains, Gage was the guy always ready to laugh. Buddy, Leo the Lion, Gage and Jake. Since grade school.

"What happened with Gage?"

"Bad deal. Had an accident, wrecked his car. Said he was drinking. You know Gage. No fear."

Jake thinking on it.

"I know that look," Buddy said. "Don't conjure up anything that adds to my workload."

"Was it ruled an accident from the get-go?"

"Call came in said there was an accident."

"Can I see the accident report?"

Buddy giving him a funny look. "Well, the sheriff... That's another story. You're gonna love this," Buddy said smiling. "Sheriff Kellogg. Old Doc Kellogg. Almost your father-in-law, wasn't he?"

The father of his high school love, Pam Kellogg. Doc never liked Jake and didn't like him a lot. The feeling had been mutual. His past was being scraped raw.

Buddy was laughing full-tilt now. "Ain't that something?"

"Who investigated the accident?"

"Deputy Bailey. Good lady, sincere and a hard worker but green as grass. We got the call and Kellogg sent her."

"Accidental death should be considered a crime scene to protect evidence and forensics. Did they secure the area?"

"You sound like..." Buddy hesitated then said, "Are you fucking kidding me? Shit. You're in the cop business, aren't you?"

Jake shrugged.

"Who you working for?"

"Can I see the file?"

"Doc's been keeping me out of things lately."

"What's the hang-up?"

"He thinks I might run against him in the next election. Haven't decided."

"Well, good luck with that. You going to allow me to see the file or not?"

Buddy looked back over his shoulder. "Maybe. Something else you should know. Gage was working for Alex Mitchell and Alex fired him. Seems they got into it about something. Bad blood."

Jake knew Gage had been fired by Alex Mitchell. Gage was evasive when Jake asked him about it telling Jake he'd tell him about it next time they were together. Jake had pushed a little but for some reason Gage was keeping his quarrel with Alex to himself which wasn't like Gage.

"What did Gage and Alex get into it about?"

"Hard to tell. You know Gage's a lot of fun, but he always at things with an attitude that can rub some people the wrong way."

Jake thought some more. "Can you get me out of here?"

Buddy smiled. "No, baby, you're a dirtbag criminal."

2

The money arrived and a bail bondsman came to bail out Jake. His sparring partners were being released at the same time.

The fat guy, Haller, said, "This ain't over, boy."

Jake looked at Haller. Black eye, blood dried at his nose and at the stain on fatty's shirt. Fatty had vomited on himself when Jake punched him in his solar plexus. "Wow, you're my first tough guy. We can do this again you want. But wash your shirt," Jake said. "And brush your teeth."

The other guy, a young guy with a narrow face, said, "Listen, Morgan. You shit your nest. Better remember us." One of his eyes was closed and swelling. That was how Jake hurt his hand.

"Yeah," Jake said. "That's the plan, walk around remembering you tough-talking guys."

An older man, carefully clipped hair, tie and a western cut suit said, "Both of you, shut-up." The man looked familiar and had come to bail out the pair.

Tommy said, "Dad, this guy started it." He gave Jake a look. "And I'm gonna finish it."

"That's enough," said the older man.

"Mister Mitchell," Haller said. "We were minding our business when this guy –"

"That's enough, Noah," said Mr. Mitchell, saying it

with a different tone than he'd used on his son. Softer. Jake couldn't remember hearing anyone calling fat boy by his real name.

"Mister Mitchell," Jake said, as a way of greeting. He remembered Vernon Mitchell from years ago. The legend was Vernon Mitchell started his empire stealing cattle from a neighbor, bankrupting the neighbor, then using the profits off the sale of the stolen cattle to buy the neighbor's farm on the courthouse steps. Couldn't remember the man's name at present.

Mr. Vernon Mitchell eyed Jake. "Who are you?"

"Jake Morgan."

Mitchell's face changed. He said, "You look different. You've...grown. What happened here?"

"Disagreement. It's over now." He looked over Fat Boy and Tommy Mitchell. "I think."

"What're you doing back here?" Mitchell said. Jake thinking that was a funny way to phrase it. Not, 'what brings you to town'. Demanding to know. Mitchell was used to being answered.

"Settle a land dispute. Believe it's with you."

"Well that's all up to the court and the judge now."

"What is the problem?"

"Nothing big. I would consider settling out of court. Would you be interested?"

"Maybe," Jake said, watching Vernon closely but getting nothing. "Gage was taking care of the place, living there since Alfred passed away. Gage was one of my best friends. Want to find out what happened to him."

"Heard he had a car wreck."

"Heard the same thing."

"Sorry for your loss."

"Gage told me Alex fired him the week before he died." Letting it hang in the air.

"I let Alex run things as he sees fit. He knows what he's doing."

"I heard Gage and Alex got crossways with each other. Know anything about that?"

Vernon's eyes narrowed. "Have no idea. Are you

wanting to sell your Dad's place?"

"First, I find out what happened to Gage." Jake scratched at his cheek with a finger and smiled. "Maybe we'll see each other around. I'm going to be here for a couple of weeks."

Mitchell looked at Jake for a moment. "Well, welcome back."

Then Mitchell left with his son and Haller.

3

Leaving the lock-up and the Mitchells, Jake walked across the town square, past the World War II soldier, resolute and stalwart in all weather, and entered the Paradise Chemical Bank, one of two banks in the town, to draw money in order to pay Sue for the Bail money she'd sent. Besides the bail money, Jake was supposed to check on his father's account and money left in the will.

The Chemical Bank was the older bank in town. Jake noticed a shiny new bank all shiny chrome and glass out on the highway when he arrived earlier. Green Summit Bank. It was three stories and gleamed in the sunlight, a beacon to community progress.

The Chemical Bank was two tellers with an attached drive-in window built onto the 100-year-old building. The foyer was fresh paint over the retro fifties-architecture. It was an old building with a face-lift. The teller, a nice young girl just out of high school, had Jake fill out some forms in order to check on all Alfred's accounts.

"It's your money but we have to jump through some hoops," she said. "We have a conference room where you can go over these in private."

He thanked her and she escorted him back to a small room with a large glass window. There was a monitor in the conference room that afforded a live view of the teller's booths and the customers coming and going. There were only two customers at that time.

Jake was examining the papers when movement on the monitor caught his eye.

Two men came into the bank. Baseball caps, Oakley Sunglasses and wearing hooded sweatshirts, their hands in their pockets. He'd seen this before. The monitor screen was soundless. The two men produced weapons, gesturing at the customers who dropped to the floor and laced their hands behind their heads. The tellers, panic-faced, were frantically digging through the bank drawers.

One guy on the tellers, one man on crowd control, weapon pointed at the two bank customers on the floor. Jake's cell phone was still at Hank's place where he'd left it on the bar. Couldn't call 911.

He exhaled, thinking come home, visit old friends, no problem. He leaned down and lifted the Glock 19 from his ankle holster. Ranger policy was to remain armed 24/7. Good policy.

Now, how to pull this off without getting any civilians killed or himself.

He gave a look at the monitor and the tellers were still stacking money. Maybe one of them was a dye pack, but no, since that Jeff Bridges movie, Hell or High Water, every lowlife in America knew better. The robbers were intent on their business, the customers were prone and safe if he could neutralize that man first.

Jake quietly opened the room door and slipped around the corner staying close to the wall. Peeking around the corner he saw the backs of the men.

"I'm armed. Don't turn around. You tellers duck behind the counter."

The tellers dropped behind the marble counter and the robber near the counter raised his hands and said, "Okay."

The crowd control thug was bolder. He swiveled towards the sound of Jake's voice his weapon raised.

Jake said, "Don't." But the man wasn't listening.

Shit.

Jake double tapped the Glock, the sound filling the bank foyer. Voices screamed. Blood flowered from the robber's throat and face. Smell of cordite burn.

The other thief started to turn but Jake stopped him. Pointed his weapon at the man's nose and said, "Rethink it."

The man nodded rapidly.

"Weapon on the floor and move away from it," Jake said it evenly, learning early on that a calm, firm voice was more unnerving to a perp than yelling and screaming. Made them realize you weren't kidding

The man's pistol clattered to the floor and he took two steps back. Jake stepped towards the bleeding robber and kicked his weapon away from the man, all the while watching the other robber. The teller robber eyed the exit doors.

"Unless you can outrun a bullet, get on your knees, cross your ankles and lace your fingers behind your neck."

"You killed him," said the man.

"Do it for you if you don't do everything I say as soon as I say it."

The man complied.

To the bank employees, Jake said, "Call nine-one-one."

***

An old friend, Police Chief Bannister, showed with two uniform officers.

"Hell of a welcome home, Jake," Cal said. Cal was a tall older man, his face creased with time and laugh lines, unusual for career law enforcement. Cal never let the job eat on him. To Cal Bannister the job had to be done and that was it. Cal made a grunting sound. "Never get used to it. The blood, the smell."

"It's nasty all right."

"I need your weapon."

Jake handed it to him.

"Come along with me," Cal said. "My guys will take care of this and I'll get your statement. Besides I have other business to discuss with you."

Jake gave his statement, in both oral and written form, to a uniform officer at the police station. He had much experience writing up reports, so he made it as simple as possible. Short declarative statements telling what happened. When he finished, he was questioned again by Chief Cal Bannister. This went on for some time until Bannister was satisfied.

"You have a history, you know," Cal said.

Jake said, "Okay, Cal, what's the hassle? It was Leo and Gage put the cherry bombs in the fountain in front of city hall."

Cal smiled and said, "Not what I heard."

"Statute of limitations?" Jake said, raising his eyebrows.

"Well, guess I'll have to let that one go, then." Cal said, "How about take a ride with me. I'll show you around town. It's different than when you left."

"In an honest-to-God police car. I can turn on the siren, right?"

Cal had been the police chief in Paradise since Cal was a teenager and all the kids liked the man. Cal would pour out their beer and take their cigarettes, telling them, "Now you know your folks don't want you messing with those things." Then tell them he didn't have the time or the patience to process them but if he caught them again, he'd sure do it.

Nobody doubted him.

Jake got in the police unit with Cal and they took a tour of the town. Pointed out the food franchises and C-stores that had replaced the local cafes and service stations.

"Thanks for intervening at the bank today," Cal said. "You may have saved some lives."

"I was lucky."

"What brings you back?" Cal asked.

"You know anything about Gage and Alex Mitchell having trouble between them?"

"Why do you ask?"

"What I heard. Alex fired him. Wondering if you heard anything?"

They drove past the high school and Cal pulled into the parking lot of the football field. The day was bright, and Jake could hear the ping of the cooling engine. Jake looked out across the field. It was green and promising, and the white chalk-lines looked like icing on a cake.

"Jake," Cal said, pulling to a stop. "Things have changed, and your return has stuck wires in people's heads awful damned quick. You upset people who like being upset."

"That right? So, you heard about my little set-to?"

"Police Chief. Finger on the pulse." Smiling.

"The Mitchells." A statement not a question.

"Maybe."

"Doc Kellogg?"

"Sheriff Kellogg," Cal said. "Best keep that in the front of your mind. What did you do make him dislike you so much?"

Jake looked across the football field and said, "I don't know. Can't figure whether it's because I dated his daughter or because I stopped. Anyway," Jake said, "she upgraded to Junior Mitchell."

Cal chuckled to himself. "Not sure that's an upgrade. He goes by 'Alex' now."

Cal reached into his pocket and fished out a pack of Camels. Jake noticed the older man's hand trembling. Cal had always been steady as an oak. Cal shook a cigarette from the pack and offered it to Jake. Jake shook his head and Cal put it between his lips and pushed in the car lighter, removed the lighter and lit the cigarette.

Cal gave a pull on the tobacco then exhaled a blue cloud out the window.

Jake said, "Gage's accident. You know anything about that?"

Cal was startled by the question. "That why you're here?"

"Some." Hedging his answer. "Not entirely. There is some land in dispute, incredibly the person contesting it is Vernon Mitchell. But for the most part I'm interested in what happened to Gage. Buddy mentioned a car wreck.

You know anything about it?"

"My authority stops at the city limits."

Jake turned in his seat to face Cal. "But you are a cop and have cop-like thoughts about such things."

Cal looked at his police radio, chewed his lower lip and took another drag on his cigarette. It was quiet between them for a long moment before Cal said, "Kellogg and I have a strained relationship. Accident seems to be the likely result. I can't see there's anything shady about it, but I don't have much information. Kellogg kept that pretty close to the vest. Fell asleep behind the wheel what they say. Drunk. Drove off that old bridge out on county road HH. That bridge should've been replaced a long time ago."

"What do you think about the investigation by the Deputy? Bailey's her name."

"Nice young lady; has a little boy. Wants to do well. Sincere person. Her husband ran off with an elementary school teacher. I don't know much else." Cal took another hit off his cigarette. "What are you doing down in Texas anyway?"

"Working for the state."

"Doing what? You seem different in a lot of ways. Same smile, same sense of humor but you're a couple inches taller and hold yourself differently. You walk different; your clothes are pressed and neat. Military?"

"Something like that."

"I know you went to Texas to play basketball and football."

"Didn't have enough arm for college football," Jake said. "So, I stuck with basketball."

"What was your major?"

Jake shrugged. "CJ."

"Criminal Justice?"

"I needed a degree in something."

Cal sat up and said, "You're a law enforcement officer."

"Some kind."

"Explains why you were armed. Why didn't you say something? What kind?"

"Texas Rangers."

"Well, well, well." Cal whistled. "What branch are you assigned?"

"Was SRT. Special Response team."

"Dangerous work."

Jake shrugged. "Recently moved to Unsolved Crimes."

"That's Homicide and serial killers, right?"

Jake nodded.

Cal opened his mouth, stopped, nodded his head a few times in realization and quietly said, "Well, you never were much for doing things halfway."

4

Next morning, the sun creased the clouds and the dew glistened with promise; a beautiful moment to sit on his Father's porch and look out across the rolling hills and multi-colored trees. Loamy smell of decayed leaves was in the air and the autumn sky had turned that forever blue. Sit and sip coffee and smoke a cigarette. One couldn't hurt.

Relax some. Learn how it works. Try.

Had some trouble sleeping. Nothing TV and movie cops will say, it works on a man, thought Jake.

One of the first things to strike him about his childhood home was the piano keyboard, the ivory keys worn and marked by his mother's hands, remembering her now. She was the stable force, the lubricant who soothed the grinding gears of a father and son, too much alike to give an inch.

Alfred Morgan, known as "Al" to friends, built the house, log home with decks front and rear with a green metal roof. Two hundred acres of good dirt for crops, and grazing for cattle. They were never rich, but they never went without, at least until Alfred started drinking.

Jake rinsed his mug and put it in the dishwasher. The floor needed sweeping, but overall Gage had taken good care of the place, so he went to find a broom. He walked to the mud room leading to the outside back door and stopped. Saw the dog dish, food in it. He looked out to the back and saw the dog pen but didn't see a dog. There was a doggy door flap on the back door. He'd only been here for a day-and-a-half and hadn't really surveyed the place.

He cleaned up, and called his old friend, Leo the Lion and asked if he wanted to have lunch in town. Leo said he could stand to eat something.

They met at the Dinner Bell Café, one of his old hangouts and one of the few still operating. It was a place served breakfast all day, and the coffee was drinkable. Actual tablecloths on the tables, matching curtains on the windows, pick-up trucks parked in the raw gravel chat. A gathering place for the locals, the town getting swallowed up by corporate franchises, one looking like the next. No charisma.

Leo the Lion came in wearing well-worn jeans, wolverine boots, a seed corn baseball cap and a long-sleeved Tee-shirt that read, "Dear Algebra, Stop asking me to find your X, she's not coming back". Leo's hair was receding, and he had a D'Artagnan beard and mustache. Leo looked and dressed less like a coach or teacher than most, but Leo was one of the best. Leo removed his cap when he entered. Jake stood and they shook hands.

"Well, superstar," Leo said. "You miss me?"

"Some," Jake said. They made smalltalk, catching up. It was like they'd seen each other yesterday. That kind of friend.

Leo saying, "So you slip into town, get in a bar fight, are arrested and then involved in a shoot-out in the bank. You're as subtle as a cherry bomb."

"You know how I like attention."

"Haven't seen you since... You missed your father's funeral. What's that about? Your family passes, you come home, and you go to the funeral. You do what's right."

"I was busy."

Leo shaking his head, his eyes fixed on Jake. Leo Lyon was the most intelligent person Jake knew. Teaching math at the local high school since they graduated from college. Leo never left Paradise, and personally considered himself to be the foremost historian of Paradise lore and genealogy. Mathematician's brain and the arms of a logger. An all-district running back who could bench 400 pounds.

"Some other time."

Leo gave him a sideways look, and then nodded. "That'll work." Jake could see his friend wasn't convinced. "Thought you were some kind of cop down in Texas."

"Some kind. Saw Buddy this morning."

"Buddy Johnson is what everyone hopes their kid grows up to be. Hard to believe he works for Kellogg. You knew Kellogg was the sheriff, right?" Having fun saying it.

Jake nodded. "Pondering why you and Buddy find that amusing. Many changes around here."

"Well, prosperity broke out and now we have cookie cutter restaurant franchises and the train station is operating again. We have McDonald's and Applebee's and the keys to happiness."

"And you never eat either place, do you?"

"On a scale of one to 'no'. Never."

"And, Vernon Mitchell got in on the ground floor of all that. Sound about right?"

"Yeah, he's got pretty fat. He's still a...hey, what were you doing down there in Texas, exactly? Hard for me to see you running off without saying anything. Seems you had a life here."

The door opened and the little bell ringer on the door sounded and people looked up. Jake too.

And, there she was.

Pam Kellogg. Now Pam Mitchell. She was alone. Leo looked at Pam and then at Jake who was looking at Pam who was looking at Jake. "Easy, Jake," Leo said, the points of his mustache rising merrily. "Don't let your hormones run away with your mind."

Pam looked straight at Jake and smiled. "Jake Morgan. The boy who got away. Oh my god, it is you, isn't it?"

"How are you, Pam?"

He stood and they hugged, Pam pressing against him longer than a moment and Jake felt things slide sideways in his head.

Pam greeted Leo and Leo returned it and she sat without being asked.

They ordered. Pam ordered a half chef salad for herself. "Have to watch my weight you know," she said.

Jake thinking she looked like she was poured into her clothes, not a pound off her high school weight, her teeth snowy white as a toothpaste ad. She smelled of shampoo and soap and the daydreams of an adolescent boy remembering quiet corners in school hallways and dark country roads with the radio playing.

"Heard you've made quite the splash?" Pam said.

"None of it was in the plan."

"So, what are you doing down in Texas?" Pam asked.

"Working."

She gave him an appraising once-over. "You're still good looking. Leo, I tried my best to corner this one, but he slipped away."

"Didn't think you were trying all that hard."

Pam pursed her lips and winked at Jake.

Leo and Pam talked about the weather, the way the town had changed, Jake not saying much, making them change the subject about the bank hold-up. As the food disappeared and the server poured coffee for the trio, the conversation shifted to the present.

"Jake," Pam said. "You haven't contributed much to the conversation."

"I'm not much at small talk."

"So, do you have anyone?"

He made a face. "What do you mean?"

"Are you seeing anyone?"

"Hard to say."

She laughed. "It's a yes or no question, Jake. How hard can it be?"

"So, what are you doing these days?"

"I got a business degree and came back home."

Leo said, "She's president of the Green Summit Bank.

The one you didn't shoot up. Plus, check me if I'm wrong, Pam, but don't you run most of the Mitchell Dynasty?" Jake seeing Leo was probing. Leo being Leo. Generally, the smartest man in the room, but didn't let on.

She gave Leo an appraising look and said, "It's a business. Mitchell Enterprises."

"Knew she'd go far," Jake said.

"And yourself?" she asked Jake.

"I work for the state."

"What state?"

"Texas."

"Doing what?"

"Whatever they tell me to do," Jake said, not ready to say anything about his job because it was a conversation stopper that made people look at him a different way and they asked the standard questions or told how some cop had screwed them.

"He's in law enforcement," Leo said.

"Really?" she said. "Why so mysterious?"

"Not my intention." Looking at her and peeling away the years he could see her again in her cheerleading outfit, fresh and young, but the present model was even more striking and possessed more presence; maturity filling in the spaces youth leaves open.

Pam looked at Leo and said, "When did he become like this?" Then back to Jake. "You're quite the conversationalist. Why's that?"

"Naturally chatty, I guess."

She exhaled and smiled. "I'm deciding if you've become more interesting," she said, "or less."

"More settled."

"What brings you back to our little town?" she asked.

Jake thumbed his coffee cup and looked at it idly. "Gage died, so I came back to decide what to do with Alfred's place. Missed Gage's funeral because my lowlife friends failed to call me." Saying the last part as he looked at Leo.

"I tried," Leo said. "You disappeared and didn't bother to keep in touch."

"True."

"As an apology," Leo said. "Pay for my lunch."

"Alfred?" Pam said. "You call your father Alfred?"

He looked at her. "That's his name."

Pam looked down at her food as if something was out of place. She looked up and said, "I'm sorry about Gage. I liked him."

"Apparently your husband didn't."

Pam gave him a look. "What does that mean?"

"Didn't like each other. Junior fired him."

"Alex," she said. "He goes by Alex now."

He nodded. "I'll write it down."

She chewed her lower lip, narrowed her eyes. "Is there a reason you're taking this posture?"

"No special reason," Jake said.

"There seems to be an edge to what you're saying."

He looked at her. "Don't read anything into it," he said but she was probably right. He wanted to know about Gage. Until then, his cop instincts warned against trusting people directly or indirectly involved. 'Heightened awareness' is what his ranger trainers called it.

"Football team looks like we're going to qualify for districts," Leo said, changing the subject. "First time in ten years."

"How long are you staying in town, Jake?" asked Pam.

"Don't know. On vacation." Hating the lie. "Deciding whether to sell the place now, rent out the property or keep it."

She brightened. "You want to sell the place?"

"Maybe. I talked to Gage last week right before his accident. Told me things were going well and that he had a surprise for me."

"A surprise?"

"Gage enjoyed stringing people along. Even his friends. Could've been anything."

"I mean, we may be interested in buying your place," Pam said.

"'We', meaning the Mitchells?"

"Yes."

"Why?" asked Jake, looking down to cut his steak, noting this was the second time a Mitchell mentioned buying the place. "Gage said there is a section in dispute. Seems the Mitchell clan has plenty of land without edging in on Alfred."

"It's a beautiful place. Nice view to the south. Vernon offered to buy it from your father before he died."

"So, he offered to buy and now we have a dispute?" Jake stopped cutting, put his knife and fork down and said, "Vernon already offered to settle with me."

"You'll get a fair price."

"The price is not an issue." Making a mental note to follow up. Wondering why Alfred hadn't mentioned it. But realizing Jake hadn't given him a chance and Gage had been circumspect. "Seems Vernon has enough land. Why was Gage fired?"

Pam patted her hair and her eyes moved to the left. "I was not involved in that decision."

"The Pam I remember knew things."

Pam looked at her watch as if an alarm went off. "I'm late for an appointment. Great to see you both. Hope to see you again, Jake."

"That would be nice."

"Maybe next time without the attitude," she said, her face tight.

She left, her perfume wafting by lightly and filling Jake's head.

"Whew," Leo said and whistled. He leaned back, both hands on the table, smiling at Jake.

"What?"

"You have such a way with women." He waved his hand as if conjuring up a vision. "There's something in the air." Leo stroked his beard before he spoke, enjoying himself now. "However, due my amazing powers of observation honed by not being you, well, let's see. You've been away for a while; the Mitchells have become bucks up with alacrity. Some things have changed, markedly, and some things haven't changed a bit."

"'Alacrity'?"

"I'm sorry; I forgot you were ignorant. Read a book once in a while. Then there's Pam Kellogg."

Jake held a hand up and waved Leo off and shook his head.

Leo saying now, "Oh yes. Pam Kellogg. You are so screwed, Jake. Can't see it, can you? You're fun to watch. She still has it and knows what to do with it. Thing is, she is more aware of it than you and will act on it. Bet on it."

"How about a break from the blinding insight?"

"You never understood the way that girl worked it, did you? Actually she's an interesting study. As are you. No doubt about it."

"Does this conversation have anything resembling a point?"

"You're in her gun sights, again. I'm looking right at it happening with a sense of nostalgic wonder and amazement." He formed a rainbow in the air with his hands. "As if time stood still. And you won't acknowledge it or worse," Leo hesitated, took a breath and said, "It's the way you want it."

"Your hair fall out, or did it fall in and clog your brain?"

"Never doubt The Lion. Pam Kellogg gets what Pam Kellogg wants."

"Mitchell," Jake said, correcting him. "Her name's Pam Mitchell."

"A name on a piece of paper, sitting in a file in the county clerk's office." Leo held up his coffee cup and saluted the air. "She is, and always will be, Pam Kellogg, the one true princess of Paradise County."

5

Alex Mitchell thinking his wife does whatever she wants. Like having lunch with her high school sweetheart, Jake Morgan. What do you do with that? Fat Boy Haller told Alex they'd had a run in with Morgan.

"He took you guys like stealing your lunch money," Alex said to him.

"He jumped us from behind."

Alex made a scoffing sound. "That's how you want me to see it, right? You didn't learn about him back in high school, so you thought you'd give it another try? At least you didn't puke this time."

Alex wasn't happy about Morgan's visit with his wife. In public view of the whole town. Everyone knew she and Morgan had been an item.

So, Alex confronted her about it. Pam was unsaddling her mare when he hit her with it, asking why she'd eat lunch with Jake and Leo the Lion.

Pam said, "Grow up, Alex. He's just someone I used to date."

"Banging him under the bleachers makes him more than someone you used to know."

"That's not how I'd characterize it."

"You know what I mean."

Using a baby voice now she said, "Is little Alex jealous?"

"It's different with him," he said. "You know it is. Where do you think I've lived all my life?"

"You mean Leo the Lion?" Smiling to herself when she said it but letting him see it. She unhitched the saddle, placed it on the sawhorse, removed the horse blanket and bridle and began currying the horse's hide.

"So, you've decided to be funny."

"It was lunch with old friends," Pam said, brushing the horse's back, a familiar exercise from years of dealing with horses. The mare stood and settled into the rhythm of the welcome brushing. "We didn't have sex or anything. That would've attracted a crowd and embarrassed Leo." She laughed.

He said, "Leo the Lion having sex with anyone isn't funny."

She stopped working the brush, picked up a curry comb and looked at Alex. "You're kind of cute when you're jealous."

"I'm not jealous. Just aggravated."

"Oh, you are sooo jealous," drawing out the words.

"You know what I'm saying but you want to avoid talking about it."

She resumed brushing again. A little harder. Longer strokes. "You don't tell me what I can do or not do, or who I talk to. Better if you remember that."

"I'm your husband; thought that might count for something."

"Sure," she said. "Who could forget that?"

"What if the situation were reversed?"

"Like it hasn't been. You think I'm unaware of your little trysts." She gestured at a bottle with the curry comb. "Hand me that liniment, would you? I think she's sore in her front left."

Alex thinking, this is what she did. No matter what he said or did or what they were talking about, she gave the impression he had no effect on her thoughts or actions or she turned it around on him. As if he were a hired hand and not the man she married. Played him off and good at it.

"Don't feel like it," he said and left the barn. "Get it yourself."

"He rebels," she said, then laughed derisively.

He could hear her singing to herself as he left.

What could you do about it? That's the bitch of being in love and he loved her. More than he wanted to love her most of the time. All of the time, actually.

Pam poured oats for her mare. Alex triggered by Jake Morgan's return to town. She smiled at that. Wasn't a bad thing. Keep the boy hungry for her.

Jake Morgan back home. After school, she'd gone off to college, joined a sorority and dated frat boys. Parties and football games on Saturday afternoons. But she studied and earned a business degree.

Jake knew about the frat boys, never mentioning it. He always knew things he didn't talk about. She could feel it the way you could smell the rain before it started. Jake went to Texas and just danced away from her.

And yet, he stayed in her head and her dreams sometimes back then.

Even now.

***

Leaving the diner, Jake stopped at a market to pick up some things for the house; groceries and other items he might need. That done he stopped at a gun shop and bought a pack of .357 ammunition for his service weapon and #8 bird shot to do some dove hunting. May as well take advantage of the season. Also, a pack of cigarettes. He could resist them. Yes, he could, but just in case.

Later in the afternoon, clouds moved in to cover the sun and Jake decided to return to the scene of the crime. He headed back to Hank's, to perhaps smoke a cigarette he shouldn't smoke, have the beer he'd didn't finish. Needed to get his mind off the shooting and the land dispute. Something, many things, were running through his head, not the least of them, Pam Kellogg Mitchell.

Jake looked at the selections on the jukebox at Hank's.

All of it dated from his dad's era. Jake was waiting for Leo the Lion to show after football practice. There was no one in the place except Jake and Hank as the evening crowd hadn't shown yet.

"Hey, Hank," Jake said. "You have anything on here from this century?"

"There ain't any other music," Hank said. "You want a beer or just bitch about my music?"

"All of it appeals to me," Jake said. He faced Hank, opening his arms. "Here's how capitalism works. You supply what the customer wants, the customer buys and commerce occurs."

"Well, here's how things work here. I put on the juke-box what I want to hear.

You gonna order or just want to hang around like a welfare bum?"

Jake had a beer and waited. The Happy Hour crowd shuffled in. Mostly locals. Everyone else went out to the highway franchises, Leo said. Guys he knew from high school greeted him, asking him what he was doing back in town offering to buy him a beer. Cigarette smoke swirling above the conversation and the clink of glasses mixed with laughter.

Leo the Lion showed wearing a hooded sweatshirt reading "Paradise Football".

Hank brought Leo a beer. It was a ritual. Leo would come in and Hank would bring him a beer instead of one of the servers.

"Hank," Leo said. "When are you going to go smoke-free and stop killing your clientele? I could die of second-hand smoke."

"Gee," said Hank, dead-panned. "That would be a loss. I'll wear a black arm band."

"So," Leo said, after Hank went back to the bar, "once again, I have prepared our boys to crush the enemy in my coach of the year style. Let our bloody colors wave or else, a grave."

"Why do you talk like an English Lit teacher instead of a football coach?"

"Because I'm not an ignorant beast who makes mistake, takes chances manages to look silly but keeps right on going."

"That's a paraphrase of Thomas Wolfe," Jake said. "Not the real quote. Read a book, my ass."

The front door opened, and Fat Boy Haller and Tommy Mitchell came in, glaring in Jake's direction.

"Not going to let it go, are they?" Leo said, watching the pair stomp to a table.

"We had an argument about French politics."

"I'm sure they had an interesting take. You'd do best to pay attention as your enemies for they are the first to notice your mistakes. And now back to current events. Jake, buddy, I've been pondering your situation. My advice for you is not shoot anyone and stay clear of Pam Kellogg."

"Mitchell."

"Whatever. I fear she has unseemly desires for your body."

"Whatever you want to believe."

"That's what you do when you don't want to address things. Just like you used to. Like with your father." Jake cut his eyes at his friend and Leo put up his hands. "I know, I know, leave it alone. You have a complicated history with Pam K now heightened by a contretemps with the two mental-deficients."

"Contretemps?"

"That's Leo the Lion, high professor of math and elocution talking. Stay on task here. Never doubt the old professor."

Leo paused and took a drink of his beer. More people came in; the smoke swirled in the air.

"It's like now, Leo said, continuing, enjoying the opportunity to expound. "You're on a collision course with a candidate for most likely to be lusted after and the blue ribbon goes once again to the winner and still champion, Pam Kellogg Mitchell."

"Do you sit in the teacher's lounge and dream up this stuff?"

"You say it like it's a bad thing. You don't want to address the situation but you'd better because she'll be coming around and...oh, hello."

Leo looked up from the table.

The juke box changed tunes.

Jake turned to see what Leo was looking at.

Pam Kellogg Mitchell.

Jake, looking at Pam, said, "Another thing, Leo. Did Gage have a dog?"

6

Pam Kellogg Mitchell walked over to the table and asked Leo if she could sit. Leo winked at Jake where Pam couldn't see it. Jake could see her entrance wasn't lost on Tommy and Fat Boy. Tommy punched in numbers on a cell phone.

"We'd be fools to miss the opportunity of your company," Leo said. Jake didn't miss the big smile on Leo's face. Pam ordered a light beer, patted her 24-inch waist and said, "have to watch my weight or nobody else will."

"Very nice," Leo said, then said to Jake, "Yes, he does." Meaning Gage had a dog leaving Pam to consider the double entendre.

"Well I can't find him," Jake said, telling Leo about the food dish and the dog pen.

"Whose dog?" asked Pam.

"Gage Burnell's. Remember him? The guy your husband fired before he was killed?"

Pam reached up and touched up the edge of an eyebrow. "Are we doing this again? Why does everything you say sound like an accusation?"

"Why does everything I say make you think you're under scrutiny?" He nodded at Tommy and Fat Boy. "We have company."

She put her hands on the table as if she were going to push away. "I don't care about them and you're being a shit again and I don't know why. Maybe you can explain that."

"He's been a cop since he left," Leo said. "Makes him less interesting, be my guess."

She narrowed her eyes and said, "So, you're a policeman now. Explains a lot."

"More than just a police officer," Leo said. "Texas Ranger."

"Much more romantic," Pam said.

Jake wanted a cigarette and a way to restart the conversation.

"Okay," Jake said. "I apologize for my tone. Don't read anything into it. I'm not happy about Gage's death coming so close to his being fired."

"I didn't fire him," Pam said.

He started to ask why she was making that a point. Instead, he said, "I know. And, it is good to see you again, Pam. You look great." He wanted to take it back as soon as he said it but it was too late.

She smiled; her shoulders relaxed. "Thanks for that."

Leo patted his chest and Pam said, "Good to see you, too, Leo. Big game Friday."

"That's why I'm self-medicating," he said, holding up the empty beer bottle. "I must look and feel my best tomorrow in preparation."

Leo's cell phone rang. He excused himself and stepped away from the table to take the call.

Jake followed Leo's departure with his eyes, but Pam kept hers trained on Jake.

"Alone at last," she said. Pam placed an elbow on the table and rested a cheek on her palm. "You're abnormally reticent. I don't remember you that way."

"You're married, Pam. Hard to get past that."

"Can't we try? What's wrong with being friends?"

"Junior may see it differently."

She shook her head, smiling with her eyes briefly closed. "You are purposely calling Alex by his nickname. Why're you doing that?"

"Fun to do."

"I was hoping you would be a little jealous."

He looked at her. "He marries the prettiest girl in Western Missouri. Who wouldn't envy him?"

She smiled at that. He felt her smile. Easy, Jake.

Leo returned and sat. "My wife on the phone." Leo's eyes left the table and looked at the entrance. "And, oh boy."

Before Jake could look, he heard his voice.

"What the hell now?" said Alex Mitchell, his jaw set. Jake hadn't seen Alex Mitchell in years. Alex looked pretty much the same, save that he was heavier, not fat, but settled into maturity. Apparently, that's who Tommy was calling.

Alex stood close to the table, saying to Pam now, "Pretty sure we had a conversation resolved this."

"You're cute when you're jealous," Pam said.

Alex made a face. "I'm not jealous."

Jake turned in his chair and said, "How're you doing, Alex? Join us."

"Can't," Alex said, edgy now, absently rubbing an unusual square Tiger eye ring he wore on his right ring finger. "We're leaving. Let's go, Pam."

"I have a beer, Alex," Pam said, saying it as if it explained everything. "I'm going to finish it and maybe have another. Why don't you sit down and enjoy the evening?"

"You know what I'm talking about, but you want to avoid it."

"Dammit, Alex, sit down," Pam said, with a little more force behind the words.

"We're going."

Shaking her head. "Grow up, Alex."

"This is the second time," Alex said, nodding at Jake when he said it.

Jake watched Tommy and Fat Boy rise from their seats, thinking go to town, have a beer with Leo. Talk about old times. What could go wrong?

Jake saying now, "Look...a...you guys want to talk, Leo and I'll move to another table."

"Sit still, Jake," Pam said. "Alex forgets himself."

The crowd beginning to notice. Jake knew Alex was in a bad spot here, standing there exposed and looking bad. He had initiated a scene and his ego would force him to look like he was in control of the situation. He couldn't retreat, and Pam would not. The Alex Mitchell Jake knew hated looking bad. This was not going well.

Growing worse as Tommy and Fat Boy moved closer.

Pam turned, pointed at Fat Boy and Tommy and said, "Go back and sit down. This is none of your business. Alex?"

Alex motioned for his brother and Haller to move back. "Do what she says."

"Fuck her telling me what to do," Tommy said, bristling.

"Aw, shit, Tommy," Alex said. "Not today."

"Come on, Tommy," said Fat boy and the pair moved back to their table but did not sit. Tommy even glowered.

Jake stood and said, "This doesn't concern me."

"There's an interesting position," Alex said. "It always concerns you."

"You're reading it wrong," Jake said. "Don't take this to a place doesn't exist."

Alex looked at Pam and said, "Let's go. Now."

Pam laughed, without humor. "Save the macho pose for the snuff queens you encourage when you think I'm not looking."

Not getting any better. Situation spiraling away. Jake was uneasy, thinking of a way out.

"Not kidding about this," Alex said, rubbing the Tiger eye ring again.

Pam shook her head and took a theatrical sip from her beer while looking up at Alex.

Alex grabbed her arm, but Pam pulled away, spilling beer on her blouse. "Goddammit, Alex. Look what you did."

"You don't want to do this, Alex," Jake said, trying to take a conciliatory tone.

"Shut the fuck up and stay out, Morgan."

Jake stood, his chair scraping on the wood floor. "I'm

not sure I can hear you when you take that tone, Junior."

Leo the Lion said, "Aw hell," as he stood. "Everybody, calm down." He made a flat motion with his hand, palm down. "Beautiful evening. Have a beer. Smile a lot."

"Don't be an ass, Alex," Pam said. "Calm down."

"Don't feel like it." He pointed at Jake and said, "It would be a good thing you keep your distance from her."

Having people point at him was on the short list of things Jake didn't care for. Wanting to say he wasn't after his wife. Swallow it. Jake blew out a breath, decided to let it go but it grated on him to do so.

"I'm leaving, Pam," Alex said. "Whether you come along or not. You won't enjoy the conversation later."

"This is your rebellion?" Pam said, giving him a triumphant smile. "You're not sitting down and I'm going to regret your conversation? Comical."

Alex left. Thankfully. Jake didn't need this.

"You should go with him," Jake said.

"Alex needs to learn I'm not livestock. Besides, a little jealousy is good for him. He's no choir boy himself."

"I prefer not to be a part of whatever is going on in your marriage."

"Don't be fussy. Aren't you happy to see me?"

"I'd feel better if you left."

Pam sat up in her seat, saying to Leo, "You hearing this?"

"Well," Leo said, with a little nod. "He's not entirely wrong."

"Okay." She stood. "You boys take these things far too seriously. But what am I to do? Good to see you again and in the interest of tranquility I will leave you to talk football and cars."

"Thanks. Good to see you again."

She left. Tommy and Fat Boy walked out behind her. Tommy gave Jake the finger.

"How high school is that?" Jake said, to Leo. "Town's changed, the idiots haven't."

Leo the Lion saying now, "You're like a brother to me, Jake; don't know many people I like as much as you but dammit, no more of this, huh?"

"I'm sitting here, she walks in bringing her shitty marriage with her and you decide it's somehow my fault. The way your mind works is incomprehensible. Whatever medication you're on needs reevaluation."

"I'll concede the point, but you," pointing at Jake as he said it. "You attract trouble and need to own that facet of your personality."

Jake looked around before saying, "I attract trouble?"

"The funny part?" Leo said, "You don't realize it and you never did."

7

Bad dreams, too much on his mind and not enough booze to chase it away. Jake tired but sleep avoiding him. What had he accomplished coming back to Paradise? Not much. Nothing good anyway.

The landline buzzed. Need to stop Gage's phone service. Jake looked at the clock. 2:00 AM. Nothing good came of calls this late.

He picked up the phone.

"Gage Burnell no longer—"

"Jake? This is Pam. I need someone to talk to. Would you mind if I come over? Please."

He rubbed his eyes with the palm of his free hand. Tried to clear the cobwebs in his head. Felt like he was dreaming all this. Let it be a dream. That would be better than the reality.

"Not a good idea," he said.

It was quiet on the other end of the connection. For a moment he thought, hoped, she had hung up.

"Alex is crazy over here. He's drunk and I'm afraid he's going to hurt me."

"Look, I'm not unsympathetic, but you coming here? Nothing good comes of that. I'm sure you have friends you can stay with. Call your dad."

He could hear her breathing on the line. "Okay, you're right," she said. "I understand. Good advice. I'll be okay."

They hung up and Jake pulled the blankets over his chest. Glad she wasn't coming but thought about it. There was still something between them and he didn't like not being in control of it. He stared at the ceiling for several minutes before sleep overtook him.

Jake dreamed deeply. His dreams were a mixture of reality where he could touch, feel, reason, and smell. But it was a muddle of locales and people. In his dream there were people that he seemed to know but their faces were wrong in familiar places where he never lived.

He felt her in his dream. She was warm, her body silky and inviting.

But it wasn't a dream. She was there. Right now. In bed with him.

"How the --?"

"Ssshhhh," she said, her hand lightly on his lips.

He sat up and she slid into him. "Pam, this can't happen."

"I know," she said, stroking his hair away from his forehead. "But I need someone. I need you. No strings. Honest. Just tonight."

She lifted herself to straddle him and he thought to push her away but hesitated and in that moment he lost all arguments against this mistake of gigantic proportions. He was drowsy but felt the arousal of her body against his, realizing and admitting he'd harbored hopes of this happening from the first moment in the diner.

This is wrong and you know better, dammit. Don't be stupid. You're a rational human being, aren't you?

Well, aren't you?

Apparently not.

And so it went.

***

Pam left before sunrise. Jake had coffee and cigarettes for breakfast with a side order of regret.

He couldn't blame her; he could've made her leave or barring that, moved to a different room. She merely offered herself and he indulged in the delight of her body, her warmth, the smell of her hair. Her urgency fueling his libido and the memory of long-ago love. Was it nostalgia, or weakness? No, he was a willing accomplice in the commission of the forbidden. It wasn't loving or tender but rather rancorous as if avenging an old wrong.

And now? Well, now, Jake old buddy, you live with it. The morning after was the toughest.

How did that old song go? 'Not quite friends...and not quite lovers."

In the morning he sat on this front deck wondering should he pack up and head back to Texas before things got worse? But Gage's death bothered him. As a law enforcement investigator, it struck him as incomplete. Too convenient. Too many questions swimming through his cop mind.

It was a remote possibility Gage's death was an accident, but Jake's instincts rejected it. The coroner had looked into it.

Still...

He heard a noise. In the back of the house.

He walked back into the house and heard it again. A snuffling noise and then a crunching sound as if someone were cracking walnuts.

Jake's heart was pounding, and he stopped to compose himself. He could feel the back of his neck tense and his blood pumping adrenaline. He stopped again to listen, taking a deep breath and letting it out halfway to relieve his tension.

Same noises, then a soft whining sound, the sound of an injured animal.

From the back porch? Had a raccoon got in through the dog flap? Coyote?

Jake entered the kitchen, slid open the door to the mud room then reached over and flipped on the light. A dog.

Growling, snarling.

Gage's dog?

The dog was lying by the dog dish, his snout in the dish but Jake could see the dog was exhausted and injured but knew better than to approach too quickly. The dog was dragging a short chain that had been snapped at a point about a foot behind the collar. The dog's neck where the chain rubbed was bare of fur and matted with mud and blood. The ribs of the animal were showing.

Jake found the bag of dog food in the room and filled the dog's bowl.

"Easy now," Jake said. "I'm a friend."

The dog curled a lip and a guttural sound emitted from deep within the animal. He kneeled and held a hand out palm down, below the dog's muzzle. The dog approached, warily, hackles raised, sniffed at Jake's hand, satisfied the dog then backed up and began eating.

Jake eased the door shut and left the dog alone.

Jake returned to his room and picked up his cell and dialed Buddy Johnson.

"What the hell, Jake? I worked the night shift?"

"I need a vet."

"A vet? What's up?"

"Gage's dog just came home, and he's hurt."

8

The veterinarian's name was Billings, a short, muscular guy wearing a Stetson and Tony Lama's. "I know this dog," said Billings. "Gage brought him in for his shots. He's a good boy. Black Lab mix. His name is 'Travis'. He's been mistreated."

"And yet," Jake said, "made his way home."

"Big heart," said the vet. "Dogs are like that. Better than most people you ask me. Someone chained him up and Travis rubbed the fur and flesh off his neck straining against it. God, I hate people do this stuff. I'll keep him a couple days until he's strong enough to come home. I can try to find him a home you want."

"No," Jake said. "I'll keep him." Knowing Gage would want that. But, wondering if he wanted a reason to keep him.

"Good. Travis could use a friend right now."

"Both of us," Jake said.

Travis was calm now and allowed Jake to scratch his ears. Travis licked Jake's hand. Okay. Good first step.

"This is not a dog that would take such treatment lightly," said Billings. "He's a hunting dog. Proud. Labs are loving animals and one of the friendlier breeds, but I would bet he'd fight back when threatened or someone threatened his owner." Jake filed that away. "We find someone with a dog bite and maybe we've got our guy. I find out who did this I'll file charges."

"You knew Gage," Jake said. "Why would anyone take his dog?"

"I don't know."

"Gage's death? You hear anything about that?"

"Just what I hear around town."

"You know anything about him getting fired by Alex Mitchell?"

Billings opened a jar of dog treats and fed one to Travis. "Well, only gossip and scuttlebutt. Hate to traffic things like that. Not good for business."

"Well, it would help me."

Billings paused, pushed by his hat with a thumb and said, "I'll tell you this much. Alex Mitchell and Gage were not getting along. There have been rumors why that was happening but that's all I care to say. People hear their vet is carrying tales they won't trust me to watch after their animals."

"I understand."

Jake thanked him and asked to pay but Billings said to wait until Travis was better. Travis would need a few days under the vet's care which meant Jake would have to postpone leaving Paradise. Realizing that he had inadvertently made a commitment when he decided to keep the animal. Billings said he would call County and ask if anyone had been treated for dog bites or given rabies shot at ER.

Jake left the animal clinic and tried to call Buddy, no answer. He needed gas so he pulled into a C-store to fill up. He had just flipped open his gas cap and inserted the nozzle when he heard his name.

"Well, well, Jake Morgan."

He turned and saw her leaning against a gas pump, one hip cantilevered and smiling a 100 watt smile prettier than a summer morning: a time elapsed photograph, from girl to woman. Unbelievable.

"Harper Bannister," he said, looking at her. "Little teeny bopper last time I saw you. Braces and skinny. You filled out some."

"How do you like it?" she said, twirling once. Having fun. And, he had to admit she looked great.

"Well, you're not the ugliest girl in the world."

She cocked her head and said, "You don't recognize a genuine 'ten' when you see one?"

"There are no tens," he said.

"Now there is."

Look at her, being cute, making him smile.

"Give your smile a nine and a half. Your eyes maybe a nine." Her eyes were more like a 12 but no use over-stating it. "Give you another nine for your personality." He liked the light sprinkle of freckles brought out by the sun.

"Buy me lunch," she said. "I'm hungry."

"Just like that, huh?"

"You're going to get a better offer?"

"Just going to keep throwing yourself at me, that it?"

"If you're lucky and play your cards right."

"It's a deal," he said.

Lunch with Harper was nice. Relaxing. Jake picked up some food for an impromptu picnic and they sat on a park bench close to the World War II memorial in the town square, the Heroic G.I. looking down on them. The sun warmed them and his worried mind over his night with Pam melted away at the vitality of Harper's smile.

A new day. He could certainly use one.

She said, "Hmm." She looked at him and then nodded as if settling on something. "This seems to have some symmetry. You think?"

He smiled, feeling it a little but said, "Two old friends, right?"

"Time passes and then we both appear at the same place at a different moment. Comfortable, isn't it?"

She was young, fresh and something new for Jake. Wash away the night before with this lovely person. People would walk by and speak to her, asking how her father was and tell him hello. She would smile and say she would do that. The world seemed to gather around her. Could he get a do-over? Could he hope for such a thing?

"So, what are you doing these days?" he asked.

"I work as a para-legal."

"That's like a lawyer, right?"

"Something like it except doesn't pay as well and you do the scut work, but I don't mind. My boss lets me off when I need to do something or just want a day off. Doesn't say anything as long as the work's done."

"What do you do for excitement?" he asked.

"Like do I go out, hit the clubs, wait for Mister Right or some semi-cowboy to buy me a drink? I don't care for that. Rather curl up on my sofa with a good book, but I like to be out and about. I run a few times a week, not a fanatic about it. I hike, swim, stay active." Looking at her, seeing the healthy glow, he guessed she worked out more than she let on. "I don't know, I like living here, always have. This is home."

"Looking at you, I'd say you hit the clubs, you'd need creep-repellant to keep the semi-cowboys off you?"

She made a face. "Asking what my sign is. Like that? Telling me I'm the one they've been waiting for all their life or some line they heard in a movie. Who needs it? What about you? You married? No? Girlfriend?"

Thought about it. Last night with Pam? That was more like an auto accident. Hit-and-run. So he said, "Nothing with a future."

"Maybe not a future," she said, "but, the way you look your past must be something. You seem flavored by your absence from our little community."

He gave her a look, one eye closed. "Careful now."

"How long are you going to be here?"

"Couple weeks." He squinted from the sunlight, surprised at mentioning two weeks. "Get things done and head back." If he was allowed to return. Being in limbo with the rangers bothering him.

"Sorry about your dad. He was a good man. So was Gage."

"Part of life."

"That's how you view it?"

"Words. All I have now. Gage was a close friend."

"He was funny," she said. "Dad stopped him once riding a bike at one in the morning. Gage had been drinking.

Dad asked him what he was doing riding a bike that time of night. Gage told him he was in no condition to walk."

Nodding his head, Jake said, "Classic Gage Burnell."

Harper ate like she enjoyed it as much as he did. Didn't talk about how she needed to lose a few pounds or what new diet she was on. No, this one ate what she wanted, didn't pose, a genuine person. A girl with a barefoot personality. They walked around the downtown area, happy to have her by his side, taking in the familiar sights shaded by time. Afterwards he drove Harper back to her car at the C-Store. When he stopped his pickup she didn't get out right away.

"So," she said. "You going to ask me out?"

He smiled. "What would your dad think?"

"I'm all grown up now and he doesn't make those decisions for me anymore."

"He carries a gun, you know."

"More reason to treat me nice. You carry one too." He gave her a sidelong look and she said, "I know about the bank hold-up. You're a hero."

"I'm not." He decided to change the subject. "There must be a dozen guys around here chasing after you."

She shrugged. "They're tiresome. One thing on their minds and it's not my eternal happiness." Her face brightened, playing with him. "Maybe I like older, mature men who stop bank robberies."

"I'm not that much older." Maybe not so mature either, thinking about it.

"Maybe I'm just interested in you. Give you a chance. Think about that."

Just like that.

"Okay," he said. "How about I take you to the game tonight?"

She smiled and it burned through his defenses.

"Pick me up at six, okay?" she said and got out of the truck. She leaned into the window and said, "I'll be hungry again, so I'll need popcorn and a couple of hot dogs at the game."

She was delightful. Been too long since a woman

made him smile. Thinking of her as a woman now. No longer a little girl.

"Anything else?"

"Yeah, I need to tell you I'm damaged goods. Just went through a divorce."

"No damage showing. Anybody I know?"

"Tommy Mitchell," she said.

Jake closed his eyes and leaned his head against the seat headrest.

Harper Mitchell? Tommy Mitchell's ex-wife?

It just gets better and better.

9

"You were married to Tommy Mitchell?" Jake said.

She shrugged. "Not my best moment."

"I know him."

Harper smiled. "What I hear." He started to ask her about that, but she said, "Police Chief's daughter. Remember? Also a para-legal. If something happens in this place, I usually know so keep your nose clean."

"Do my best."

***

Jake sitting on his front porch, his, realizing it. The porch, more like a deck jutting out from the front of the brick ranch house, looked out across the lawn and the fields, seeing the barn and remembering delivering winter calves, his bio teacher called the process 'parturition', sometimes having to reach in the cow's vaginal tract, nasty but warm, feeling good on freezing hands. Summers with hay down his shirt damp with perspiration, smell of dirt when the plow or a disc tore into the land. He had good memories of farm life, but it was never a destination. Well, it had been once, but time and circumstance changed things. Not always for the better but usually forever.

Watching the smoke trail from the cigarette, something bubbling at his subconscious, cop curiosity kicking in. He walked to the back and around the area around the dog pen. He could see where tire tracks had left impressions, but they could've been from Gage's vehicle.

But where was Gage's vehicle? Remembering Gage had sent him a photo of a new SUV. What was it? He hadn't seen it. It wasn't the car Gage wrecked. There were only two vehicles on the farm now other than Jake's. Alfred's Ford pickup which needed tires and a car covered with a tarp. The vehicle under the tarp was an old Lincoln Mark IV Jake had attempted to restore and given up on years ago. Weird that Alfred hadn't gotten rid of it.

He kneeled and examined the ground around the pen and noted what looked like footprints. A lot of them. Different sizes.

He noticed a disturbed area where the grass was twisted and broken. Something most wouldn't notice but Jake's training triggered him to watch for such things. A struggle? He looked closer and saw three sets of footprints. One small, and two much larger. Gage was 5-9, 160 pounds. He didn't make those prints. Too big for the small set, not big enough for the other two.

Fat Boy Haller was a large man. Don't jump to conclusions, a lot of people had big feet. The small prints were interesting.

Back in the house, Jake went through Alfred's and Gage's files and documents. Also a pile of unopened mail. Gage was a highly organized person, one of the reasons Jake had entrusted him to serve as caretaker for Alfred's place. Jake tried Gage's laptop, but it was pass-worded. There was a four-drawer file cabinet with farm bills and documents in it. Bills, tax receipts and tax filings.

Bills and paid receipts arranged by month. Taxes arranged by year.

All of it neatly filed and in order.

But, the last two months were missing and no tax files or bank statements for the present year. They were gone. Everything gone since Alfred died? Where were Alfred Morgan's files? Where were Gage's personal files? Conspicuous by their omission. No reason for Gage to remove them. Or was there? Something Jake needed to check.

Jake pulled the old files out of the drawer and set them on the kitchen table, giving each file a careful look. After an hour he had separated a few from the rest. There were a few phone numbers, some doodles and a couple of notes Gage had written to himself.

Jake called one of the numbers and a secretary at the county recorder's office answered. Recorder's office? That would be one of many things. Deeds, mortgages, certificates of titles and many other documents and records and ranging into coroner certificates, bankruptcy filings and land titles. Something to do with the land dispute? Wishing Gage had given him more information. What was the surprise Gage mentioned?

Jake asked if their office received a call from a Gage Burnell? The secretary told him she just started working there and didn't know, offering to ask someone and have them call him.

Jake hung up and called the other numbers on his land line.

Two of them were businesses. Law firm of Benchley and Robinson and the State Highway patrol. He didn't know what to ask either of them, so he apologized and said he had the wrong number.

A third number was a recording. He recognized the name on the caller ID.

Pam Mitchell.

He clicked the button to break the connection.

Thought about it.

Time for a look at Mitchell Enterprises.

10

Jake drove out to Mitchell Enterprises' liquid fertilizer plant where Gage Burnell had been fired. When Jake and Gage were in high school Mitchell Enterprises had started with a trailer and a couple of low silos and had now mushroomed into modern low slung office building, with several airport hangar sized metal buildings and giant fertilizer tanks. He took a good long look and drove on.

Leaving the plant Jake returned to town to pick-up Harper. He saw the police lights in his rearview mirror. He wasn't speeding and his license was current. Taillight out or his truck matched the description of someone they were looking for? He pulled his truck over to the side and the police unit pulled in behind him.

Seeing Sheriff 'Doc' Kellogg get out of the unit told Jake it wasn't a busted taillight.

What could be more perfect?

"Hello, Doc," Jake said, when Sheriff Kellogg approached his door.

"License and registration," said Kellogg.

Jake started to protest. He was a law enforcement officer and knew there was no probable cause. He also knew he was a stranger in a land turned strange. He was on a lonely stretch of road and it would be his word against Kellogg's, the county's elected protector.

"Did I do something wrong, Doc?" Jake asked with as

much civility as he could muster.

"Wait in your vehicle, sir," said Kellogg. Officious was a strange posture for a man who had known Jake since he was a kid. Something up.

Jake watched the sheriff walk to his unit and get inside. Kellogg would run his plate through the computer. By now Kellogg would know Jake worked for the Texas Department of Safety. Would that make any difference? What could he charge him with? Nothing Jake could imagine so what was this about? This is not going anywhere you can't handle. Let him have his little roust and enjoy the football game with Harper Bannister. Don't let him push your buttons.

Kellogg returning now.

Jake turned on his cell phone video recorder.

"Step out of the vehicle, sir," said Kellogg. 'Sir', when he knew his name. Curious.

Jake opened the door and restrained the urge to say something and Kellogg asked him to accompany him to his unit. Jake did as he was asked. Commanded? What could you do?

Jake sat in the passenger seat and waited.

Kellogg said, "You're wondering why I stopped you."

"It occurred to me," Jake said, looking out the window at a cornfield, half of which had been harvested, bent stubs of corn stalk robbed of its seed.

"I want to talk to you." No violation, no probable cause. "Heard you're a Texas Ranger now."

Jake said, "Are you surprised? I promise to be a good citizen and get one of those "support your local sheriff" bumper stickers. How's that?"

"Don't get smart with me."

"The explanations would be too much trouble."

Kellogg stared at the side of Jake's face, saying nothing. It was quiet. Jake looked out the windshield. It was a police trick. The uncomfortable silence. But the phone recorder wouldn't last much longer and may have already finished.

"I didn't think much of your hero act at the bank. Ever

think what could've happened to the customers?"

That's what we're trained for, thought Jake, but he wasn't going to argue with Kellogg.

"No, you didn't," said Kellogg, continuing. "Just playing hero. Like you were back in high school playing quarterback and sneaking my daughter out late at night."

"That what this is about? If that's all I'll be going now."

"You'll go when I say. I got a call you were snooping around Mitchell's Chemical facility."

"You have snooping laws?"

"You had some trouble with the Mitchells recently."

"I'm concerned about Gage's death."

"What does that mean?"

"You investigate his death?"

"Of course." Sheriff Kellogg paused, took his ticket book and tossed it up on the dash of his SUV.

"You knew Gage had some trouble with the Mitchells, specifically Alex before his accident."

"I notice you had some trouble with the Mitchells yourself. What does that have to do with his accident?"

"Just interested. Would you mind, as a matter of professional courtesy, if I review your files on Gage's death? Just to satisfy my curiosity. I'm sure it was just an accident, but he was my friend."

"As I mentioned, you were involved in a row outside of Hank's."

"Made bail and the witnesses support my statement. It'll get tossed."

"I don't want trouble, but my daughter was seen with you on two separate occasions since you hit town. I remember you and her years ago and I was against it. Still am. Stay away from Pam."

Jake turned sideways in his seat and faced Kellogg. Getting to it now. "You stopped me because you think I'm after your daughter?" Who put him onto that? "Funny how your mind works."

"I don't like you being around her. I mean it. Got rid of you once so don't start up again."

Like old times. Remembering how Doc couldn't control Pam so he would intimidate the boys dating her. Jake had ignored him, and Kellogg never liked him. Old times, bad times.

"Using your badge to work out personal problems diminishes you."

"Just stay away from her."

"This is the worst roust in the history of bad rousts. Why not just bust out my tail ight with your night stick and write me a ticket?"

"Don't tempt me. I don't want any trouble, but I wanted to make sure we set the ground rules."

"Let's get something straight. You don't like me, and I don't think about you except for moments like this. I'm not after Pam. Think you can remember that? If Alex can't keep her at home that's nothing to do with me."

Kellogg's jaw muscles tightened, and he pointed his finger at Jake. Jake fought the urge to slap Kellogg's hand away.

"Listen up, Mister Texas Ranger." Whatever Kellogg was going to say he swallowed. "This is my county. You're not welcome here."

"Explains why there was no parade."

"Always thought you were smart, didn't you. Now get out of here."

"No kiss?"

"Keep talking," said Kellogg. "I'll get tired of it."

Jake got out of the car and walked around to Kellogg's side and leaned against the window. He could see that Kellogg had his hand on his service weapon. Theatrics.

"You gonna shoot me, Doc? Dial it back. Just want to ask you a question."

"What?"

"Somebody beat hell out of Gage's dog. Why? Which of Gage's vehicles was involved in the accident that killed him?"

"It was a Dodge Charger. That satisfy you?"

"He just bought a Dodge SUV, but I can't find it anywhere. Why is that? I ask around and no one seems to know what happened to it."

"I have no idea. Maybe his fiancée has it."

"Did you personally investigate Gage's death? Or did you assign someone?"

"I looked into it. All you need to know."

"You sent a Deputy. Lady cop named Bailey."

"You knew the answer but asked anyway. You're way beyond the line."

"Were there witnesses?"

"Get in your truck and leave. We're through here."

"I'll get back in my truck but I'm not leaving. I'd like to see the autopsy report and if there are witnesses. With your permission I would like to interview them."

"You have no jurisdiction and the matter is closed."

Jake placed a hand on the door handle of his pick-up, then turned and said, "One more thing, Doc."

"What?"

"Gage's accident? It isn't controversial, or is it?"

Kellogg ignored him and walked to his unit and burned rubber when Kellogg pulled out onto the highway. Jake felt the wind of the vehicle as it passed by him inches of where he stood waiting to get in his car.

"I get under everybody's skin," Jake said aloud. "It's like a gift."

11

Back in town, Jake drove by two more Mitchell holdings – a grain elevator and a New Holland tractor dealership – then picked up Harper and drove to the stadium. The air was cool and crisp. Smell of popcorn and autumn nights. Football weather.

The Paradise Pirates versus the state-ranked Hilltop Diamonds. Biggest game since the days of Leo, Buddy, Gage and Jake. The four horsemen without a clue.

Jake found Leo the Lion on the sideline and wished him luck.

"It's kids playing a kid's game," Leo said. "We'll bite their heads off and drag 'em back on their shields." Jake gave him a funny look and Leo laughed then said, "Sometimes I'm so full of shit I can hardly stand it myself. Our kids will show up."

Jake and Harper found seats and Harper mentioned she had no popcorn.

"Sure," Jake said. "You want to come with me?"

She made a show of patting her hair and batting her eyes. "Perfect tens do not fetch popcorn," she said, her eyes sparkling like sunlight blue water. "I need to save our seats, anyway. Place is packed."

Jake made his way to the concession stand and that's

when he ran into Buddy Johnson, wearing a PHS Security Jacket.

Jake said, "Moonlighting?"

"Needed a job. Kellogg fired me today."

Jake looked around. He nodded for Buddy to come with him and the crowd parted as they walked away from the concession stand. They moved near the tall cyclone fence and Jake asked him what happened.

"Because of me?" asked Jake.

"No." Shaking his head. "That wasn't it. He did mention it though. He didn't like you getting credit for taking out the bank robbers. See how you are? I filed for sheriff yesterday and it seems to have unsettled him. Who knew he was so touchy?"

"You'll make a good sheriff."

"When I do, my first act will be to remove the riff-raff. But I'll give you 'til sundown to get out of town, boy."

"I leave, what'll you do for crime?"

Two high school boys started to walk out of the stadium, Buddy telling them they weren't coming back inside, and he added, "I know you, so don't try it."

Then turning back to Jake, he said, "Besides the SRO job here Cal said he'll put me on the city force."

"Cal's as good as it gets."

Buddy nodded his head towards the grandstand. "I see you're here with his daughter. Good call. Best girl in town not married to me."

Jake bought popcorn and two cokes and returned to his seat next to Harper.

"Buddy's going to work for your dad," he said to her.

"My idea. That way he can keep an eye on Pam Mitchell. Make sure you don't make any clandestine moves her direction."

He looked at her for a moment, deciding. "What's that about?"

"Don't be offended. I'm not some starry-eyed little girl."

"Well, you are all grown up for sure."

"All part of being a perfect ten."

"Nine and a half," he said. "Maybe."

"We'll see if you hold to that assessment later."

***

Leo the Lion's Pirates beat the Hilltop Diamonds on a late drive and a short field goal. The biggest win in Paradise history. There was an after-game party at the Country Club. Leo asked Jake to come out and help him celebrate. Jake said okay.

The Paradise Country Club wasn't out of town and it wasn't very country. Arnold Palmer 18-hole golf course and two swimming pools. The old public course with its sand greens and weathered clubhouse gone now, replaced with gabled clubhouse with dining room and a large bar and lounge area right out of Caddy Shack. So nouveau riche it made his teeth hurt.

Leo was the center of attention. Everybody wanted to shake his hand and be part of the victory. Affirming the bloodlines, establishing the pecking order. Leo the Lion climbed the mountain and brought the possibility of a state playoff to Paradise and that hadn't been done since Jake was a senior, so the victory was vicarious for those who could join the party.

Glasses clinked, voices swelled and drifted away. The alcohol flowed and the voices became louder as the evening progressed. The room swarmed with well-wishers, wannabes, beef-and-bourbon businessmen and the self-proclaimed elite of Paradise schooling around the honored guest, the math teacher slash football coach with the D'Artagnan mustache. Leo saw Jake and Harper and pushed through the well-wishers to get to them.

"Congratulations, Coach," said Harper.

"Aw shucks, ma'am," Leo said. "It's nothing any run-of-the-mill genius couldn't have pulled off."

"Your public is all astir," Jake said, looking around. "Can I still be your friend?"

Leo looked around the room. "Yeah, it'll last until we lose, or I don't play the right person's kid. I have no illusions about any of this. I love the game and the kids. This part...well..."

"So, why are you here?"

"Bask in the glow of temporary celebrity, of course," Leo said. "Turns out, I hunger for attention. I'm a hero and I didn't even have to shoot anyone at the bank." Leo winked at Jake then said, "It's one of those things I do to help the kids out. Booster club gives us money for uniforms and other things. They paid for the new locker room and the sprinkler system for the field."

"What a whore," Jake said.

"Yeah," Leo said. "But a whore with a new locker room and sprinkler system. Try not to act loutish in front of my fans."

Vernon Mitchell walked up and put his arm around Leo. He smelled of Scotch and aftershave.

"Great game, Coach," Vernon said. "This is great for our town. You did a hell of a job preparing them."

"Jake here came up with the game plan," Leo said, that look Leo had always had when he was messing with him. Jake had forgotten the delight Leo got making Jake uncomfortable.

"Well," Vernon said, clearing his throat, uncomfortable now. "Thank you, Jake."

Jake said, "I had nothing to do with it. Leo's messing around and covering his modesty."

"Anyway," Vernon said, "a great night for our community. We're growing. Just one more thing that'll pull in business and more people. A... hello, Harper."

"Vernon," Harper said, nodding. "How's the airport thing coming along?"

"That's maybe off in the future," he said. "Working on it though."

"Airport," Jake said. "Paradise is getting an airport?"

Vernon's eyes shifted to the back of the room. "A small one. It's not like we'd be flying to Paris. Jumping off place for small airlines to hit places like Las Vegas,

Branson and Nashville. There's some interest. We're just in the talking stage right now. If you ain't moving you're going backward." He waved to someone. "Gotta run." He nodded at Harper and left them.

"What's this about an airport?" Jake said.

"Just something I knew they were talking about while I was a part of the Mitchell crime family. They were pretty excited about it, too."

"Where would they put an airport?"

"I don't know. I'm out of the loop these days."

Jake considered this new development but didn't know how it fit anything unless it had to do with the land dispute. He switched his attention to Leo the Lion.

"Even Vernon gives you praise."

"And deserving."

"Your modesty is staggering."

"Good to know you finally acknowledged my modesty."

"You have none," Jake said.

"Never did," Leo said, toasting Harper with his glass. "Never will. Modesty is for the weak who fail to recognize their inner greatness."

"You are so full of it, Coach," said Harper. Jake realizing Leo would've been one of Harper's teachers. Time didn't march on; it sprinted over the horizon and left a trail of shimmering memories.

Pam excused herself to go to ladies and Jake saw Pam walking his way.

"Some game, huh?" Pam said.

"Pam," Jake said, and nodded at her. Sheriff-Daddy wouldn't like this. So, bonus. Bedding Pam was right there between them and made things different. Not in a good way. He should've known better. Thinking of the joke about a guy naming his penis because it made all the important decisions.

"I see you're baby-sitting my sister-in-law," Pam said.

Jake scratched his cheek with a finger and said, "Looking at her she seems fully formed."

A little twitch at the corner of her mouth. "She's cute.

Latched on to you first chance she got."

"I don't know that's the way I'd put it. She can probably have her pick."

"And yet, she chose you," Pam said, close to him now. "Isn't that wonderful?"

"You and Alex straighten things out?"

"He's drunk. We need to talk."

"What happened to no strings attached?"

"I don't deserve that."

"Pam, we need to let this fade. Yesterday's news. Not that you're not attractive or that I don't care for you, but it's no good. Did you know your father stopped me today and warned me to stay away from you?"

That caught her attention. "What?"

"It wasn't a suggestion. More like any second I'd be night-sticked, handcuffed and charges filed. Wonder where he got the notion I was after you?"

"Not from me."

"He mentioned the incident at Hank's and today Buddy Johnson was fired."

"I don't know what you're talking about."

"What's this about an airport?"

"How do you know about that?"

"Your inebriated father-in-law mentioned it."

"The whole family talks too much when they're drinking." She made a face. "It's like a disease with them."

"You know anything about Gage's death?"

"Just what I hear, and you're changing the subject. What about us?"

"There is no us. We knew each other for a brief moment years ago. We're different now. You're married and I'm a long way from home. I'm not part of this place anymore." And realizing it more than ever. "We revisited our attraction last night and that was probably a mistake. Not a mistake like you think. Pam, look at it logically. We're several years of doomed dramas and dreams that aren't coming true if we push it. We'll both be ahead if we quit now."

"I don't want to stop," Pam said.

"Has to."

Pam bit her lower lip, started to speak but...

Harper returned now and said, "Well, Pam, how are you? Have you lost weight? You look great. You look even younger than you are."

Pam wet her lips, "Why thank you, Harper. You're looking...well, yourself."

Harper slipped her arm under Jake's elbow. "How's Alex?"

"He's fine."

Jake noted the brief flicker in Pam's eyes.

"You ready to go, Harper?" Jake said.

"Sure." Harper looked over and nodded in the direction of Alex who was talking to Shari Langston. "Whoops, looks like you'd better go rescue your husband. Shari's community stuff, you know. Bye, Pam."

They left. But not before Pam gave Jake a look that spoke of unsettled issues. He had managed to pile more garbage on top of the other garbage his life was becoming. He'd deal with such things as they occurred.

Yeah, that's what he'd do. Doing a bang-up job so far.

Outside, Jake pulled Harper closer and said, "That was one way to sugar-coat contempt."

Harper placed her hand on her chest and with a broad southern accent, said, "Why, Jake Morgan, I have no idea what ya'll talking about."

He could get used to having Harper around.

Yes, he could.

12

Jake sat on a cranberry colored sofa, Harper next to him, in Harper's nice little two-bedroom in an older tree-lined street. It was decorated in muted pastels, impressionist prints on the wall and it smelled of cinnamon and clean linen. There was a gray kitten and a salt-and-pepper miniature Schnauzer named Bandit playing on the floor. Norman Rockwell could have designed the place.

"What do you think about Gage's death?" he asked.

"In what context?" said Harper.

"Just throwing it out there."

"You mean did anyone in the Mitchell family have something to do with his death?"

"Anyone. Not just the Mitchells."

"Hard to think someone would hurt Gage. Maybe it was an accident. They happen."

"You're probably right. But you live here, know people and you have a good mind. Give me some of that female intuition stuff."

"That's a myth, Mister Misogynist, but who knows?" She stroked the gray kitten. "You sound like a suspicious cop."

"Maybe." He told her about being stopped by Sheriff Kellogg.

She gave him a look. "And why do you suppose he did that?"

Realizing he'd just stepped in it. "He has some idea his daughter has designs on me?"

"Does she?"

"I can't do anything about what other people think."

"Nice sidestep," said Harper.

"Alex Mitchell fired Gage and days later he has a wreck. Alfred died before that. Now the Mitchell's want my land."

"You didn't attend either funeral. And the first-person reference to your father is telling." She stroked the kitten and said, "You're holding back."

"I guess I don't see where I have a response that will help you understand. Do you know why Gage was fired?"

"Seems Alex and Gage had personal issues."

"Such as."

"Ask your old girlfriend."

"Was there something between Gage and Pam?"

"Just talk. I shouldn't have said anything. Don't make me out the jealous girl. I know Pam and she knows how to get what she wants and is not shy about doing whatever it takes. She's not going to leave you alone," Harper said. Harper didn't miss a thing. He would have to be careful about her. "Don't be surprised I see it. You're not the first for her. What are you going to do about that?"

Jake shifted on the sofa and said, "Yesterday's box score."

"Not what she thinks. I can see it in her posture. She sees you as a possibility. Why would she think that?"

Harper was boring in and Jake uncomfortable with her questions. Why did Pam think that? The gray kitten batted at Bandit with a paw. The Schnauzer flinched but leaned down and nuzzled the kitten.

"Pam and I were together back in the day. That help?"

"And she looks to fast-forward to now." She searched his face, his eyes, feeling her look. "There's more. I know her, have watched the way she does things. Know when she is in seduction mode. Observation not intuition. Anything else?"

"My choices haven't always been the best," he said.

Life was never simple. "Sometimes I require a lot of for-giveness. Can you give me that?"

In the background Adele was singing 'Melt My Heart to Stone'. It was quiet between them. She folded her arms over her chest and moved ever-so-slightly away from him.

"I have to be able to trust you," she said. "And, you need to trust my feelings for you. Neither of us is perfect. No one is. We have to allow each other to make decisions based on that trust. I've had a crush on you since junior high. You didn't know that? Of course, you knew, you're too aware not to. There's still some of that. There could be more than just a crush developing between us. You want to go into that with secrets?"

"No." He shook his head. "No, I don't. But this is not going to be pretty."

In a quiet voice she said, "Okay, that's fair, go ahead."

He told her. Told her about Pam's visit the night before. About the scene at Hank's place. She didn't interrupt or ask questions until he was finished.

"So, are you going to stay away from her?"

"Yes."

"Because of her father or because you don't want her?"

"Because of you, I guess."

"Guess?"

"I don't want anything like last night, ever again."

"So, one more sport fuck for old time's sake? Another item for the school paper's gossip column?"

"Keep in mind there was no you at that time."

"So, a nostalgic ride. Once more into the breach. That it?"

"Don't overthink it. You asked for the truth. I provided it."

"I know," she said. "This is more difficult than I imag-ined. Like you, I have history with Pam and the Mitchells. I need to let that go."

"I have no desire to be Pam's boy toy nor to be known for the fastest hips in town. Not something I seek. Pam was years ago. I walked away from her for the very reasons you mentioned. All of this is ancient history. Last night was like a car wreck."

The kittens back raised and turned and ran from the room. Bandit took a couple of steps to chase her and stopped, then took out after her. Harper rested her chin on the back of her hand. With her teeth in a straight line, she said, "I need time to think about this."

"Sure."

"You're right," she said, "it's not pretty."

But there it was.

"One more thing," said Harper.

"Sure."

"You don't wonder how she got in your house?"

13

The next morning Jake was at the county courthouse, his boots echoing on the ancient wooden steps up to the second-floor recorder's office where he was led to the map room. He searched for his place and found it, saw the boundaries. He looked up property owners of the land adjacent to it and recognized the names. Alex Mitchell, Tommy Mitchell, Vernon Mitchell and Pam Mitchell.

Wow. Alfred's place was surrounded by Mitchell property. The purchases were made within the past eighteen months. Now the inquiries about buying the place making sense. The Mitchells wanted the farm. It was sitting right in the middle of their holdings. But, what did it mean? There was talk of an airport and maybe they wanted the farm as part of that project. Nothing criminal about procuring property and extending your holdings. Land was a marketable commodity.

Still...

Gage and Alfred both died within the eighteen-month period of the land purchases. Maybe a coincidence.

Jake hated coincidence.

Jake sought out the county coroner, a local doctor. He doubted the M.E. would tell him much but his experience was you checked everything. Whatever you were wishing to turn up could be anywhere.

The coroner, Dr. Majuri, a medium sized man with a

middle-eastern accent, made a tent of his hands, resting his elbows on his desk as he listened to Jake's questions.

"I was a friend of Gage Burnell," Jake said. "He was killed in an auto accident recently."

"I remember it. Tragic."

"Was there another vehicle involved?"

"I only examined the...a...body. The sheriff's office investigated the scene."

"Was he drinking?"

Dr. Majuri studied Jake. "What are you looking for here?"

"I'm a law enforcement officer in Texas," Jake said. He produced his star with the words 'Department of Public Safety, Texas Rangers' embossed on the circle. "Like I said, Gage was a friend."

"You are perhaps out of your jurisdiction," said the coroner, smiling. "But you are an officer of the law and as a matter of courtesy I will tell you this. His blood showed, if memory serves, high levels of blood-alcohol content. Over the legal limit."

"Never knew Gage to drink much. When we were younger Gage was generally the designated driver. Why would he get drunk and drive his car off a bridge?"

Looking over the top of his bifocals he said, "You are asking me to make a value judgment. I examine and propose medical theories of a person's passing. Hopefully, I am accurate. Mister Morgan, I see strange things in my work. Dead spouses stabbed post-mortem, carbon-monoxide suicides, once found an old woman who had been dead for over a week sitting in her rocking chair, the television tuned to the Playboy channel. The average citizen does not see these things."

"May I see the photos taken at the scene?"

"The sheriff has those. According to state statutes they could not be disclosed except to close relatives."

"Were there any post-mortem wounds or anything that may suggest previous injury?"

"Meaning?"

"Bruises, contusions or cuts that were present prior to

the accident."

"Well... " Majuri thinking about it now. "Hard to make that determination as the body was badly damaged in the...a...crash. There were, naturally, contusions and multiple cuts and abrasions. I will admit I found that odd."

"Your final determination was accidental?"

Majuri nodded.

"Which of those injuries was most responsible for his death?" Jake said.

"None of them. The cause of death was suffocation resulting from aspiration of fluid."

"What?"

"You didn't know? Your Mister Burnell drowned."

14

Jake drove out to the old bridge on HH. There was a significant drop off as the ground over the creek was elevated. He could see the tracks and trail of Gage's vehicle where it tore weeds and ripped turf. He got out of his truck and walked down the bank. There was no suggestion that Gage had tried to stop, walking down to the creek's edge he saw were the bumper of the vehicle had dug into the shallow sediment of the creek.

There were several footprints on the slope but that would be consistent with people recovering a body and pulling the vehicle out of the creek. There were signs of boots or shoes sliding down the bank.

He looked closely. Thought about it. Sliding marks. The gouge in the sediment and shore looked as if the truck had stopped right there.

Meaning the vehicle had not fully gone into the creek.

How did Gage drown? It was a large running creek and deep enough. Did Gage exit the vehicle, disoriented in a drunken stupor or from injuries incurred during the crash and stumbled into the creek face down? It was possible. Jake had once investigated a drowning as a possible homicide, but the victim was drunk and high on crack, passing out. Still, what explained the injuries sustained by Gage the M.E. described? He had more questions for Majuri and wanted to interview Deputy Sheriff Bailey.

Cal had said Bailey was a good person.

He called Majuri's office and waited. Majuri came on the line.

"Yes, Mister Morgan. What can I do for you?"

"One more question, Doctor Majuri. Was there a full autopsy done on Gage's body?"

"Why, no. He was rushed to the med center. I examined him there and determined the cause of death was suffocation resulting from aspiration of fluid even as I related earlier and that is on the death certificate. There is little doubt he died from drowning. Sheriff Kellogg accepted that finding. As I mentioned previously, I did perform a blood test."

"Would Gage's blood-alcohol content be high enough that he would be black-out drunk?"

"It varies with each individual so it would be hard to say. Is there a problem?"

"I don't know," Jake said.

"Let me know if I can help you further. As the county ME I can only suggest certain things. I am not infallible. Determination of reason is the province of law enforcement. Again, much sorrow for your friend's passing."

Jake thanked him and broke the connection.

He dialed Buddy Johnson.

"Can you hook me up for a meeting for me with Deputy Bailey?"

"I can try."

"Have you been out to the site of Gage's accident?"

"Been there but didn't examine it. Why?"

"Something's not right. Gage sustained multiple injuries but that isn't what killed him. The ME marked it as an accidental drowning. But from what I've seen out here—"

"Dammit, Jake, are you out at the bridge?"

"Yes."

"Hang on, be there in ten minutes."

Buddy arrived in street clothes. His day off. They stood on the bank and looked down at the creek bed.

"Man, you're right," Buddy said. "I don't see how he

got cut up if what you're telling me is a fact."

Jake saying, "It's a fairly steep grade and he could've bounced or rolled on the way down. If he wasn't wearing a seat belt he could've been tossed around and tore up by the steering wheel, gear shift and debris in vehicle. We don't know if there was another vehicle involved which would create other questions."

"Drowning's weird though."

"You didn't know?"

Buddy removed his baseball cap and scratched his head. "No. Sheriff just said it was a wreck. That's all he told me. Word around town is the wreck killed him. I told you Doc's been keeping me on the outside of things. He was unhappy the day you had your little scrimmage with Tommy and Fat Boy. I made a joke about it, pissed him off, telling me citizens getting assaulted wasn't a joke, but then he doesn't have much of a sense of humor. And now I'm fired so my access is gone."

"I come to town and I start asking questions and you're fired. That bother you?"

"Some."

"What about Bailey? Can you set something up?"

"I don't know. I'll try but she could hesitate she thinks Doc won't like it and he won't. She's got a kid and her husband ran off and left her to pay the bills he ran up. She's going to be reluctant to do anything Doc won't approve, and lose her source of income. You know I never knew how Kellogg got the nickname, "Doc"?"

"He was a medic in the military," Jake said. Another thing to think about. Why hadn't Kellogg been concerned about Gage's injuries if he knew Gage had drowned? A medic would have questions.

"Bailey's not going to buck Kellogg," Buddy said. "May be better if I ask her about her investigation."

"Ask her if she saw other footprints when she arrived on the scene."

"Yeah," Buddy said, nodding. "Yeah, that's a hell of an idea."

"Another thing."

"Yeah."

"I want to see the car."

Buddy nodded. "You're a lot of trouble."

"All this at no extra charge."

15

Saturday morning Jake decided to take shooting practice. He fired his personal firearms along with his service weapon, setting up targets for both combat and competition shooting. Groupings were good, glad for that, wanting to stay sharp. Afterwards, he cleaned the weapons and planted a pair of red maple trees, something constructive. Jake's mind was sharper and more focused when doing manual labor. Digging the hole, he thought about last night and his discussion with Harper hoping their relationship was not stillborn.

Now thinking about what he had seen at the bridge. Buddy said he would attempt to draw information from Deputy Bailey that would be useful. So far, Jake had only suspicions most of which could be explained away but his experience had taught him to chip away and continue to gather evidence.

But he was running out of time. He now had only a few days to learn what happened to Gage before returning to Texas to face the music...or be reinstated. If he was not cleared of the specious charges, then what?

Jake had finished digging the first hole when he heard the rumble of the Camaro burning up his lane. One of the newer Camaros, with the throwback look, throwing gravel and trailing a plume of dust.

Aw hell. Not now. Not today. It was Tommy Mitchell.

Tommy got out of his car and slammed the door. Without preamble he jabbed a finger at Jake, saying, "You stay away from my wife, Morgan. Stay away from my brother's wife, too."

"Do you take intelligence reducing meds?" Jake said. "Get back in your car and get out of here before I change your day."

"She's my woman, Morgan." He was swaying a little as he said it. Drunk or stoned before noon. What a special guy.

"That's not accurate," Jake said. He wiped perspiration from his forehead with the back of a sleeve. Who needed this? "Doubt she ever was. She's her own woman. That's what guys like you don't get. She's free to do what she wants."

"Don't make me say it twice."

"Repeating it make you feel better? When you're finished scaring me, let me see your taillights get small before this escalates and you finish your drunk act at ER."

Tommy leaned against his car and crossed his ankles. "You think you're some kind of swinging dick, don't you?"

Jake really smiling now. Tommy could be unwittingly entertaining. Jake jammed the shovel in the ground to make it stand erect, wiped off his hands and said, "Did you hear that on TV, Tommy? Nobody really talks like that."

"Don't fuck with me, buddy."

"I'm not your buddy and your threats are boring."

"You think I'm bluffing?" Tommy said, his bluster diminished by his unsteady stance.

"I don't have thoughts about you at all. We've already seen what happens when we're are at odds. But guys like you gotta be shown, right?"

"You need to pack it in and head back to wherever you came from." Jake noting that Tommy apparently didn't realize Jake lived in Texas. Tommy wasn't the guy who mentioned Pam to Sheriff Kellogg.

"I was born here," Jake said, wondering why he said it.

"I'm going to get her back," Tommy said. "One way or another. She's my bitch, no one else's. I can't have her I'll fix it so no one else can."

"What does that mean, Tommy?" Jake stepped towards Tommy not liking Tommy's choice of words, feeling the heat and the red cloud forming behind his eyes. "Is that something you want to have said? You talk about her as if there is no weight for saying things like that."

"That a threat?" Jake could see Tommy was losing the heat of his bluster.

"Seeing your future. You touch her and your life will never be the same. Now, get off my place before I drop-kick you down the lane."

"Maybe it won't always be your place."

Hell of a thing to say. Jake wondering about that.

"Do I have to count to three?" Jake said.

Tommy got back in his car and ripped a donut in Jake's drive.

Jake leaned on his shovel and shook his head, trying to remember who said, 'May you live in interesting times'.

***

After Tommy Mitchell left, Jake planted and watered the trees and did chores around the house. He took a break for lunch and called Harper, no answer. He left a message for her to call him back.

That done he decided to take another look around the place and in particular the dog pen. Something wasn't right. The pen was secure and well-constructed. It was clean and the hinges and fastenings were not damaged so Gage's dog, Travis, didn't break out of the pen and run off. So, why did Travis for days? Was Travis with Gage when his vehicle went off the bridge? The chain spoke against that. Where did the dog get the injuries?

Jake had the broken chain from Travis' collar. He looked at it again, examining the break. The chain was a good one. Too strong for a dog, even a good-sized Lab to break. A chain link had been cut clean as if with wire cutters. Travis had bloodied and bruised up his neck trying to break loose, but the vet had said the damage was fresh like the dog was trying to get away from someone.

Someone cut the chain.

Why not just turn the dog loose? Why cut the link?

Did Travis' injuries have anything to do with Gage's death?

Where was Gage's second vehicle?

Okay, Jake, take a look at it. There's a vehicle missing, an SUV, a Dodge Ram if he remembered right. Gage didn't just drive off and leave it anywhere. The wrecked vehicle was a car, not an SUV.

In any investigation the simplest explanation was often the best. Occam's razor. Someone had reason to get rid of the vehicle. Someone had reason to take Travis, and someone let the dog loose and cut the chain.

Jake decided to take plaster casts of the footprints and the tire tracks near Travis' dog pen. Wondering now if any of them would match the prints at the bridge slope. It was a long shot.

One good clear print looked about a size 14 and two smaller footprints. Jake removed loose twigs and leaves from the large one, very carefully. Used his cell cam to photograph the prints and tire marks. That done, he cut up a heavy cardboard computer box he found in the garage and made a ring around the print. He mixed up a bowl of Plaster of Paris and after spraying the prints with a can of men's hairspray so the plaster wouldn't stick, he poured the mixture into the cardboard ring until the print was full and the pasty mix touched the cardboard. This would make a negative cast. It was the old school method, but it would do the job. He did the same with a good tire print. Now he had one of each. Whether that would lead anywhere was another guess. Could be anything and probably nothing but it was a start.

He left the casts to dry and did a sweep of the house Gage had lived in the last few months. Find something, anything.

He pulled the comforter off the bed, examined the sheets, pulled them then checked the mattress. Tiny brown spots. Blood? Maybe, but it may not mean anything. Thinking about getting Sue, his lab tech friend, to run a test but maybe he was pushing it too much, him gone and their relationship hitting that blip where both went different ways.

Too early for making the assumption about blood? Missing personal files, the land-buy off and Gage's death had gears grinding in his head. He didn't believe in gut reactions but his were making a racket.

So, he called Sue.

"What now?" she said, when she answered. "You need a favor, right?"

He admitted it.

"Knew it," Sue said. He could hear her low laugh. "What is it this time?"

He told her about the blood on the mattress and she told him to send him the samples. "Also, send me something with your friend, Mister Burnell's, DNA on it for comparison and a sample of yours for a control variable."

"Like what?" Jake asked.

"Your friend's toothbrush or comb. The blood samples, you know how to do that. And from you anything like that but no used condoms."

Playing with him.

"Something else," Jake said. "Run some tire print photos I can text you see what kind of tires left the marks. Also, can you run records on a guy named Noah Haller? Born here in Paradise?"

"Whatever tickles you just suits me to death," she said, turning the idiom upside down.

***

Two in the afternoon Tommy Mitchell was shit-faced and buzzing like a cheap clock. He was supposed to be doing his foreman job at Mitchell feed elevator but what the hell, huh?; he was the boss and they owned the damned place, could do what he wanted. He stopped at a liquor store and picked up a twelve-pack of Coors and a pint of Jim Beam.

And man, did Mr. Beam slide down easy after a couple of beers.

He was still worked up after going out to the asshole's place and needed to level out. That Morgan asshole had some mouth, threatening him as if Tommy was nobody harshening Tommy's mellow. The guy giving him tough guy looks like he knew Tommy and knew things about him. He'd love to get the guy down and work on him. But how? The guy had been all over him and Haller the other night. So fast.

There was another cunt needed an attitude fix besides Harper. His sister-in-law, Pam. She'd be ticked off he was drinking, always on his ass and she took big bites; but he avoided her when he could. Way he saw it you wore a tampon every 28 days you weren't in charge of shit.

Still, Pam wasn't no pork chop. She was U.S. prime with a wicked tongue. She'd give him the look and then start in on him with her nasty mouth.

He took a slash from the beam and washed it down with a good swallow of the beer. Feeling better. Plenty of sunlight left to score some weed, mellow out. Find a nice place to sit and waste the day.

Tommy looked in the rearview mirror, touched this cheek and saw the purple-yellow bruise. Jake Morgan. Boy, you couldn't come at him straight up. The guy took Fat Boy Haller like he was a kid. Both of them. Man had some training somewhere. Wasn't no street fighting stuff. Some kind of martial arts but not like the movies. Somebody said it was an Israeli commando way of fighting, Krav Maga, what they called it. Man, he'd like to catch him in the sights of his .30-06. Pow! Let him have it, watch his eyes glaze over. Teach him he should never have come back to Paradise.

Or.

Or, face him down, man to man. Old west style. Imagining it. Staring the asshole down, calling him out into the street, see who was the fastest gun in Paradise. Telling the guy to pull on the count of three, Tommy pulling on two.

Yeah, that was the way. Asshole wouldn't figure that. Doc Kellogg didn't like the guy and maybe look the other way. Hell, Doc would have to go along he wanted to remain as sheriff was the way Tommy saw it.

Why was he drinking alone?

What he could use right now, what with the beer buzz, was the weed and a little trim. He knew a little girl in town whose husband slept during the day that could take care of Tommy's urge, but when he called she didn't answer.

How about? Aw, should he? How about Harper fucking Mitchell? A little afternoon reconciliation was in order wasn't it? She'd be at work this time of day, but he could wait.

Hell, he knew where she kept her hideaway key. She didn't know that. Be waiting when she came home from work.

Surprise baby, daddy's home.

16

Last time they spoke Gage told Jake he finally decided to marry Hanna Stanislaus, his high school sweetheart, gave her an engagement ring. They were hot and cold as a relationship for years most of it Gage's fault. Gage would do something crazy or just tick her off as he was prone to do, and they would break up. Never for long, though. Small towns were like that. You count on ending up with the one you started with. Hanna is the next place to get some answers.

Hanna ran a dog-grooming place called the 'Puppy Palace'. He entered the lavender painted building and was met with the aroma of shampoo and animal musk. Hanna was happy to see him.

"I have trouble thinking about Gage," she said. She had a Shiatsu pup looped on a tall table, clipping his coat. "Keeps me awake nights. It's a terrible thing. He was a good man. And, I'm worried I can't find Travis. He loved that dog."

"I found Travis," Jake said. He told her about Travis coming home and his injuries.

"Who would hurt Travis?" she said. "Such a sweet boy. Gage was crazy about Travis. Went everywhere with Gage. We both love dogs and that's one of the reasons we get along so well." She stopped clipping the little dog. She looked away, took a breath and placed a hand along her cheek, her eyes moist. "I miss him."

"He was an original. You said Travis went everywhere with Gage? Would he have been with Gage during the wreck?"

"Maybe. Like I said, they were pretty close."

"Did Gage chain Travis when he wasn't home."

"A chain?" she said, asking it as if it were a strange question. "No. Never. Gage detested chains and never used one on Travis."

"Did Gage seem depressed or down in the dumps lately?"

"Gage? You know how he is...was." Stopping for a moment again. She placed a hand behind her neck as if pained. "He was always in a good mood or at least a goofy one. I don't think he was ever depressed or bored. No," she said again. "Not depressed. Ever. Gage thought the world was made just for him to have fun. Consequences never entered into his thinking."

Travis was Gage's constant companion. Travis would not have run off nor would he have left Gage. Dogs don't do that. Travis would not have left Gage at the wreck nor would he have allowed him to drown. File it away.

"You know anyone want to harm Gage?" Jake said.

Hanna dropped her eyes then appeared to be thinking about it. "Maybe...but no."

"You started to mention someone."

"No. I just...it's nothing."

"Anything helps."

"Do you think Gage was murdered?"

"Didn't say that." Cryptic now. "Someone took his dog and abused it. Like to know who did that?"

"I would hate to falsely accuse anyone."

"You wouldn't be."

Hanna sat down, folded her hands in her lap and looked at them for a moment. Then she looked up at Jake.

"I just would...rather not. Let me think about it."

Jake was trained to watch people, look for behavior tells, and Hanna was holding back. People withheld information for different reasons. Sometimes it was personal items that really didn't matter but sometimes there was a little gem that fit everything together. He would save it for another time. He could come at her a different way at a later date and a different setting.

"Jake, may I have Travis?" said Hanna. "It would be something to hold onto that was part of Gage."

"I can think of nothing better," Jake said.

Leaving the Puppy Palace and promising Hanna he would tell the vet to give Travis to her, Jake decided to stop by Harper's and see if she felt better about things. She was troubled by the revelation of his tryst with Pam but did not go on about it or act childish and jealous. Still, it set her back, he saw it in her, felt her pulling back and he understood why she would feel that way. Didn't help him feel better but there it was.

When he pulled up to Harper's drive, he saw the Paradise Police unit parked at her house. Must be her dad, is what he thought.

But it wasn't Cal Bannister's car.

7

Jake buzzed the doorbell and a uniformed Buddy Johnson opened the door. "Come on in, Jake," Buddy said. "We're about done here."

Jake entered and saw Tommy Mitchell on the floor, hands cuffed behind him. Tommy's hair was disheveled, and his eyes glistened with alcohol poisoning. The smell of stale marijuana radiated from him. Harper wasn't in the room.

"Where's Harper?" Jake said. "She okay?"

"I'm fine," said Harper, entering the room. She straightened her hair and he could see the redness on one cheek and the torn buttonhole on her blouse. "No thanks to this idiot. Tommy, you come around again I'll hit you with a baseball bat."

Jake noticing Tommy's knuckles were scraped and swollen.

"How'd you hurt your hands, Tommy?" Jake asked.

"Smacking you," Tommy said hissing it.

"Never laid a hand on me. You're a lightweight. Who else you been fighting?"

"What's he doing here?" Tommy said, ignoring Jake. "The fuck're you doing at my wife's house?"

Again with 'the wife' thing.

Jake saying now, "Did you hurt her, Tommy? Did he hurt you, Harper?"

"Are you fucking him?" Tommy asked Harper.

That was enough.

Jake took quick steps and snatched up Tommy by his hair and bent him over a chair. "It's coming," Jake said. "You won't let it go. Just show up here again. I fucking dare you."

"I didn't have these cuffs on," Tommy said.

"Take his cuffs off, Buddy," Jake said.

Jake felt strong hands pulling him away from Tommy. "Dammit, Jake," Buddy said. "Leave off. You're complicating things."

Jake let go, blood throbbing in his neck.

"He's fucking dangerous," Tommy said. "Arrest him."

"Shut up, Tommy," Buddy said. "Or you'll be eating those cuffs." Buddy reached down and lifted Tommy off the floor by his cuffed arms as easy as if he was picking up a pillow.

"Ouch! Damn, Buddy!" Tommy said.

"Behave and it won't happen a lot."

"Wait until Kellogg hears you're abusing innocent citizens."

"I don't work for Doc anymore," Buddy said. "You need to keep up with current events. And you've never been innocent long as I've known you. You're lucky I took the call and not Cal. He has reason not to care for your dumb ass in the first place." Buddy looked at Harper and said, "Do you want to bring charges?"

"Maybe," she said, she glared at Tommy, burning a hole in him with her eyes. "I have three hundred sixty-five days to file."

"Yes, you do," Buddy said.

"Throw him back, let him grow up," she said.

Buddy leaned down closer to Tommy's shoulder. "Hear that, Tommy," he said. "You mess with her again and you're looking at assault and attempted rape."

"And trespassing he comes on my property again," said Harper. "I'll file a complaint about that."

"Bother her again," Jake said, with more venom than intended, "and I will become a permanent fixture in your life."

Buddy shaking his head and looking tired. "Will you shut up, Jake? I'm handling this."

"Rape?" Tommy said. "I didn't rape her, she's lying."

"Attempted rape. Assault. Pay attention," Buddy said. "You want that told around, Tommy? Kind of dampen your romance with the local girls. Not many of them want to date a guy charged with attempted rape."

"As if anyone would date him otherwise," said Harper.

Buddy uncuffed Tommy and led him away. As they were leaving Tommy said, "I'll be seeing you around, boy."

"Be careful you don't see me too often."

"Both of you knock it off," Buddy said, shoving Tommy outside.

Jake alone with Harper now. She left to change her blouse and returned wearing a sweatshirt with the words 'Paradise Football' on the front.

Jake sat on the cranberry sofa where they'd sat the other night. This time, though, Harper sat in the matching wingback chair. Though they were in the same room he felt the distance between them.

"You okay?" he asked.

She surprised him saying, "The question is are you okay?"

She was working up to something. He waited.

"Jake," she said, "I care for you. The anger? I think you try to hide it but... First, there's Pam and you've been in a fight first day back and for a brief moment it looked like you wanted to cripple Tommy."

Jake looked at his hands and said, "I don't like men who abuse women."

"I understand but Buddy had control of the situation. It's not I don't appreciate your concern...and I realize much of it is your feelings for me, which is not a terrible thing."

Jake told her Tommy had already made an appearance at the farm.

"Making the rounds," she said. "No wonder you're wound up. Tommy can do that. When I got home Tommy was here, waiting for me." She brushed a lock of hair behind an ear. "He found a hideaway key. He wanted to negotiate a reunion. I told him to get out and he tried to get next to me telling me how much he loved me and wanted me back." She was shaking her head. "Tommy never loved anyone but Tommy. God, I have no idea what I was thinking or what I saw in him."

She stopped and looked out the window briefly and then back at Jake. Jake wasn't going to hurry her.

Harper continued, saying, "I phoned dad's office and Buddy answered and showed up, but not before things got physical and the idiot tried to force himself on me."

Jake didn't know what to say so he said nothing.

"I really want to be alone right now, Jake."

"You sure you're okay," he said.

She nodded. "Yes. Just go. Please."

"Okay," he said and got up to leave. With his hand on the door handle, Harper had something else for him.

"Jake?" He turned as she walked towards him. "One more thing. You see the difference?"

Her eyes searching his face. He waited for her to speak.

"When Tommy showed up, I turned him down. That's how you deal with someone out of your past who is no longer part of your future."

He started to say something, thought better of it, and left.

What do you say when somebody slapped you with the truth?

You tried to learn from it. That's all.

18

So far Jake didn't have much. Tire prints and foot casts wouldn't help unless he could determine a crime occurred. Gut feelings and 'hunches' are for television. Was he hoping he could go after the Mitchells? His own prejudices against them clouding his reason?

Tommy's damaged hands, along with what he'd learned looking at the accident scene, piqued his interest. It was not enough to assert a homicide yet neither did it satisfy Jake that the investigation of Gage's death was thorough and professional. Stay after it. As for the jurisdiction thing, he would try to stay under the radar with Kellogg. Right now, he wanted to see the car Gage was driving when he ran off the bridge. Go see Buddy and work that out.

***

Buddy Johnson, in his new capacity as Paradise P.D. officer, led him to the chain link fence impound area where Gage's vehicle was kept.

"The city and the county share the impound," Buddy said, turning the key in the padlocked gate leading into the impound area. There were cars, trucks and SUVs of all descriptions and repair. The ground was raw with dirt and scattered chat. "Kellogg can bitch but he can't do a thing about it."

"You had a chance to see Gage's car?"

"Not until today."

"What was he driving?"

"He just bought a Dodge Ram SUV, but he had a Dodge Charger. Nice one about four years old he kept waxed, looking like it came off the show room floor. Burnell liked the Mopars." Buddy pulled out a creased document and read from it. "Red Dodge Charger R/T." He folded it up and put it back in his pocket.

"Where's the Ram? It's not at my place." First time he had referred to Alfred's farm in first person.

"It's missing?"

"Unless you know where it is, yeah."

Buddy shaking his head now. "You're telling me his other vehicle is gone? No one mentioned that. That's strange. Let's look at this one first. See it anywhere?"

"I see one matching the description," Jake said, looking across the lot. "But that can't be it." He pointed at a red Dodge near the back of the lot.

Buddy stared at it. "Man, it looks like it." They walked towards it. "Yeah, that's it, but shit."

"Yeah," Jake said. "The damage isn't extensive. How could that cause the injuries described?"

"I didn't even know he drowned until you told me," Buddy said. "I did some checking and the official version is Gage ran off the bridge, got out of the car and passed out face down in the water. Said that's how they found him, face down in the creek. Told you. Kellogg kept me in the dark."

"Travis wasn't with him."

"The dog?" said Buddy. "What makes you say that?"

Jake stared at the car for a long time, hands on his hips, before saying,

"You should've followed things up, Buddy."

"Yeah? And you shoulda showed up at the funeral. Don't come at me like that, Jake. I love you but that won't keep me from holding you upside down over a toilet."

"Someone could've called me."

"You didn't stay in touch. You left and we didn't hear

anything from you for years. Missed your dad's funeral, too. What is it? You have some other personal issues you want to lay off on me?"

"Don't start on me."

They glared at each other for an uncomfortable moment.

"I ain't your problem, Jake," Buddy said.

Jake nodded and held out a hand. "Okay, you're right. Truce?"

Buddy nodded. He shook a cigarette out of a pack.

"When'd you start smoking?" Jake asked.

"The day you came back. Quit for years. See how you affect people?"

Jake saying now, "I want to look inside."

"I don't have a key," Buddy said.

"That's okay," Jake said, producing a pair of driving clothes he brought with him. "Window's broken, I'll just reach inside and unlock it. Doggone kids must've climbed the fence and vandalized it. They're always up to something."

"That window ain't bro—" Making a face and saying, "Aw shit, Jake. Don't do that."

"Give me your stick."

"No."

"Gotta be a rock somewhere." Jake began searching the grounds.

Buddy looked around, turned away from Jake and handed him the collapsible baton.

"Don't watch," Jake said. "Plausible deniability."

"This how you do things in Texas?"

"We're not in Texas," Jake said, extending the baton. "I'm a private enterprise operation. We don't look into this no one else will." Moving to the passenger door side so he didn't disturb the driver's seat he whipped the baton backhanded at the side window and it disappeared in an explosion of broken glass. He tugged on the driving gloves and lifted the door latch, then tripped the door locks. That done he walked back around the vehicle and opened the driver's side door, looking inside.

Buddy stood by, shaking his head. "Man, you are something else entirely. You remember I'm running for sheriff, right?"

Jake examined the interior, careful not to disrupt the crime scene. Thinking of it that way now even though it was not considered a crime scene by Sheriff Kellogg.

"What are you looking for?" Buddy said.

"Hang on." Jake examined the floorboard seeing the dust one would find in this part of the country. Checked the back seat. Checking under the passenger seat he found a couple of unusual items. Used toothpick and a tin of Skoal. Toothpicks and smokeless tobacco would narrow the possible users to only several hundred men in the area. Pretty thin unless he could get a DNA profile; an impossibility unless he could prove evidence of a crime. He gathered up dust samples and placed them in some zip-lock bags he'd brought along. He didn't have a forensic setup but he did have Sue. He also scraped the brake pedal, noticing a strange substance embedded in the grooves.

He noticed the driver's seat was pushed all the way back. Gage was five-foot-eight and that position would not be comfortable for a person of Gage's size. Someone else driving the car.

"Was the car towed or driven back?" Jake asked Buddy.

"They're always towed. Liability question if we drive them."

"Wish we could dust for prints," Jake said.

Buddy grunted. "I'll see what I can do, you come up with anything."

Jake reached under the dash and popped the trunk, got out and walked to the rear of the vehicle and looked inside. He was surprised by what he saw or rather by what he didn't see. The carpeting had been removed from the trunk. Frayed carpet pieces were scattered around the trunk area.

"Well, look at that," Jake said.

Buddy looking over his shoulder said, "I know what you're thinking."

"Someone didn't want anyone to examine the contents of the trunk like blood on the carpet."

Buddy nodded, then sighed. "Gage was a fanatic about this car. He wouldn't let me smoke in his cars. He wouldn't tear that carpet out."

"The driver's side is a mess. He had cuts and bruises yet there's no blood I can see in the car. Not consistent with the injuries the ME mentioned. Bet we don't find any fingerprints besides Gage's either." Or, just thinking it now, Maybe Gage was killed elsewhere and moved to make it look like an accident. Drowned Gage and drove his car off the bridge? Possible. Someone moved the seat back and it wasn't Gage. Jake leaned in and made a closer look at the trunk interior.

"Look at this." He pointed at grey flakes on the spare tire.

"Cigarette ashes?" Buddy said.

Jake nodded and said, "Whoever killed him forgot not to smoke at the scene of the crime."

Buddy dropped his cigarette and stepped on it. "Hang on a second. Come on," Buddy said. "Scene of the crime? You talking homicide? Why would anyone kill Gage?"

"I don't know." But he had thoughts about it. He wanted Buddy's input without bias.

Buddy said, "Who'd be that mad at Gage?"

"Question is," Jake said, shutting the trunk lid. "Why go to the trouble to make it look like an accident? If it's a homicide, it was planned and would take more than one person to pull it off."

"Why's that?"

"The bridge is in a remote area miles from town. Wouldn't be good to be seen walking back to town. They needed a second car meaning at least two men were involved."

Buddy threw down his cigarette and stepped on it. "That's only true if he was murdered."

"Know what I think?"

"I'm afraid to ask."

"I don't believe he was in the car when it went off the bridge."

"How you figure?"

"At the bridge you could tell the car didn't go all the way into the creek. I think it possible he was drowned elsewhere then placed by in the creek. Too many footprints at the site and now too many people walking around down there to check it out. I'm not buying Gage stumbled out of the car and drowned."

"But it is a possibility. He had a high blood-alcohol reading."

Jake dusted his hands and nodded. "Maybe. The killers couldn't risk getting Gage trapped inside where they couldn't get him out. They wanted to see the body. Make sure he was dead."

Jake walked around the Charger, checked the front bumper and then along the panels under the doors. Mud was caked on the front and underneath the car. He lay down and slid under the vehicle. No damage to the front suspension. He got out from under the Dodge, dusting off the back of his pants and said, "I want to see the accident report."

"Sheriff's got it and I don't work there anymore."

"What about Cal?"

"Jurisdiction problem. It's county. Kellogg won't give either of us a smell and don't get any sick thoughts about breaking into the office."

"I wouldn't do that."

Buddy widened his eyes and snorted. "Hell, I don't know what you would do. Seem to do whatever you want. Case in point," he said, nodding at the car. "Slow down, Jake, before we end up in jail, which tends to be a negative factor in an election campaign. You come up here and storm around like a goddamn Texas cyclone. You gotta listen to me. Slow the fuck down and go at this legally."

"How? If this is what I think it is then everything I need is going to be out of my reach. That doesn't bother you?"

"Hell yes, but I'm not wild as you. You've always been like this. You just can't run straight through everything."

It was quiet between them for a long moment.

"You're fucking one surprise after another," Buddy said.

"I've been away."

"Don't make me wish you still were."

Jake laughed.

"Here's what we have," Jake said. "No blood in the vehicle, some various sediment and dust particles on the floorboard that could be nothing, contusions and cuts but no blood in the vehicle but the trunk carpet removed and discarded. The victim, uh... I mean Gage drowned in the creek. I wonder?"

"Wonder about what?"

"Need to talk to Deputy Bailey. Or, you do."

"Damn, Jake, this a lot to take in."

Jake nodding his head. "It is."

"Could get us in some shit."

"Yep."

"And you don't give a damn what anyone thinks?"

"Nope."

"What the hell, huh? Okay. What're you thinking?"

Jake put his fists on his hips, looking at the car. "If Gage died somewhere then was moved to the creek, we need evidence of that. If we get that evidence, then we can get the state patrol to open up a homicide investigation."

"You're awful careless with that 'we' shit, white boy," Buddy said.

"C'mon, if we're going down in flames let's do it right. You know you're in and can't wait to run it down, either."

"Yeah, well," Buddy said, shrugging. "What the hell, huh? Way I figure, we go down, we may as well do it in style."

19

What had Jake learned so far? Nothing that would pry open an investigation into the peculiar death of his friend. He would need more information and a motive anyone would have to kill Gage, and at the moment he had zip for a motive. Had Gage stumbled onto something that got him killed?

He wanted to know the content of Gage's lungs to determine if they were filled with creek water or some other fluid or even if it was water from a different source. Suffocation by aspiration of fluid did not necessarily mean water. Forensic science had made remarkable progress and could determine not only that it was creek water it could pinpoint the source. If not creek water, then what? And what was the material he'd removed from the brake pedal? He had no crime lab to make a determination. All he had was possibilities and suspicions, but his cop radar was buzzing.

Tuesday morning the high school had an early dismissal and Leo the Lion gave the team a day-off so he called and asked if Jake wanted to try out the Country Club golf course. Jake agreed and found Gage's clubs in the front closet.

The club course was well-maintained. The fairways and greens looked like cake frosting. Jake remembered the old public course with its gravel parking lot, sand greens and bare spots in the fairway. He also remembered Gage and himself jumping the fence and playing holes three through eight without paying. The Country Club course was contiguous to Mitchell Agri-Business and their Chemical-Fertilizer plant. Not surprising.

"How do you afford a membership on teacher's pay?" Jake asked Leo as they got their clubs out of the truck bed.

"Booster club pays," Leo said. "Just another perk in my success saga. And now, as so often happens you are about to learn there is one more thing I'm better at than you, you pitiful lout."

They went to the clubhouse and Leo signed in Jake as his guest and paid for a cart along with a twelve-pack of beer and a cooler.

"Stoking carbs, Leo," said Jake. "We must fortify ourselves for this athletic event."

Leo had called ahead for a 2:00 tee time. The course marshal told them the 1:45 twosome had not shown up yet. Leo pointed out that those who were early were on time and those who were on time were late.

The course marshal said, "This group is probably exempt from that."

That was when a cart pulled up containing Vernon Mitchell and Doc Kellogg, both dressed in Country Club monogrammed shirts and hats.

Leo looked at Jake and smiled. "And the hits just keep on coming," he said.

The two older men got out of their cart and Vernon greeted them. "Hello, boys. Good day for it, isn't it? Not many left now. Sorry we're a little late, Pete," he said to the course marshal.

"No problem, Mister Mitchell," said Pete.

Leo looked and silently formed the words, 'no problem' to Jake.

"Are you boys waiting to tee off?" Vernon asked.

Leo telling them it was okay they could wait. Vernon invited them to join them for a foursome. The invitation hung in the air like a cloud. Doc Kellogg looked like he'd swallowed a golf ball.

Jake cut his eyes at Leo who was shaking his head telling Jake 'do not accept'. Jake leaned on his driver and said, "I'm not sure Doc would like that."

"He's okay with that," Vernon said, "aren't you, Doc?"

"Sure," said the Sheriff, without looking at anyone.

"Let's forget our difficulties for today and have a nice round."

"What difficulties?" Jake said. "I'm just happy to be home again. Hell, I may move back here."

Leo rolled his eyes.

"Team scramble?" Vernon said. "Best-ball and ten dollars a hole, hundred bonus?"

Jake aware Vernon was baiting them. Vernon and Doc might be hustling them. Well, let it be what it is. He would love to take their money.

"A little rich," Jake said. "How about a buck a hole and if I win, I get a free club membership?"

"What do I get if I win?" Vernon said.

Jake smiling now, "I'll give you this nice set of Great Big Bertha Drivers and matched set of Ping Irons."

"I already have a good set of clubs."

"But these are Gage Burnell's," Jake said. "Figure you'd like to have them for their sentimental value, if nothing else."

Doc Kellogg's lips were set in a firm line. Vernon's eye darkened, but he recovered quickly. He laughed to himself and said, "Okay, hotshot, dollar a hole is fine and a club membership if you and Coach win. You won't need to throw in the clubs. Five dollars a stroke for total score."

"Suits us," Leo said. "Your time is our victory."

Vernon teed-off and sent a ball straight down the fairway about 200 yards with Kellogg nearly matching that. They were both veteran golfers so winning would be difficult. Jake teed off and his ball sliced into the rough on the right. Fortunately, Leo hit a nice shot 225 yards out on the left side of the fairway.

They got in their carts and chased after their tee shots. When they stopped, Leo opened a beer and offered one to Jake who declined. Leo was shaking his head.

"Just had to blaze one under his chin, didn't you?" Leo said. "Couldn't just let it go. Boy, you never stop." Leo made a grunting sound and took a swallow from his beer can. "Try to remember Doc carries a gun in his golf bag."

"And you think I don't?"

Leo gave him a look. "Are you...are you kidding me?"

"Taurus nine. Right back there in the ball bag."

Leo squeezed his eyes shut, then opened them and said, "You're scaring me. When did you become this?"

"Leo," Jake said, as they stopped to allow Vernon to line up his second shot. "You've never been scared one day in your worthless life."

***

Vernon and Doc took the first hole and after 13 holes Vernon and Doc had a 7-6 advantage.

"Damn, they're good. We're lucky to say close," Leo said. "Time to go into a prevent defense. I'll fake an injury and we'll leave."

"No."

"You're a masochist."

"Determined optimist. You need to improve at observation."

The 14th hole was a long par five by a creek that bordered Mitchell Agri-Industries on the right. It was a hole for big hitters. Straight with bunkers at the front of the green and one in the middle of the fairway. The kind of hole that looked like an easy five but there was danger.

Vernon got off his best tee shot of the day and he was in good position to shoot the green for an eagle or at least a birdie with two good shots. Leo hit a decent drive that was 50 yards short of Vernon's. Jake addressed the ball and looked down the fairway. Leo was in good position so Jake was thinking he could load up and go for a winner.

Jake took a John Daly wrap-around backswing and brought the driver forward. 300 plus yards, but the ball tailed right into the rough on the right side.

"That's too bad, son," Vernon said.

"Playable," Jake said.

Vernon laughed and got in his cart.

"Are you out of your mind?" Leo said. "What're you thinking? Mine's the smart play."

"You're right. But, your powder puff hit's short and if mine's playable; we have to use it if we're going to keep up. C'mon, live a little, take a chance. What've you got to lose?"

"My money."

They stopped their cart and Doc Kellogg hit his best shot of the day. They watched it rise and fall on the green 20 feet from the green.

"Right on the playground," Vernon said, exultant. He waved to them as they drove up to the green."

"See?" Jake said. "We need the extra distance. Do you see the pattern here? I'm right again."

They pulled the cart up next to the rough and began looking for the ball. They found it but it was further right than Jake had hoped. The ball was near the creek bank and out-of-bounds. A gentle breeze blew through the trees as Jake spotted the ball.

"Yeah," Leo said, hands on his hips. "Let's play your ball. Two-stroke penalty. I'm proud to be part of this team. We lose this and I'm gonna wrap a lob-wedge around your neck."

"That's quite a statement for a pacifist."

They stepped out of the wooded area and Jake dropped a ball for the two-stroke penalty. Leo had the best ball but was still short of the green. They were going to lose two, maybe three strokes on this hole.

As they drove their cart up to hit their approach shot, Jake asked, "Why use the lob wedge."

"I can't hit my lob for nothing."

20

Buddy Johnson took the call on his cell phone. It was Jake.

"What's up?"

Jake said, "Do me a favor and research all of Mitchell's holdings."

Buddy looked at the paperwork on his desk. It had piled up in the last few days as he acclimated himself to his new duties with Paradise P.D. His ashtray was full with cigarette butts. Wishing he had not resumed that nasty habit. His kid was in a kindergarten concert later and he promised he would go.

"What else I have to do?" Buddy said. "You know I look forward to running your errands. How do you – " Buddy began, then said, "Where are you?"

"On the 15th tee down eight holes to six."

"You're increasing my workload."

"I'll buy you a beer at Hank's."

"No," Buddy said. "A steak dinner and no delay in paying up."

"Done," Jake said and broke the connection.

***

Pam Kellogg Mitchell's office was on the second floor of the Green Summit Bank Building where she conducted most of the Mitchell family business along with running the bank. Pam was wearing a black business suit with a matching skirt and a blood red blouse.

There were plaques and awards, along with her MBA Diploma on the wall. Pictures of Pam with local business-people, celebrities and state politicians on the wall. Large aerial photo of downtown Paradise behind her.

Her secretary buzzed her and said her husband, Alex, was on the line. Alex chasing Shari Langston was the last straw. Pam told the secretary to say she was busy and would call him back later. She wasn't going to call him but it was okay to give him a little hope.

Five minutes later her secretary entered her office and said a lady was here to see her. Harper Bannister.

Well, that's interesting. The day was picking up.

"Show her in," Pam said, waving a hand and returning to her work.

Harper entered and sat without being asked. Harper wore a white silk blouse under a collarless blue blazer over a pair of tan pleated slacks. She crossed her legs and leaned forward; her hands folded comfortably on her knee.

"It's good to see you, Harper," Pam said. "What can we do for you, today? Would you like a cup of coffee?"

Or a poison apple, thought Harper, smiling to herself. "So, we're going for polite today? Okay. First, no thank you regarding the coffee. As graciously as one can pose an indelicate question, what is going on with you and Jake?"

Pam pulled her head back in mock surprise, saying, "I'm a married woman."

"As difficult as it might be to expect, I would appreciate a straight answer. If there is something going on, that's fine. I just want to know for myself."

Pam leaned forward her forearms on her desk. "What makes you feel you are in a position to ask anything of me?"

"I'm amazed you think everyone is overwhelmed by you," said Harper. "See, I don't have a penis, therefore I remain immune."

"Well, meow," Pam said. "You come here to insult me

or to gain information about some mystical relationship with Jake Morgan?"

"That," said Harper, "and what you had going with Gage Burnell."

"This is your idea of polite?" Pam said. "Not surprised. Not only are you indelicate, you likewise have no practice with etiquette. I am put off by you and your tasteless insinuations."

"No answers then? Wanted to hear your side of things. But then you always project your suspicious nature on others. Jake told me about your appearance at his place. Thought it would be entertaining to hear an abridged version of what is going on in your love life."

"There was nothing between me and Gage. Now, if there is nothing else I can enlighten you with, I have things to do."

"Always wonder how you have time to get any work done where you have your clothes on."

"Why don't you take a five-minute break from being a bitch and access the non-crazy of your brain and let's talk straight."

"You have no practice with honesty," said Harper. "You take the scenic route when you want something. Probably how you got rich." Harper looked around the office for a moment before saying, "But, to be fair, just because you marry rich boys doesn't mean you're a whore."

Pam removed the half-glasses from her face and said, "That's just a little beyond – "

"I meant," Harper shrugged with her palms upturned, "you were a whore way before you married Alex."

Pam chewed at the corner of her lower lip and exhaled.

"Always a treat talking to you but you've over-stayed," Pam said. "I'm sure you hoped to unsettle me yet, as so often happens, you're still a boring little shit. So, leave now. Before I call the sheriff."

"Sheriff Daddy? He's out on the golf course. Jake sent me a text from the Country Club. But I'm going. I would think histrionics were beneath you. You're slipping."

Harper got up to leave, pleased with her performance.

As she neared the door, she turned and said, "I note that you didn't deny you're in heat for Jake. So, it's on, girl-friend."

"I'm not your girlfriend."

"And now I learn you're unable to discern sarcasm."

***

"That's a birdie for us," Vernon said, carding the 14th hole. "Double bogey for you? That gives us eight holes to six for you and you're down four strokes with only four holes left.

Jake took out his driver and limbered up. He took a practice cut. "Love a challenge." He accepted a beer from Leo and offered one to Vernon. Vernon and Doc had been pouring Scotch over ice into red Solo cups, Doc sipping his between puffs on a cigarette.

"No, thanks," Vernon said, expansive now. In a good mood from the alcohol and the score. His face was flushed, and his mouth was slack. Maybe this was the right moment.

Jake said, "How about ten bucks a hole and five bucks a stroke for the final four holes and we keep the first four-teen as a done deal?"

Leo looked at him, his eyes wide. Jake winked back at him and lit up a cigar.

"Your funeral," Vernon said, addressing his tee shot.

"Regarding funerals," Jake said. "I missed Gage's. Were you there? A shame him drowning in a creek. Odd way to die isn't it, Doc? I thought it was injuries from a car wreck. Did you follow up on the crime scene?"

Doc Kellogg looked straight ahead. "Wasn't a crime scene." Doc teed off and hooked a shot into the rough.

"Aw," Leo said. "Bad luck."

"Any accident is a crime scene, Doc. You know that."

"You learn that at Ranger academy? Come home to teach us hicks about law enforcement?" Kellogg walked back to the cart and rammed his driver back into the bag.

"Just making conversation." Jake took a drag on his

cigar, exhaled a blue-grey cloud and teed up his golf ball. Placing his cigar on the ground Jake hit a nice shot five feet to the left of the green. Leo topped that with a beauty that rolled up onto the green of the par four hole.

"Wow," Jake said. "Maybe an eagle, huh? Nice start wouldn't you say, Doc?"

Kellogg didn't look at him or say anything, instead slamming back his red cup then filling his cup again. Vernon drove the cart forward with a lurch causing Doc to spill some of the liquor.

"May have struck a nerve," Leo said, to Jake.

"All part of my secret evil plan," Jake said.

"Better work, I can't afford the loss. You do realize I'm a poor public-school teacher. Why'd you press the bet?"

"I'll cover. This is my game. They're drunk and getting pissed off."

"And you want them mad?" Leo said, shaking his head.

"Yep."

"Twain says anger is an acid. When will you be going back to Texas?" Leo said. "I don't know how much more fun and friendship I can sustain. You always did like it out on the ledge. You and Gage."

Leo and Jake picked up two strokes when Doc and Mitchell bogeyed the 15th hole, while Jake dropped a nice 17-foot putt for a birdie.

Down two, three holes left.

Between holes, Jake began sharing old war stories with Leo about the good times they had with Buddy and Gage. Jake making sure Doc Kellogg heard it, especially the part about how Gage always had to be the designated driver.

"Never nailed us for DUI, did you, Doc?" Jake said. "We always made sure to have Gage along as designated driver. Sure could handle his beer."

"We going to play golf or hold a class reunion?" said Doc.

"I just find it strange..." Letting it hang.

Doc turned away, took a practice swing with his driver, and said, "What was strange?"

Vernon looked at Doc with a sour expression.

"You know," Jake said, sticking the needle in now. "I heard how Gage was drunk the night he had his accident. This was funny to me because Gage never drank much. You ever see him get drunk, Leo?"

Total fiction as Jake had seen Gage drunk, maybe not black-out drunk but Gage liked to light up the night and had done so more than once. So had Leo.

"Not one time," Leo said, picking up on Jake's line.

Jake pulled on his golf glove, wriggling his fingers into it and said, "So, there you have it, Doc. A guy not given to being drunk drives off a bridge, gets out of his car, stumbles into a creek and drowns. That didn't strike you as something to follow up on? I mean, I would've."

"He'd just lost his job," Vernon said, getting his own dig in. "I heard he was having problems with his fiancée. Maybe someone else was plowing his field."

Beautiful. Vernon wanting to come back at Jake, booze loosening his tongue. Gage having problems with Hanna? Maybe what Hanna was holding back? Something to check with Hanna.

"Fired, not lost his job," Jake said. "You know, Doc, you're probably right," Jake said. "You being a long-time lawman. Sorry I brought it up."

Kellogg spit on the ground, lined up his tee shot and duck-hooked into the trees on the left. Vernon followed with a worm-burner that bounced along the ground and rolled into the fringe on the right side of the fairway. Inebriated and pissed off. Not conducive to good golf. Leo and Jake both hit beauties and won the hole.

The 18th hole was a par three. A small island on the lake with a man-built path to reach it. There were only two ways to play the hole. When you teed-off you either landed on the green or you splashed. It was the toughest hole on the course. Built to ensure you wanted a stiff drink when you got back to the clubhouse.

Total strokes were now tied but Jake and Leo had a lead in total holes, 9-8.

Jake stepped up and said, "In the water or dancing on

the lawn." He waggled his pitching wedge and swung. The ball rose high in the air. They watched as it soared over the water, hit the green, back-spin as it dug in and rolled five feet to the right of the pin.

"I choose to dance," Jake said.

"Shit," Vernon said, softly.

"Knew you'd be good for something if I waited long enough," Leo said. He put his wedge back in his bag and said, "It's Miller time. Not going to waste my energy. Believe you boys are properly bow-dicked at present. You'd think I'd be tired of winning, but...not."

Both Kellogg's and Vernon's tee shots were wet. Doc took his 9-iron and threw it in the lake.

"C'mon, Doc," chided Jake, feeling good about things. "Just a game."

Kellogg turned and pointed at Jake. "Don't push me, Morgan. I've had about enough of your mouth and your insinuations."

"Relax," Jake said, feeling in control for the first time since he'd come back to town. "Beautiful day, good company. Besides, you have enough stress with an election coming up. Be tough to beat Buddy though. I really like Buddy's chances. He's popular and honest. Tough combination to beat."

Vernon Mitchell reached into his golf bag and producing his wallet he fished out a hundred dollar bill. "Here," he said, "this should cover it."

"Would you like some change?"

"The only change I want is your location," Vernon said.

"C'mon be a gracious loser," Jake said. "We'll give you a return match. Give you a couple Mulligans."

"Don't hold your breath," Mitchell said. "You won't learn, will you? So, I'll make it clear. You need to give serious consideration to haul you Texas ass back south and do whatever you did there. There's nothing for you here." He drew himself up before saying, "Less than nothing you keep prodding me."

Smiling now, Jake said, "Don't forget my membership.

A deal's a deal. May move back here and take advantage of it."

Vernon pointed at Jake, his face reddening. He shook his head and got back in his cart with Doc and they headed for the clubhouse at a quick pace.

"They seem disconcerted," Leo said, handing an icy beer to Jake. "Damn, Jake, those guys draw a lot of water around here and you went right at them. Good to know you still have a knack for spreading sunshine wherever you go. How do you manage that?"

"Naturally affable, I guess," Jake said.

Leo said, "Affable may not work this time."

Jake scratched behind an ear and said, "Either way, it's on now."

"The gauntlet thrown," Leo said shaking his head. "I guess you know what you're doing?"

"I don't know what I could've done to make you think that. I'm just poking at them, see what happens."

"Bear in mind, old buddy," said Leo. "You beard the lion in his den you could end up missing a hand."

21

Jake got a call from his Captain Parmalee, back in Texas. Parmalee telling him he was not pleased to get phone calls from law enforcement agencies in other states informing him one of his people was insinuating themselves into a closed investigation.

"Not only that," said Parmalee. "How in the hell did you get involved in a bank shooting? You ever do anything that isn't chaotic?"

Jake could understand Parmalee's ire. So, Kellogg and Vernon had gone over his head. Very telling.

"Two armed men in the bank," Jake said. "I gave them a chance to surrender. One chose otherwise."

Concerning Gage's death Jake telling his Captain there was evidence something was wrong and why bother to call Parmalee if there was nothing to it? The captain telling Jake to stay out of it.

"Don't know if I can do that," Jake said.

Quiet on the other end. "Jake. Listen to me. We cannot provide cover for you. You do understand what a leave of absence in your situation is? This is an excessive force complaint. You put the man in the hospital. If you get on the wrong side of this thing in your hometown then it's possible Austin will terminate your service. I wouldn't like that. You're a fine ranger with a promising career, never see anyone shoots as well as you, but consider my position and the position of the department. We do not interfere in other jurisdictions without being invited."

"So, if invited I can go forward with the investigation."

Jake could imagine the captain sighing. "Take my advice for what it's worth. Stay out of local troubles."

Parmalee broke the connection.

At least Jake knew what the stakes were. No job, no future, surrounded by enemies, and stuck in the place he had long wished to vacate.

He checked back with Buddy Johnson regarding Mitchell holdings in the county. Buddy told him he would email the list.

"Thanks."

"I hope you're not getting in deeper than you can dig out," Buddy said. "Heard about your golf game. Would've loved to see Doc's face when you mentioned the election."

"It was a tender moment."

***

It was dove season, so Wednesday morning Jake called an old friend and gained permission to hunt a silage-cut cornfield. A day outdoors would get his mind off his captain's warning and allow him to sort through the convoluted chain of events that led to the homicide of his friend. Calling it homicide now.

Jake loaded up a small cooler with soda and a couple of sandwiches and by midafternoon he was sitting in a row of uncut cornstalks and waiting for the grey birds to fly in for a late afternoon snack. It was a cool autumn day with the temperature hovering in the 50s, the sun warm.

He reached into the cooler and pulled out a red Coca-Cola can, dripping with moisture. A dove swung low over the field like a missile and out of range before Jake raised his shotgun. He knew there would be another.

He settled the crimson can back in the cooler and got ready. A pair of doves flew his way, and as they passed, Jake opened up with the shotgun.

Stepping out of cover, Jake walked through the raw

stubble of the harvested part of the field. He placed the butt of the shotgun on the rough ground for support, leaning down to pick up a bird when a sudden jerk on his shotgun wrenched it from his hand. The shotgun collapsed then the delayed report of a high-powered rifle Jake. Jake tumbled to the raw stubble.

He rolled and scrambled to his feet zig-zagging across the field. Try to reach the windbreak hedgerow and get cover. Move. Another shot slashed the ground at his feet before he reached the hedgerow and was able to dive behind the tree line. He placed a hand against the trunk of a tree and looked back across the field, then quickly put his head back. A round ripped into the tree and then the crack of the weapon.

Who was shooting and from what point? From the delayed sound he knew the shooter was far off.

He'd left his cell phone in his truck. His shotgun was shattered and useless. His sidearm would be useless against a long-range target. Jake belly-crawled along the hedgerow to get distance and cover from the shooter.

He rolled over on his back and exhaled. Placed a hand on his chest and breathed out of his mouth to slow the adrenal rush. For the first time he felt a pain in his left wrist and a sensation in his left thigh. He looked down and saw it – a sprinkling of blood and shards of wood in his thigh. The bullet hitting the stock, shattering the stock splintered wood digging into his leg.

Several minutes passed like hours before getting up. Distant sound of a vehicle starting.

He stood and felt a twinge from the injured leg. The cuts were slight but annoying. Limping into the field, he retrieved his ruined shotgun. The stock was ripped up, the fragments white against the varnished veneer of the stock.

He retrieved his dove and headed to his truck. Get his phone and call it in. To who? Doc Kellogg? That probably wouldn't work. Remembering the late reports of the rifle before the bullets struck the ground and the tree. Had to be a 150 to 200 yards away. A shooter confident in his ability and Jake lucky to be alive.

Someone wanted him dead.

He heard the sound of a second vehicle starting and receding in the distance. He tried to look up to see if he could locate the disappearing vehicle. He did.

It was his truck.

Well damn.

22

Jake hoofed it to a farmhouse and got a ride from the farmer he knew, man named Millen. Jake called Harper telling her where he was headed and asked could she give him a ride. He told Farmer Millen why he was afoot.

"Did you see who was driving?" Millen asked.

"No. Happened too fast. Formed an opinion though."

Millen pointed at Jake. "You're bleeding."

Jake looked at his hand and said, "Yeah. You can drop me by the police department, you don't mind."

"Sure."

Millen dropped him off, Jake offered to pay, but the old farmer waved him off.

Harper was waiting for him. He related the incident.

"Who would do such a thing?" Harper said.

"Makes me wonder why. Tommy that reckless?"

"Tommy is one possibility," she said. "I have a second candidate in mind."

"Who would that be?"

"You're not going to like it."

"You're going to say Pam Mitchell."

"And you're going to dismiss it without consideration."

"There would have to be two people involved." He shrugged. Two people. A shooter and a driver to hotwire my truck. "Could be anyone. She's as viable as anyone, I guess. Either way, they'll abandon my vehicle at some point." Thinking, the same way they abandoned Gage's SUV. "I'll report it to your dad and see if he can locate it."

When Jake related the incident, Cal shook his head. "I'd like to help but there's not much I can do." He explained that the location of the incident was out of his jurisdiction, but he would attempt to glean what he could.

Cal said he would look into it and report it to Kellogg.

Jake said, "How far you think that'll go? He'll only be sorry they missed me."

Cal said, "I have little choice. I wouldn't like it were the situation reversed. It's something Doc can't just sweep under the rug. He'll have to at least take a look at it, and I'll see if I can tag along when he checks the site of the shooting."

"Well, thanks."

"You think this has anything to do with Gage Burnell?" Cal said.

"What do you think?"

"Same as you," Cal said.

***

Cal located Jake's truck behind an abandoned blacksmith shop, a landmark from the past, just inside the city limits. The driver's side window was shattered. Wires hanging down beneath the steering column. Jake and Cal walked around the pick-up and checked underneath. No explosives or unusual wires. Jake opened the gas cap cover and white residue around the cap. Sugar. He had the truck towed to a garage where they could remove the gas tank and check for damage to the motor. Someone didn't like him enough to shoot at him and vandalize his truck.

The killers or Tommy?

Jake couldn't be without transportation, so he called a rental agency and they had nothing available until the next day. He remembered his old project car. The Lincoln he never finished. It would at least run, that is if it would start after all these years. Cal gave him a ride out to his place and asked him if he needed anything else. Jake said if he needed a ride to the rental car agency, he'd call Leo or Buddy, and thanked Cal.

Jake walked out to the garage where the old car sat preserved like an art exhibit under a light fabric tarp.

It was a 1969 Lincoln Continental Mark III he tried to restore before he left for Texas and then lost interest. No, that wasn't it. He didn't want to be at home with Alfred. Alfred had bought it for him in a good time and they had worked on it together until the drinking started and Jake could no longer tolerate his father's drunken rages.

Jake tugged at the dusty cover on the vehicle. When he uncovered the car, he was staggered by what he saw underneath.

It was gorgeous. The primer coat was covered with several coats of a deep jet-black lacquer gleamed from multiple waxings shining through the thin film of dust. The chrome dazzled and the tires were new Michelins. He opened the door and smelled the aroma of the black leather seats. There was a new stereo radio with a CD player in the dash, a departure from the vintage restoration.

It looked like it had just rolled off the showroom floor decades ago from a time of big block Detroit power. Actually it may have never looked this good, even new.

He sat for a moment and let it wash over him.

Son of a gun. Alfred had finished the car. Alfred, his father.

Jake turned the key and it started up, the engine a whisper. There was an old Temptations CD in the glove box and when Jake played it his head flooded with a million thoughts. What could have been, what never was, how he would be able to reconcile this new vision of a father he didn't allow in his life.

"Jake, you are an unforgiving asshole," he said aloud.

He rolled the convertible top down and backed out of the garage onto the raw graveled lane, regretting having to subject the pristine vehicle to dust. When he hit the highway, the ancient luxury car swept away the miles like a cloud.

Thinking of Alfred as Dad again. Could he do that?

Okay, that works. Thanks, Dad. Sorry I waited too long.

Since Jake's truck was found in town making it a city police matter. Cal could examine the vehicle for hairs, prints, and request information from Sheriff Kellogg. Good luck with that.

Jake didn't hold much hope finding anything. It had been a cool day and the driver could've been wearing gloves. Definitely wearing gloves if they were the same people who had set up Gage's "accident". Two of them. One to hot-wire and drive Jake's truck; one to drive the other vehicle. The Mitchell clan could shoot. All of them. Pam also if he remembered right.

But most of the people in and around Paradise could shoot. This was Midwest farm country and every farmer and his kids learned to shoot and hunt early on in life.

It was time to go right at the Mitchells. Keep the pressure on. Saturday morning, Jake had breakfast with Buddy and Leo to tell them what he had in mind. What he had in mind was driving out to the Mitchell place and confront them about Gage and his truck.

Leo looked around the diner. "Got a team meeting to go over game film. Sorry, you know I'd love to go out there and risk my career and serious injury but not today."

Buddy was off-duty and agreed to go along. "Sounds good to me," he said.

"Could hurt your election chances," Jake said.

"How many votes you think I'll get from the Mitchells and people associated with them? Also, I'm with you that Gage didn't die in an accident. Besides, sounds like an interesting afternoon." Looking at Leo staring at him now and Buddy saying, "What?"

Leo looked at Buddy and said, "You find this interesting because you and Texas here are seriously disturbed individuals."

"Well, vote for me."

Leo pointed at him, like shooting a pistol. "Soon as your check clears."

23

It was an unusually warm afternoon, as Jake and Buddy drove out to the Mitchell place: the sun glorious, the air smelling of agriculture and autumn. The vintage Lincoln rolled majestic and silent, radial tires singing its highway song to the Motown beat. They passed by Pam and Alex Mitchell's house -- that's what it said on the mailbox – Pam and Alex Mitchell. There was a horse stable behind the place with a white rail fence surrounding the stable. It wasn't one of those plastic rail fences you saw anymore; it was real wood and it gleamed in the sunshine with a fresh coat of paint.

"Smells of money, doesn't it?" Buddy said. "Where'd you get this car?"

"Long story."

"Meaning you don't want to talk about it?"

"Dad restored it for me."

"'Dad' now?" Buddy chuckled. "Welcome home, Jake."

Jake smiled.

They drove until they reached Vernon Mitchell's place. The two Mitchell ranches were contiguous to each other, only a paved road separating them. Jake noted that the pavement stopped about one hundred yards past Mitchell's driveway; a testament to Vernon's influence as county commissioner. Moreover, it demonstrated his contempt for anyone who might think to complain about it.

The Mitchell compound was large and sprawling with a long, paved lane leading back from the road. Double M Farms read the sign as they entered the drive. The house was a large rambling ranch with a wrap-around porch and three-car garage. There was a free-standing metal garage building for more vehicles. South of the house was a metal building not quite large enough to house an aircraft carrier where the combines, tractors and other implements would be. There was a bulldozer used to build terraces and dig out ponds alongside the building.

 Jake heard music coming from the back of the house. The two friends walked around the house, and in the back there was an impressive swimming pool, covered for the fall.

When they saw Jake and Buddy the music played on, but the voices stopped.

***

Pam Mitchell could not believe it.

Jake Morgan.

Surprised Jake would show up. Here. Like this. But, thinking about it she knew it was so like him. Jake only knew one way. Straight up and right at you. Buddy Johnson was with him in street clothes which made him look even bigger than when in uniform.

She could not suppress her inner satisfaction at his appearance. She nibbled the inside of her lower lip anticipating the dynamics of his appearance and how it might liven things up. This is what she had always liked about Jake Morgan.

He was a danger zone with legs.

She was getting bored anyway.

***

All the Mitchells were there except Tommy, the person Jake most wanted to see. There were a couple of beefy guys among them, along with Fat Boy Haller. Pam was sitting in a lounge chair, resplendent in white shorts and a pink sleeveless blouse. There was a small dog, a Yorkie, yapping energetically when it saw Buddy and Jake.

Pam shushed the dog and smiled at Jake. Alex didn't. The two beefy guys and Fat Boy didn't. Vernon seemed amused.

"Hello, boys," Vernon said, the good host. "Sit down and have something to drink. There's beer in the cooler. Bourbon and ice on the table. Help yourself."

Jake shaking his head. "I'm here about other things."

"Why ruin a beautiful afternoon?" Vernon asked.

"You wouldn't do that would you, Jake?" Alex said. "You're usually the life of the party." He got a look from Pam, so he changed his tone. "Just kidding. Sit down and have a beer, Morgan. You too, Buddy."

The Yorkie started barking again and Pam placed her hand around the dog's mouth. "Be quiet, Muffy."

Jake fishing for a reaction saying now, "Maybe you should have Tommy and Fat Boy quiet little Muffy. They know how. Isn't that right, Fatty?"

"Watch your mouth," said Fat Boy.

Jake looked at Haller, then at Vernon. "Where is Tommy, today? Like to speak with him."

"He's not here."

"You'll do."

"There's no reason for you being here," Vernon said.

"Really? I've been shot at and had my truck stolen."

"That doesn't concern anyone here."

"Maybe. Never hurts to look into things. Also, I'm not very happy about Gage's death. Not buying the accident angle."

"You're in the wrong place for that," Alex said.

"Why are you like this, Jake?" Pam said. Vernon glared in her direction. It wasn't for approval. Pam was unmoved by it.

Jake looked around. "Gage was intuitive. One of the reasons I liked him, and I liked him a lot. He saw something or knew something and now he's gone. Why'd you fire him, Alex?"

Restlessness and hard looks around the pool. Good. Having Buddy there didn't hurt.

"Had reasons," Alex said. "And they were my own."

"A week later he's dead. Called it an accident."

"And you don't?" asked Alex.

"Too convenient for some."

"I don't care for your insinuations," Vernon said.

"Kellogg or someone here called my cCaptain. Somebody is afraid. If you accept the premise Gage didn't die in an accident it opens up possibilities. I'm thinking Gage made the mistake of associating with people who would give no more thought to killing him and kicking his dog than what they have for breakfast."

The two beefy guys got up from their lawn chairs. One of them with a rust-red buzz-cut said, "Had enough of your mouth."

Buddy knew the redhead and said, "Barb, sit down so you'll be able to stand tomorrow."

"Not afraid of you, boy," said Barb. Steve Barb was his name.

"Takes brains to be scared," Buddy said, smiling. "Call me 'boy' again, though. I love that."

"You want boys want some shit. Who're you?" said the man sitting by Barb, a curly headed young guy with thick arms sticking out of his Tee-shirt. He threw down a cigarette he'd been smoking and stood. Both Barb and Curly head wore work clothes. Mitchell employees.

Vernon made a slashing motion with his hand. "Stay out, Robby." Guy's name was Robby. "You too, Steve. We're not going to have any of that here." He pointed at Jake. "You don't have any respect for a man's home, do you? You arrive uninvited yet I extend hospitality and you repay it with insults and allegations. I don't understand you, son. Why can't you just sit down and have a beer and a neighborly visit? You seem determined to make me dislike you. We play a round of golf together and you use the occasion to aggravate the sheriff."

"Doc only has two emotions. Pissed-off or constipated."

Vernon said, "I have tried to be gracious. I think anyone here would agree."

"I'll allow you're doing better than I would the way things are shaking out."

"Believe I'm going to have to ask you to leave."

Jake nodded. "Calling my captain won't stop this."

"Nobody here called your superiors," Vernon said.

"Superiors?" Turning to Buddy, Jake said, "Do I even have an equal?"

Buddy shaking his head and smiling, "Not for conversation anyway."

Pam leaned forward from her lounge, started to say something and held it.

Jake saying now, "Understand that I'm going to keep kicking over rocks until I find out which one of you is under it. There's damage and it's been sloppy. Mistakes were made and they're going to cost someone. Maybe someone here."

"Be careful you don't overvalue your abilities," Vernon said. "No one here had a thing to do with Gage being murdered."

"Didn't say he was murdered. I'm saying he didn't have an accident."

"Leave. Now."

***

"Well," Buddy said, as they walked back to the car. "Nobody can say you weren't polite. That is, nobody who was born before the Lord Jesus Christ. You ever even read any books on etiquette?"

Jake shook his head. "I wanted a reaction."

"You got that and here comes the second wave."

He heard his name. "Jake." It was Pam. "Wait up," she said.

Jake and Buddy stopped and Pam walked over to them. She looked at Buddy for a moment, saying nothing.

Buddy nodded at the Lincoln and said, "I'll...a...warm up the car."

Pam brushed a wisp of hair from her face and said, "Why are you so angry?"

"Thought I explained that."

"No," she said. "Why are you angry at me?"

"I'm not. Unless, you're mixed up in this."

"Since you returned you've been sardonic and sullen when you're around me." She lifted her chin an inch. Her face softened and she said. "Except for one brief moment."

"How'd you get in that night?"

"The door was unlocked."

"It wasn't. Why did Gage have your cell phone number?"

"He used to work for us," she said. "What are you saying, Jake? Is that what has you creased? You think something was going on between Gage and me? You have a sick mind, Jake Morgan." Her face changed.

"You know, Pam, I've seen your act before. Do you ever experience real emotion or are you always on?"

Her mouth fell open as if she had been slapped. "Why? Why do this to me?" She took a deep breath and her cheeks turned a rose color. "I never got over you. Did you know that?"

"Yeah," Jake said. "That's why you married the yuppie and later hooked up with Junior and the Clanton Family."

"Jake." She stopped, looked down at her hands, and then lifted her face. "Jake, can't we talk about this some time?"

Jake shook his head. "How's that going to help anything? We did our talking years ago." He let out a small breath, relaxing his shoulders. "What we had was good then. We all want to feel like we did when we were young." Thinking about his dad now. "That's why Buddy stayed and especially why Leo the Lion is working at the same school we all went to. That's why the other night happened. Nostalgia sneaks into our thoughts and moves us to attempt to recover things that are unattainable. It was a good time and we have good memories of it. But that's all they are. Memories. You can't bring it back. We're different now and the changes are what they are."

It stopped her for a moment. She searched his face for something, anything. But Pam was not a person to give in. She said, "Listen to me. Just say you'll talk to me some other time. At least give me that."

Shaking his head.

Pam looked back over her shoulder. So did Jake and saw Alex standing beside the house, looking right at them, twisting the Tiger Eye ring absently.

Perfect.

Pam saying now,. "Maybe I have information that will help."

Jake chewed a corner of his lip. "We'll see. All I can say."

Jake left her and walked back to the car. Buddy was sitting in the passenger seat. Jake slid in under the steering wheel."

Jake said, "Went swell, didn't it?"

Buddy scratched as his upper lip, smiling now. "You know when you said coming out here wasn't the smartest thing you ever did? Well, that was only the second dumbest thing you've done today."

"Be careful, Buddy."

"You telling me you don't have something going with Pam? Holy gee gosh, partner, you and Pam are a live soap opera."

"You and Leo, huh?" He put both hands on the wheel, shaking his head then turned in his seat to look at Buddy. "Both of you think you have insight."

"Well, there's something going on and you just poked the hornet's nest with your dick."

"Colorful way of putting it."

"I'm a black man, and we are wise in the ways of sexual adventure."

Driving back to town it was working on him. The thing that was bothering him was this:

The lonely figure of Alex Mitchell standing in the background over Pam's shoulder. Alex Mitchell standing there realizing his wife wasn't faithful. An image that stuck in Jake's head.

Hell of a time to start feeling sorry for Alex Mitchell.

And Vernon warily watching Pam.

What a family.

What a homecoming.

24

Driving back, Jake got a call from Cal Bannister. It was as Jake had predicted. No fingerprints on the truck. Nothing.

"Sorry, Jake," Cal said. "We'll stay on it here. By the way, did you and Buddy go out to the Mitchell place?"

"Maybe," Jake said.

Quiet on the other line. Then, "Don't screw around, Jake. This isn't the time for it. I'll need to speak with Buddy when he gets back."

"Have you seen Tommy Mitchell around town?"

"That's why you went out to the Mitchell's," Cal said. "Be careful elevating this scenario. Doc Kellogg doesn't need more reason to become involved."

"He's already involved. Could've been anyone who stole my truck but I'm thinking Tommy is the best candidate."

"We don't have a positive ID so leave it alone until we have more information. I have more reason to burn him down than you. Dammit, Jake, I can't have you running around like this was the Wild West."

"Sorry about that, Cal."

"I've got an idea may fix it."

"Meaning?"

"Come in with Buddy and I'll explain what I have in mind."

He broke the connection. Jake looked at Buddy. Buddy

saying now, "Am I in trouble?"

"Probably."

"What I get for hanging around with you."

"Like a dream come true, isn't it?"

"Always has been, Jake. Always."

***

Cal's idea, which he revealed only after castigating both Jake and Buddy was to appoint Jake as a "Police Auxiliary Officer".

"Gives you legal status," Cal said. "Besides, I've talked with your Captain Parmalee. Though he says you're a pain in the ass, which is general knowledge, he says you're one hell of an investigative officer. I could use a good investigator."

Cal reached in his drawer and produced a badge, handing it to Jake, who accepted it.

Jake nodded. "Parmalee good with this?"

"Not entirely but was more comfortable when I told him why I wanted you."

"Why's that?"

"I think Gage Burnell was murdered here in town and transported outside the city limits."

"Why do you think that?"

"Just a hunch. Still working on it but I have limited intel. I'll give you more when I get more."

"Do I get a car with siren and one of those snappy uniforms like Buddy's?"

Cal looked at him and smiled. "Not just no, hell no. Basically you're going to work undercover."

"I'm a secret agent? Do I get a double-O?"

"Maybe for IQ," Buddy said.

***

Sometimes you go back to basics. When there is a death the first person to interview is the spouse, or in this case, the fiancée.

Hanna Stanislaus. Either tie her into it or eliminate her. It wouldn't be the first time the obvious suspect wasn't the killer. He wanted to know whose name she wouldn't mention before and this time he could do it officially.

Jake Morgan, auxiliary police. Watch out, criminal element.

Hanna agreed to meet him at the Dinner Bell for lunch. Hanna arrived ahead of Jake. She looked different today because she wasn't wearing the smock and her hair was down. She was dressed up and he'd forgotten how attractive she was. Even her body language was different.

They ordered lunch and after the server left, Jake said, "I want to talk to you about Gage. I hope you don't mind."

"That's fine," she said, she turned her head, giving him a sideways look. "I was halfway hoping you had another reason."

The café door opened, and Harper walked in. She saw Jake sitting with Hanna. She stopped, smiled and shook her head. She turned and walked back outside. "Excuse me," Jake said to Hanna, and then hurried outside to catch Harper. She was opening her car door when he said, "Wait a minute, Harper."

Slowly, she turned and looked at him. "What?"

"I need to explain what I'm doing."

"You don't have to explain yourself to me. You're a free agent."

Jake opened his hands to her, shaking his head. "It's not what you think."

She placed a fist on her hip. "What is it I 'think'?" she said. Jake looking at her. Wow, she could get mad.

"Give me a break." He told her that Cal had enlisted him and what he was doing talking with Hanna. How he was attempting to cover all his bases as he looked into the circumstances of Gage's death. "I'm trying to put things together. I'm sure someone killed Gage and I'm going to find out who that person or persons were. Talking to his fiancée is part of that."

Harper pursed her lips and smiled at him. "Okay." Shaking her head now. "I'm sorry Jake. But I have a reason for feeling like that. Maybe not a reason, but there is some history there."

"I don't know what you mean."

"Sweet little Hanna in there?" said Harper. "Hanna is one of the many reasons I divorced Tommy. She gets around. Start with that."

25

He thought about what Harper said as he walked back into the restaurant. This would change his line of questioning and he would have to be careful not to put Hanna on the defensive. He wanted Hanna off-balance but not where she would walk out on him. He needed information and people had different hot buttons and different keys to open them up.

Hanna may have had an affair with Tommy Mitchell and...maybe someone else she was hiding. What else was going on? Better, who else was getting it on with whom here in Paradise place? How to untie this Gordian knot? He'd left Texas and landed in a Midwest soap opera.

When he returned to the café, he was aware of Hanna's body language. As Jake sat, she leaned forward in her seat, brushed her hair away from her neck. Jake could smell her perfume. The jukebox was playing, and the lunch crowd was chattering away. If a stranger walked in, he or she would just see a normal small-town restaurant filled with nurses, accountants, farmers, bank employees and retired men and women enjoying lunch. Just another flavor of Americana.

But Jake saw it differently. As he always viewed things since the day they handed him his star. The curse of the investigator. People had hidden agendas. Some of those agendas were shadowy. How dark were Hanna's secrets?

"Do you know Harper?" she asked.

"Yes," Jake said. "For many years. Her father and I are good friends."

"Is that all?"

He ignored the question. "I'm going to have to be a little indelicate here," Jake said. "I hope you don't mind."

There it was a faint change in her facial muscles. If he wasn't looking for it, Jake wouldn't have noticed it. She leaned away from him and said, "It's fine."

"Look, Hanna," Jake said. "Gage was my friend and I'm not going to ask this to hurt you but, was Gage...a, did he ever stray during your engagement?"

The server brought their order. Cheeseburger and fries for Jake. Club Sandwich and tomato soup that had the consistency of blood for her.

"You mean did he have an affair?"

"Like that. Yes."

Hanna looked down. A tiny incisor chewed on her lower lip. "Well." She let out a breath. "Well, yes, I had suspicions. It would've been unlike him. But I don't know. There were just some things that seemed odd."

Jake sat quietly. Waiting. Sometimes, in an interview, silence would draw out the interviewee. She stirred soup with a spoon, re-arranged her knife and fork. She took a small portion of soup on her spoon and delicately tasted it. She dabbed at her lip with a paper napkin.

She looked up, blinked twice and said, "You want to know who I think it was, don't you?"

He nodded. Waited again.

She put her spoon down, leaned back against the seat and placed folded hands in her lap. "This is hard," she said.

"It is."

She thought about it some more. "Would you mind if we ate first and then we can talk about this?"

Jake was pretty sure he already had his answer except for the 'who' part. He had a good idea of the identity, but it wasn't solid. Hanna was holding back. He was sure of it. She had a secret. One possible secret he knew about or had information from Harper. Hanna and Tommy. Tommy and Harper. Harper and Jake. Jake and Pam. Pam and Alex. Gage and...who?

He feared he knew the answer and suspected it from the first but would not allow himself to believe it because it robbed him of something. Changed the way he looked at himself, at Gage, and his past. Pam had access to the house; Gage had her phone number hidden in his file cabinet. Pam and Gage?

Did Hanna know? Or just suspect? What else did Hanna know or suspect?

They ate in silence for a few minutes.

Time passed and the working crowd began to scoot chairs, leave tips and return to their jobs. Jake and Hanna finished lunch, Hanna barely touching hers and asked for a container to take her sandwich back to work with her. Jake ordered coffee. The server filled their requests and Jake asked for the ticket.

"I probably need to get back to work," Hanna said, without preamble.

"Who was the person?" Jake asked.

"It's indelicate," Hanna said.

"So's murder."

Her eyes widened. "You don't think that? Really? Oh my God."

"A suspicion. Who was the woman?"

She made a face as if the soup had gone sour. "You're... so blunt. This isn't easy."

"I'm sorry for that. Gage was my friend. He was your fiancé. We both have reason to learn what happened and achieve some semblance of closure. You want that, don't you?"

She nodded. "Yes." She took a breath. "I have a conflict that hinders revealing who she is."

"What's the conflict?"

"I have a lien on my business. With Green Summit bank. Does that help?"

It did, but Jake pressed on. "What about Gage?"

"There were...well, some things I wasn't sure about

with Gage. Like I said, we had a few problems just like anyone does in a relationship. Gage never looked ahead. I don't think he understood, no, that's not it. He lived in the present moment. That was a problem. I'm a planner and an organizer. They say opposites attract and Gage was such a free spirit. Well...Gage would do things and never stop to think about the unintended effects of his actions."

"Did you argue over your suspicions?"

She stopped for a moment as if thinking of what she was going to say next.

Jake said nothing.

She shook her head slowly and looked blank. "I'm not sure I can do this. I'm not sure if it happened. And...and there's more. I, well I wasn't...I can't do this."

"I think you are sure, and you can do this." From experience, Jake knew people were generally expansive about who they think is hitting on their spouse or beloved. They wanted the guilty to pay because in their imagination it was happening whether there was an adulterous relationship or not.

"I really have to go," she said, rising from her chair.

"Pam Mitchell?" Jake said.

"What?"

"Was it Pam Mitchell?"

Hanna looked around the room as if she were about to slip the silverware into her purse. She leaned forward, and in a voice just barely audible, she said;

"Maybe."

"What about Tommy Mitchell?" Bang, hit her with it.

The blood drained out of her face. "What? Why did you say that? What are you saying?"

"I think you know."

She pushed her chair back and stood.

"Hang on," Jake said. "I apologize. That was indelicate."

"I had nothing to do with Tommy," she said. "That was just a rumor around town. He hit on me, but I turned him down."

"Please sit," Jake said. "You really need to sit for the

next thing I'm going to ask. I promise I mean no harm. You are not the focus of this and anything you say will not be shared."

She looked towards the door, then sat. Her arms were crossed, and her facial muscles were tight. Jake had seen the look many times before in an interrogation. The person being interviewed wasn't looking forward to the question but wanted to know what the interviewer was holding in reserve.

"I don't want to hurt you," Jake said. "Not my intention. But, to find out what happened to Gage requires questions that make people, even innocent people, uncomfortable. It's the way it is. We both want to know what really happened to Gage. Someone stole Travis and treated him badly. Someone didn't like Gage and wanted him dead. I think they used the dog to get at him."

Her mouth turned down and she swallowed. "Okay. What is your question?"

"Who was the person you would not mention the day I spoke to you at your business?"

"That was a slip. I mean—" She exhaled.

"Did you stray from your relationship with Gage?"

"No." Defiant. "We were on a break, that's all."

"So, you were on a break, right? And someone stepped into the picture."

Her face was blank for a moment before she gathered herself and said, "Gage and I argued about...well, about Pam Mitchell. There. I noticed her showing up a lot and didn't like it. He denied it but wouldn't keep her away. I told him I had enough, and we were split up for a time."

"And during that time?"

"I was asked out by a younger man. Silly, isn't it? Well, I wanted some measure of revenge on Gage."

"You're not the first and Gage should've respected your wish to avoid Pam."

She nodded. "Thank you for that."

"Who was it?"

"Steve Barb. You don't know him. He works for the Mitchells. Just went out with Steve a couple of times.

Gage and I reconciled, and we got engaged."

Steve Barb. The employee at Vernon Mitchell's place.

"How did Barb feel about that?" Jake asked.

"He was very angry. Kept calling."

"Did you tell Gage?"

Shaking her head now, looking embarrassed. "No. No, I didn't. But Gage asked me about it."

"Was Pam more than just a suspicion?"

"Yes." Animated now. "She's puts herself out there. You should know that better than anyone, right?"

He was quiet.

"Well," said Hanna, triumphant now. "Don't like being questioned, do you? You think people in town don't see her chasing after you?"

"Thanks for meeting me," Jake said.

She placed a hand to her mouth. "Oh, Jake. I'm sorry. I had no right to say that."

"Well," Jake said and nodded. "Maybe you did."

26

"You shoulda been there, man," Steve Barb said to Tommy Mitchell. They were standing outside the Mitchell's grain elevator and feed store in town. "That asshole Morgan came out to your Dad's place and got in everybody's face."

"So, what did you little girls do?" Tommy Mitchell asked.

"Nothing," Steve said. "Mister Mitchell said he didn't want that at his home. Vernon said let it go. Hey, your brother sat there and didn't do anything either. Pam gave him one look and he sat there like a puppy. The guy had Buddy Johnson with him. Like to smack that spook. I was ready to go but Vernon stopped me."

Tommy looked at him. "So full of shit, aren't you? Buddy would rip your head off and laugh about it. Morgan though?" Thinking about how Morgan had taken down Haller. So quick. Steve here had a big mouth and a quick temper combined with low intelligence so maybe he could use him to get back at Morgan.

Tommy said, "So, what are you little Nancy-boys gonna do? Let Jake Morgan punk you out like that? It's like your noses bleed every twenty-eight days."

"He took you and Fat Boy out," said Steve.

"True." Nodding his head, playing along. "That's true. But Fat is just big, and Morgan caught me off-guard."

"Heard otherwise," said Steve, nudging Robby with an elbow.

"Yeah," said Robby.

They were big enough. Both bigger, well thicker, than Morgan. Morgan was taller and quicker, hell, much quicker. Barb took on Morgan, it was a win-win. Either way, Tommy got something out of it. Morgan got his ass kicked or if the opposite happened, that would shut Steve up for a while. Steve could get on your nerves in small doses. Morgan too.

Tommy saying now, "Tell you what. You guys whip up on Morgan and I'll give you a hundred bucks each. How's that sound?"

"Sounds like you want someone do your dirty work," said Robby.

"Shut up, Robby," said Steve, placing the side of his hand against Robby's chest. "Hang on a minute. I don't need Robby."

"I think you do," Tommy said, setting the hook. "This Morgan, he's a bad boy and you guys aren't used to bad boys."

"We'll see," said Steve.

And, just like that, Tommy knew he had him.

***

Alex knew he should've been out at the plant getting things done. Instead he was pulling a "Tommy" and was on his second double bourbon sitting in the lounge at the Holiday Inn out on the highway. He ordered a beer on the side with the second bourbon, the only person in the bar.

"Pulling a Tommy" was what they called it when somebody blew off their responsibilities and got drunk or generally disappeared. Little brother was becoming increasingly unstable since Harper divorced him. Tommy had never been what you would call reliable. Tommy could surprise you but now these surprises were coming more often, and each seemed to be more self-destructive than the last one.

Alex's problem now was Pam. He didn't realize she could still get to him. She spent the afternoon with him and the family when Morgan and Johnson had come out. Morgan. He wondered about Pam talking to the guy before he left. Goddamn her, right in front of his family and his employees. Morgan and Pam? Were they – ?

No, don't think about that. Thinking about it made it worse. He knew they used to be an item, but Morgan was interested in Harper, that's what he told himself.

He looked around the lounge, noted the bored bartender and the standard motel décor. Muzak muted through bar speakers. No atmosphere.

So he left some money on the table and headed downtown.

To Hank's place.

***

"There you go," said Hank to Jake. "I added some new stuff to the jukebox just for you. I expect a tip so get your money up."

Hank's idea of "new stuff" was more of the same. It just hadn't been on the jukebox earlier. Jake smiled and punched in some Tom Petty, some Johnny Cash recorded just before he died, and a little Roy Orbison, how long had Orbison been gone and Hank called it "new".

Jake was waiting on Harper who had some extra work to get in and they were going to get together later so Jake was killing time. It was gradually getting better with her.

He had misjudged Hanna with his first impression. She had not seemed the fem fatale her past might suggest. Maybe she wasn't. Never understand the numbing ennui of small towns. The town's ambience had changed, it was different for him now, but Hank was Hank and...Leo the Lion was right. Pam was Pam Kellogg. Always would be. You could not marry that out of her.

And Jake's feelings about his dad were different. Better.

Thinking about all this when Alex Mitchell walked into Hank's. Alex started walking towards Jake's table. Now what?

What a life.

27

Alex Mitchell listed like a small boat at sea as he staggered toward Jake. Alex lifted a hand just above his waist and gave a wave to Jake.

Hank saying now, "Watch yourself, Mitchell."

Alex waved both hands. "No, no. It's cool. Ice cold." He looked at Jake and asked if he could join him.

Why not? Jake pushed out a chair with his boot.

Alex sat, pointed at his chest and said, "Fill 'er up, Hank. High test. Beam and a Bud, please."

Hank made a face but brought a can of Budweiser and a filled shot glass and sat them on the table.

"Put it on my tab," Jake said. Hank gave Jake a look, but Jake nodded, and Hank walked back to the bar.

"Feeling guilty? Gonna make you feel better about yourself you buy me a drink?"

Jake watched Alex for a moment, before answering. "Don't believe I'm in the mood for it so go a different direction."

Alex started looking around the room as if not remembering where he was.

"You all right?" Jake asked.

"Yeah, sure," Alex said, and then laughed a drunken chuckle. "I'm fucking copacetic. Was any better I'd throw a party. How you doing?"

"Looks like you've already been partying."

"Not so you'd notice. What goes on inside is not always mirrored by appearances."

"Early, isn't it?"

"Not when you have reason. I've got things – ." He paused to point a wavering finger in Jake's direction. "Things to think about I want to get outside my head. You ever have that?"

Jake sipped his beer and waited. Listening to drunks talk was a chore.

"Look, man," Alex said. "I don't want to keep this thing going between me and you. You know about this thing, right?"

Jake said nothing. Let him talk.

"Okay," Alex said. "Maybe you don't. Doesn't matter. Just two guys sitting here drinking beer and shooting the shit." He threw back the shot and then took a pull on the beer. He sat the beer down, grunted and said, "Damn. That'll put the snakes back in the basket for a while."

Jake sipped his beer. What he really wanted was a cigarette. Two days without one at this point and maybe he was on the verge of kicking the habit. Funny the way things worked out. Both of them thinking about Pam and now he was sitting here with the husband of a woman he'd slept with, a chance encounter working into his day.

Jake looked at Alex and waited.

Alex said, "You're wondering why I'm here talking to you? Coincidence? Or divine intervention?"

"Could be it's a small town and not many destinations."

Alex shrugged. "Anyway, here we are, you and me, like a couple of old buddies when basically we never really liked each other."

"I don't dislike you."

"No?" Alex surprised.

"Don't really like you much, either."

Alex laughed. "That so? Sometimes the things that may or may not be true or the things that are said are not said are the things that dictate relationships and shared histories."

Surprising insight for one so medicated.

Jake said, "You get kind of lyrical when you're drinking. Never knew that about you. I get jumped by your little brother and fatty, then your Father and Kellogg decide I need to get out of town by sundown and you know, it sets a man to watching his back. Gage is dead. I'm not okay with that. Someone shot at me and stole my truck. Maybe you have a better candidate for that than I do."

"You got something going with my little brother has nothing to do with me. I can't help the way he is. He's a pain in the ass and does what he wants and imagines no collateral damage."

Jake didn't miss the mention of Tommy.

Jake saying now, "Life is full of consequences we don't see coming."

"Is that a double entendre? Or you making threats?"

"I was going for philosophical but can't always pull it off." Jake leaned back and considered Alex. Where was this guy headed?

Alex took another drink then said, "Things are in motion I can't stop and maybe don't want to do that. It's not really personal. You're in the wrong place at the wrong time. Not by design, for sure, but – ." He stopped talking, looking inward, losing his train of thought.

"What things are in motion, Alex?"

Alex waved a finger in the air. "No. You don't get to do that. There's nothing diabulous...malev—" Struggling with his speech. "No, wait, nothing. There's not anything going on should bother you. That's the straight of it."

"You know, Alex, whatever's happening around here starts with Gage getting killed a week after you fire him. You don't see that. The way things are you don't get to call it off because you're liquored up and spouting cracker barrel observations." Rising up inside of him again. "Gage was my friend. That's in the way of things and it's not going away until I learn what happened."

"I don't know what happened to him."

"You don't know how he died?"

"Well, yes, I know that. Wish it hadn't happened."

"You're aware of the unhappy coincidence?"

Alex nodded, his head drooping momentarily.

Jake saying now, "Why did you fire him?"

"That's business. And, private. We don't get everything in this world." He blinked and said, "And you don't get that."

"Was it because of Pam?"

"The fuck're you saying?" Woke the boy up.

"You know what I'm saying. Did you suspect Gage was bopping your wife?"

That one hit the mark. Jake meant to do that. For a brief moment, Alex was sober, sitting up and starting to speak, but the moment passed.

"You're full of shit."

"You may be right about that. There are people believe you fired Gage for personal reasons."

Alex's eye looked away. He took a deep breath then another hit on his drink. "I don't know what assholes think. When was I placed in charge of everybody's problems? Hell with that." Alex squeezed his eyes shut, then opened one to look at Jake. "What I really want to talk about right now are women and their effect on plant growth."

"You want to talk about women? Or just want to talk about Pam?"

"I'm asking," Alex said, trying to pull himself together to say what he wanted to say. "You ever have hope that one day it'll all come together, and things will be peaceful, and you'll be as happy as you think you want to be?"

"I think you have to work real hard on that one."

Alex pounded the table, waving a hand in the air, and said, "Hank, another round here, dammit. We're dying of thirst and starved for answers to life's mysteries."

Jake could see Hank bristle. Jake held up a hand and nodded at the proprietor. Hank brought the drinks and gave Alex a hard look, then glared at Jake. Good ol' Hank.

The booze was taking over and doing the talking and thinking for Alex which was good for gaining information but sometimes the information was spotty. Alex had that faraway look as if not focusing on the now. Jake wanted to hear from him. Keep him talking by nodding in affirmation.

Alex said, "I used to be fine. Things were good. Had girlfriends and didn't care whether they loved me or not because I for sure did not love them or even care if they were around. Then, there was Pam. She's the whole package. Looks, brains and can turn your day around she smiles at you. You left town, thought now she's mine forever. Next thing I know she was married to some frat-rat. You know those guys, little chickenshits and their rush parties, not knowing they're pussies. I told everyone I didn't care, she was a bitch and I stayed drunk for about six months, jumped every girl I could get in my truck or my bed. Things were fine and I'd more or less forgotten about her." He took another pull on the beer, wiping his mouth with a sleeve, then continued. "She came back, sonuvabitch, she came back and suddenly she was mine." He stopped talking and looked off in the distance. "Well, as much as she could...belong to anyone. Now I wonder if I can get back to being fine."

Alex's head drooped. He looked at Jake as if wanting a response.

"If you're looking for 'happily ever after' you married the wrong woman. Pam is about Pam being happy."

Alex leaned forward in his seat and jutted his chin out, but the boozy smile remained on his face. "I should be offended but—" He belched, and his eyes were rheumy "—there is some truth in it."

"An observation." Actually Jake was seeing a side of Alex he never noticed before or maybe he just didn't care to see it. He sort of liked this Alex. Alex had always been intelligent. An honor roll student in high school. Popular most of that time. Rich always. But maybe not that happy. "You happy, Alex?"

"What?"

"You happy way things turned out?"

"I don't know. That takes a lot of thinking. How do you know if you're happy or not? You know any happy people?"

"I think happy people know they're happy." Wondering about himself. "While I do understand your feelings and am aware of the power that woman has to influence the direction of a man's day, I can't help you with any of this."

Alex's head lolled slightly, and his eyes were unfocused. "Well fuck you then." Pointing at Jake with a listless hand. "Fuck you and fuck your pal, Burnell. I'm unhappy because I want Pam. I cheat on her for revenge for what she's done to my psyche." His psyche? Alex scarred in a way Jake couldn't see but it was there. In a way that Jake shared with him.

Alex still talking saying, "'Cause my head is jammed-up with her and sometimes she is all I can think about while I'm doing this other thing which is living my fucking life, whatever that is. And now I'm stuck...between hating your guts because of her and realizing...not your fault."

"Nothing is left of you, each time you see her," Jake said, remembering the Catullus poem he'd memorized from college. Citing now the entire phrase, "'Godlike the man who sits at her side, who watches and catches that laughter which softly tears me to tatters: nothing is left of me, each time I see her'."

Alex stared at Jake for a moment, his eyes unfocused. He began twisting the Tiger eye ring. A habit.

"Damn. Besides, being a poet." Alex put both hands on the table and said, "Are you fucking my wife?"

"Getting to it now, are we? I get the feeling you want me to say something to ease your mind. But I don't have any of that either way. If your head is in a dark place, it's none of my doing." He leaned back in his chair and said, "Ever watch heat lightning out over the horizon and the thunder rolling in behind it? Well, sometimes that's all life is. If we're in each other's way, which is not my purpose, that's just something that's rolling in. You can watch it, but you can't stop it."

"Clarify for those of us who might be, you know, drunk."

"I can't help what's coming. Doesn't mean I don't sympathize with what you're going through, just that it's there."

Alex was listening but Jake could see a man lost in thoughts colored by alcohol, talking to himself as if Jake wasn't there. "Nothing's like it used to be, like it's supposed to be. You know," Alex said, to his beer glass. "She never cries." He looked up at Jake. "You ever notice? Never seen her cry. Doesn't even tear up."

Jake thought about that one. Alex was right. Thinking of a line from a song. She never cries like a lover.

28

Leaving the bar Jake walked to the rear parking lot where his rental was parked. He saw the two men get out of a car and walk his way. They were wearing light jackets against the night air. Not locals. They shut off their vehicle which had been expelling a cloud of smoke, suggesting they had been sitting there for some time with the engine idling.

Thick wrists and heavily knuckled hands. He'd seen men like this before. It was one of those things he knew instinctively after dozens of felony arrests. Thuggus Americanus. Some of them ended up in Texas prisons or in the county lock-up. Some of them he'd put there himself. The type of bar room toughs found in many towns. No skills save a propensity for violence.

They stopped and looked at him.

"Hey," said one of them, a dark-haired guy same height as Jake. The other guy was shorter and built like a professional wrestler. "You know a good place to eat in town." Walking in Jake's direction as he said it. If he really wanted to know the answer there was no need to walk towards him.

Jake looked at them and said, "Stay where you are."

The pair took two more steps in Jake's direction.

Jake said, "I mean it."

The men stopped.

"What's the problem?" asked the dark-haired man.

"Where's that southern hospitality, Tex?"

"I'm all out."

Tex, huh? Information going out and that was all Jake needed to know.

The man said, "Wait a minute. Want to show you – " The man reached inside his jacket. Jake interrupted the man's movement by producing the Taurus and holding it down by his side where they could see it and be able to achieve an understanding of their situation.

"I see the inside of your coat," Jake said. "There's going to be a loud noise."

"What the hell is going on?" said the man. "There's no reason to be unfriendly. I don't have a gun. Shit."

"Peel your jackets," Jake said, making a languid movement with his gun in the men's direction. "Slowly. Either do it or put your faces on the ground and we'll go from there."

"You gonna shoot us?"

"Not if you get those jackets off."

"You won't shoot," said dark-hair.

"Better believe me," Jake said.

The two men looked at each other then slowly removed their jackets without taking their eyes off Jake. No weapons on either man.

"Anything else?" said dark-hair.

"Yeah," Jake said. "This place here? Hank's?" Nodding in the bar's direction. "Great cheeseburgers. The proprietor has kind of an attitude, but prices are fair, and the beer is cold. You boys have a nice stay, but I don't want to see you again. Get that? I have an idea who sent you, but you show up in my orbit again I'm going to make it a point to help you find a way out of town. Put it on my calendar."

"You threatening us?"

"Don't know how you could miss it."

"What're you gonna do? Gunfight at high noon?"

"Some imagination you got. That's not bad, though." He nodded at them. "Promise you'd lose. Get that? You'd better." He tucked his sidearm away. "You boys have a nice evening."

***

Buck fever. Jake had a touch of it now. That's what they called the reaction when a big whitetail deer would just appear like a ghost and you got the shakes or froze, staring at the woods, not seeing anything for a couple of minutes, thinking did that happen? He'd heard of guys jacking a lever action gun empty, or ejecting a bullet magazine, without taking a shot, forgetting to pull the trigger.

Jake feeling that now after fronting the two men. They weren't much, just local stuff; still there was a light trembling in his hands and shoulders and a little dryness in his mouth. Fear wasn't any help, so you tamped it way down and did what you had to do. Despite the moment and the danger and all the questions, something else was on his mind. It was Harper. She was at his place when he got home, and he feared he may have inadvertently put her in danger.

Harper Bannister. She was something special.

He could hear Sue's voice in his head telling him she had told him so and that, 'you're hooked, buddy. A little scary? You bob and weave and then out of nowhere it hits you. Didn't expect that did you? She's cute. And smart and fun and intriguing in a way you never seen before. Something new. Can't stop thinking about her, can you? Like now. It's all good, no hard feelings, Jake, we both knew someone would blaze one inside and you wouldn't be able to knock it back. Your only recourse is to go with the pitch or bail'.

That's why Harper was here now, with him. She had called and came out to his place. They talked for a time and she had fallen asleep on his couch, next to him. He watched her sleep, breathed the freshness of her and smiled while he watched a late movie on the television.

But wasn't following the plot.

***

The two men, named Mac and Gene, which Jake confronted behind Hank's place decided not to leave town. Well, Mac decided that, not Gene. Gene had been a pro wrestler for a time. Small venues, not the big-time on TV with Hulk Hogan or Triple H. Then he was a bouncer at a bar. He'd broken some noses, put some guys in ER, done some collecting work but he'd never been a shooter.

"I didn't like the Texas asshole talking shit at me," said Boyd Macklin. It was morning and they were having breakfast in their motel room someone else paid for. "I fucking hate smart ass goat ropers."

The other man, Gene, said, "Morgan isn't a Texan, he's from here. You shouldna called him 'Tex'. He made us when you said that. You said it yourself," said Gene, trying to calm his partner down. "He ain't gonna scare like we were told so let it go? He's nobody."

"I need to settle this." Gene watched Macklin load up a Glock 24 pistol.

"Don't do that. C'mon."

"May need it the cocksucker starts with his mouth."

"You want to go back to prison?"

"Wasn't so bad. Worse is this fucking cracker running his mouth at me."

"Do what's smart. Forget him."

Macklin stood and shoved the pistol into his waist, covered it with a jacket.

"You coming or not?"

Gene sighed heavily. They drove out of town in a used 2014 Buick.

Gene thinking to himself this wasn't the smart move.

***

Unbelievable, Harper was thinking.

Harper watched Jake get up from the breakfast table, look out the window, walk back to his bedroom and return with a handgun, then telling her, "Visitors. I need to go out and say hello. Stay inside and give your dad a call, get Buddy out here."

"What?"

Just like that and without explanation he slipped out the back with the weapon.

Would she ever understand him?

What happened next made her think maybe not only would she ever understand him...she may never even know him.

***

Jake watched the black Buick creeping up his lane. The same car the night before in Hank's parking lot.

Jake went to his room, got his weapon out of the nightstand, heeled a magazine into the butt and racked in a shell. That done he told Harper to call her dad and then eased open the back door and slipped quietly outside.

He came around the corner of the house, behind the two men who were just getting out of the car and adjusting their jackets.

"Morning, fellas," Jake said coming up behind them, his weapon down alongside his leg.

The pair whipped around, surprised.

"Shit," said the man built like a linebacker.

"I thought we were clear about your future," Jake said.

The darker man, who stood on the driver's side, saying now, "You don't tell me where I can go or can't go."

"True," Jake said, getting ready. "But there are consequences when you don't."

"We're not going."

"I see that. Now what?"

The heavy-set, wrestler type, looked at the darker man, then he said, "I don't even want to be here. This is his idea. Let's talk, see if we can calm things down."

"I'm through talking to you two. I meant what I said. Get on the ground and lace your fingers behind your necks."

"Are you fucking kidding?" said the darker man.

"Did it sound like that? I was going for authoritative."

"It ain't happening, cocksucker."

"Name-calling. So, not going to be friends," Jake said, saying it like to himself, shifting his eyes from one man to the other. Deciding. "It ends here. It ends now."

The two men spread apart.

"Don't do that," Jake said. "Either of you moves again I'm taking that one down."

"There's two of us," said the darker man.

"I can wait while you call up reinforcements," Jake said.

"Some mouth you got on you, asshole."

"Goddammit, Mac," said the heavy man. "What the hell are you doing? He has a gun. This is no good."

"Doesn't have to be this way," Jake said, his eyes level on the man named Mac, deciding the other man wasn't a worry.

"We can just go our way," said Mac. "That what you're saying?"

Jake shaking his head. "No. You're trespassing and threatening so you're going inside for a day or so. Toss your weapons and get your faces in the dirt."

"You're arresting us?"

"Beats the alternative."

Mac, bulled-up, saying now, "You can't be serious."

Jake relaxed now but his eyes hard. "Better believe me."

Mac said, "This ain't the Wild West, boy."

"Toss 'em or it starts."

"All right," said Mac. "You win this time."

"Every time."

Mac laughed, said, "Fuck you". Reaching inside his jacket for his weapon when Jake shot out the driver side window next to where Mac was standing. Mac jumped and his hand came out of his jacket, empty.

"Next one dead center. Two fingers, left hand, the weapon in the dirt and then you also on your stomach."

The other man, the wrestler surprised, his mouth open and staring. What just happened?

"Believe me, now?" Jake said.

The wrestler got on the ground.

***

Jake cuffed both men with zip-tights then walked back into the house got his Ranger handcuffs. Harper stared at him while the phone rang at her father's office. Jake walked back outside and re-cuffed the men, then walked back inside and picked up his coffee cup and took a sip. Harper watched this, amazed, as Buddy Johnson answered on the other end. She said, "He's right here," and handed the phone to Jake and Sheriff Candidate Buddy said, "You did what?"

Jake told him he had two men in custody.

"In custody?" Incredible. "You understand neither of us has jurisdiction? You seem unable to keep that in the front of you."

Jake told him that's why he called him and did Buddy know any state troopers would be willing to come out and take a look. Buddy telling Jake the sheriff wasn't going to be happy and how would it look, Doc's election opponent bringing in outside law enforcement? Jake telling him he'd completely forgot to consider Buddy's electoral campaign while he was shooting up the guy's car.

Giving up now. "Okay," Buddy said. "I know a trooper I trust."

After talking to Buddy Jake asked the heavy-set man, Gene, if he wanted anything. Coffee or a beer?

"I drink it how?" asked Gene held up his handcuffed wrists.

Jake made a show of thinking about it, pointing at the interior of the Buick. "I can cuff you to the steering wheel and you can use the other hand."

"This is what you do? You shoot at people then serve drinks?"

Jake nodded at the other man sitting on the ground

cuffed behind his back, who the wrestler guy, Gene, told him was Boyd Macklin. "Well, he gets nothing for being rude. I didn't shoot at you. Yet."

Gene's eyes widened. "What's that mean? You gonna shoot us?"

"Nope. Unless you screw up when I get you a beer. I've got some Bud and a couple Heinekens."

Gene looked at Jake and said, "You got any light beer? I kinda need to watch my weight."

***

Harper watched Jake walk back outside put one man on the ground and then stepped on the man's back while he cuffed the other man to the car steering wheel.

Then a really crazy thing. Jake came into the house, took a beer out of the refrigerator and she said, "You want a beer after that?"

"It's for the fat guy."

Really? She didn't know whether to laugh or...well, laugh.

29

Cop lights danced as Buddy Johnson showed with a state trooper named Fred Ridley. Ridley went six-foot, slim waist and weight-lifter shoulders. Uniform crisp and clean. When the trooper got out of his unit he carefully seated his Smokey the Bear hat on his head. Buddy introduced them.

Ridley watched Gene drink beer from a can, his other hand cuffed to the steering wheel of the Buick.

"You gave him a beer?" said Trooper Ridley.

"He was thirsty," Jake said.

Ridley smiled at that, squinting and giving Jake a sideways look. "You're not going to be trouble, are you?"

"Don't mean to be."

"Texas Ranger, huh? You shoot a lot of cars down there?"

"Said he wanted a bullet-hole Buick."

Ridley looked at Buddy. "What have you got me into here?" Then to Jake, Ridley said, "You're aware this is not your jurisdiction."

"I hear that a lot."

Ridley went to work, first removing the cuffs from the steering wheel, then placing them in the back of the patrol unit. That done the muscular Trooper walked back to the Buick. "You shot out the window?"

"I was aiming at his tires."

Ridley said, "I'll bet."

"Both men were carrying. Their weapons are on my deck."

Ridley studied Jake for a moment, shrugged and walked over to secure the handguns.

Ridley pulled their ID, returned to his unit and called in requests for a white male, Boyd Macklin, birthdate, 7-16-71. Also for a white male, Gene Hamtramck, birthdate, 3-4-65.

Ridley nodded at Harper Bannister. "You witnessed this?"

She nodded. Her lips were pursed, and her arms folded under her breasts. "Yes. I did and it was something to see."

"Happen like he said?"

Nodding again. "Yes."

"You his girlfriend?"

"We're deciding."

Ridley chuckled at her oblique reply, then said, "You're made for each other. Bet the conversations are interesting."

Ridley's radio crackled and he got the information he wanted. Both had jackets. Macklin had a sheet with local authorities. "Mostly assault," said Ridley. "Some county time. Picked him up myself for DUI. The other guy? He got hauled in a couple times for bar fights. Couple weekends in county lock-up. Nothing big. Looks like Macklin graduated to assault with a deadly weapon. Looks like you put a bad guy on the bench."

Jake shrugged. "Doing what I can."

"Also a bank hold-up."

"I was lucky."

Ridley looked at Jake. "Is this something you do a lot?"

"Give beer to bad actors?" Jake said.

"Shoot up vehicles. Shoot bank robbers."

He shrugged. "Not so you'd notice."

"Wonder how you manage to attract the attention of such people."

"People are naturally drawn to me."

"Trying to decide whether I like you or you're trying to annoy me."

"The former's my preference," Jake said.

"Tell me what led up to this."

Jake related the problem with the two men the night before.

"You think someone hired them," said Ridley.

"Or pointed them in my direction."

"Officer Johnson says this might be a dicey situation with you and Johnson being close. You don't like the sheriff?"

Jake smiled, looked at Buddy.

"Jake is a good man," Buddy said. "Unpredictable but a good man."

Ridley nodded. "I have to go to the sheriff with this. It's procedure and I have no choice." He chewed his lower lip with a tooth. "But I'll go in with you when you report it."

"Thanks," Jake said.

Ridley reseated his hat and said, "We know all about Sheriff Kellogg. Promise you."

30

"You forced them into a showdown?" said Kellogg, leaning in when he said it.

They were at the Paradise County Sheriff's office, Jake, Buddy, Cal, Harper and Trooper Ridley. Kellogg asking questions of Jake. Jake was seated in a padded chair, Kellogg towering over him.

"Offered a citizen's arrest but they weren't having it," Jake said.

Kellogg removed his Stetson, placed it on his desk and looked at Trooper Ridley. Ran a hand through his hair. "This is not how things are done. Local police calling in a state trooper instead of calling me. Makes me think you don't trust me."

"Should I?" Jake said. "You've already established you don't like me."

Ridley, his arms folded over his Sam Browne strap, looked at Kellogg, saying nothing. Looking at Jake again, Kellogg said, "I don't like people getting shot in my county."

Jake nodded. "I shot their car."

"I'm going to have to take you into custody, Morgan."

Ridley intervened, saying, "I don't think that'll be necessary. It was a good shooting. You can do what you want but believe that is a mistake. Both men have records for rough stuff. Two armed men, with assault records, show up at this man's place and you don't think they had improper motives? I would advise you to investigate the scene and talk to the other man, Gene Hamtramck. Hamtramck is ready to give a statement in exchange for immunity. He's going to tell you, off-the-record, that Macklin went there to assault Morgan."

Jake could see Kellogg chewing the inside of his cheek.

Ridley saying, "According to Mister Morgan, Hamtramck did not draw a weapon or make any threatening statements or movements."

"I even provided refreshments," Jake said.

Kellogg started to speak, changed his mind and left the room shaking his head.

Two hours later and a taped statement from Jake and he dropped off Harper at home and now was on his way back home. At home Jake experienced a strange feeling that something was out of place, not inside his head but in his physical surroundings he couldn't put his finger on. He'd felt it yesterday for the first time as if something had changed in the house. He was not yet familiar with the way Gage set up the house but there was a rhythm and sensation to a home that resonated and that was broken.

His cell phone rang.

Jake decided he'd better give his captain a heads-up. Not the kind of thing Parmalee would appreciate hearing second hand.

He called ranger station B and told Parmalee about his encounter with the two thugs and the other incidents. He left out the visit to the Mitchell ranch as he was pretty sure the conciliatory tone would vanish.

After Jake finished, Parmalee said, "Maybe you should come back to Texas before you get into anymore mischief. Let the local law enforcement officials handle this."

"The sheriff is not a friend. He's unlikely to investigate Gage's death and may be a party to covering it up."

"You're paranoid."

"Heightened awareness."

Pause. "What am I supposed to do with you?"

"How about a promotion?"

"Does it occur to you that while you are...that your question is poorly timed?"

"So, that's a no?"

"Son, this isn't funny. I appreciate your situation and your feelings and factor those in with your youth and your settled demeanor. However, you place me in an untenable position if this blows up in your face. People tend to take an unfavorable view of rogue law enforcement people shooting up the landscape. Realize that if you are wrong about any of this you could be in the unemployment line."

"I know you'll have my back."

Jake could hear Parmalee exhale into the phone. "Have your back? Jake, there are political realities and procedures regarding how we conduct ourselves as law enforcement officers. Why doesn't that connect for you? Sometimes I wonder why I endure your nonsense."

"Maybe because I'm a lot like you were before you got a desk with a nameplate."

"Not in a million years."

"I've heard the stories," Jake said.

"Don't believe everything you hear."

"Don't worry, boss," Jake said. "I don't."

"Well," said the captain. "I'll do what I can at this end but don't presume upon it. And, don't call me boss."

"Thanks."

"Don't get ahead of yourself. You may not have reason to thank me. One more thing."

Jake waited.

Parmalee said, "Looks like you're going to be all right on the other thing. The wife changed her story and said her husband deserved it and if you hadn't intervened, he might've killed her. The guy's out of the public arena for nine months and you're off the hook."

"Okay."

"Doesn't mean you're free to beat the shit out of every perp you encounter in the future. Or, shoot them. Remember that. We'll see you back here in a few days."

New lease on life. Don't screw it up, Jake.
Telling himself that but sometimes...

***

After the phone call, Jake decided to take a look at the
west fence line. It was a pretty good walk to the area,
but he wanted to clear his head. He looked at the sagging
fence and knew it would be a project to fix but it would
have to be done.

A lot of things would need to be done. He had to head
back to Texas soon. How to keep the farm up? He could
hire someone or rent out the place. Or?

Sell it.

As we began to walk back to the house, he heard a
vehicle coming up his lane. Before he could get back, he
could hear the sound of the vehicle leaving. Probably saw
he wasn't home and left.

He hoofed it back to the house, got a beer out of the
fridge and the landline rang and the phone ID read "unknown". He hesitated to pick it up thinking it was a solici-
tor wanting him to purchase some double-paned windows
or siding.

He answered it.

A voice, muffled and unrecognizable, said, "Get out of
town. Today."

"Who is this?"

He heard the click of the phone as the party hung up.

Crank call?

Jake punched in Buddy's number told Buddy about the
cryptic call.

"You beginning to think someone doesn't like you?"
asked Buddy.

"With my fetching personality? How could that be
so?"

Jake absently patted his pocket for a cigarette, remembering he wasn't smoking. Still a bit unsettled by the
shooting incident.

"Don't doubt Vernon Mitchell's very long reach in this
area."

"I don't. That's not it."

"What?"

Jake said, "Vernon strike you as someone who doesn't plan well?"

Buddy shaking his head, then looking at Jake. "No. No, he doesn't. He strikes me as ruthless and tough. Not a killer though. What're you saying?"

"So far, things seem fragmented. Some things are well-planned and open like Sheriff Kellogg or someone calling my captain and hiring bar thugs to confront me. Others, like stealing my pick-up are more the act of people making it up as they go along. This would be more like Tommy who still thinks Harper belongs to him."

"I noted she spent the night with you."

"Be careful, Buddy. Nothing happened. She just fell asleep on my sofa."

"Uh huh. So, that's your story? Don't screw things up with her. She's the real deal."

Jake imagined Buddy smiling at Jake's chagrin regarding Harper. "I don't know if you've noticed it or not but there's a lot of untoward sex stuff going on in this town when the sun goes down."

"You mean like my sister-in-law Shari Langston and Alex Mitchell?" Surprising Jake. "Makes my wife sick. She gets enough from the peckerwood ass wipes around here about being married to a black man."

"You're black?" Jake said. "Wow. I just thought you had a really good tan."

Jake watched the Paradise Country Sheriff's SUV coming up his lane. Inside was Sheriff 'Doc' Kellogg. Jake walked outside and continued to talk to Buddy.

"Gotta run," Jake said. "Looks like the sheriff is here."

"Easy, Jake," Buddy said. "Lay back and be cool. Part of his job to follow up on the shooting, even a self-defense shooting so this is just routine. You got your way at his office and you've already pushed him enough. He's got the hammer here. Keep calm and don't light him up."

Jake nodded to himself. "Yeah, believe you're right."

"Stay out of trouble," Buddy said. "Good to be home isn't it?"

Sheriff Kellogg got out of his unit, putting on his Stetson and adjusting his gun belt. He had a deputy with him.

"Sorry about this," said Kellogg. "You're not going to like this but I'm going to have to rope it off as a crime scene."

"Not the house, just their car."

Sheriff Kellogg thought about that.

"If you have to close down the house, then do what you have to do," Jake said. "Whatever's best but I hope you won't be offended if I talk to an attorney about that."

"Well," said Kellogg. "We'll see. Not doing that at the moment."

Kellogg and his deputy went about their duties, checking the scene, taking photos of the Buick. Jake showered and changed clothes. Kellogg and his deputy were gone by the time Jake fired up the Lincoln to go see Harper. As he got to the end of his lane, he met Pam Kellogg Mitchell. Her window whooshed down, and she said, "I came as soon as I could."

The statement was perplexing. 'As soon as she could'?

"What do you mean?"

"I heard about the shooting. Are you okay?"

"Yeah. I did the shooting."

"We need to talk," she said. "I think it was Tommy."

"Tommy?"

"He stole your vehicle I think."

"I need more than that. You have anything concrete?"

"He hates you because of Harper."

"Well, I appreciate the information. Why're you telling me this?"

Her face softened and her lips parted before saying, "I tried to stay away, tried not to be drawn to you, but I can't. I still love you, Jake."

Jake looked in the rearview mirror back at the car covered with yellow police tape. Leo the Lion was right. Pam Kellogg would always be Pam Kellogg and whether it was men, money or power, Pam Kellogg knew how to get what she wanted.

So, what to say?

He said, "I believe you."

She looked at Jake. All the soft light gone and in its place was a look in her eyes he had not seen before.

It wasn't love.

31

Jake considered possible suspects for Gage's killing.

The Mitchells were a possibility. All of them. They had many businesses and perhaps that was the key. The businesses that interested Jake the most were their chemical fertilizer plant and their grain elevator. Jake noted something caked on Steve Barb's boots Sunday at Vernon's home. Did it look like what he had found on the brake pedal of Gage's vehicle?

The chemical fertilizer plant was located outside city limits. However, Mitchell's grain elevator was located in town. Right where a dedicated auxiliary cop could see it.

It wasn't a slam dunk because every farmer on every farm in the county had sacks of fertilizer and feed that may match what he had found in Gage's auto. Almost a dead end unless he could definitively match the residue in Gage's Dodge Charger to materials found around the elevator or the fertilizer plant. So, it was circumstantial evidence at best, but investigations were put together a piece at a time. Sometimes the most innocuous things became important, even conclusive.

He was sharing this information with Harper. They were sitting on Harper's back deck to watch the sun fade into a warm golden orange.

"Pam could be right about Tommy," Jake said.

"Steve Barb works at the fertilizer plant and the grain

elevator," said Harper. Her cat leaped up on Harper's lap, while Bandit had curled up at Jake's feet. "And so does Robby Warner. So does Tommy. They move around. I struggle thinking of Tommy as a killer. I mean, he's an irresponsible jerk, but a killer? I don't see that."

"Why'd you marry him anyway?"

"I'm attracted to creeps." Big smile and letting it hang.

"Touché," Jake said. "You know, doesn't take a lot to create a murderer. Circumstances can turn anyone's thoughts to homicide."

"I don't believe that."

"Most of the people I've arrested were ruled by impulses that—" shaking his head now, "—were inexplicable. I once handcuffed a woman who'd stabbed her boyfriend with a letter opener. Said she did it because he kept changing channels on the TV, and it was driving her crazy."

"What about Pam?" said Harper, arching an eyebrow. "You thought about that?"

A sick thought was Pam had a key to his house. The only explanation for how she showed up the night she visited him. Pam had a connection with Gage. Pam's thought processes had ever been inexplicable, partly because she was a woman and largely because Pam Kellogg was an extraordinarily talented person who was smarter than all the Mitchells put together.

And, perhaps smarter than Jake.

"I'm not excluding anyone at this point."

"A murder mystery," said Harper. "One involving cover-ups, intrigues, violence, sexual indiscretions and a tall boy back from Texas."

"People who've killed once have nothing to lose by eliminating witnesses."

"I'm worried about you."

"Why's that?"

"Something happens to you I have to go back to the semi-cowboys wearing polo cologne."

"You don't like the semi-cowboys?"

"Don't like Polo cologne. Smells like junior high boys."

***

Jake left Harper, telling her he had a couple of things to do and would be back later. On the road he looked at the gas gauge. It was low. He remembered there was a couple of credit card gas pumps in front of the Mitchell grain elevator. Two birds with one stone?

He pulled into the parking lot and eased next to one of the gas pumps. Jake zipped his debit card, opened the gas cap, pulled the hose from the pump and shoved it into the gas tank. He looked up at the grain elevator looming and towering over the low city skyline.

Jake saw the two men walking his way. What a co-incidence. Steve Barb and his partner, Robby Warner. Jake turned away, much like you do a dog, ignoring it and letting it know its growling didn't mean much.

"Hey, asshole," said Barb.

'Asshole'? Unbelievable. Pump the gas and do what you came to do. Check out the elevator then see Cal. Afterwards go back to see if Harper wanted to make it an evening. Maybe a nice dinner. Better than dealing with a couple of mental defectives who may or may not be killers.

"Didn't you hear me?" Barb said, flicking a cigarette away.

"I was ignoring you. You miss that part?"

"Want to talk to you."

"That works because I've been meaning to talk to you."

"Yeah, what about?"

"Where were you the night Gage Burnell was killed?"

"What's it to you?" said Barb.

Jake smiled, shaking his head. "They told me you were a gifted conversationalist, but I had no idea you were so articulate."

Jake watched Robby, circling away from Steve, moving to the outside of Jake's peripheral vision. Here we go.

"You got mouth problems you know that?"

Jake keeping his eye on Steve. Guy was bulled up. What was this? Were they considering an assault? Right here in town? Did Vernon have so much power they weren't concerned about an arrest? Robby didn't look like he wanted trouble but both of them big enough to bring trouble. There was no one else around.

"Look," Jake said. "Let me fill up and we'll talk. How's that?"

"Fuck you," said Barb.

"Well, never mind. Just back away and I'll see you some other time. Maybe in an official capacity."

"Heard you took two guys in town a few days ago," said Barb. Starting to escalate. Jake hadn't figured on a confrontation and wasn't ready for it. Scrape of boot leather against raw pavement behind him. Robby moving further out of his vision. This could turn ugly and he was trapped between the Lincoln and the gas pumps in a town that no longer knew him. A town without pity for a Texas visitor.

"Well," said Barb. "We want you to understand we're not those two guys."

Barb was a talker. Wanted to tell how it went down later. Never knew a talker that did anything unless they came at you sideways or had the deck stacked in their favor. Robby was a follower. Barb was wrapping a strip of hard rubber around his hand. Not good. This was going to happen. Jake turned to look for Robby while putting the gas nozzle back in its holster.

"You morons are looking at an assault charge you come at me. You want trouble I'll accommodate you, but not here."

Robby had moved to within two steps of Jake. Jake spun and said, "You keep coming, Robby, I'll knock the taste out of your mouth."

Barb moved in and hit Jake behind the ear, the hard rubber wrapping making it more painful. Jake's head filled with starbursts. Crunch of teeth grinding.

Jake recovered and caught Barb on the shoulder with

an elbow, then kicked out at Robby but instead of taking out Robby's kneecap, Jake's boot merely scraped the side of the man's leg and now the two men had him down between the car and the gas pumps with no room to maneuver.

Jake tried to cover as they worked on him, punching and kicking out to try to get them off. He felt their fists and the hard ground underneath him. Someone yelled. They had him down and there was no way out. These were big men. Hard men. He was going to take a beating, so he folded himself up to lessen the impact. Ride it out, Jake.

Tire skidding on gravel, a door opening and then...

"Get off him," said a familiar voice, then a beastly sound. A guttural bellow he had heard many times years ago by an all-district linebacker busting through blockers.

Leo the Lion had snatched Steve Barb and now had Barb dangling over Leo's head like an Olympic power-lifter, Barb's belt and shirt gripped in Leo's fists. Barb squirmed but the alternative was a hard fall onto unforgiving pavement. As Robby backed away, Jake got to his feet and stalked Robby.

"No more," said Robby, his hands out in front of him, imploring Jake. "We're done, okay?"

"I'm not," Jake said. He was breathing hard as he punched Robby at the base of his throat. Robby threw his hands to his neck and coughed for air. Jake started towards Robby but stopped when he heard Leo yelled out at him.

"Jake. Stop," Leo said, his voice under the strain of his power-lift of Barb.

Jake turned toward Leo and shocked by what he saw; Steve Barb suspended over Leo's head.

"Damn, Leo," Jake said, amazed. "Put him down."

Leo surged with adrenaline, his chest heaving with effort. His eyes darted right, then left, as if confused, then embarrassed. People were gathering. He sat Barb down and Barb stumbled to regain balance, his face drained of blood, and registering disbelief. He had been physically lifted, like a sack of feed.

Robby, who had been coughing and spitting, said,

"Shit," the words coming softly from his mouth.

"You two guys need to give some thought about your life choices," Leo said. "This is bullshit and you can do better, Robby. Find someone else to hang out with."

"Sorry, Coach," said Robby. Barb had his head down. Dawning on Jake that this pair had played football for Leo and listened to him.

Leo pointing at Barb now and saying, "As for you, I have no expectations. You don't realize being a man requires more than you give to it. I'm done with you; don't come around. I don't have any use for you."

"Coach, I – "

Leo interrupted, saying, "I don't want to hear anymore from you. Move away right now."

A Paradise police unit pulled up, its siren whooped once, and a uniform officer got out and told everyone to "stand down".

Jake felt the corner of his mouth and when he looked at his fingers there was a smattering of blood. Back of his neck felt like he'd been hit with a hammer.

Barb and Robby were perp-walked away by the officer like a couple of schoolboys who had been reprimanded.

"What was that?" Jake said, to Leo. "What you just did?"

Leo shrugged, looked away. Embarrassed?

"Wow," said a kid nearby. "You see Coach Lyon?"

Jake watched Steve and Robby disappear into the police car, touched the corner of his mouth again, making him wince, then said, "Whatever it is," Jake said, "you still got it."

"You all right?" Leo asked Jake. "You never were a beauty, but you look like hell. I'm glad to see you again but you'll be better off back in Texas until things cool down here. You cool down too." Jake was silent and Leo searched his face for a long moment, then decided something. "But you won't stay away, will you?"

Jake said nothing, dusting his clothes.

Leo shaking his head. "Why do you make being your friend a high wire act?"

Jake smiled and said, "You're not enjoying this?"

Leo seemed lost in thought. "I don't...care for things like this. I'm not a fighter." He let out a breath. "You... You make pacifism hard work. Glad I got here when I did."

Jake rubbed his shoulder and said, "You're glad? I'm ecstatic you showed up."

32

Leo filled up his vehicle and left. Jake walked over to the Mitchell grain elevator and examined the grounds then back behind the plant to the railroad tracks.

Seeing something now and thinking he'd found what he was looking for.

When Jake pulled into her drive Harper was glad to see him. That is until she noticed the corner of his mouth was swollen and bleeding and his clothes were torn and dirty.

"What happened?"

He touched his mouth. "Oh this? Couple of guys wanted me to put high-test in my car and I wanted regular."

She folded her arms and gave him a look telling him she wasn't in the mood.

"I guess I should see what the other guy looks like," she said.

"They're fine. Lost this one. Hadn't been for Leo showing up you would be visiting me at ER."

"Not sure you shouldn't be there now."

"Don't make a thing out of it."

"Who was it?"

"Barb and Warner."

"That's the second one since you came back. Childish to get into fights at your age."

"When I lose anyway. They didn't give me much choice."

She unfolded her arms and reached up and touched his cheek. She told him to sit and left the room. He heard water running and cabinets being opened and shut. She returned with a damp cloth and rubbing alcohol. She cleaned his cuts with the cloth, and he flinched when she dabbed at them with an alcohol-soaked cotton ball.

"Ouch!"

"Quit being a baby."

He told her about what happened and how Leo had come to the rescue. In the nick of time just like the movies.

Jake asked her if she had some zip-lock baggies he could borrow.

"Why do you need that?"

"I have to go back to the Mitchell grain elevator."

"Why would you do that?"

"Found something maybe."

"What do you think you found."

He shrugged. "Could be a waste of time. But there was some strange residue in Gage's Charger and I saw something like that on someone's shoes. Possibly the same thing at the elevator."

"When did you look at Gage's car?"

Harper's dog bounced over to be petted so Jake scratched behind his ears. "Cute little guy."

"Don't avoid the question," said Harper. "How did you manage to see Gage's car? It's in the impound area."

"How do you know where it is?" Jake said, having fun delaying his answer.

"I'm the chief's daughter and I work in a law office."

He told her about visiting the impound area with Buddy Johnson.

"They took the carpet out of the trunk?"

"See? You know where I'm going with this."

"Someone did kill Gage."

He nodded. "Cigarette ash in the trunk. Gage didn't smoke. My problem is I don't know why he was killed."

She sat for a moment, shaking her head. "Poor Gage. Such a nice fun person. No wonder you're attracting violence. When did you get like this?"

"Like what?"

"You have an attitude and a death wish. Are you un-aware what has been happening to you?" Exasperated now, she said, "Is it worth all this trouble?"

"Trouble?" He smiled at her; his swollen lip made him wince when he did. "What trouble?"

"Don't patronize me," she said. "I get worry lines on my face, I'll poison your food." She smiled back at him.

"Aw, she cares."

"Quit putting yourself in these situations."

"If you think about it, I'm not, rather people are seek-ing me out. If I'm taking flak it means I'm over the target."

He told her about how Pam had shown up as he was leaving his house.

She stopped cleaning him up and gave him a sidelong look. "What did she want?"

He told her that Pam said she was the one who called to warn him and that she still loved him. It was quiet for a moment while she considered that.

"I knew it. And," she said. "What did you say to that?"

He told her.

Harper stared at him in disbelief. She closed her eyes for a moment, a smile forming and then started laughing. "You told her, 'I believe you'?"

He shrugged, his palms up. "That's bad?"

Shaking her head now she said, "No woman wants to hear that. I'll bet that set her on fire." She smiled again and shook her head. "You are such a guy. I'm sorry for being – ." Her voice trailed off as she searched for the words.

"Jealous?" Jake said. She liked the way his eyes looked when he smiled at her.

"That's another thing you don't say to a woman. You really know nothing about the opposite sex, do you?"

"I know I could be falling for you."

She smiled, then said, "I believe you."

33

Leaving Harper Jake stopped by Paradise PD to speak
with Chief Cal Bannister. Jake wanted to share his
thoughts on Gage Burnell's death. He intended to lay it
all out – the scene at the creek, the missing carpet in the
trunk of the Charger, the cigarette butt and ash and finally the residue on the brake pedal and carpet which may
match what he found at the Mitchell grain elevator.

It was all moot when Cal stopped him.

"You're not going to want to hear this," Cal said, from
behind his walnut desk, his papers and flyers neatly arranged as a checkerboard. He picked up a pipe from a
pipe holder affixed to an ashtray and began filling the pipe
with Borkum Riff. "Sheriff Kellogg just arrested a man
for the murder of Gage Burnell."

Jake fished his shirt pocket for cigarettes that weren't
there. He said nothing for a moment.

Cal nodded at Jake. "That's right. Homicide."

"Admitting to it," saying it more to himself. "Odd.
When?"

"An hour ago."

"No," Jake said. "When did Doc decide against Gage's
death being an accident?"

Cal screwed up his face, exhaled. "That? I don't know."

"I believe it possible Gage was killed in town then
transported to the scene of the accident."

"What?" Cal smiled and said, "You sound like a cop instead of a troublemaker which most would call you at this point. But you have insight. I've got your dance partners in the holding cell." Cal placed a hand on his chin, framing his mouth with thumb and forefinger. "So, let's hear what you've got."

Jake shared his findings. The cigarette ash, the missing trunk carpet, the residue on the brake pedal and Steve Barb's tossed away cigarette. Cal listened without interruption, as immovable as an Egyptian monument. When Jake finished, they both sat quietly for a moment. Pipe smoke hovered in the air between them.

"First," said Cal. "Who let you in the impound area?" Jake gave him a look and Cal said, "I don't want to know, do I? Okay, how does anything you told me establish a homicide occurred in town?"

"A guess," Jake said. "Consider I've been targeted? I believe it is happening because I'm close to something someone doesn't want known. I found this." Producing a baggie filled with what he'd found at the elevator he handed it to Cal. "I found the same substance in Gage's car. Removing the carpet liner from the trunk suggests, to me, the killers transported Gage in the trunk. Blood residue would show up had they not."

"Killers? You think there's more than one?"

"The killer couldn't drive two cars. One driver to transport the body and Gage's car and one to pick-up the driver. One man would have a helluva time trying to lift Gage into the trunk then take him out and drag him to the creek."

"That assumes quite a bit."

"You explain it then."

Cal, his pipe stuck in the corner of his mouth, nodded slowly. "Pulling the carpet is hard to explain, but it doesn't mean Gage was in the trunk. The sediment you have here is from the elevator, but dozens of locals walk through the place daily."

"Gage was a big boy. What'd he weigh? About one eighty? You ever drag one hundred eighty pounds of dead deer out of the woods. That's a lot of dead weight."

"Still, Kellogg says he has the killer."

"You don't find that convenient?"

"Meaning Kellogg decides at this moment to change the accident to homicide after you ride him about it and start an unauthorized investigation?"

Jake sat back. "Auxiliary Police. That's me."

"It's thin. But not bad."

"Would give you jurisdiction to investigate. You can mount an investigation at your discretion."

"A parallel investigation. That'll piss off Doc."

"A bonus. My guess is they don't want to know what really happened and want it to go away. Doesn't necessarily mean Kellogg is complicit; might only mean he's worried where a real investigation would lead. Who does Doc have in custody?"

"I don't know."

"Can we go see the guy?"

Cal stood and set his PPD hat on his head. "Thought you'd never ask."

Kellogg was less than excited to see Cal and Jake.

"What is he doing here?" said Kellogg jamming a thumb in Jake's direction.

"Works for me," Cal said.

Jake suppressed the urge to flash his auxiliary police badge. Probably not that impressive.

"Congratulations on the arrest," Jake said, going for sincere. He extended a hand. "Sorry for doubting you."

Kellogg gave a sidelong look at Jake's hand. "You're with PPD? How'd you manage that?"

"Temporary," Cal said. "Can't deny he has the background and he isn't charging me. Good work on your arrest. How about it, Doc? We see your killer?"

Kellogg thought for a moment before nodding. "All right. Come on." He walked them back through the lock-up to a door with a small window, a fretwork of wire within the heavy glass. "There he is," said Kellogg. "Terry Bill Pennell. I'm sure you've arrested him before, Cal."

Jake looked through the window at the tattooed man with a scrabble beard, bed scrambled hair and zig-zag tattoos down one arm. What struck Jake was not the man's appearance but the size of Pennell.

"That's him?" Jake said.

"Yep. He'd made threats on Burnell's life and we found Burnell's credit cards on him. Used one of them and we ran it down."

"So," Jake said, looking askance. "This is the guy, right?"

Kellogg guarded now. "What're you getting at?"

"Terry Bill managed to overcome Gage, drag him out of his car, and drown him? Wow. Terry Bill must have superpowers no one knew about. Gage was a pretty tough guy. And a guy size of a bag of potato chips manhandles him?"

"We have the credit cards and the threats."

"So how did this guy, looks like a meth addict on a diet, manage all that?"

"There was a blow to the back of Burnell's head that may explain it."

"Really? The coroner didn't mention that when asked."

"He missed it," said Kellogg, his jaw set. "And that's another thing. You had no right to inquire about that. You've been doing a lot of things you should not, that is, you haven't had standing to ask."

"So, how did Terry Bill get back to town? Did he walk? He had to have help. Do you have an accomplice yet?"

Kellogg looked confused for a moment. "We're working on it. That okay with you?"

"It's peachy. You care if I take a look at Gage's vehicle?"

"That's secured evidence."

"Carpet was torn out of the trunk. Why would anyone do that?"

Kellogg's face darkened and his ears rose as the skin around his jawline tightened. "How would you know that?"

"Anonymous tip."

"You know you're a goddamned nuisance? We have the credit cards; we have the dead body and that's all there is to it. Like to stir things don't you, Mister Big Time Texas Ranger. Always thought you were smarter than everyone, didn't you? But not this time. I'm through explaining things to you. The sooner you leave town the better I'll like it. Now, get out of my jail."

"Look, Doc, it took two men to drag Gage out of the car and drown him or drag him into the creek, not to mention the beating Gage was given. Was the blow you mention on the left or right side of Gage's head?"

"You're not listening."

Kellogg stomped away leaving them to stand by the lock-up door.

"I think he's warming up to me," Jake said, watching Kellogg leave.

Cal was shaking his head slowly. "I'm gonna have to throw in with you that you're on to something. I don't know how I missed it."

Jake nodded at the window of the lock-up. "You know what? Kellogg's gone. How about we interview the perp while we're here?"

Cal pushed back his hat. "Doc's not going to like that. But, why not?"

"We're not going to get on Doc's good side, anyway." Jake knocked on the window. "Hey Terry Bill. Got a second?" Holding up a pack of Camels now. "Yours if you talk to me."

Pennell stood and shuffled to the windowed door, there was a small opening at the bottom of the window. "Yeah? Okay."

"First we talk. How did you kill Gage Burnell?"

"Man, I didn't do that. I look like a killer?"

"They come in different shapes and sizes. There's no particular look."

"Man, I'm mindin' my own business kickin' back in my trailer with a bottle of wine and a joint when Kellogg and his brown shirts crash my door and go all ISIS on me. Shit. Telling me I'm under arrest for murder. I say, 'murder', who'd I kill? They don't give a shit what I'm tellin' 'em. They rough me, cuff me and bring me here. I had to eat the roach 'cause I thought that was my bust. Burnt my tongue. Have no idea what's goin' on. Havin' a bad day, man."

"You threaten Gage Burnell?"

Terry Bill snorted, then said, "Don't even know the man. I mean, I see 'im around but it's not like we hang out. Besides, Burnell's a crazy fuck. I'm gonna threaten somebody like that?"

Jake smiled letting Terry Bill know he was on his side. "They say you had his wallet and credit cards."

"Yeah, that? Fuck man, that's a hell of a thing. Nobody's gonna believe me when I tell how I came by that."

"Try me."

"Was in my fuckin' mailbox." Terry Bill stopped and watched Jake for a reaction. Jake raised an eyebrow. "Yeah. Somebody put it there. Had eighty-three dollars and those cards in it. I thought wow, my lucky day."

"You didn't think maybe turn it in?"

Terry Bill snorted. "You fuckin' kiddin'? Money falls outta the sky and I'm going to be Joe Citizen? I don't have a job and need the bucks. Stupid to use the card."

"What do you weigh?"

"What?"

"Your weight."

Dubious now. "I get a prize?"

Jake held up the cigarette pack. "Sure."

"About hundert' thirty five."

Jake gave Cal a look. Cal chewed his lower lip. Jake handed the cigarettes through the slot and started to leave.

"Hey," said Terry Bill. "What about me? I didn't do nothin'."

"More than you think," Jake said. "You helped me and that may help you. Only thing you're guilty of is theft and ugly tatts."

"Aw man, why you goin' that way?"

"Believe you're about to become a free man. Happen to know a good lawyer."

"Dude. You do that and I'll buy you a carton of smokes."

"Afraid you'd steal them."

"'At's right, give Terry Bill shit alla time. Everybody on my ass today."

"I'm trying to quit myself."

As they were leaving Cal said, "Terry Bill didn't do it, did he?"

"Nope," Jake said. "He did not. You have a cigarette?"

34

"How about these accommodations, huh?" Jake said to Steve Barb and Robby Warner as they sat in the holding cell at Paradise P.D. Jake and Cal had returned to Cal's office after leaving the sheriff's office. Barb and Warner were lounging on the hard benches in the cell. "Cal runs a clean hotel."

"Whyn't you fuck yourself?"

"I'm at a loss how to counter such a witty comeback?"

"We'll be outta here in a couple of hours," said Barb.

"Sooner," Jake said. "You answer some questions."

"How's that?"

"I'm a forgiving guy. Maybe I drop the charges and you two ballerinas go back to scratching your pelts with your mouths hanging open."

"Why would you do that?" said Robby Warner.

"You know a guy named Terry Bill Pennell?"

"Yeah, he's a doper. Little popcorn fart."

They didn't know Terry Bill had been arrested. Filed it away.

"Either of you see Gage Burnell the night of his accident?" Keeping back the homicide determination.

"Why you keep asking that?" said Robby who then looked at Barb.

Barb said, "We didn't kill him."

Jake saying, "I ask if you saw him, you say you didn't

kill him? It's like talking to grade school kids. You're answering questions I didn't ask. Just like the day at Vernon Mitchell's. Everyone wants me to know they didn't kill Gage. What kind of cigarettes you smoke, Barb."

"What's that to you?"

"Want to see if you'll lie to me. You strike me as an individual who would lie even if the truth would be better."

"Not tellin' you nothin'."

"Double negative, Barbie boy. Not useful in proper discourse."

"You're so fucking smart, aren't you?" said Barb, jumping up from his seat. "You don't know shit 'bout nothin'."

"Enlighten me. Oh, I'm sorry. I mean, tell me what I'm missing."

"Shut up, Steve," said Robby. "Shit. He's pumping you."

"Better listen to your friend, Barbie. I'm pretty tricky."

"Stop calling me that."

"Did you see Gage Burnell the night he died?"

Smirking now as if he had hidden inner knowledge. "I don't remember. Think I was working late."

"What about you, Robby?"

"Same as him."

"Either of you know anyone mad at Gage?"

Robby glanced at Barb then quickly away.

"What about you, Steve? Can I call you Steve since you don't like Barbie? Like to be on a first name basis."

"Don't know anything 'bout that."

"Were you mad at Gage?"

Silence while Barb glared at Jake. "I get out maybe we dance again."

"Love to. All I'd want for Christmas." Jake saying now, "You dated Hanna, Gage's girl, but then she and Gage got back together. Told people she didn't like you much. Heard that angered you. I know it would've angered me."

"I don't need that cunt."

"Need to wash the C-word out of your vocabulary. I don't care for it."

"Fuck you." More force this time.

"The F-bomb again," Jake said. "Well, Barbie, we'll see who gets the last fuck here. You boys get cold, feel free to cuddle."

***

"You have a unique interrogation style," Cal said, settling back in his office chair.

Jake opened his hands and said, "They're idiots in a big hurry to say they didn't kill Gage and worried about the cigarette thing."

"You think there's a match?"

Shaking his head. "It's a different cigarette than the one I found. But people change brands and DNA might give me something. It shook him up when I asked about it. Doesn't mean either of them is a killer but, you know small towns. People talk and they may have heard something. Can you keep them here?"

"They called a lawyer already," Cal said. "But I have an anonymous tip they may've been involved with Terry Bill Pennell in a homicide."

"Anonymous tip?"

"Sounds good as anything."

"Cal," Jake said. "You're a beautiful man."

"By the way, stay away from my daughter," Cal said, smiling.

"Think you're alone on that? Nobody wants me to see their daughter. Kinda hurtful."

"She's too good for you," Cal said.

Jake shrugged. "Can't argue that."

Back home Jake had doubts about his investigative reasoning. It had a few holes. Holes big enough for a first-year law student to walk through. No way to charge anyone as no prosecutor would take the case even if Jake knew who to arrest and he didn't.

The landline was ringing, and Jake looked at the caller ID. Vernon Mitchell? Jake answered.

"Yeah, Vernon, what can I do for you?"

"Got a proposition for you. You mind coming by my place and we can talk? You know the way."

Jake agreed to it.

Jake drove to the Mitchell ranch. On the way he called Cal Bannister.

"You remember we talked about how Vernon Mitchell bought his land off a guy after stealing his cattle?"

"What're you thinking?" Cal said. "That's about as close to an urban legend as we get around here?"

"C'mon, what's the name?"

"That'd be a guy named Yoder. Franklin Yoder. But hell, that's forty odd years ago."

"Whatever happened to him?"

"I don't know. Disappeared. Don't know if they just moved away or what happened."

"Thanks."

Jake arrived at the Mitchell ranch, got out of his car and Vernon greeted him at the door then led Jake inside to Vernon's home office which spoke of money and conquest, albeit garishly. Photos of Vernon with senators and congressmen and a couple of country-western stars. Overlarge cherrywood desk that made Jake feel like they were sitting in different time zones with Vernon seated at his executive chair. There was a ten-point whitetail and an antelope head mounted on the wall, with brass plaques describing the date and type of weapon used to take the animals. Jake had hunted for many years himself, with a rifle, bow and lately with a handgun. Never once did he consider displaying their heads on a wall. To Jake, the hunt was an implicit agreement between himself and the deer not to humiliate the animal after killing it.

"You got a couple of my workers in jail downtown," Vernon said.

Jake picked at some lint on his sleeve and offhandedly said, "I'm got some cuts and bruises. Why they're inside."

Vernon raised a hand showing his palm. "I know,"

Vernon said. "Don't blame you being honked off at them. They're good boys though and I need them."

"Why would you need them?" Thinking perhaps Vernon didn't want them talking to the police. Or, maybe once again Jake was allowing his distaste for the Mitchells to influence his mind.

"I do anything to get you to drop charges?"

Jake thinking about it now. Was he offering a bribe? Perhaps dangle interest in front of the man.

"Maybe," Jake said. "What're we talking about?"

"I cover your medical expenses and a little on top of that. How's that sound?"

"Not bad," Jake said. It sounded terrible, even sordid, but he wanted Vernon to take the bait.

Vernon was quiet a moment, drumming his fingers on his desk, as if considering something.

"You know," Vernon said, "I can sweeten the deal."

Jake tried not to smile when he said, "I'm listening."

"Your pickup was damaged and you have incurred expenses. What would be fair compensation?"

"Hard to say. What do you have in mind?"

"New truck and five thousand dollars to cover incidentals and compensate you for your trouble."

Jake pretending to think about before saying, "What about the two guys working for you drove out to my place to assault me?"

"I don't know what you're talking about."

Jake stared at Vernon for a long moment and said, "Not yours? I'll let you have that one. Here's the thing, every time I look into Gage's death I run into opposition from your people or your sons."

"I regret that. Would you like a drink?"

Jake shook his head. "I've gotta head back to Texas soon and I don't know, with Gage gone, I can't really keep the farm up. I've got a price in mind and maybe we can get your workers out of the lock-up in addition to what you've mentioned. What do you offer?"

"That's pretty steep for those boys. Just want them out to get back to work."

"Thought you wanted to buy the place."

"Changed my mind. Don't need it."

Well, well, well, thought Jake. "What changed your mind?"

"You going to take my offer or not?"

"I think we're pretty clear how I feel about you and your workers."

Vernon's eyebrows constricted. He was catching on. "You're playing with me, aren't you, boy? You think that's something you want to have done? Here's the way I see you. You're a goddamned nuisance."

"Everybody says that."

"Your mouth is going to cost you yet. I don't like the things you've done since coming back here. First it's beating up my son and Noah and then what's going on with you and my daughter-in-law."

Bingo. It was Vernon clued in Doc Kellogg. Why would Vernon do that?

"You're making an intuitive leap about Pam," Jake said.

"You think I miss the way she looks at you? I know Pam better than she thinks. Used to having her way, riding Alex, digging in her spurs when she wants him to do what she wants rather than what's best for him?"

"So, what's best for Alex?"

"None of your damned business. I'll deal with her later."

"You want to clarify that? Deal with her how?"

"Don't keep nosing into my business. Others have tried."

"Is that a threat?"

"I don't make them. I predict the future."

"That's fairly transparent. Whatever happened to Franklin Yoder?" There, hit him with it before he was ready, and Vernon hesitated one beat too long before responding. "You know anything about that?"

It shook him.

"What? I don't have any idea what you're talking about."

"They disappeared and you picked up their land on the cheap."

"That's enough of your crap. You're a sick nasty individual. You know your way out, right? I don't want to see you out here again. Ever."

"We're together on that one."

"I've tried twice to get along with you and in return I get a lot of mouth and bullshit accusations. I'm through playing games with you, son. Get the hell off my property and be careful where you go when you leave."

Jake stood, looked down at Vernon and said, "Guys like you scare people. You're a fucking bully. You don't scare me and if anyone needs to be careful it's you."

As Jake backed out of Vernon's drive, across the road he saw Pam talking to Fat Boy Haller. They were intently examining something between them Jake couldn't see. Pam was dressed in cut-off shorts and a halter top. Had to admit she looked good. They didn't notice as he drove by.

Wondering about Vernon's change of mind? Why was Dad's place no longer a priority? Whatever Vernon was looking for or hoping to create it wasn't on the Morgan property. Why had Vernon thought it was there?

Or was it somewhere else? Even then, what would it be?

***

Back home Jake fired up Gage's laptop and used his access code to gain entry into the Texas Department of Safety's TxDPS secure website. He knew it would set off bells and whistles back in station B but he needed information. Accessing records from an unauthorized site, like Gage's laptop, was always checked. He ran the name, Franklin Yoder, Paradise, Missouri. One hit. Reported theft of grazing cattle. 1971. Cattle rustling. No arrests. Wild West stuff. Last known address? Paradise. Nothing after that.

That done, Jake ran Yoder's name on an online search engine. Several names came up. Three Franklin Yoders and one F. Yoder. Only two of them would be about the right age. He called the phone numbers. One of them had recently died but the person answering said the man never lived in Paradise. The second Franklin said he was deployed to Vietnam in 1971 and also never lived in Paradise. F. Yoder was a woman.

Dead end. The guy had just disappeared.

What happened to Franklin Yoder?

Knowing when he found out, Jake may have the key to locking up Vernon Mitchell for a long time.

Jake remembered something his dad, Alfred, once told him after Jake threw three interceptions in a junior high school game. "It is a long old road that has no curves in it."

35

Sheriff Doc Kellogg was in his police unit when the call came through. Kellogg wheeled his vehicle around and raced north on highway 27, siren wailing. Dispatch notified the hospital and Kellogg had a county ambulance trailing behind him. Doc was shattered by the victim of the shooting.

Vernon Mitchell shot, maybe dead. What did it mean? Who would do such a thing? This could not happen at a worse time for Kellogg. An election coming up and well, the other plans he had.

When Kellogg arrived, a neighbor was there. "I was returning an auger Vernon leant me but when I got here no one answered and I'd just talked to him on the phone an hour before."

One shot right in the middle of his face, a killing shot. Two more in the chest were post-mortem. Nose tore off and his false teeth hanging from his mouth. A nine-millimeter SIG Sauer pistol lay on the floor. No forced entry. Someone Vernon knew or had let in was the shooter. The neighbor? Unlikely but would have to be considered.

The only person around the place was the hired hand, Noah Haller. Ask him about it. A tech showed up and dusted and bagged the gun and a spent shell casing.

"Got prints," the tech said.

Maybe this one wouldn't be tough to solve after all.

Two birds with one stone.

However? Why leave the murder weapon?

Morgan?

***

Jake's cell phone lit up and it was Buddy Johnson.

"Where are you?" Buddy asked.

"Home."

"You own a SIG Sauer pistol?"

"It's my service weapon."

"Is it a nine-millimeter?"

".357. What's this about? Somebody got shot, right?"

"Vernon Mitchell. Do you own a nine?"

Jake paused a second to take that in.

"You still there?" Buddy said.

"I do. A Taurus. You need to know I was just there an hour ago talking to him."

"You were at Mitchell's place? Shit, Jake, what're you thinking? You're sticking your dick in everything. Kellogg's going to be all over you. You know that."

"How'd it go down?"

"It was personal. Left the weapon on the floor."

"Left the weapon." Thinking about that. "No one is that dumb, well strike that. I've met some truly dumb people in my life. Leaving the weapon suggests the killer wiped the gun or...wait."

"What?"

"If I'm smart why leave the weapon for police to find it?"

"I see where you're going," Buddy said. "Wow, that's something. Framing someone else."

"Well I didn't shoot him."

"I know you didn't. But Kellogg will want you for it. He'll be hungry to hang it on you. What the fuck were you doing at Vernon's place?"

"He offered a bribe to drop assault charges on Barb and Warner."

"That's not going to sound good when you tell it in

court. You're in the mix for this one, Jake. Don't over-react but you know Kellogg will be coming and will do back flips to hang it on you."

"You could be right."

"Sure calm for someone in the middle of this."

"Should I run around in circles and scream?"

"Just keep your head and don't be a smartass when you're questioned?"

"Do I do that?"

"Not going to be your straight man, Jake. This is a fucking shitstorm and I need my quarterback to call the right signals."

They broke the connection and Jake heard the crunch of gravel on his lane. He picked up his Taurus nine and looked outside.

Getting paranoid. It was Harper.

"Dad told me about it. This is awful," said Harper as they embraced. "What's going on with the Mitchells?"

Jake telling her he was with Vernon right before he was shot and killed.

She stood there and stared for a long moment, shaking her head. She said, "Why? What were you doing there?"

He explained.

"Wow. This is not good. Jake, what were you thinking? You hear from Sheriff Kellogg yet?" she asked, leaning back from his embrace. "You know you're going to."

"Not yet, but he'll be here with a net and a club. He's not happy about your dad and me doubting Terry Bill Pennell's involvement in Gage's death."

"Terry Bill would be the type to follow and could've been in on any attack on Gage if he had people to protect him."

"True. But, he's the kind of guy who'd turn the others to make a deal. Terry Bill isn't a stand-up guy. No, he's a false narrative. I just don't know why Kellogg lit on him as a killer yet."

They walked inside, Jake made coffee and they sat at the kitchen table. Harper rubbed her arm and shook her head at the situation. "This is terrible. What is going on you haven't told me? Don't hold back. I'm a cop's daughter and I'm used to this stuff."

Jake said, "There's quite a bit going on. Enough that I can kind of piece together what's going on and why there is so much activity."

"Enough to get people arrested and hopefully not yourself?"

He shook his head. "Vernon made a cash offer, a bribe, for my silence. That suggests he had things to hide. I had him down as orchestrating Gage's death and now I don't know what or who it might be. I can't figure why anyone would kill Vernon."

"You realize, if I didn't know you better, I would guess you did it. So you'd better come up with something or, well, I don't want to think about that."

"It was possibly...doesn't matter. Throwing everything off is Vernon being killed. Don't understand why that happened or who benefits."

He told her about the legend of local rumors about Franklin Yoder's disappearance and not being to locate the man. "And there's one more thing that needs checking."

"What?"

"I need to know what happened to Pam's first husband. She met him in college. Rich kid. I remember correctly he died in an accident. He was from Nevada. Believe Las Vegas was where it happened. Seems to be unhealthy to be involved with Pam."

"More reason for you to stay clear of her, little boy," Harper said, wagging her finger at him.

"Noted."

Jake dialed Texas Ranger Captain Parmalee's number and told him what he had in mind regarding checking on Pam's first husband's death. Parmalee hesitant at first but said he would clear the way for Jake to talk with Vegas Metro as a Texas Ranger.

They waited until Parmalee called back and said, "You're good to go."

Jake called LVM and requested any information that

Vegas Metro would have on the death of Pam's first husband. The officer in charge of the investigation was unavailable so Jake left his cell number, hung up and said, "I'm going to take another look at the grain elevator."

"Why?"

"With Vernon dead they may decide to close the elevator in observance. If it closes that gives me a chance to walk around the place without being interrupted."

"That'll be a couple of days from now. You're probably going to be answering questions and unable to move about freely. Besides, they're not going to let you within a hundred yards of the place. They find out you visited Vernon before he was killed, they'll be all over you. Better to have someone else look."

"Who?"

"Me."

"Not good."

"Oh, it is," she said. "I worked there when I was married to Tommy. I may have accidentally kept a key to the place."

He considered her for a moment and then said, "That's breaking and entering."

"Not if a girl was looking for the earring she'd lost and maybe it was in the office. You have a better plan?"

He didn't. "I'll think about it." Be interesting to learn if Vegas Metro gave him anything about Pam's first husband's death.

Wonder when he would hear from Sheriff Kellogg.

36

Jake decided to be proactive, so he drove to the sheriff's office to report his visit but Kellogg wasn't there.

However, the lady deputy, Bailey, was there. She was an earnest young lady a little overweight but with an honest face. Jake thinking his luck was improving.

"What can I do for you, sir?" said Bailey.

"Where's Doc?"

"Sheriff Kellogg was called away. I don't know when he'll be returning."

"I'm Jake Morgan."

"I know who you are," said Bailey, her mouth downturned.

"I need to report that I was with Vernon Mitchell prior to the shooting. I was in his house. He was fine when I left him. I will cooperate anyway needed."

She looked at him, uncertain how to proceed. "Well, that will be helpful. But I think you should talk to Sheriff Kellogg. I'll take a statement if you wish."

"You investigated Gage Burnell's death, right?" Jake said.

Again, the disconcerted demeanor.

"It's okay," Jake said. "I'm a cop. Texas Rangers. I am also working for Paradise PD as a volunteer investigator. Gage Burnell was a close friend. Who took the call on Gage's accident?"

"The dispatcher. A... it has been upgraded to a homicide."

"I heard. I talked to Terry Bill."

Her eyes widened at that. Suspicious of Jake now.

He said, "Surprised? Deputy, I need information you may possess. I don't believe Terry Bill Pennell killed anyone and suspect that Gage was killed someplace other than the bridge."

"Why would – ?" Stopping herself.

"Good question," Jake said. "Why were you tagged to investigate the scene of the accident? And further, why did you determine it was an accident that has turned into a homicide?"

"I don't know. I don't think I should be talking to you."

"If there's nothing to this then you have nothing to hide. Do you?"

She chewed her lower lip, deciding, and then told him the dispatcher took the call, gave it to Kellogg and Kellogg sent Bailey out to look into it.

"It was a routine accident, so Sheriff Kellogg sent me."

"Who called it in?"

"It was anonymous. Someone called and said a car went off the bridge."

"Anyone there when you arrived?"

"No."

"You didn't find that odd? An anonymous caller and no one there when you arrive. Did you meet anyone coming on the road?"

"Of course."

"Anyone on HH? It's a pretty remote county road."

"No. Wait. Yes, I did."

"Do you remember who it was?"

"It was an SUV. A Dodge Ram I think."

Jake was taken aback by that. Gage's Dodge Ram? He kept it to himself. He tamped down his enthusiasm. Besides the circumstantial evidence in the Dodge Charger, this deputy possibly seeing Gage's Ram leaving the scene was juicy. The killers or at least one of them had driven the Ram. He tried not to salivate and drool.

"How many people in the Ram?"

"I don't know." Sound of a door opening and closing outside. "I...I'm not sure I should be telling you this."

"No, you should not," said the voice of Sheriff Doc Kellogg. "Morgan, I'm detaining you for questioning in the homicide of Vernon Mitchell."

"I may not be much help."

"Where were you around 3:00 this afternoon?"

"On my way home. I had just spoken with Vernon at his home."

"Did you kill him?"

"No. I'm here to tell you I had been with Vernon and to offer my cooperation." Jake nodded at Deputy Bailey.

"He did," said Bailey.

"I'm going to have to arrest you."

"Based on what?"

"You were the last to see Vernon Mitchell."

"Except for the person that shot him. Believe I will exercise my right to have an attorney present."

***

Harper's boss, Attorney-at-law Jerry Jessup, showed within the hour and advised Jake not to make a statement without Jessup attending. Jake telling him he had nothing to hide. Jessup was adamant and Jake apprised the attorney of the situation.

"You were there at Mitchell's prior to the shooting?" asked Jessup.

"I didn't shoot him. There was a weapon left at the scene and it wasn't mine. Fingerprints will show I had not handled the weapon."

"How did you know there was a weapon left at the scene? How do you know the weapon wasn't wiped?"

Jake telling Jessup about his phone conversation with Buddy Johnson. As for the question about the weapon being wiped Jake said, "Because I think someone is either really dumb or really smart. If the weapon is clean, then they're framing me. If there are prints, they're either stupid, angry enough to kill in fit of passion or they're attempting to frame another person. I told Kellogg I was on the premises talking to Vernon, so they don't turn up any forensic evidence proving I was there and hold back that information."

Jessup nodding his head, said, "Okay. We'll go with that. But, that's all. Anything else, goes through me, understand?"

"Sure."

"From what Harper tells me you need a hobby." Jessup turning his thoughts inward and saying now, "You've had multiple run-ins with the Mitchell family, including a fight with his son and accusations of infidelity with Alex Mitchell's wife."

"Where'd you get that?"

"Privileged information."

Harper.

Jessup continuing said, "Your history with the Mitchell family speaks to motive. Okay, just the fact you were at Vernon Mitchell's prior to the shooting. Is there anything else?"

Jake nodded. "Need to tell him I saw Pam Mitchell and Fat Boy Haller within close proximity prior to the shooting. They may have seen something."

"And that's all."

"I also own a nine-millimeter Taurus semi-auto pistol. It has been shot and cleaned recently. The killer used a nine. May have to reveal that in case they try to say I left a phony weapon at the homicide scene."

"Not just yet," said Jessup.

Deputy Bailey arrived and led Jake and Jessup to the interview room. It was a small room, one window, with ink tattoos burned into the desk. Kellogg came in and sat facing Jake, Kellogg's patent leather holster made a sound as he sat. Jake once again stated he had been at Vernon Mitchell's home prior to the murder.

"What were you doing there?"

"Vernon requested a meeting," Jake said.

"What was the meeting about?"

Jessup shook his head. "That's all for now."

"He has more information," said Kellogg.

"He has the names of two possible witnesses for consideration."

"Who?"

Jessup nodded at Jake, who said, "Noah Haller and Pam Mitchell may have seen something. They were outside Pam's place when I left."

"What were they doing?"

"That's all I have," said Jake. "They may have seen something."

"That's pretty flimsy. I'll talk to them, but I want to know what you were talking to Vernon about."

Jessup shook his head at Jake. Jake sat back and said, "That's all."

"Are you going to make me arrest you, Morgan, for the murder," said Kellogg.

"Based on what?" said Jessup.

"He was on the scene at the time of the murder and has been threatening the Mitchell family previously."

"Pretty thin, even for you, Doc," Jake said.

Jessup cut his eyes at Jake. "Be quiet, Jake," said Jessup. "Doc, you can hold him, but I don't know how you can make this charge stick. My client is cooperating and you're making your call before the evidence has been assessed. You do this you're going to have egg on your face."

"I don't care. He had motive and opportunity. I've watched him go out of his way to irritate and annoy Vernon. He's admitted he was at the scene of the murder very close to the time of the shooting. We have fingerprints and we have the murder weapon."

Jake smiled at Jessup. "Told you."

"You were right," said Jessup.

"My fingerprints are on file with the Texas Rangers," Jake said. "They'll be happy to share them with you or I can give you my fingerprints right now. Either way that will demonstrate I didn't touch the murder weapon."

"We're not going to do any such thing at this time," said Jessup, admonishing Jake.

"Then we're done here, except for this," said Kellogg rising from his seat. "Jake Morgan, you're under arrest for the murder of Vernon Mitchell."

Jake stood and placed his hands behind his back. Hated being cuffed but no use creating more problems. Being charged with a homicide was a pretty big enchilada.

Deputy Bailey entered the room. She had a worried look on her face. "Sheriff, I need to tell you something."

"Not now."

"You're going to want to hear this."

"First cuff Morgan and take him to a holding cell."

"I don't think that will be the right thing to do in light of the information we have. It regards evidence from the techs."

"Well, what is it?"

"The gun was stolen from Alex Mitchell's home. It was stolen by Noah Haller."

"Who told you that?"

"Your daughter, Pam Mitchell."

37

Fat Boy Haller was handcuffed and chained to a U-bolt in the floor of the sheriff's police car. Siren screaming over his head looking through the metal fretwork on the backseat. He was scared. It all happened so fast. He still couldn't get his head around it. One minute he's working on the farm, minding his own business and the next thing he knows Doc Kellogg's deputies show up, guns drawn, telling him to get his face on the ground then cuffing him, not bothering to be gentle about it either. Face down in the dirt and then off to the county lock-up. They processed him through, Haller protesting he didn't shoot his boss, but they read him his rights like on television. Telling them he had nothing to hide because he didn't do it. Why kill the man who paid him? Why kill his best friends' Father?

"How does that make sense?" he told them.

***

Buddy called Jake and told him Kellogg had taken Fat Boy Haller into custody.

"I was there when they brought him in," Jake said. "Not arresting me ruined Doc's day."

Jake filled Buddy in on the events of the past few hours. Wheels turned in his head. Haller shoots Mitchell.

Why? Jake remembered the first day he arrived and Vernon treating Haller not like an employee but like a family member, calling him 'Noah', not 'Fat Boy' or 'Haller'. Still, people sometimes killed even those people they liked for motives that only made sense to the killer.

"Haller's dependent on the Mitchells for his livelihood," Jake said. "And he's dumb and too loyal to cut that lifeline."

"Seen crazier things lately. Besides he would still have Alex and Pam to pay him."

Jake said nothing.

"What're you thinking?" Buddy said. "It's never good when you're quiet. You stay in one place until there is more information."

"Sure. There's something wrong with this. I don't see how Fat Boy gains anything by killing Vernon."

Buddy, not convinced, said, "Dammit, Jake, don't make this more difficult."

"Vernon was looking for something from me. I brought up a name to him. Franklin Yoder. See what you've got in your files on Yoder."

"Aw, hell. Don't have me chase rabbits. I got enough on my plate without that."

"Listen to me, Buddy. Yoder disappeared forty years ago, and Vernon Mitchell bought the guy's farm on the courthouse steps. I think it possible Vernon killed Yoder, and someone found out about it. Maybe Gage. Or someone in the Mitchell orbit had reason to kill Gage. It's also possible Vernon or even Alex thinks Gage told me something. Vernon wanted my silence and he doesn't want Steve Barb and Robby Warner to talk to Cal. I believe Gage was killed elsewhere and transported to the bridge. Maybe killed in town. I'd like to get inside the grain elevator."

"Well that's only possible if Cal can prove that the killing occurred somewhere besides the site of the accident. Do we have enough yet?"

"Not yet but maybe."

Heard his friend exhale on the other end. "All right.

Your experience can be helpful. Killing the community's leading citizen, whether we like him or not, is not helpful and will bring the media and a lot of pressure."

***

Forty-eight hours later, The Paradise County prosecuting attorney arraigned Noah "Fat Boy" Haller in the County Circuit Court at 11:00 AM Friday morning, the day of the Vernon Mitchell visitation and funeral. All Mitchell businesses were closed.

This was the opening Jake wanted.

Haller was being represented, paradoxically, by the law office where Harper worked as a paralegal. Jessup was handling it.

"His fingerprints are on the gun and the spent shell casing at the crime scene," said Harper, as they drove to town in the Lincoln Mark IV. "The glass gun cabinet in Alex and Pam's house was broken into and one of Alex's pistols missing and it was the murder weapon."

The radio had Luke Bryan singing about 'drinkin' beer and wastin' bullets', the swampy guitars buzzing as power poles and rural scenery clicked by.

"Fat Boy will take the fall for this one," Jake said. Jake saying the scenario too pat and too stupid, but Haller wasn't overly bright. He saw a signpost on a fence that read, 'No Hunting'. "When it's this tight a fit Kellogg is going to close out his investigation and the prosecutor is going to see an easy win. Why make more work? Law enforcement people aren't often like they're portrayed on TV. If it looks like they've got the right man, they stop looking. PA's like things tied up neat. Can't blame Doc for that."

"But you have your doubts," she said.

"I do."

"Couldn't it be someone else?"

"Who?"

"Maybe Vernon's daughter-in-law." She mentioned Pam as if not wanting to say it or not wanting him to react.

"We'll see what Vegas Metro tells me."

"Pam Mitchell is capable of doing anything a man would do. I've watched her fire employees. She enjoys it, likes power and using it. She's a nasty person. Look at your little 'tryst'. She's a sexual terrorist."

"Wow. Sexual terrorist."

"Don't be a smart ass."

"It takes a cold heart, burning passion, or extreme hatred to pull the trigger on someone you know. Pam would have no reason." But thinking Pam may have plenty of reason, remembering Vernon's words that Vernon would 'deal with her later'. "I don't see what Pam gets out of this."

"She gets to run everything."

"She's already running everything. Also, knowing her it's hard to think of her as a killer."

Harper made a face, then looked out the passenger side window. "I don't want to hear about her anymore."

They were quiet for several moments, the silence of their thoughts and emotions a barrier between them.

"You're thinking," Harper said. "About what?"

More to himself, Jake said, "Something's still not right."

"People are killed, there are attempts on your life and you decide something's not right? I no longer harbor doubts that you're a genius."

He shrugged. "Are you better for it though?"

"Who do you think would shoot at you?"

"The Mitchell brothers and Haller are possible. Not Alex, gut feeling. Besides Alex is smarter than the rest. He always was. I believe someone kidnapped Travis or even Gage."

"Kidnapped?"

He told her about the plaster foot casts he'd made and the fact that Gage's vehicle was missing. "You once asked me if I wondered how Pam got in my house and I did ask but she didn't answer. She has a key. Gage had her cell phone number, but it was hidden away. Something has created all this. Something obscure. I believe the catalyst is Franklin Yoder."

"Who?"

Jake shared what he had learned about Yoder and the local legend that Vernon Mitchell started his empire by illicit maneuverings. "Yoder vanished from the face of the earth. No death certificate, no forwarding address."

"You think someone killed him? How does that work? Neither of us were alive at that time."

"It was Vernon's start and he would be the only person with reason, and he benefited when he bought their land. Most people kill over money or jealousy."

"Vernon's dead now."

"Yeah." That fact screwed up his meme that Vernon Mitchell was behind everything happening. "That complicates things. Doesn't explain Gage's death unless he knew about Yoder. I don't see Vernon getting his hands dirty on Gage. Steve Barb had reason and maybe Alex Mitchell." He glanced sidelong at Harper, her sitting in the passenger seat, and said, "May have to include Pam as a possible."

He gave her a big smile.

She raised her eyebrows but didn't smile back.

"Sorry to mention her name again," he said.

She looked at him, being cute now. "Shut up."

"Anything you say."

"There. You're learning."

38

Tommy Mitchell was surprised by his emotions. His sense of loss over his father's death had more impact than he would have guessed. The tears came and he couldn't stop them. He loved the old man and now he was gone. Tears dried and composed for the funeral. Fucking Haller killed his father. Some friend. Didn't understand it but Pam told them Vernon was going to fire Fat ass.

Tommy's father lay in a coffin at the Evergreen Funeral Home, there's a shitty name for a place where you take dead people. People he knew came by the visitation ceremony to offer their condolences, Tommy chain-smoked in his dark blue suit, being asked to smoke outside. Wearing no tie, no tears now, he thought about his future and intermittently took surreptitious sips off a flask of Wild Turkey. What he really wanted was a hit on some good weed, but not here. His head wasn't in the same place as the event. Unsure how to deal with it. Get this funeral over and then figure out what to do next.

Pam and Alex were there, Pam in a black dress, looking like a movie star with her legs showing, Alex looked like a zombie, as if somebody woke him up in the middle of a dream.

"You okay?" Alex asked him.

Tommy nodded. "Thanks, I'm okay." They hugged. Hell, the guy was his brother.

Pam was greeting people and smiling, thanking them for coming. He looked at Pam and she looked back giving him a funny look. What? She walked to the door, and then with her hand on the knob, looked back at him and nodded with a flirty wink. Outside?

Okay. So he followed her. She was over to the side of the parking lot now and waiting for him, nobody around, asking him if he had a cigarette and, "maybe a sip out of that flask you think you're hiding".

You think you're so damn smart, don't you, was what he wanted to say but instead he shrugged and said, "Who cares anyone sees it? I'm in mourning. Can't you tell? Got a suit on and everything."

She accepted a cigarette, smelling her perfume as she leaned over to take the flame. He lighted it and she placed a hand lightly on his arm, lingering there, him feeling the warmth. She smelled like a million bucks and he caught a little cleavage. Why was he thinking about that with his dad lying inside a box?

She surprised him saying, "Get a good look?"

He said, "You want guys to look, way you dress and act."

She gave him a funny smile like she knew something or like she was in control asking him did he like what he saw? Always turning things around on a guy. He was aroused, hating it, but still caught by her smell, her look, and those legs.

"Maybe we can work something out," she said.

Looking at her, trying to figure out her meaning. Looking back at him, half-smile on her face, then taking a drag on her cigarette. He had to admit the bitch was smoking hot.

"What do you mean?"

"Depends on what you think I mean."

He gave her an up-and-down look of appraisal, chewing on it in his head, damn, it'd be worth it wouldn't it? Look at her; she's ready. She wants it.

Tommy said, "What about Alex?"

She smiled, crossing one lovely ankle over the over,

leaning against a black SUV, careful not to muss her dress, putting some breath in it and said, "What about Alex?" Shining it back on him but still leaving the meaning open to interpretation, felt the bourbon swimming around in his head. This was some dirty shit in his head but man she was spinning his wheels.

He didn't know what to say so she said it for him. "I got a bottle of Pappy Van Winkle out at my place. How about you come out and drink real bourbon instead of that convenience store bullshit?" she said. "Alex has to stay here, take care of some of tomorrow's funeral arrangements. We both need to get away from this. Nobody will think anything of it."

His mouth was dry, but he said, "Sure."

She let her fingers delicately trace his jawline. "See you there."

Wow.

***

Jake pulled the Lincoln Mark IV behind the grain elevator. Harper produced the office key and showed it to Jake.

Jake said, "There is a sneaky side to you that concerns me going forward."

"Says the man about to illegally break into a place of business."

***

Tommy Mitchell drove out to Alex's place. Pam called it 'her place', Tommy thinking of it as Alex's, wondering if Pam thought dad's ranch was now 'hers', Pam hard to figure but boy could she ever sell her stuff.

Stereo played hip-hop, got his motor revving with Tech-Nine rapping through his speakers. He found a joint in his glove box and fired it up getting his mellow on; toking on some top drawer weed, mixed in with swallows off the flask. Synergy was good for you, saying it out loud, laughing at himself.

Shiiittttt, feeling good now.

Everything was going to be all right, baby. Get his sister-in-law in a compromising position and show her who was boss. Yeah. Who's your daddy now, girl? And, he'd have something to hold over Pam, the cunt's, head. Pulling into the driveway now thinking, things were about to change.

Too late and what the hell anyway?

He'd always been a what-the-hell guy. Why change?

39

"I'll check the office," said Harper as they entered the office of the Mitchell Enterprises' grain elevator. "You go ahead and do whatever you need to do inside the plant."

"I'm uncomfortable you being here," Jake said. "This is nothing but a preliminary look. Nothing I learn here can be used in court. I just want to see if I'm on the right track."

"No access without me. Besides, it's exciting."

"It's not a movie. This could go south so quick we're caught."

"I'm just a poor little girl, thought she'd left an earring in the office and can't find it anywhere and know anyone would understand me being out here looking for it."

"Yet maybe not as understanding that I'm with you."

"I'll pout and look sincere and give it back if we're caught."

Shaking his head, Jake saying, "I don't know which of us is crazier."

"I do," she said, batting her lashes.

Jake walked back to the floor where employees would bag up feed corn and looked around, hoping to find something to prove Gage may've been killed here. If Haller was one of the killers he might go down for a different killing. It was a jumbled mess of intrigue, greed and sex but somewhere there had to be an element to tie it all together.

Jake checked the sump area and the rancid stench of rotting grain assailed his olfactory. Wondering why they just didn't throw Gage in the pit and call it an accident. That's when Jake noticed it.

The grain sump. Floating on the rancid pool of decayed grain was a sediment that looked similar to what he'd found on the gas and brake pedals of Gage's Dodge Charger. It was also on the floor around the sump.

Meaning that the killers were likely employees of the Mitchells or one of the Mitchells. Not just random farmers. One would have to be around the silage pit to get the sediment on their boots. He would need a search warrant and a forensic match. That might be a tough get but at least he was amassing circumstantial evidence.

What to do next? What to look for? He walked around outside behind the facility into the lot behind it where the elevator fed train cars from a long spout.

Then he found it.

Dog tag. Travis' name on it with Gage's phone number. Blood splatter on some gravel. The dog's blood or maybe belonging to Gage? Jake wrapped the dog tag and gravel in his handkerchief. So now he could prove that Travis was there but again it was circumstantial. He'd take what he could get.

"You find anything?" Harper asked him as they prepared to leave the facility.

He nodded. "I need lab work which will be the trick."

"How about you? Find anything in the office?"

She cocked her head and smiled. "Hardly anything," she said, "Just some plans for a proposed airfield along with a relief map of property to be included. Got photos too. Aren't you glad I came along?"

40

When Tommy Mitchell opened the door to his brother's house he noticed it wasn't latched properly, asking her what was wrong with the door and Pam telling him Haller had forced it open to get Alex's gun and she needed to get someone out there to fix it and would he take a look at it.

Tommy looked at it, running his fingers over the freshly splintered wood. "The facing will have to be replaced and a new latch installed."

"Can you take care of that when you have time?" she said. "That would be great. Alex is just − ." She tailed off shaking her head. She still wore the black dress but had kicked off her shoes and was barefoot. Her calves and ankles were smooth and perfect, thought Tommy. Love to get those things locked up behind his neck. Damn, the woman looked good. Tommy saying, "You mentioned Pappy Van Winkle."

She lifted the hair off the back of her neck and the aroma of her perfume filled his head. She poured the 23-year-old bourbon into a heavy rocks glass and handed it to him.

He took a sip. It warmed and tingled his mouth like liquid sunshine.

She put her arms around his neck and kissed him long and deep, her tongue searching his mouth, Tommy feeling the stirring and his breath catching. She let him go and led him to the couch. He followed docile as a lamb.

She pulled him down to the couch and said, "There are certain things I like."

"Whatever you say, lady."

"Tear my dress off."

"Wha——-? Really?"

She said, "Really." Breathing it out.

Tommy tore at it, not believing how aroused she became when he did. Set him on fire too. Shit, this could be the best he ever had, the taboo added to his excitement. They staggered to the bedroom, coupled as one. Urgency fired his need. They collapsed on the bed and as he entered her, she clawed at as his back and neck really digging in and hurting him. She had to be drawing blood, but he didn't care as he drove himself hard into her, as she tore at him.

***

Alex Mitchell left the funeral home and called Pam but got her recorder. Now what? His father lay in a casket and his wife nowhere to be found. Tommy either. Everything left to him. Like always. Alex gets the scut work while Tommy gets drunk or high and Pam and Dad did the business planning. Well, that was how it used to be. Things would change. Finally, things would even out for him. He hated it that he was thinking like that because he loved his father, despite his faults, but had to plan and look logically at the future.

Alex was headed home to change when he met his brother, Tommy, flying low, a flashing crimson streak, on the way back to town. What was his big hurry?

***

Vegas Metro, called Jake back concerning the death of Pam's first husband.

"Nothing here," said the female voice, a Lieutenant Tara St. John. "We had our suspicions but nothing to get traction on. No way to indict her. It was a thorough investigation and we autopsied the victim. It looked dicey, we had questions and perhaps missed something, but we didn't have anything prosecutable. I still have thoughts that she got away with something. Don't like that feeling."

Jake thanked her and broke the connection. A dead end yet added to Jake's suspicions. Maybe Fat Boy Haller had something worth hearing, Needed to interview Noah Haller. Harper talked to her boss, lawyer Jessup, telling him, "You get a free experienced investigator, Jerry. And he has training."

The meeting with Noah Haller, AKA "Fat Boy" Haller, took place over the objections of Sheriff Kellogg but Jessup had already checked with a judge and brought the okay from the magistrate in writing, so Kellogg was reduced to sour expressions.

First thing out of Haller's mouth? "You got a cigarette?"

The things they thought of, their lives on the line. Like the guy Jake interviewed who cut up his girlfriend with a broken bottle wanting to know if this was going to affect his résumé, telling Jake he applied for a job at a local factory. Then there was the woman who shot-gunned her husband's mistress, telling Jake she'd killed the woman instead of her husband because she saw the woman before she saw her husband, and had a hang-nail driving her nuts and did he have some fingernail clippers?

Second thing Haller said was, "I ain't tellin' you nothin'."

"How do you think this ends?" Jake leaned down, elbows on his knees. "They have your prints on the weapon. Does that register in your head? I'm here on behalf of your attorney which means I'm on your side. I want to know about Gage Burnell," Jake said. "You give me something and we'll look into what you're telling us."

Haller looked apprehensive, biting his lower lip. "Why should I trust you?"

"You don't have much choice," Jake said. "You're washed out of friends. How do you think the Mitchell brothers feel about you right now?"

"What do I get in return?"

"I don't have anything to give you except find the real person killed Vernon."

Haller crossed his arms and leaned back in the wooden chair. "Fuck it. I'll take my chances." The big man sat back. Haller let out a huge breath. He smelled of body odor. "All you get for now. I didn't shoot Vernon."

"I were the prosecutor," said Jessup, "you, Mister Haller, will take the full weight for Mitchell's death. This is a lock for the PA and I don't foresee an alternative outcome. Noah, I'm being honest. I am at a loss to find anything that could possibly turn this in your favor unless we get a handle on something that exonerates you. You have to help us if I'm to effectively represent you in court, or you're going to prison."

"You don't give us something you're tying our hands," Jake said.

Then Haller did something strange. A look of confidence came over Haller's face and he said, "I won't go down for this. Bet on it."

Jake looked at the man for a long moment, considering the man's statement. "What are you telling us?"

Haller lifted a big paw and waved off Jake. "All I'm saying."

Jake mystified by the man's response. Was he that stupid or... Or, did he have information that would compromise someone?

Jake and Jessup left the lock-up. Okay, according to the information Harper found at the grain elevator office there was a new highway and airport but none of it was planned for his Dad's place.

Why had the Mitchells been interested in purchasing the place and then reneging? Jake was convinced it hinged on Franklin Yoder's disappearance. It was thin, almost ephemeral but he wouldn't let go. Wondering about his part in this. His nostalgic night with Pam was stupid and may have been a catalyst for the events since.

As if she read his thoughts, Harper said, "None of this is your fault."

"Hope you're right. Haller's looking down a hole where he's inside for the rest of his life but he's not talking and doesn't think he's going down. He's either the dumbest person I've ever met, or someone is offering him a lifeline. I have no idea what that would be, and I don't see how he extricates himself from this."

"So, what do you do next?"

"I'll convince your dad to authorize a homicide investigation and include the grain elevator. The trick will be to get a judge to go along with a search warrant."

"What are you looking for we don't already know?"

"I have no idea," Jake said. "But I'm running out of time."

***

Back at his place Tommy thought about what just happened and how stupid it was. He didn't feel right about it. He had scratches on his back and neck and Pam had bit down hard on his lower lip, drawing blood, as he exploded inside her. It was Guinness Book sex.

When they were done, she told him he'd better get out of there before Alex got back, almost pushing him out the door. Deciding she's a crazy bitch and no longer wondered why Alex couldn't keep her happy or why Alex thought she was getting boned by the Texas boy. The girl liked sex. More than any girl he ever banged.

Pam had given him some cocaine and the mixture of coke, dubawana, and high-test whiskey blurred his thoughts and dulled the pain, but it was wearing off now, so he felt the scratches on his back. She bit his lip, as if trying to bite through, vampire shit, and it hurt. When he checked the bathroom mirror his lower lip was an angry purplish color and swollen like a bee sting.

He needed ice and hydrogen peroxide. He was still jacked up by the coke and knew when he crashed he'd sleep for about two days.

He looked like shit.

How would he explain this lip? How was Pam going to explain the torn dress?

***

What's a couple of broken fingernails, thought Pam, as she changed into different clothes being careful about the ripped dress and especially the semen stain on the hem line. She wasn't going to wash up, just yet. First, she made a call to her father's office but asked for Deputy Bailey, instead of her dad. They told her Bailey was posted out at the Morgan place.

Even better.

She asked for Bailey's cell number and though the dispatcher hesitated, Pam insisted and knew the guy would do as she asked: the man's boss her father, the Sheriff of Paradise County.

Pam hung up the landline and used her cell phone to place the call to Deputy Sheriff Bailey.

Bailey answered and Pam put the right amount of distress and pain in her voice when she told Bailey she needed the deputy to come out to her place and "bring a rape kit but please don't say anything to Daddy".

41

Tommy heard the doorbell and then a loud banging on his door as he got out of the shower. He looked at his cell phone. 6:30 PM. What the hell? He'd passed out. Damn, his head fuzzy with alcohol and drugs and his back and lip burning with cuts and bruises? Naked, he padded to the front room.

"Who the hell is banging on my door? Fuck off."

"Sheriff's Deputy, Paradise County."

Deputy Sheriff? He peaked through the window and saw the police unit and then the female cop, Bailey.

"What do you want?"

"Talk to you."

"Go away."

"Two ways to do this," she said, through the door. "Let me in and we talk and maybe reach an understanding, or I get help and we process you."

Process him. What the hell? He ran a hand through his hair, telling her to let him put on some clothes. He pulled on some jeans and a tee-shirt, no shoes, then went back to open the door, letting Deputy Bailey in.

The deputy came in and dropped a bomb.

Son of a bitch. Tommy was scared, terrified. Shit, why didn't he think things through? The fucking cunt had bow-dicked him.

***

Sue, the ranger lab tech, called Jake with the forensic information Jake requested. Lab techs, like Sue, were the brains that never slept or took vacations. Unlike field officers, lab techs loved their work, enjoyed solving puzzles and extricating gold from minute bits of forensic evidence. Having a good relationship with these people was a must and sped up investigations.

"The blood samples belong to your friend, Gage," she said. "They match the DNA on the toothbrush you sent. Doesn't tell us much. People bleed in their homes. However, there's a couple of other things involved here that are of interest. One of the blood samples you sent doesn't match Mister Burnell's or your father's DNA. But it does match the DNA of the female hair sample you sent." There was a pause before she added, "One wonders why you have a female hair sample or how you procured it."

"Professional investigator."

"And an asshole who uses his ex-girlfriend to investigate the DNA of whoever this present woman may be."

"It's not like that."

"Got your check for the bail bucks. How'd that turn out?"

"They dropped the charge."

"Can I do anything else for you? Wax your car, shine your shoes?"

"As a matter of fact – "

Sue laughed at the other end. "Okay what have you got?"

He told her about the sediment samples, the cigarettes and the blood on the gravel."

"Fed-Ex it overnight and I'll see what I can do."

"You're the best, Sue."

"Sure. Anyone ever tell you that you're lovable in an irritating way?"

42

"I don't know how we proceed with the information you have from Haller," Buddy said. They were in Buddy's office at his new position with Paradise PD. His office more spare then Cal's. "In fact, you have no information and this is a county matter. These people don't like you, Jake and forget charm. You can't even spell 'tact'."

"Pam said she still loves me."

Buddy made a face, pointed at Jake. "You." Shaking his head. "There's something wrong with your head, man. How's that supposed to help sort this out?"

"I have evidence from the Mitchell plant and some DNA information." Jake shared his information about the blood samples and his visit to the chemical plant.

"Where do you get DNA analysis?"

"I sent it overnight to a lab tech friend of mine in Texas."

"The big surprise is you have friends," said Buddy. "It's good to know but its circumstantial," Buddy said. "Any family member, even and especially Haller's DNA is going to be in Vernon's house and the grain elevator."

"True. But if it matches we have a thread to pull on see where it goes. You and I are going to get the PA to open Gage's homicide investigation as an incident occurring in town and include the grain elevator."

"You're dreaming."

"I'm going to vote for Kellogg."

"You don't get a vote, Tex."

"May decide to live here."

"Don't threaten me like that."

The phone rang. Buddy put it on speaker.

"Buddy," the dispatcher, a female, said, "Get in here, quick."

Buddy left the room and was gone for a couple of minutes. When he came back into the office he said, "You're not going to believe this."

"What?"

"Fat Boy Haller made bail and then skipped."

One damn thing after another.

***

First, Jake would find out who provided the bail money. That might give Jake insight into Fat Boy's peculiar confidence. Attorney Jessup gave Jake the name of the bail bondsman and it was the same one Jake had used, named 'Fritz' Delmar.

***

Fritz Delmar looked more like a farmer than a bail bondsman, thick wrists and broad shoulders, weathered skin.

"I used to work on a ranch in Oklahoma," said Delmar. "Work petered out and I went into this work, which, so far has been mildly lucrative since you showed. You're kind of a boon for business but you're the first client I ever had on both ends of these things. What can I do for you?"

"I want the name of the person who provided the bail money for Fat Boy Haller."

"Yeah, I'm screwed if he's not found."

"Want him found?"

"Hell yes. I'm out a hundred grand I don't have laying around."

"I'll find him for you."

Delmar thought about it. "You have any experience?"

"Some."

"Yeah, what?"

"Texas Rangers."

Delmar snorted. "Shit, whyn't you say so? I'll pay you two thousand you bring him back."

"Instead of the usual ten to twenty percent, right?"

"You done your homework. You know, I can find him myself."

"And risk injury and time away from the office."

"Had to do it before. I have my own guys."

"I'll bet they're great finding drunks and meth heads. Besides, I may already know where he's hiding." A bluff, but Jake played it.

Jake smiled. Delmar made a sour face.

"Shit," said Delmar. "You work awful hard at being difficult."

"Not really all that much work."

"It's a deal then," said Delmar. "Maybe I'll have more for you do this right."

"I'm just in it for the sport." Jake Morgan, manhunter. Wearing a lot of hats these days. Jake saying now, "Again, who was it provided the bail money for Haller?"

"The person who provided the cash wished to remain anonymous. They paid extra to ensure their anonymity." Delmar smiled in triumph.

"So you're not going to tell me."

"You bring back Haller and I'll tell you then."

"Quit jerking off. You're going to be out more than the cream on top. The name?"

Delmar shaking his head and saying, "Plus, you find Haller for two grand."

"I'd hate to play poker with you. All right, I'm in."

Delmar held up two fingers like a 'V'.

Jake smiled. "You're kind of a hard case yourself."

"I think," said Delmar. "This could be the beginning of a beautiful friendship."

43

Jake knew it was important to be the first person to find Noah 'Fat Boy' Haller or at least be first to find his corpse. In Jake's mind Haller's death was the most likely scenario. Someone didn't want Haller around to talk. Haller too thick to understand that whoever bailed him out was the first step to have him disappear or 'disappeared' believing Fat Boy would either be killed or allowed to head out for a place he couldn't be found. The former was the likely end. No loose ends.

With Haller in the wind Sheriff Kellogg issued a statement regarding plans to capture and prosecute Fat Boy. The Mitchell estate was offering a reward which would surely complicate things with phony leads and drunken cowboys and farm hands getting in Jake's way.

A possible ending could be a shootout where Fat Boy Haller was killed. No way was Haller going to be allowed to return and talk. Jake pretty sure Kellogg was in on the dodge. But first, Jake had another string to pull. He drove up to the school to see Leo the Lyon.

Leo was on his plan period and Jake caught him in his office, working out a math lesson plan with Mozart playing on a Bluetooth speaker.

"Mozart?"

"Stimulates the mind," Leo said, without looking up. "The rhythmic meter is mathematically embedded."

Looking up now, Leo said, "Oh, it's you. Allow me to translate. Mozart good. Make kid smart."

"You actually plan your classes?" asked Jake.

"Some of my students have a different attitude towards the learning task than did you, Mister 'I'm da quarter-back'."

"Who is the most knowledgeable person in town on Paradise lore and history?"

Leo gave Jake a pained expression.

"Besides you," Jake said. "You are obviously without a peer for our generation, but I need a senior citizen."

"That's easy enough. That would be Vienna Dalrymple."

"Missus Dalrymple's still alive?" Jake remembering his teacher.

"Not just living, thriving. Seventy-four and getting younger every day. She is religious about her daily journal, though she calls it her 'diary'. She calls about once a week and asks how things are going at her 'beloved school'.

Mrs. Dalrymple had been their high school English teacher. Taught at Paradise High School for 45 years before retiring. Leo gave her a call and she agreed to meet with Jake.

"Said she would be interested in hearing from one of her 'problem students'," Leo said with a smile.

Vienna Dalrymple met Jake at the door of her Victorian style home. She had prepared tea and a plate of Danish cookies. Jake didn't drink tea but accepted the proffered cup. It was better than expected.

"So," said Mrs. Dalrymple. "What are you doing these days, Jake?"

"I work for the Texas Department of public Safety."

"On the highway department?"

"Texas Rangers."

Her eyes widened, put a hand to her throat and she said, "Oh my." Saying it as if it were further evidence of the collapse of Western Civilization. Jake sipped his tea to cover his smile.

"I have three more diplomas than anyone would've guessed," Jake said.

She laughed. "I'm sorry for my reaction, Jake. You were so... I don't know, distracted by a certain young lady as I remember."

"I need some information from you, Missus Dalrymple, if that's okay."

"I don't know much about Texas."

"This is local stuff. Do you remember a man named Franklin Yoder?"

"Frank? Why yes, I do. He and my Roy were good friends. Such a shame about him."

"What was a shame?"

"The way he was railroaded by that Vernon Mitchell, may that nasty man rest in peace."

"Whatever happened to Yoder? He seems to have disappeared."

She set her teacup down. "It's the oddest thing. It was like he and his wife vanished from the face of the earth. So sad. Roy and I tried...but, wait a minute."

Mrs. Dalrymple left, and Jake could hear her in another room, shuffle of books. Jake tried the cookies. Delicious. Maybe put a few in his pocket. She'd expect him to still be on the dodge and up to mischief. Mrs. Dalrymple returned with a couple of brown notebooks and began leafing through them. Jake sat quietly sipping tea wishing it was coffee.

"Yes," she said, happily. "Here it is. January 4, 1975." She began reading from her diary. "Roy and I return from Christmas vacation with Roy's family. We are very concerned we have not heard from our friend, Frank Yoder, nor his wife, Caroline, since they failed to show for the school Christmas party two weeks ago." She looked up from her reading. "Caroline was on the faculty then. She taught Home Ec. They call it FACS now." She continued her reading. "Roy called today and learned that Franklin's phone had been disconnected. Roy was worried enough he took action and drove to the Yoder's home only to find it abandoned and a Public Notice taped to the front door. The notice proclaimed that the home and farm were 'placed into receivership by a bankruptcy judge effective, Jan. 1, 1975. Sale of property and contents will be sold at public auction, tentatively for March, 1975'."

She closed the journal and her eyes became sad as if looking off into the distance past and reliving the emotions.

"I never saw either of them again."

Jake sat forward. "They disappeared without a word?"

"Yes. And Vernon Mitchell bought the place. I think, and I shouldn't say this as it was a rumor, but I believe Vernon Mitchell pilfered their cattle and sold them to make his fortune. Franklin didn't have insurance on his stock, and they had a bad year with their crops."

Both of them, thought Jake.

Jake told Mrs. Dalrymple about his attempts to find Franklin Yoder and was unable to run him down or even find a family member.

"Frank was an only child," she said. "His father and mother died leaving Frank the farm."

"Anything else?"

She sighed. "I'm not sure what you mean."

"Any other dealings of consequence between Franklin and Vernon Mitchell?"

"Well, yes there is." She placed a finger alongside her cheek. "Vernon dated Caroline prior to her marriage to Frank."

"How did that end?"

"Badly. Vernon was a ferocious young man. A drunkard and a bully."

Thinking about that, Jake said, "Did anyone investigate the Franklin's disappearance?"

"I believe the sheriff did so. Wait." She leaved through the brown notebook found what she was looking for. "Here," she said. She turned the notebook around and handed it to Jake.

The article headline was: Paradise County investigates Disappearance of Local Couple. Jake read silently, digesting the single column report. The first sentence caught his eye.

Paradise County Sheriff, Robert Burnell, has opened an inquiry into the disappearance of long-time Paradise county residents, Franklin and Caroline Yoder.

Gage's dad.

"Friends of the Yoder's assert the couple left for a Christmas break vacation to Florida around December 22 or 23, 1974. This was an annual trip and it did not surprise their friends they were gone.

During this period the Yoder's farm and property was seized by the court and will be sold in the spring of 1975 at public auction..."

Jake put down the notebook. "Sorry for the loss of your friends."

Mrs. Dalrymple shook her head. "It was most disturbing. They lost their farm and Vernon took it over. Since that time the gossip mongers have concocted disquieting scenarios to explain away their disappearance. One of the ridiculous theories by these ninnies is that Frank killed Caroline and then killed himself because their daughter was actually Vernon Mitchell's bastard child."

Jake held up a hand and turned his head to one side. "Wait. There's a daughter?"

"Oh yes. I believe I have her address. Her name is Christine McKee. She was adopted by an aunt, who was single at that time. I doubt she knows what happened, but you can try. She was quite young when her parents disappeared. Not yet of school age. Do you mind my asking why you're interested?"

"I believe the Yoders were murdered and so was Gage Burnell and possibly the two things are related."

She put a hand to her breast and her mouth fell open. "How horrible. Poor Gage. Such an entertaining young man. He was the clown of your little group. I once gave him an assignment to read a passage of James Joyce's Ulysses. He made a rather inappropriate yet humorous remark concerning Joyce's writing style."

"Do you remember what he said?"

She nodded, smiling, then shaking her head. "Gage was very sharp but never used it to his advantage. He was a carefree spirit, almost in rebellion to his button-down father, a fine man. It was a very funny review, but I had to be stern with him and make him re-write. His initial response was, 'A boring screed written by a potato-eating drunk. I use my copy as a door stop'."

"Sounds like Gage." Jake feeling a pang of regret that his friend was no longer alive.

"Pardon me for a moment and I'll get Christine's address. At least her last known address." She left and returned with a hand-written post-it that she held out to Jake.

Jake accepted the note and said, "How intense was the relationship between Caroline and Vernon Mitchell?"

"Caroline was a beginning teacher and Vernon was a local boy, rough around the edges. I've never bought his gentleman farmer act. He is, well was, a deceitful and duplicitous man who has his tentacles in many businesses in the county. Vernon had his eye on Caroline. She was quite a beauty in those days. She allowed him to escort her around for a brief time in high school before she cut him off when she was dating Frank. Vernon would not let go. Even after they graduated Vernon kept after her. Frank warned him off, threatening to punch him in the mouth but Vernon wouldn't let go until Frank did just that one evening in town. Frank had to be restrained, I'm told, to prevent him from hospitalizing Vernon."

Jake sat back. "What about the child, Christine?"

Mrs. Dalrymple colored slightly. "Well, Caroline was pregnant at the time of their wedding. In those days you did the right thing. Caroline would never have considered an abortion. It wasn't done. Not around here."

Jake thanked her for her time and prepared to leave. Mrs. Dalrymple prevailed upon him to take some cookies with him. Didn't have to steal them after all.

Cookies and a shotgun wedding.

Small towns, huh?

44

Deputy Sheriff Sharon Bailey was anxious about her promise to Pam Mitchell not to inform Doc about Tommy forcing, well raping, his daughter. The young deputy couldn't sleep last night and this morning she chewed both thumbnails down to a raw, pink nub, now throbbing with irritation.

She needed this job since her no-good husband left her with two kids to feed and care for. The medical insurance plan offered by the county was a good one as was the dental plan. Things Bailey would not have if she were terminated.

Her primary focus was to keep her job; a job she had trained for and taken JC courses in college. It was a dream she'd had since she graduated high school. Become a law enforcement officer and hopefully catch on with the Highway Patrol or on the police force in a large city.

Maybe law school if she could swing it. She had long-term goals, chief among them raising her child in a secure home.

These things were on her mind.

What if Doc learned of the rape before Bailey could tell him about it? It would be hard to explain, and Bailey had already seen how touchy the sheriff was about his daughter, Pam. Pam, for her part, was the topic of much police gossip, none of which ever reached Doc Kellogg's ears. Hell no. That would be the end of that person's career, you bet.

She was going to have to tell him and soon.

But, man, did she dread doing so.

Doc Kellogg was not a man who handled bad news well.

***

After his talk with Vienna Dalrymple Jake decided finding Fat Boy Haller would have to wait. Buddy said he'd keep him posted if Haller was found and Jake asked Leo to do a little research on Haller's habits and background.

"It's time your wealth of Paradise history actually works to our benefit," Jake said, to Leo.

Christine McKee's address would require a three-hour road trip across the state. Another day lost. Only two days left. Before heading there Jake wanted to shake things up a little. He decided a visit with the person he believed bailed out Fat Boy Haller was in order.

Jake entered the Paradise Bank and asked to see the president, Pam Kellogg Mitchell.

"May I tell her your name and the nature of your visit?"

"Jake Morgan. Need to borrow a large amount of money. Considering buying a farm."

"Would you prefer to see a loan officer?"

"No. Missus Mitchell is expecting me." Actually the last thing she expected.

"I'll tell her you're here," said the teller, a fresh-faced young girl, smiling a helpful smile. Maybe he'd open an account here.

The teller left then returned, her face flushed. "I'm sorry, but Missus Mitchell is busy right now."

"That's her office back there, isn't it?" Jake said, pointing.

"Well, yes but – "

"I'll just go on back."

"Wait."

He ignored her and pushed open the door to Pam's

office, the teller following him.

"Good morning, Pam," Jake said as he entered. No one in the room but Pam who didn't look busy, in fact, she seemed annoyed. You come home and no one is happy about it.

"I'm sorry, Missus Mitchell," said the teller. "I told him you were busy but – "

Pam held up a hand and said, "It's okay, Naomi. Won't you sit down, Mister Morgan?"

Mr. Morgan? Pretty formal for someone who proposed love and devotion. Harper was right, he had angered Pam Mitchell. Jake sat.

The teller left them.

"What do you want, Jake?"

"Why'd you bail out Fat Boy?"

"Why do you persist in irritating me?"

"I asked you second."

"Okay. None of your business."

"I'm not playing with you, Pam. This is a homicide investigation and I believe it's tied to Gage's death."

"I don't see a badge."

"Auxiliary officer," Jake said, with mock pride. "Paradise PD."

"What?"

"Either you provide a plausible explanation for your unusual interest in bailing out Vernon's alleged killer or I'll begin to equate that with complicity."

"Grow up and use your head."

"Best to tell it now."

She pursed her lips, containing herself before saying, "I don't believe he did it."

"What makes you say that?"

"He was helping me at the house the day Vernon was shot. A terrible thing." She was switching gears now, going with the innocent little girl mourning the loss of a family member. Her voice shaking. "I sent him to do something on the farm. He couldn't have done it."

"Did you watch him do this thing you sent him to do?"

"No."

"Were you in the house while Haller was away as he said he was?"

"No." She put a finger to her lips and a faraway look came into her eyes. "I left right after that. Took a ride on my horse."

"So, you don't know where he was."

"I'm certain he did as I requested."

"The weapon was stolen from your house. I saw you and Haller together just before Vernon was shot."

"How'd you see us?"

"I was at Vernon's prior to the shooting."

"Maybe you did it?"

"Sure, I walked past you, broke into your home, stole the weapon, walked back across the road, using the power of invisibility so you wouldn't see me. Too late for that scenario anyway. Look, Pam, you're the person accused him of stealing the weapon and they have his fingerprints on the weapon and a positive residue test."

"I hated telling them Noah had stolen the gun. Still, I just thought he wouldn't do such a thing."

Jake watching her closely, remembering Pam's talent for affecting emotion. She was damn good. She was intelligent and practiced at gauging people's reaction to her charms.

"You didn't hear a shot?"

"No."

"Where is Haller?" Jake said.

"I have no idea."

"I don't believe you."

"That's because you've become cynical and insufferable. What happened to you, Jake? You used to be a lot of fun. Why would I want to hide him?"

"I don't know, why would you hide him? You know the answer."

"I'm out a lot of money if he doesn't return in time for the trial."

"And, perhaps gaining many times more what you lose."

"What the hell does that mean?"

"So, tell me where he is or might be and I'll run him down and turn him in to Doc."

"Well," she said, making a show of considering it. "Give me some time and I'll see what I can do."

"Do you know someone named Chris McKee?"

There it was. She hesitated a beat before saying, "Who?"

Just a flicker but he caught it before she composed herself.

45

Jake drove east to Jericho, Missouri, the home of Christine McKee. Driving along he made mental notes of vehicles that accompanied him on the trip. One stood out as it turned off at the Jericho exit and followed him a few blocks into town before turning off. A dark green Toyota Camry.

His guarded nature heightened by recent events caused him to take a circuitous route to his destination. Confident he'd lost the tail he continued on his journey.

Christine McKee lived in a modest frame home in Jericho, Missouri, nicely landscaped with oak trees turning harvest colors and a rock garden.

When McKee opened the door, Jake was taken aback. Same slender face and brown eyes. A lovely middle-aged woman, Christine McKee could pass as Alex Mitchell's older sister. Jake tried not to stare as she invited him inside.

"Are you all right?" she asked as Jake sat.

"Yes. It's nothing. I just – . Thank you for allowing me to visit."

Mrs. Dalrymple vouched for Jake, so McKee was happy to receive him and had prepared coffee and cookies in advance of his arrival. Cookies again. Small town hospitality was going to damage his health. At least she had coffee instead of tea.

"Vienna said you were quite the rounder when you were in her class. 'Rounder' was her word. She said you had some questions about my parents. I'm afraid I won't be much help. I was barely out of diapers when they disappeared."

Jake was quiet, digesting the information, watching mannerisms that seemed familiar.

"Are you sure you're all right?" she asked again.

"They disappeared?"

"I hardly remember them. I was placed in a foster home for a brief time until my Aunt Sharon, Mother's sister, was allowed to become my guardian. Vienna kept in contact with me for many years though I've only met her once or twice. A very nice lady. She was, I believe, close friends with my parents."

"You know a man named Vernon Mitchell?"

She gave him a quizzical look. "Strange. You're the second person to ask that question."

"Who asked before me?"

"It was a couple. I've forgotten their names though I'm of a mind they were not using their real names."

"Why do you think that?"

"A guess, but they were very careful to make sure they used each other's real names repeatedly as if afraid they would forget them."

Jake happy to find Mrs. McKee was sharp, observant. "When was this?"

"About six weeks ago."

"Can you describe them?"

She gave a description of the pair. The man sounded like Gage Burnell but could be someone else. The woman she described as 'quite beautiful, even stunning and assertive'. The woman asked most of the questions. Jake asked if their names were 'Pam' or 'Gage'.

"No," she said. "I certainly would've remembered the name 'Gage'. Unusual."

"How about the name Alex Mitchell?"

Shaking her head now. "No. What is this about?"

"Your parents' disappearance may have some bearing

on a homicide investigation back at Paradise." Hedging on why a Texas ranger, acting as an auxiliary officer was involved on such an investigation. He showed her his ranger star. "Do you remember anything about your parents that might help me?"

"Texas Ranger?" She pursed her lips in thought. "I can't think of anything at the moment."

"Almost anything has a possibility of providing an investigative avenue. Something left to you, photos, memorabilia, anything. You never know what will help or at least give me an insight into the personalities involved."

She nodded and said, "I'll be right back." Mrs. McKee left the room briefly and returned with a Florsheim's shoebox, its edges brown and timeworn. Also, a couple of age-faded yearbooks from 1967 and 1968. She set the items on a table then removed the shoebox top, setting it upside down on the table. Inside were photos, some clippings and other memorabilia.

"You are welcome to look through these things," she said. "I hope it helps."

Jake sat and began removing the articles separating them into different piles. Black-and-white photos in one small stack, color photos in another. Clippings in a stack, and miscellaneous memorabilia in a pile to one side.

The clippings were family reunions, picnics, little children, the usual stuff families accumulate. The photos were helpful as they were dated with names on the back of the photos allowing him to be able to pick out Caroline and Frank Yoder. One color photo dated 4-16-68 struck his eye. It showed a young Caroline Yoder, by her maiden name, Friedebach, smiling and showing off an unusual ring. It was a square shaped tiger eye. A smaller version of one he'd seen before. Jake sat the photo aside and went through the rest of the material but didn't learn anything.

He picked up the yearbooks and leafed through them. Fortunately, there was an index in the 1968 Paradise High School yearbook, and he looked up the page numbers for Mitchell, Vernon and Friedebach, Caroline. There were five cross-referenced pages listed. One was their composite class picture, the type they hung in hallways in schools the alumni would come back and search out; two more were in clubs they both were members of. But there was one photo that stood out for Jake.

It was a candid of a young Vernon Mitchell, who looked very much like a larger version of Tommy, with Caroline. Vernon had Caroline by the waist and a laughing Caroline was showing off two similar rings: one larger than the other on her left hand.

"Do you have a magnifying glass?" Jake asked Christine.

"Yes. I'll get it." She did so and handed it to him.

Jake looked closer at the old photo. Two Tiger eye rings. The larger one a dead ringer for the ring Alex Mitchell wore. Could it be the same ring? He sat back and thought about that.

"You wouldn't have any of your mother's jewelry, by chance?"

She nodded. "As a matter of fact, I do. Would you like to see it? It's mostly costume jewelry."

While she was gone, Jake decided to check the index for Yoder, Franklin then cross-referenced with Friedebach, Caroline. Only one page. And it showed Franklin and Caroline hand-in-hand in their graduation gown. They were a striking couple. Caroline was a beautiful young lady whose smile spoke of life ahead. Frank was tall, fair complexioned with kind brown eyes. They looked very happy. The kind of people who knew they were happy. Did that happiness rankle Vernon Mitchell? How deep was his resentment that he waited almost six years for revenge? What triggered such murderous vengeance?

Something happened during their senior year, whereby Caroline threw over Vernon for Frank Yoder. Jake remembered Mrs. Dalrymple had said Caroline Yoder was pregnant when she married Franklin.

Jake wondered if he was looking right at the source of Vernon's jealousy as Caroline returned with a hexagon-shaped jewelry box decorated with ornate blue flowers. She handed it to Jake. Jake looked through the items and found what he was looking for wondering if someone else had been looking for it years ago.

It was the smallish woman's Tiger eye ring. One other ring was missing that Jake was interested in finding and now sure he knew who wore the other.

"Do you have your mother's wedding ring?"

She shook her head. "No, she must have been wearing it when they disappeared."

Jake held up the Tiger eye ring. "You ever wear this?"

"No. It was my mother's, so I have kept it to remember her. Anything about her."

"How'd you come by your mother's jewelry?"

"My aunt saved it for me. Mom had visited Aunt Sharon just a few days before her disappearance and had taken her jewelry with her. This is odd. A few years ago, I offered to give Aunt Sharon a couple of pieces to remind her of mother and well... when she saw the Tiger eye it upset her. I asked her about it, but she said, 'it just reminds me of another time'."

"I would like to speak with your aunt," Jake said.

"She died last year. There is no family left save me and my husband and our two sons, both married now."

"May I keep this ring, temporarily?"

"Well." She hesitated. "What are you thinking? Why would you want it? She trailed off.

"I don't want to upset you," Jake said. "But I don't think your parents disappeared. I believe they were killed."

"I've heard that dad murdered mom and then killed himself. Just horrible."

"No," Jake said, shaking his head. "That did not happen."

Her eyes closed and she exhaled. "You have no idea... God bless you. What a relief to hear that. So glad someone knows my father would not do such a thing. Then who?"

He exhaled, feeling compassion for his nice lady. "I believe the man who did it and I'm fairly satisfied he's the one, has recently been murdered and that's why I'm here."

"What?" Christine put a hand to the side of her mouth. "How awful. And you think the ring helps you do what?"

He shrugged. "Not sure but it's a powerful coincidence."

"Take it then, for as long as you need it."

"Also the yearbooks and this photo, if you don't mind." Jake held up the photo of Caroline and the ring.

"Whatever you need. I only ask you return the items when you're finished and that you share what you find."

"Okay. One more thing and this is a hard one."

Christine nodded her head slowly. "All right. What is it?"

"I know this is sudden," Jake said, "and it's going to sound unusual, but I'd like a hair sample from you if you don't mind providing one."

"What?" She began laughing. "Vienna warned me that you had an unusual sense of humor. Why would I do something like that?"

"In fact, if you pluck one or two from your head that would be helpful in clearing up something." A hair follicle was more accurate for a DNA test than a cut hair and he wanted a one hundred percent match. "Perhaps a blood test."

She placed a hand to her mouth, surprised. "What are you hoping to learn from all of this?"

"Maybe nothing," Jake said. "I can't really say at this point and I don't want to be unnecessarily intrusive. If I'm wrong, it could be distressing to others and even to you. You'll have to trust me. I promise to share what I learn."

"You believe it portends to something else."

Jake nodded. "Yes."

"Okay," she said. "Okay, if you think it will help, I'll do it. All of it."

46

Leaving the McKee home Jake drove two blocks and sat in the parking lot of a Baptist Church, empty on a weekday. From this point he could see the front of the McKee home through a pocket monocular he carried with him.

He waited.

Within ten minutes the dark green Camry drove by the McKee home and then disappeared around the corner.

Jake waited some more.

There it was again. The green Camry drove slowly by and then stopped in front of the house. A smallish round balding man in a tan raincoat got out of the car and walked to the door, and pushed on the doorbell, the main door opened but not the storm door. The man was talking yet the door wasn't opening. He pulled on the door handle and it opened partway when Caroline pulled it shut.

Jake started the Lincoln and drove back to the McKee house. Jake watched the man and Caroline in a tug-of-war with her door. Jake pulled the Lincoln in front of the Camry blocking it and jumped out of his vehicle. The man saw Jake and he bounded off the steps and ran to the Camry but Jake intercepted his flight.

"Get out of my way," said the man.

"What're you doing here?"

"I don't have to tell you anything."

"You could be wrong about that. Consider size difference."

"You're bigger, so what?"

"And you don't think that will be sufficient?" Smiling big.

The man started to walk around but Jake grabbed the front of the man's raincoat and pulled him back, twisting the man's coat in his grip. The man squirmed to get loose, but the coat slipped up behind his neck and Jake held firm.

"See how easy that was?" Jake said.

"Get your hands off me."

"Talk to me or you talk to the police."

"Who're you?"

"You already know that, or you wouldn't be here."

"You're imagining things."

"I'm starting to imagine you with a broken nose."

"I'm a licensed private investigator," said the man.

"Who sent you?"

"I won't reveal that."

"Already know who did. Someone in the Mitchell family."

The man began to look uneasy. "Doesn't matter. I'm leaving."

"Not until you answer some questions."

"I will not."

Christine McKee walked across the lawn and joined them; she was visibly shaken but composed herself. "He tried...tried to break into my house. What're you doing here?"

"I just wanted to ask some questions."

"She doesn't want to talk to you, and you forced entry. That's B&E, assault, and trespass. Could be a problem for you with the local authorities. Might even pull your ticket."

"I'm leaving." He started to pull away, but Jake gripped him tighter.

"Your name and I want to see your license."

"I don't have to show you shit." Still struggling but not loosening Jake's grip.

"I'll show you mine if you'll show me yours," Jake said reaching into his pocket. He produced his Ranger Star. The man looked at it, then at Jake, deflated now. "I... I didn't know."

"Now I see yours or you're going downtown and things escalate. You've involved yourself in a homicide investigation. You could be charged as an accessory after the fact. Sound like fun? Good thing I arrived when I did wasn't it, Missus McKee?"

"Yes, it was," she said, picking up on Jake's line. "He was making threats and I was worried for my life." Smart lady.

"What? No," said the man. "I was just going to ask what you were talking to her about." The man reached into his jacket and showed Jake his private investigator license. His name was Wayne Cross.

"Why are you here?" Jake let him go.

"Gathering information," he said.

"Why Missus McKee?"

"I was charged to follow you. When I called back my client wanted to know what your business was with Missus McKee."

"And?"

Cross tried to maintain some dignity while being held, so he said, "May I ask why you are interested in Missus McKee?"

"Sure," Jake said. "But I won't give you an answer."

"I showed you mine," said Cross, hopefully.

"One-way street, Wayne," Jake said. "You don't have anything to trade."

"May I leave now?"

Jake looked to Christine. "What do you want to do, Missus McKee?"

"You won't see me again, Lady," said Wayne Cross. "I promise."

"That's nice, isn't it? We're all getting along now. Maybe go bowling as a group later," Jake said, then to Mrs. McKee, "I believe we can cut this one loose."

Christine nodded. "Let him go." She took her cell

phone and snapped a picture of Wayne Cross, P.I. "My husband sees him around here, a trip to the hospital will be a sure thing." She leaned in and said directly to Cross, "He used to wrestle in college as a heavyweight and he's very protective."

Jake looked at Christine McKee now, seeing a different person than the cookies and coffee Mrs. McKee.

Jake saying now to Wayne Cross. "I see you again, even by chance, my shadow falls on you, I'll rip your fucking eyes out. Got that?"

Cross looked up at Jake, exhaled heavily, shrugged his coat back into place and nodded his head twice. "Got it."

47

Jake returned to Paradise. In his possession a small box containing hair follicles of one Christine McKee. She promised to send him copies of the lab report on her blood test. He also had Caroline Yoder's yearbooks and the small square tiger eye ring.

His next steps would have to be measured and careful. Wayne Cross was sure to report back to Pam Mitchell or whoever sent him.

He stopped at PPD to see Cal Bannister before heading home, hoping to see Harper but she was running background for Jessup at the University Library in Jamesville. Jake then checked in with Cal Bannister.

"Anything on Haller?" asked Jake.

Cal shaking his head. "They're still looking."

Recalling his training at the Florence Ranger facility in Texas. "Fugitives are like rabbits," his trainer, an ex-Marine with combat experience, told him, "They run for a while but then they sit. The trick is to determine where they decide to hunker down and hide. And often it's close to home or someplace familiar."

Where would Fat Boy go? Where would he hide? Checking the man's background, Haller had only lived in Paradise and rarely ventured very far outside the county. Once outside the county limits Haller would be uncomfortable. He would have to eat, sleep and have shelter so

Jake was figuring a fifty to one hundred-mile radius.

Would Haller have had time to get to his place and pick up supplies? Doubtful as that would be the first place authorities would check, that is, if Doc Kellogg really wanted to find him and law enforcement would seal it for the investigation.

For Haller's flight to be effective he would need funds and supplies? Would he go to a relative's place? No. that would be the second-place law enforcement would look.

Unlike Texas, where Jake could tap into a budget, here he had limited resources, but he had training and a nose he trusted. Checking with Leo the Lion Jake learned the Mitchells had a lake cabin located about an hour's drive south of Paradise. Would Haller go there?

Jake believed Pam, for whatever reason, lied about knowing where Haller had gone to ground. She bailed him out and if she did that what else was she doing for him? The lake cabin? It was a long shot but a starting point and worth checking.

Jake loaded his service .357 SIG, also his father's Remington pump shotgun, the home defense model that held 6 rounds. He loaded it with buckshot backing that with a slug load. Cowboy up. He placed some provisions in a hunter's rucksack and put all of it in Leo the Lion's dilapidated pick-up, a Ford F-150 from another era that was rusting behind the wheel wells, and the heater didn't work.

"Why do you need my pick-up?" Leo had asked, suspicious of Jake's request.

"You get to drive around in style in dad's Lincoln."

"Are you going to tell me or not?"

So, Jake told him of his intention to find Haller and that not only would Haller recognize the Lincoln, but that Sheriff Kellogg would notice it.

"I've also been followed by a private detective," Jake said. "Don't want to pick up another one. They're watching me."

Leo thinking about it. Not excited about lending out his truck. "Okay, but I go with you."

"No."

"I could help."

"I'm telling you something, Leo." Making his friend understand, calm but serious. "You're a football coach. I played football but you coach, and I don't, wouldn't be good at it. There's a reason for that. This is the same thing. Just like you know how to game plan, this is what I do. You're the real deal, you're tough and smarter than me, but I'd be worrying about you the whole time."

"I can handle my end."

Jake considered Leo before saying, "Haller may not go peaceably. I can shoot to kill if I have to. Can you do that? Kill Haller?"

Leo dropped his head, knowing the answer. "You know I can't. Disturbs me you say that with such coldness. I know you but I don't know some things about you."

"There it is. Sorry, not this time."

"Well, good luck," Leo said, shaking his head now. "No one can say you're not relentless."

"Intrepid," Jake said. "Rangers are intrepid."

Leo saying now, "Be careful, Jake, the world would be less fun if you weren't around."

***

The Mitchell's lake cabin had a view of a large private lake, bordered by White Oak and Pine rising away from the cabin, the lake blue and placid in the pale rose-colored dawn.

Jake had driven to the place before daybreak wearing camouflage and a baseball cap. He settled in to observe the cabin seventy-five yards up the rise where he could glass the area with his binoculars. He spooked a deer coming in, the animal near invisible in the pre-dawn light. He parked Leo's pickup a half-mile away and hiked in, carrying his rucksack and the shotgun, his service weapon holstered at his hip.

Wondering now if this was a complete waste of time and effort. He could be sitting watching an abandoned cabin while Fat Boy was two states away. The lake breathed a cloud of fog over the valley. As the sun rose over the lake, piercing the fog, Jake noticed a glint of sunlight reflecting off a metal object. The bumper of a vehicle? In the vapor it was yet hard to tell.

He waited. Then he waited some more. Surveillance was patience. Years of deer-hunting as a kid made this almost a joy particularly in such a setting. A cool morning breeze rising up from the lake rustled the oak leaves and within an hour the animal life of the forest adjusted and accepted his presence, an acceptance that most never experienced. Squirrels barked and scampered, birds whistled and chased. Familiar smell of damp earth and pine.

He felt at peace with the quiet morning and finally, at peace with what and who he was. He was a cop. A Texas Ranger. This is who he was, what he did and that had changed him from the careless high school quarterback he once was.

What that would mean going forward with Harper was the next chapter and as yet unknown.

The morning passed uneventfully. No one came or went so he moved to get a better angle on the glint of metal he'd seen earlier. Carefully he picked his way through the woods, keeping to the shadows until...

There it was. Dodge Ram SUV. Gage's missing vehicle.

Remembering now a photo of a proud owner who sent him a text photo of the vehicle. A friend.

Was Gage's killer here? Haller? Or someone else?

Crazy to have it here. Confident no one would check on it? He pulled out his cell phone to take a picture but, damn, he'd forgotten to charge his phone. Dead.

Who was here? Move in or wait it out?

Silently Jake made his way down the hillside careful to keep in the shadows of the forest. That's when he saw a vehicle appear and head up the rough road. Leaving now it had been hidden from Jake's view by the cabin. A car he recognized.

Cadillac convertible.

48

Doc Kellogg thinking things were fouled up and getting worse, Vernon murdered and Haller skipping bail, when Deputy Sheriff Bailey came into his office and said, "Doc, I need to tell you something. In private."

Kellogg nodded, saying, "Shut the door."

Bailey thanked him and stood until Kellogg offered her a seat.

"How is the search going?" Bailey asked, trying not to appear nervous but wetting her lips.

"Not well. Going to be heat if we don't find him soon. The media is going to eat me alive. Have to find Haller."

"He's saying he didn't do it."

Kellogg stared at her. The room was quiet, and she could hear herself breathing.

Kellogg sat up higher in his executive chair his chin raised and looking at his deputy. "Listen, Bailey. They all say that. Prisons are full of men who say they didn't do it. Noah Haller is a liar. Been a liar for his entire life. He's dangerous. He's killed and has no reason not to kill again now. I don't see him wanting to return to jail. He's willing to do anything to get out of this. Why he ran."

Bailey considered Kellogg's response, before speaking again.

"Well, sir," she said. "There is something else you should know." Gathering her courage now. "Something I was asked not to share with you."

And then she told him.

He didn't like it telling her, no yelling that she had a job as his deputy and loyalty was one of the requirements.

"Damn it, Sharon. What the hell were you thinking?"

"I didn't want to hurt Pam," Bailey said, knowing it sounded weak.

Kellogg's chest heaved, his lips pursed. He picked up his coffee cup and threw it across the room where it bounced off the wall, hit the floor and shattered.

"I'm sorry," said Bailey, about to cry.

Kellogg seated his hat and stomped to the door. "Clean that up. And don't ever withhold information from this office again. Ever."

He slammed the door as he left.

Now things were even worse than the sheriff thought. Nothing to do but ride it out and do what he had to do. Tommy Mitchell would pay, and Vernon would not be around to intervene.

Thinking, dammit, Vernon, I told you that boy was going to break your heart someday. Just didn't realize it was going to be posthumous.

Time to deal with Noah Haller.

***

Tommy had few choices left. Deciding now to head out of town until things cooled off, which was probably what his bitch sister-in-law wanted. How did it get like this? One minute, things are going great, and the next, everything gone to hell. That asshole from Texas comes to town and everything goes to shit and the hogs eat it. Taking after his girl, ex-wife, whatever she was.

Lay low for a few days. Think. Get his head clear. Score some good weed, some beer and maybe some tequila to work on.

But where to go? Someplace to kick back, consider his options.

The lake cabin. Closed down now for the approaching winter months. Yeah, that'd work.

***

Jake looked through the lake cabin window, cupping his hands against the glass to cut the glare and saw Haller, his back to Jake, something laid out before him. Hard to see through the screen window. The television boomed loudly. Walking around to a back entrance he picked the lock, a skill not taught at ranger training, and slipped quietly inside, the television covered his entry.

Haller was sitting at long wood-hewn table playing solitaire, an open can of Miller High Life and a half-empty bottle of Jim Beam on the table. Also a stack of money and a semi-auto pistol.

Jake thumbed the hammer back which made an audible 'click' and said, "Black Jack on the Red Queen," startling the big man.

"You," saying it to Jake like an accusation.

"Me."

Jake moved to the side where he could watch Haller. Haller looked at Jake, Jake smiled back at him. Haller's eyes moved to the pistol on the table, thinking about it.

"Never get there in time," Jake said.

The big man huffed, making a face. "How'd you find me?"

"Followed your odor. Surprised no one told you about that. Hands behind your neck, lace your fingers together."

"What if I don't?"

"You're a homicide fugitive, I'm a duly appointed officer of the law with a .357 who doesn't like you. You work it out."

Haller complied. Jake removed the gun from the table, ejected the magazine and slid the action to pop a cartridge in the air which he caught with his free hand, smiling as he snatched it out of the air. He nodded at the pile of cash.

"How much there?"

"What?"

"Who's paying you off?"

"I don't know what you're talking about." Defiant but his confidence slipping away.

"I saw her leave. You're too big to hide under the bed. Why was Pam here?"

"She's helping me."

"Helping you do what?"

"Not telling you shit. People don't like you you know?"

"Kind of dashes my political aspirations. What's her interest?"

Nothing. Mean-mugging now. Being a tough guy. Jake took the butt plate of his SIG Sauer and rapped Haller's laced fingers.

"Fuck," Haller said, flapping his hands in pain. He started to rise and as he did Jake kicked the chair out and Haller crashed to the floor.

Haller attempted to scramble to his feet, but Jake stepped on his shoulder. Shaking his head now and saying, "No. Like you down there. No more thinking you can talk ugly at me. I'm beaucoup pissed off about Gage's death and not sure how long I can maintain my composure. When I ask a question, you give an answer. You don't, I'm taking you back, maybe not alive. That compute for you, shit-for-brains? Why's Pam helping you?"

Resigned to it now, Haller said, "She knows I didn't kill Vernon."

"How does she know?"

"Because I didn't do it."

"Her father thinks you did it, the evidence says you did it. I know guys like you. Every tough guy inside is innocent, just like you. They just keep saying it over and over but they're still marking the days off and keeping their ass against the wall so nobody tries to date 'em in the shower. How're you different?"

"I liked Vernon. He treated me good. Tommy's my best friend. Why would I mess that up?"

Jake asking himself the same thing.

Haller saying, "I didn't do it. My fingerprints were on the gun because I fired it to show Pam how to – " Dawning on him now, eyes wide, mouth open. "I handed her the gun."

"And?"

"I don't know." Staring off into the distance.

"Losing interest. So you handed her the weapon and then?"

"Said she didn't know how to fire it and wanted me to show her, so I did. After that she sent me to fix a cattle waterer, one of those automatic ones, that was... shit, it wasn't broken." The guy putting things together in his head.

Jake marveled. Did the man know how stupid he was? The big man made a face pondering it. Jake wondering if it made Haller's head hurt to think.

Jake said, "So, she sent you to fix something that wasn't broken, and someone busted into the house, stole Alex's handgun, walked across the street to kill Vernon and left you dangling. That what you're telling me?"

"Had to be someone did that, didn't it?"

"Ask yourself why break into one house, steal a weapon to kill someone across the street and then leave the weapon with your fingerprints on it, yours Haller, and no one else's. Was Pam wearing gloves when you handed her the weapon? Catching on yet?"

Dawning on the guy now. "Motherfucker," said Fat Boy, almost to himself.

"How used do you feel right now?" Pam pretending to be his friend so he wouldn't talk. Why would Pam kill Vernon? Why would anyone? Vernon wasn't a great guy, but Jake didn't see any reason to put his lights out. Too many people's fortunes tied to Vernon.

"Fucked, ain't I?" said Fat Boy.

"Christmas is going to suck badly unless you talk to me. That's Gage's Ram outside. You drive it?"

"I didn't know whose it was."

"You don't know anything I want to know, do you? Just got miracle here, that's what you're going with?"

"What?"

"You drove Gage's truck. Want to tell me about that?"

"Get me out of here and I'll tell you."

"You kill Gage?"

"No." Shaking his head, looking different now. "I'm

no killer. I'm serious. Gotta believe me. I'll help you."
Anxious. Wanting Jake to believe him.

"You don't know who killed Gage then that's two ho-
micides you're going to take the full weight. Makes you
a repeat offender. The needle in your neck or your new
forever home in an eight by twelve with no toilet lid. They
do have an exercise program where you could lose some
weight, make yourself more appealing to the bull-queers.
You didn't kill Gage but you know something about it.
Better talk."

Defeated now.

"Okay."

Jake waited.

"We took the dog. Stole his truck. All we did."

"Who's 'we'?"

"Me'n Tommy. Supposed to be a joke. Tommy thought
it'd be funny, panic the guy."

"Why would he want him panicked?"

"Alex fired Gage. Tommy made a smart remark to
Gage about getting fired, Gage telling Tommy he could
fix it so Gage could entertain the nurses at ER. Tommy
a little afraid of him, Gage kinda scary, got crazy eyes.
Tommy's a weird guy, too, always wants payback."

"Never heard why Alex let him go. Was Gage not doing his job?"

"You don't know why?"

"You hear me asking, right?"

"Alex thought Gage was fucking Pam. Tommy made
an issue about it. With both of them."

"Both of who?"

"Alex and Gage. Tommy and Alex don't always get
along. Tommy don't like Alex and Pam bossing 'im
around so Tommy started riding Alex about Gage and
Pam doing the ultimate naughty."

Jake thought about that. Explained a lot and confirmed
his thoughts.

"So how did Gage die?"

"I don't know."

"Losing patience with you."

"We took the dog like I said. Took it to the elevator. Just holding on to him. I would never hurt one. I like dogs. Tommy called Gage and told him he had the dog, messing with him, so Gage drove to – "

"He drove? The Dodge outside?" The killers used Gage's Charger not the Ram for the accident.

"Yeah, but that's all we did. We were kidding him about us hiding the dog, Tommy pimping him, telling him we put the dog in the silage pit. Burnell, he got all pissed off, showed up threatening us."

"Who hurt the dog?"

"Tommy did. The dog wouldn't listen to Tommy, snarled at him. Tommy kicked him a couple times, but I made him stop."

Jake let that simmer. "I'll square that with Tommy later. Okay you were at the elevator, then what?"

Haller starting to answer when Jake heard a vehicle pull down the lane to the cabin.

49

Tommy saw Burnell's Ram SUV, wondering why it was here. They had hidden it after Gage threatened them, crazy shit, over a dog. Thinking back now to the night they took Burnell's dog. Shoulda known better. Burnell being a crazy dude. They'd hidden the truck in an old abandoned garage on the south of town and planned to tell him later but then Gage died. They stowed it in the garage at the old Grange house. Somebody found it and was driving it. Only he and Fat Boy knew where it was.

Shit.

Fat boy was here at the cabin. Had to be.

Now what? Not bad. Tell people he found Fatty, turn him in and make the sonuvabitch pay for killing his dad. Hell yes, be a hero, make Kellogg think twice about prosecuting him for rape, which it wasn't, even if it was his own daughter. Wishing he'd never touched her, fucking woman was radioactive.

This could fix things, get him back to some kind of redemption.

He parked back up the drive where it would be hard to see his vehicle. Creep up on his old buddy.

Tommy slid out of the truck, gun tucked in the back of his jeans. Looking forward to the surprised look on Fat Boy's face.

***

Jake noted the shadow and a flash of light flicker through the windows. That's how he saw the vehicle arrive and Tommy Mitchell get out of the car.

"Tommy's here," Jake said, smiling. "This is going to be fun. Well, for me, not for you."

"He'll kill me," said Fat Boy, worried now.

"He's pretty mad at you." Working Fat boy, nodding with a smile when he said it, enjoying himself. "And he does have a gun. Sticking it behind his back now. Tommy, you sneaky boy, you. Wonder why he brought a gun to see you?" He paused, then said, "Oh yeah, now I remember. He may be under the mistaken impression you killed his dad. But you just tell him you're innocent, and it'll all work out."

"You have to protect me."

"I don't know," Jake said, shrugging. "He looks dangerous. Maybe I'll just ease out the back door and see what happens."

"What if he shoots me?"

"I'll arrest him for murder. I can see it now, 'prodigal son returns, apprehends fugitive and his killer'. Sounds pretty good. Always wanted to be a hero."

"You can't do that." Panic in his voice. "You're a cop – " stopping to think about it now like he just realized it.

"Then talk. And do it quick. Here he comes."

"Okay, okay. Look, we took the dog." Coming in a rush of words now. "Burnell showed up with a gun, pissed off. We were just messing with him. When we saw the gun, Steve told – "

"Steve Barb."

"Yeah. Then what?"

"Barb 'fronted Burnell when he showed. They started arguing. Burnell hot and not scared of anything. Willing to take everyone on. Wanted his dog back."

"What were they arguing about?"

"A woman. What else. Hanna whatshername."

"Anyone else there?"

"Barb's buddy, Robby Warner."

"That's it?"

"Yeah."

Thinking about it now. "How mad was Barb about Gage going back to Hanna Stanislaus?"

"A lot. He went after Gage when he showed up. They got into a fight."

"Who won?"

"Burnell was winning until Warner jumped in and they beat him pretty bad. Tommy liked it for a while, but I made them stop."

"Two against one. Sounds like them. Then what?"

Fat Boy swallowed. "Gage didn't look so good. We told Gage the dog was okay, but I don't know if he knew what we were telling him. Gage wouldn't quit. Kept getting back up no matter how bad they beat him. Said he was going to square things with all of us. We got out of there while Barb and Warner held onto him. Tommy and me took the dog and chained him out at Tommy's until we could think what to do. I couldn't stand to see the dog penned up. Tommy wouldn't take care of it wanted me to kill it after we found out Burnell was dead. Couldn't do that, so I cut his chain and told Tommy he broke loose."

"Tommy shoot at me that day I was hunting?"

"No."

"Who?"

"Shit," Haller said. "It was Pam."

"Well, well," Jake said, to himself. He had considered that, but part of him, the part that was a high school kid didn't want to accept it. Harper had been right about that. "You were the other driver?"

"Tommy was passed out drunk, so we took him along. You pissed her off at her dad's place, wanted to scare you. After Pam shot at you, laughing her ass off, we took off in Tommy's truck and left him. Pam's idea was have you think Tommy shot at you. Tommy didn't have any way back to town, so he took your truck. She wanted to kill you; I promise she could've. She can shoot good as anybody I know."

Something else to file away. Pam shot at him, wanting to blame Tommy. She could shoot and was good at it, according to Haller.

"Yet she had you thinking she didn't know how to shoot a handgun. She come on to you or just show you a little?"

Haller put his head down, sheepish.

Jake moved to the window, wondering why Pam would shoot at him, Pam involved in everything. He hadn't seen it. Blind to it. He watched Tommy walk stooped over as if it made him invisible, getting closer. "Almost here."

"Shit," said Fat Boy. "Do something. Tommy's got no sense when he's mad."

"Sit tight," Jake said, putting the SIG in a holster on his hip. He didn't need another shooting. The authorities might not overlook a second one in one week. "I won't let him shoot you."

"How you gonna do that?"

"Magic. Haven't you been watching me?"

***

Tommy excited now. This was going to be so fucking good. He threw open the door, gun drawn.

"Put it away," Jake said.

Tommy wheeled around, his gun at his side. "Shit! Why?"

"Because you don't want to shoot him."

"Maybe I want to shoot you," Tommy said.

Jake moved his jacket away to reveal the SIG Sauer on his hip. "Being stupid doesn't mean you have to get shot."

"I've got mine out, motherfucker."

"Check the safety."

Tommy turned the pistol to look at it and when he looked up Jake had his gun pointed at him.

"See the difference, Tommy? This isn't the movies. Put the gun down."

Tommy struggling with it now. "Maybe I don't care what you do."

"Sure you do." Tommy making him tired. "People pretend they don't, but the reality is everyone wants to continue." Jake raised his weapon higher. "Put it down."

Tommy dropped the handgun to his side, his shoulders sagging. "What about this asshole killed my dad."

"Well, I don't know. Maybe we talk about that, compare stories see where that leads us. After we're through talking, you think he did it you can shoot him. And, what the hell happened to your lip?"

Tommy's hand went to his mouth. "Long story."

"Goddammit, Tommy," said Fat Boy. "Don't shoot me. I didn't do it."

"Shut up," Jake said.

"You're going to let me shoot him?" Tommy said.

"Of course not. Just funning around."

"You think this shit's funny?" said Fat Boy.

"Most things are," Jake said, "you look at it right. And now boys, we're all going to sit down, have a beer, and talk. And don't screw up. Remember, I don't really like either one of you."

50

"So, big deal, I took your truck," Tommy said to Jake. Tommy and Fat Boy were sitting at the long table, the solitaire cards still spread on the table. As Jake promised they both had a beer in front of them, this seems to be a new thing he was doing with bad guys. Refreshments. Jake Morgan, concessionaire to the criminal class. "I was passed out, woke up when I heard shooting. I just wanted the hell outta there. I didn't shoot at you. I did you'd be dead."

"Keep talking tough, Tommy," Jake said. "It confirms everything I think about you. How'd you get this stupid?"

"This fat fuck here," Tommy said, "killed Dad. I'm gonna get you for that, Fatty."

"He didn't kill your dad," Jake said.

That stopped Tommy. "What? How do you know?"

"He had no reason."

"It was Pam," Haller said. "She set me up. Frame job like in the movies. She had me shoot a gun then used it to – "

"Mother fucker," Tommy said, perking up. "Are you fucking kidding me?" You could see him chewing on it. "Damn. Fucking cunt did same thing to me. She's telling I raped her."

This surprised Jake. "What?"

Tommy told them how Pam invited him out to her

place where they had a sexual encounter.

"She bit my lip, clawed my back and I dropped my dick down her like an oil well. I didn't rape her; she asked for it."

"With your smooth delivery and colorful language. How could she resist?"

"Then she called a deputy come out and tell me I might be charged with sexual assault. Rape even. Total bullshit. Sonuvabitch, she screwed me over and wanted me in prison."

"Both of us," Haller said.

"Woman deputy?"

"Yeah, Bailey's her name. Scared shit outta me."

Pam used Bailey rather than calling her father. Consider that.

"Have you been arrested for rape?"

"No. Bailey just said Pam was thinking it over. Hadn't told Doc yet."

Also remarkable. Holding the faux rape over Tommy's head. Statute of limitations was years. By the time it had passed Tommy would either be compliant with Pam's authority or she could damage him with the allegation backed by Deputy Bailey. She already had Alex in her pocket, so Tommy was a logical step. Neutralizing opposition, that is, if she was the person pulled the trigger on Vernon. But why kill him? Did she inherit? Would get that eventually if she stayed hitched to Alex. Was there another reason? Still not sure who killed Gage but Barb and Warner were emerging as leading candidates.

And, what had Vernon been after?

"She set us up, Tommy," said Fat Boy. "Shot at this guy. Bet she has plans to push Alex out of the way and get all the money. She was just here though and bailed me out. Why would she do that? I'd bet – "

Jake interrupted. "It'll go better if you don't talk a lot and try to remember thinking isn't your long suit."

"Yeah, Fatty," Tommy said.

"Eat shit," said Fat Boy. "I didn't kill your Dad."

"So you say."

Like talking to kids.

"Shut up, the both of you." Listening to them made his head hurt. "How old are you guys, anyway?"

Jake putting things together formulating his next step. If he could trust Haller's story, Pam's frame was a good one. No one was going to believe Haller over Pam Mitchell, especially when her father was the investigator. Haller had run making him appear guilty and Pam had paid him well to do so. Haller too thick to see through it.

"You guys know about the planned airfield?"

"What they want me to know," Tommy said. "I get a salary and a profit-sharing percentage. Pam and Dad run everything. Alex ran the fertilizer plant and the elevator. Acts like Alex is more special than Jesus. Since mom died, I get shit on. Me'n Fat Ass here took care of the farm and the cattle."

"Better quit the names, Tommy," Haller said. "Startin' to get mad at you."

"So what? You gonna sit on me, you fucking hippo."

Jake put a hand to his forehead. "How about you save the pre-school spat for the county lock-up? Just answer my questions or I turn you over to Doc and you can take your chances. I'm sure he'll love hearing how his daughter set you boys up. Sound like something you want a shot at?"

They glared at each other for a moment but settled down.

"So," Jake said, to Tommy, "you were your mom's favorite?"

Tommy looking at him with a sour expression. "You a psychiatrist now? She just didn't let Dad shit on me."

"But Alex and Pam ran things."

Tommy shrugged. "Mom thought Dad favored Alex. Heard her say it."

"Either of you know a man named Franklin Yoder?"

Shaking their heads now, like BBs rattling in a tin can.

"So, we're back at the elevator, Barb and Warner ganging up on Gage with you two watching. I should pistol-whip both of you for that." Feeling heat rising behind his neck. "Or just shoot you and let Doc sort things out. A fugitive murderer and the guy raped his daughter. Both appeal to me but doesn't get things done. Who killed Gage?"

"Had to be Barb and Warner," Tommy said.

Jake believing them but needed more.

"Was this fight close around the silage pit in the elevator?"

"Yeah," Tommy said. "Yeah, it was. How you know that?"

"And you two left with Travis and Gage's Ram?"

"Who's Travis?" asked Tommy.

"The dog, stupid," Jake said, with a little heat. "You didn't even know his name; just like to beat up animals? So you left and Gage was still with Warner and Barb. Didn't you make a connection when Gage ended up dead?"

"Told us he had an accident," Tommy said.

"Who told you?"

"Well," Haller said, "Vernon."

Tommy nodded. "Yeah."

"Yet you didn't say anything about the fight?"

"Dad said it would look bad we said anything, that it was an accident and we'd be going to jail as accessories."

Jake thought about it. The pair of them was certainly stupid enough not to connect the dots. Vernon covered for Steve Barb. Vernon wanted Gage dead.

"We had his dog and his truck. I didn't have nothing against Gage 'cept he shot his mouth off at me. We took the truck when we grabbed his dog. Ok, probably not smart, looking back." Tommy looked at the bottle of Jim Beam, Jake nodded and Tommy took a good tug on the whiskey, wiped his mouth and said, "When I heard about him dying, was afraid they'd blame us, you can see that, right, so we hid the truck in the old Grange building. We didn't want to take it back to his place, well, your place, and get caught with it. Stupid here was supposed to take care of the dog but he pussy'd out."

"I ain't killin' no dog."

"You know, Noah," Jake said, using Haller's first name

to establish some closeness, a device he'd learned watching some of the veteran investigators. 'Their last name shows them they're nobody to you, their first name makes them your buddy'. Jake continued, saying, "Letting Travis go is a huge plus in your favor. Travis is all right now thanks to you. It convinces me you did not kill Vernon."

Haller gave Tommy a self-righteous smile.

"As for you, Tommy," Jake said. "Hurting that dog? When this is done, I'm going to put you on the other end of that."

"That dog tried to bite me."

"I can't understand why you're not a favorite with animals."

"Okay, I shouldn't have done that. So, what now?"

Flipping Fat Boy to Doc could result in Pam's perfect frame working. There was no way Doc objectively investigates his daughter. Doc had motivation to burn both Haller and Tommy once Pam charged Tommy with sexual assault.

Pam was smart. Always two steps ahead of everyone, including Jake. Doc was closely aligned with Vernon Mitchell. That was another factor. How much did Doc know about Franklin Yoder's disappearance?

Jake could not turn the dickheads over to Doc. They'd be railroaded into prison sentences and no matter the satisfaction such an outcome would afford Jake, he couldn't allow that. Much as they deserved to be hung out to dry, especially Tommy, Jake knew he would need to take steps to protect these two mental defectives.

What a world.

"I hate myself for what I'm going to do."

"What?"

"I'm going to help you both, keep you out of prison. Somehow get you out of this thing. But I need things from you," Jake said.

"What's that?" asked Tommy.

"Give me your word you and Haller won't come out of hiding until you hear from me, and I need a key to your Dad's place. Stay here and don't call anyone. No one.

Promise me. Otherwise, I'm giving you to Doc and you roll the dice."

"What choice do we have?" Tommy said, sour expression on his face.

Jake laughed. "Absolutely none."

51

Jake used Tommy's cell phone and touched base with Lawyer Jessup, regarding the fugitive Haller, telling the attorney what he had learned from Tommy and Fat Boy.

"I bring in Haller," Jake said, "No way he gets a fair shake. Pam Mitchell framed him; you know what Kellogg will do with that."

It was quiet on Jessup's end for a long moment, Jake thinking the connection had been severed when Jessup said, "It's byzantine. You can't harbor a fugitive. You'll have to return him, Jake. Call Kellogg and have him pick up Haller."

"No. I'm afraid Haller wouldn't make it back to Paradise alive."

"What are you telling me?"

"I can easily imagine a scenario where Haller is killed attempting to escape."

"That seems implausible and even cynical."

"No, it's plausible and likely."

"You obviously don't trust Kellogg. You think he's capable of such a thing?"

"His daughter's involved. I don't trust Haller to keep his mouth shut. We're talking about a guy whose head is a gumball machine. Whatever's in his tiny brain rolls right down to his mouth and out without consideration of consequence."

"I can petition for a change of venue, but all of this is going to be complicated by his escape from lawful detention. Bring him in, Jake."

Jake knew the attorney was right. But he wasn't ready to do that yet. "Give me twenty-four hours and I'll bring them in."

Jessup wasn't happy about it but, "I don't know what else I can do if you won't accept my advice. I don't know where they are so, grudgingly, you have twenty-four hours."

Jake had one more thing to do before bringing in Haller. He needed to ascertain if Haller and Tommy were telling the truth. Someone was lying and it was highly possible it was the pair in front of him.

"You're going to give us up?" said Fat Boy Haller.

"Should, but not now. Relax and do what I say and maybe you stay out of prison, which is where Kellogg will put you, have no illusions about that. You boys sit tight and get along."

"Why can't we just go to town and tell what really happened. That we was framed?"

Shaking his head, Jake said, "You couldn't possibly be as thick as you seem."

"You're no smarter than me."

"I guess maybe you are, after all," Jake said, chuckling to himself. "You tell Doc anything you told me, and he'll smoke you and your little playmate here. It's his daughter. God, why do I have to explain this to you? You'd need to accept I'm your only way out of this."

"As for you, Tommy, I think you had the right idea to come here to lay low, but Pam may be out to check on Fatty. She's been here and who knows when she'll be back again."

"She won't be back for a while," Haller said. "She gave me enough money and food to last a couple weeks."

"Both of you need to stay as far away from her as possible until this thing is resolved. If she does show, Tommy, you stay hid."

"I want nothing to do with her." Tommy, smarter than

Haller, was considering things. "You think she killed Dad?"

"I don't know. Maybe. There's a lot I don't understand yet."

"I don't know if I like this."

"I'm trying to imagine a scenario where I give a damn what you think or what you like. You want to confess to Doc I give you leave. I'd as soon watch you tied down on the interstate during rush hour as help you, but my fantasies often go unrealized."

"What?" Haller said, confused.

Jake nodded. "You seem intent on making my point regarding your intellect."

"What?"

"Exactly. Did you even graduate from high school?"

"You're so fucking smart," Haller said.

"Third in my class. You can look it up."

52

Jake sat in Buddy Johnson's Spartan office – government surplus metal desk, worn vinyl upholstered swivel chair, Jake telling Cal about his talks with Haller and Tommy leaving Pam out of the equation for the moment. Jake didn't want anyone see him in Cal's office and Buddy was out on patrol. Also telling Cal what he learned talking to Vienna Dalrymple and Christine McKee excluding the mystery couple who descriptions fit Gage and Pam and also excluding his suspicions about the parentage of McKee.

Cal lit a cigarette and sat back in his chair. "You really need to turn Haller over to Kellogg."

"Not yet."

"Not your decision, Jake, your evidence is circumstantial and your witnesses are a couple of part-brains who'll piss down their legs at a hearing. And you don't know they won't choose to ignore your warning and wander back into town telling everyone what you've done. They do that'll come back on you. Turn 'em in and get clear. You're going to get your tail twisted trusting those guys. Kellogg is never going to pin this on his daughter and we have no standing to impeach his authority. Same problem we've had since the beginning."

"But there is probable cause to investigate Gage's assault at the grain elevator leading to his homicide. That's where it started. Not murder but murderous assault. That could lead to a manslaughter charge. I'm not letting go of this, Cal. Barb and Warner are dirt bags. Doc only changed Gage's vehicular accident finding to a killing when I looked into things so he threw Terry Bill in jail as a scapegoat. Haller skips and I bring him back and he's cut loose again or worse."

"Maybe Barb killed Gage in a jealous rage and it has nothing to do with the Mitchells."

"Possible. He had a motive, but I believe Gage had something they didn't want known. More to the point, something Vernon covered it up."

"Vernon's dead."

Jake nodded and said, "For a reason though. I think Haller is being set up to take the fall."

"Who paid Haller's bail, which was kept secret, not to mention it stinks he was released. Doc has to know this looks bad with an election coming up."

"I made an arrangement with the Bail Bondsman." Jake told him about the deal. "I bring in Fat Boy and he gives me the name of the person fronting the money."

"Fritz Delmar?" Cal whistled lowly, shaking his head. "He's the only guy I know who'd go along with such a deal. You and that pirate make quite a pair. He's your match in some ways."

"You say that like it's a bad thing. I already figured out it was Pam Mitchell. That was affirmed when I saw her leaving the lake cabin and Haller said she was helping him."

"Information just dribbles out from you, doesn't it?" But Cal smiled. "So Pam bailed out Haller because you think she framed him. It's a good one, I'll admit, if it's true. By the way, had to let your buddies, Warner and Barb go. They made bail."

"Learn anything from them?"

"Not much."

"Nothing on Tommy being charged with rape?"

"Nope."

"Pam's holding that in reserve to keep Tommy in line."

"Word around the campfire says Doc is furious at Tommy and wants to talk to him. Apparently, his deputy, Bailey, spilled the beans. No charges yet, without Pam's filing, but hate to be Tommy when Doc gets his hands on him. Like me, Doc's getting old, but he's got a lot of hard bark on him. He survived Vietnam as a medic and he's no coward. Something you need to keep in mind."

"Didn't Doc work with Gage's Dad when Mister Burnell was sheriff?"

"That's right. Doc was his deputy."

Thinking about that now. Something there, right at the back of his mind but Jake couldn't bring it forth at the moment. Decades of secrets, molding and souring with time.

"Give me one of those cigarettes," Jake said.

"Not while you're seeing my daughter. I don't want her smelling like an ash tray. Already smell your cologne when I'm around her." He raised an eyebrow.

"Don't be one of those dad's, Cal," Jake said, smiling as he said it. "Speaking of which, is it possible Doc has a sense of the way a real investigation of Vernon and Gage's murders might be headed?"

"Could be. Hate to think it. Doc used to be a square shooter but anymore with his daughter marrying into the Carrington family – "

"Who?"

"Dynasty. TV series. You don't remember...hell, you were a little kid and you're dull to boot." Winking. "Doc and Vernon got to be best buddies after the marriage. Pam got even tighter running Mitchell's empire though of late I'm noticing some cooling between her and Vernon which may have something to do with you and some unpleasant times gone by. Vernon favored Alex and I'd guess he wouldn't like you raiding the henhouse. They are 'times gone by' right?"

"Harper and I have already hashed that out if that's your concern."

"Good."

Jake pondered what to say next, deciding. Might as

well say it. He couldn't trust Cal Bannister, he couldn't trust anyone. "Somewhere out on the old Yoder place or near my place are the remains of Franklin and Caroline Yoder. I think Vernon killed them, disposed of the bodies and took over the Yoder farm."

Cal leaned forward and put a hand on his desk. "Hell of thing to come up with. I'll allow you haven't been twiddling your thumbs." Cal looked at his desk then back at Jake. "I suspected such a thing for some time. Gage's Father thought the same, couldn't find a handle. No corpus delicti. There was no evidence of a crime, people who vanished. Sheriff Burnell retired about the time you and Gage started high school and Doc took over." Cal rubbed his jaw and chin with his hand, let out a breath. Shaking his head now, Cal said, "What you're saying could be true, but Vernon's dead so how does the information help us? Can't prosecute Vernon anymore. Seems an ice-cold case with the murderer dead."

"There's one person who knows everything."

"And?"

"That's why Vernon's dead."

"Revenge?"

"No. Anger, maybe inheritance."

"Alex killed his father?"

Jake said nothing, waiting on Cal.

"You're not saying it was – ". Cal said. "Yes, you are. Pam Mitchell? The cigarette in Cal's mouth nearly fell out of his mouth. He caught it in time. "What're you telling me? Why would she do that?"

"I don't know." Not telling Cal what he had in mind.

"Don't hand me that gut feeling horseshit. We're not going to operate like that. This is real life."

"Has to be her. Think about it." Jake repeated the incident as Fat Boy Haller had related it to him.

Cal stubbed out his cigarette, leaned back in his chair, hands laced together over his heart. "It's almost perfect. The perfect crime committed in full view with the perfect fall guy. We can't go after her because of Doc and his jurisdiction over the case. Vernon's dead so he has nothing to say about it. We need, or you need, to find more evidence she's involved and pulled the trigger, and finding people who will testify against her is going to be tough. She neutralized Tommy by holding a rape charge over his head. She's got a lot of plates spinning. Always was smart."

"She has Alex in check also."

"You sure?" Cal said. "Word around is that Alex has a girl on the side."

"Shari Langston."

"What don't you know? Does Buddy know this?" Jake nodded. Cal saying now, "Why do you think Alex is under Pam's thumb?"

"Alex told me."

Cal removed laced fingers from his chest and moved them to the back of his head. He smiled a half-smile. "Alex Mitchell, who hates you, told you this. You get around, don't you? I'm beginning to appreciate you're a hell of an investigator. You're sneaky about it. Most see you as a hothead."

Jake shrugged. "Can't control what people think. You have Warner and Barb assaulting me. You have Tommy and Fat Boy witnessing Gage's assault in the grain elevator by the same pair. Speaks to motivation."

"How to connect the dots? Tommy afraid to testify. Pam has him by the 'nads. You yourself said there will be no fingerprints in Burnell's vehicle."

"The absence of fingerprints in a five-year-old vehicle demonstrates cover-up as we form our hypothesis. Besides, they don't know whether we have fingerprints or not. Bring Barb and Warner back in, threaten 'em, scare 'em. Tell them you sent out the fingerprints and none of them are Gage's."

"I just cut them loose."

"Different charge. Man one. They're dirty whether they killed Gage or not."

"How am I going to do that? I don't have witnesses."

"You do, Tommy and Haller."

"Again, sketchy. Then there's Doc who will holler

when he learns we're conducting a parallel investigation."

"Doesn't like us anyway."

"There's another problem."

"What's that?"

"I ever tell you the prosecuting attorney is Pam Mitchell's cousin."

"Who?"

"Darcy Hillman. She was the daughter of Geraldine Mitchell's sister."

"I remember her from school." Darcy and Pam were close in high school. "Have they got a lock on this?"

"No. Darcy's a fairly straight shooter. Maybe we get Barb and Warner on the assault charge for beating Gage but I don't see how we get to Pam Mitchell."

Jake thought about it. "Haller told me Pam sent him away from the house after getting Haller to put his fingerprints on the weapon that killed Vernon."

Cal following Jake's reasoning. "And all Pam has to do is provide Haller's alibi and Haller will owe her his freedom. She already provided his bail. She covered her tracks. We do not have access to the scene of the homicide, and she is confident Daddy won't pursue her. I'd say we can forget pinning Vernon's killing on her."

"No, I won't do that. She's been too ruthless. She's caused too much carnage. You with me on prosecuting Barb and Warner?" Jake said.

Cal lit another cigarette, took his time inhaling the first drag, and blew a cloud of blue smoke, before saying. "Yeah. I don't like them getting away with assault and a possible homicide in my town. Second, I don't like what's been going on here for the past few years. Something's wrong, I've felt it; could do nothing about it until you kicked in a rotted wall and now we can see what's on the other side."

"Maybe we can push this past the election for sheriff and get a better shot. Can Buddy beat him?"

"Not unless something happens between now and the election to change things," Cal said, lifting his chin. "Kellogg's got connections and backing."

"Let's see if we can change things. I think and will soon know if Alex Mitchell has an older sister."

"He doesn't have—" Cal stopped, giving up. "Are you kidding? Who would that be?"

"Franklin and Caroline Yoder's daughter, Christine."

Cal exhaled a breath letting it flutter through his lips. "Jake, if you're right this is a hell of a thing. If you're wrong, they'll flush us both right down the pipes and piss on us while we're down there."

Jake nodded. "Yep."

"Promise me you won't do anything extra-legal."

Jake said nothing. Better that Cal didn't know what Jake's next move was going to be.

"Just gonna sit there and not promise."

"Plausible deniability."

"Shit," Cal said. "Your mind must run one hundred MPH."

Cal was right about one thing. They were both flushed if Jake was wrong.

53

Jake parked the Lincoln behind the enormous hangar out-building at Vernon Mitchell's estate. No one would see it. He had made sure Pam and Alex, who lived across the road, were in town before driving out.

Jake walked past the swimming pool and across the deck to the rear of the house. Tommy had given Jake a key to the house, so Jake walked around the rear of the place to the front door, careful to watch and listen for approaching vehicles.

There was a sliver of tattered yellow tape on the front door where the police line had been removed by the sheriff's department. Kellogg, satisfied Haller was the killer felt no need to continue his investigation. "Premature foreclosure, Doc," Jake said, to himself as he took Tommy's key from his pocket.

Jake thinking he was on solid ground, legally. He had no warrant but an heir to the home had willingly given him a key and permission to enter. Tommy was finally good for something.

Jake wearing leather driving gloves. He brought along a large tape measure and a laser pointer. He would use his cell phone for photos as Kellogg would not make available crime scene photographs. Wondering how much of the crime scene had been contaminated or scrubbed. Kellogg had already made his decision so Jake held little hope he would find anything conclusive, but things were often overlooked in an investigation or in this case, purposely disregarded.

Jake entered, careful not to disturb anything, and took photos of the hardwood floor. The hardwood floor showed a darker square shadow where an area rug had been removed. A brown stain showed on the boards where Vernon Mitchell bled out his life.

Jake knew Vernon had been shot in the head, the killing shot, and twice in the chest. Very carefully, Jake examined the wall and found what he was looking for. There was damage to the wall behind a large drape. It lined up where the victim had been standing. A chunk of drywall lightly spattered with blood speckle. He knew it had been a nine-millimeter shell. The techs dug the bullet out of the wall for forensic examination, so the bullet hole had been altered slightly.

Jake pulled back the curtain and looked back to the faded blood stain on the hardwood floor. The bullet lodged at a point approximately two feet above Jake's head. Jake took out a pocket laser and raised it above his head and lit a path back over the top of the blood spatter. Knowing Vernon's height, Jake made a calculated guess at the point where the bullet had passed through Vernon's head and entered the wall.

The angle suggested the first shot had been at Vernon's head or face, who had been standing when shot.

The angle also made it implausible for Fat Boy Haller to have been the shooter. Haller was 6-4 and unless he'd shot from the hip, he could not be the shooter. A head shot from a projectile exploded from the hip was possible but unlikely. Killers did not take chances shooting from the hip for a head shot. He would raise, aim and fire straight out down his sight path along his arm. Additionally, the bullet trajectory would be at a lower angle as Haller was taller than Vernon.

The shooter was shorter than Haller. Much shorter, suggesting a below average sized man or an average sized woman.

Haller was telling the truth.

54

Jake called Trooper Ridley before driving to Troop A HQ where he submitted Christine McKee's hair follicle sample to the highway patrol's lab technicians via Trooper Fred Ridley. His boss, Lt. Browne, gave the green light to the submission, even fast-tracking it.

Jake filled Ridley in on what he had learned at Vernon's home.

"You got the son to give you a key? How?"

"Charm."

"You'd have to borrow it," said Ridley. "Tell me about it."

Jake told him of his talk with Tommy and Haller.

"You realize that could be construed as harboring a fugitive."

"I don't know what you're talking about and I don't know where they are."

Ridley placed his hands on a hip and his service weapon. "You didn't tell me, if it comes up."

"What comes up?" Jake said, opening his arms in a 'what're-you-talkin'-about' gesture.

"Keep it that way. Don't string this out much longer. Sam won't like this. I'll give you a day then I will beat it out of you."

"Sam Browne's his name?" Jake said to Ridley at the mention of Lt. Browne's first name. "Like the belt you guys wear over your chest?"

"He's heard all the jokes," said Ridley. "He has a good relationship with the techs, and he trusts me, so they'll do a hurry-up on this. He's a hell of a guy so try to restrain your impulse for being cute and withholding information."

"I can do that."

"Can you?" said Ridley, looking over the top of his sunglasses.

***

Barb and Warner balked at providing information whereupon Cal officially charged the pair for "assault and battery with intent to commit mayhem" in the attack on Gage Burnell.

Cal kept Jake out of the proceedings, including the interview of Barb and Haller. "Kellogg will holler as it is. He'll holler louder if you conduct the interviews. And, it'll poison testimony and give their attorney grounds to question my investigation."

Cal was right on both counts.

"What the hell is going on, Cal," said an irate Sheriff Kellogg, showing at Paradise PD. "I already have Pennell in the lock-up for this and an unknown co-conspirator which eventually I will uncover."

"Well, that's damn good police work," Cal said, unmoved. "I'm going after Barb and Warner for assault and perhaps wrongful death charges."

"What do you hope to gain from that?"

"Find out what happened."

"You've been listening to Morgan. Damn it, Cal, this looks bad and you're pissing me off."

"I don't want to do that, Doc," Cal said, rolling an unlit cigarette in his fingers. "I just want to take care of things here in my town. I can't allow people to assault citizens and not investigate. Why, that'd look like I was protecting someone." Cal smiled and nodded at Kellogg and the implication was not lost on the sheriff.

Kellogg left.

"Doc's unhappy with me," Cal said when he told Jake afterwards.

"Join the club."

***

That afternoon Charles Langley of Langley, Pope and Hardy, showed up demanding the release of Barb and Warner. Langley, sharp in a dark suit, French cuffs, understated cufflinks, dove grey tie, manicured fingernails and just the right touch of patrician confidence.

Langley shook hands with Cal Bannister but did not extend the same courtesy to Jake. Subtle intimidation. Played this game before, thought Jake.

"Mister Morgan," said Langley, "is it true that you were involved in an altercation with Noah Haller and Thomas Mitchell?"

"Yes."

"What precipitated your attack?"

Jake sat quietly. Several moments passed. Langley said, "I will amend that. What precipitated the altercation between you and Mister Mitchell and Mister Haller?"

"Bad manners and false courage," Jake said.

"And what did you do then?"

"I subdued them."

Cal covered a smile with a hand.

"Did you receive any injuries?"

"A slight jarring of my dignity."

Langley gave Jake a lingering look letting him know he was not amused by Jake's answer. Jake smiled back at him. Langley doing his best to intimidate.

"If they initiated the altercation and there were two against one, most would conclude you would've sustained injury. Why were you unscathed?"

"They're not very good at it."

"Good at what?"

"Fighting."

"And you are."

Jake said nothing, brushing lint off the sleeve of his jacket.

"Do you have animus towards Noah Haller?"

"I don't like him, but I don't think about him much."

"And yet, these two men, the same men attacked you are now your witnesses against my clients."

"Not mine," Jake said, nodding in Cal's direction. "His."

"Where are these witnesses?"

"They're under protection. I will produce them soon."

"When?"

"Soon."

"You're a Texas Ranger," said Langley. "Why're you involved?"

"I hired him on as an auxiliary investigator," Cal said. "He has expertise that no one on my staff has."

"Yes," said Langley, smiling wolfishly. "I looked into your background, Mister Morgan. Seems you're on administrative suspension."

"Was. Not now."

It set Langley back but recovering, Langley said, "Well, it has been interesting talking to you men."

"An honor for me," Jake said.

Langley started to say something, instead he smiled and said, "I will arrange bail for my clients."

"Who hired you?"

Langley smiled at Jake and said, "Have a nice evening, gentlemen." And left.

Cal saying, "You don't know who Langley is, do you?"

"No."

"No way Barb and Warner can afford him."

"To me that means we're right about who is backing them."

"Seem to be. And Jake, like I said, Langley's bad medicine. He didn't care for your conversation."

"His problem."

"You don't give an inch, do you?" Cal said.

"Pam hired them," Jake said.

"Or Alex?"

Jake hadn't considered that, but Cal could be right. That could either be an innocent thing or one more damned variable.

55

"Told you," Buddy said.

Buddy Johnson lit a large cigar and offered one to Jake, who accepted it. They were in Hank's, along with Leo the Lion, the three friends seated at a round table near the back of the place, a pitcher of beer emblazoned with a Heineken logo on the table. Jake sharing with them part of what had transpired over the past week. Buddy knew most of it. Jake even shared the late-night visit from Pam Mitchell which revelation the two men were railing on him about.

"Told me what?" Jake said.

"You can't stomp around breaking windows on cars, break into private businesses to impress your girlfriend and conduct an investigation in an un-cop like manner."

"Oh that." Jake admitted Buddy was right. "Yeah, that's right. Still worked."

"So," said Leo the Lion, dressed in coaching clothes. "You did diddle Pam Kellogg even as I predicted."

"You didn't predict it."

"Did I not say she had designs on you, and some things never change?"

"If it helps you."

"Then you're admitting I was right and as a consequence admitting you were wrong."

Jake shrugged. "Okay."

"We need to document this occasion. On this date Jake Morgan, clumsy wood-hippy, has confessed to being wrong for the first time in his life."

Jake frowned. "Not the first time."

"Were you wrong not to attend your father's funeral?" asked Leo.

Jake looked at him. "Is this going to end at some point?"

"You said, 'later' and now it's later. I'm wanting to understand not impose."

"Jake," Buddy said. "We're your friends. Your brothers. Enough is enough. We know your troubles with your dad and we're with you, you know that in spite of your being, you know, a jackass at times."

Jake looked down at his beer, untouched. "It was a mistake. I should've been here."

It was quiet between the trio for a long moment.

"I understand it," Leo said.

"Same here," Buddy said.

"Doesn't make it right," Jake said.

"No," Leo said. "It does not. But you can go forward from here."

"Sure," Jake said, nodding. "You know, Leo, sometimes and only on rare occasions you and Buddy Bear here are actually helpful in your own pathetic style."

"You must study the past if you would define the future," Leo said.

"Is that a Leo-ism?" asked Buddy.

"Confucius," Jake said.

"Confucius anticipated I would say it," Leo said.

"Drink more," Jake said. "Pontificate less."

The front door of Hank's burst open and in walked Alex Mitchell.

"Oh boy," Leo said. "Watch your topknot, Jake."

Alex stomped along the hardwood floor straight at their table.

"You son of a bitch," Alex said, jabbing his finger at Jake. "You piece of shit."

Jake said nothing.

"Get up," Alex said, yelling it.

"No."

"You're a fucking coward."

"That's not why," Jake said

Alex clenched and unclenched his fists, breathing in fits before he turned and left.

The three men were quiet a moment.

"Well," Jake said. "Guess she told him."

"Those Mitchells," Leo said. "It's like as kids they wanted to grow up to be chancre sores. Never seen anyone as prone to outbursts. Jake, you've been stomping a mud hole in the Mitchell Empire," Leo said. "How about Harper? She know about Pam?"

Jake nodded, slowly turning his beer glass on the cardboard coaster. "I was honest with her about Pam and we're working it out but, who knows?"

"Don't under-sell her," Buddy said. "Harper's sharp, thinks for herself. You'll be all right."

"I want to talk to Bailey one more time."

"All right," Buddy said, but she may not want to talk to you."

"I'm amazed anyone talks to you," Leo said.

"You could be onto something," Jake said.

***

Buddy called Deputy Bailey, trading on his friendship with her again but concealing the fact that Jake Morgan would be part of the meeting. Buddy asked Bailey to meet him in her sheriff's unit, Buddy and Jake in Buddy's PPD car. As she pulled up and stopped, she saw Jake and her mouth fell open.

"What's he doing here?" she said.

"Come on, Sharon. This is important."

"Already told what I know about the accident."

"This is a different thing."

Bailey looked up at her rearview mirror then out her passenger window. "I've done enough."

"I want to know about a problem between Tommy

Mitchell and Pam Mitchell," Jake said.

Her eyes evasive, searching for an escape route. "I don't know if that's –"

"Already talked to Tommy and got his side."

"When? Doc can't find him. And if you talked to him why ask me?"

"I want the truth."

Bailey visibly paled. "I can't help you."

"Sharon," Buddy said. "Have to trust me on this one. You're a good deputy and want to do what's right. This is important."

Bailey pursed her mouth before saying, "Okay. Not here, though."

She told them to meet her at the Border Café, a restaurant catering to truckers on Highway 27 sitting across two counties – Paradise and Truman. There were several gas pump-islands, some of them oversized and reserved for sixteen-wheelers, smell of diesel fuel, dusty steel and warm rubber. Inside were items of various practical use along with Tee-shirts and baseball caps emblazoned with slogans such as: 'Wake up, kiss ass, repeat' or "Retired: Gimme my F'ing discount'. The place bustled with noise and activity. They met Deputy Bailey in a booth and sat.

Bailey looked around as if wolves were about to leap out at her from under the seats.

"What do you want to know?" said Bailey. She twisted the watch on her wrist. "I don't have much time."

"Did Tommy sexually assault Pam?" Jake said. "Or is it possible she set him up?"

"Set him up? How?"

"What did Pam tell you?"

"That Tommy broke into her house, there were scratches on the door, and he forced himself on her. She tried to fight him off, but he was too strong. Her dress was torn, she showed me the semen stain on the dress. He had a swollen lip when I saw him."

Jake thought about that. "Why would Tommy need to break into his brother's house?"

She shrugged. "Maybe she slammed the door shut on

him when she saw him coming."

"He's been in that house hundreds of time. Why shut him out now? Why would he decide at this point with his father killed to go have a jump with his brother's wife?"

A restaurant server, a young male, asked for their order. They ordered coffee. Buddy ordered a slice of cherry pie to go with his coffee. "Keep my strength up."

When the server left, Jake said, "Go through the entire scenario as Pam related it to you and what you observed as a law enforcement officer."

Bailey telling how Pam said bring a rape kit because she had been sexually assaulted and not to tell her father, Doc Kellogg. Bailey went to the home where she met a distraught Pam who described the scene of the attack, including the broken door and her torn dress.

"Did you administer the rape test?"

Bailey nodded.

"Does Doc have that evidence?"

Uncomfortable now. "Yes, he does."

"But Doc hasn't acted on it."

"No."

A father had access to evidence his daughter was raped but hadn't acted on it. Tommy damned well better stay hid.

"What was Tommy's reaction when you confronted him?"

"He was frightened and panicked. He denied it, said she invited him to her home for sex, even giving him bourbon and cocaine."

Pam had access to cocaine. Her father had the rape evidence. Things becoming dangerous. Dangerous for everyone. Jake was running out of time. He had to report to Texas within the next 36 hours.

"Did he seem to be telling the truth?" asked Jake.

"How would anyone know that?"

"You watch them. They have 'tells'. You're a cop how long?"

"Three years."

"Over that time have you had notions about whether

people were telling you the truth or not?"

"Of course."

"So," Jake said. "The problem in this situation is you're dealing with two manipulative people; well Pam's manipulative and Tommy is just a spoiled shithead. When Tommy denied it, did his denials seem plausible?"

"You know, his reaction wasn't what I expected. He didn't try to act like it was no big deal. Told me she, Pam, asked him to treat her rough. Tear her dress. Said she bit his lips and clawed his back. Showed me the scratch marks."

"Did she have any marks on her?"

Bailey shaking her head, perplexed now. "No. No, she didn't. Just the torn dress."

"Where did the rape take place?"

"In her bedroom."

"He carry her in there? That was Pam's story? And you weren't supposed to say anything to Doc. But you did tell him, didn't you?"

"Yes."

"Why?"

"Afraid to hold back."

"You were concerned about Doc's reaction if he found out about it and you didn't tell him?"

"You bet."

"So, you were more afraid of Doc than Pam?"

"That's a good question. I need the job. Doc can be well, vindictive. But, Pam." She stopped.

"Well?" Jake said.

"You ever meet someone looks at you, convinced they can just reach out and take a dump on your life? Someone so sure they're above everything and everybody? It's unsettling. Well, that's Pam Mitchell, and yes, she scares me."

The server returned with their order, setting down the coffee and Buddy's pie. Jake trying to imagine Tommy over-powering Pam and forcing her into the bedroom risking his brother showing up and catching him. But maybe that's what Pam hoped. When it didn't happen, she called Bailey. Possible.

"How's Doc taking it? Is he angry?"

"Boiling."

"Why hasn't he gone after Tommy?"

"I think...well, Pam talked him out of it."

"Doc's a father and therefore not restraint friendly. He'll go after Tommy at some point. He made any threats against Tommy?"

Bailey looked at Buddy and said, "This is too much to ask, Buddy. I'm going to leave. I shouldn't have told you anything, especially about Sheriff Kellogg. I'm sorry but that's all you get. It's bad enough people seeing me talking to you when you're running against him. I'll deny telling you any of this. I have a kid to look out for and I need this job. Don't ask for more."

"I win," Buddy said. "You'll have a job."

"And if you don't?" She stood and left without touching her coffee.

"What do you think?" asked Buddy, watching her leave.

"Everyone's afraid of Pam Mitchell."

"But, you're not?"

"Wary of her. I'm not stupid. I'm interested in your thoughts, Buddy. You know Bailey, worked with her, she trusts you. What do you make of what she told us?"

"Bailey's a good officer. She's smart, smart enough to know where her best interests lie. I don't see her as career law enforcement; doesn't have the temperament, too nice, but she has decent instincts about people. Afraid of Doc because he can terminate her employment. She's afraid to buck Pam because of the first thing, and also because of her, what is it? 'Female intuition' about Pam, which assessment you've had some experience with."

"From what she told us, and I have shared with you, is Tommy telling the truth or did he rape Pam?"

"The day Tommy broke into Harper's house, when I got there he was just standing there in the room. He wasn't after her at that moment. They kind of pushed and shoved around but Tommy wasn't violent with her, just drunk and wanted to see if she'd give him some. Sorry about the phrasing."

Jake nodded.

Buddy continued. "Tommy didn't rough her up, but he did grab Harper. He was more worked up about you being there than he was at Harper for calling me. Those Mitchell boys are possessive of their women, or they're pussy-whipped and can't let go. You know Pam, she slipped into your bed real handy, didn't she? If she had a thing with Gage, that tells us a lot. I don't like Tommy; he's an asshole, but he gets plenty of trim around, him and Alex both, yet both are intimidated and manipulated by Pam and do little about it, unless Tommy did rape her which we have to consider. Pam is a tough, smart woman and has power in this community. She uses her sex appeal like a weapon and holds mortgages and deals the cards in the Mitchell businesses. People are truly concerned about such things. Alex doesn't blame Pam for jumping your bones; Alex blames you."

"And maybe he blamed Gage and had reason to kill Gage."

"Pam has a lot going on but seems unconcerned. Confident she can walk past this. You don't back away much from such things and I don't know if you have the ability to watch out for yourself. The irresistible poontang meets the immovable asshole. You and Pam, huh? Man, you come back to town and it's just like the old days. You and Gage stirring things up."

"How's that?"

"Gage always down for fun, not considering consequences and you always ready to take things on, even if it not smart. You never had an 'off' button, boy."

"People change."

"And you think you've progressed? Man, that's funny shit right there."

56

Harper was going to need a heads-up, thought Jake.

"The stuff with Pam on that night may come out and be talked about around town," Jake said, sitting at the dining room table, looking at Harper, seated to his right. "I'm sorry."

"Jake," said Harper. "I'm a divorcee who was married to the biggest jerk in the county. You told me all about her and it doesn't matter. It only matters how we react to it."

"People will say it happened after I met you."

"Let 'em talk. My mother ran off with the Methodist preacher when I was ten. Haven't seen her since. I got through it."

"Sorry about that. Hurt, didn't it?"

"Yes. A lot. Just like you've been hurting about your dad. I had my father to get me through it. You had no one and kept it bottled up inside like you do most things. Your mother died and you and your father were left alone in close proximity to each other, each bearing the loss, stoically, and I'll bet neither of you talking about it."

"Alfred was—"

Harper held up a hand.

Jake amended his words. "Dad was drinking heavily. I didn't like the way he was."

"You ever think he was in pain about his life, maybe about the loss of the woman he loved, watching her die a little bit at a time? We all have a life and we're the only ones who know everything about ourselves. Everyone holds things back. You don't know what was going through his head and heart, what dramas he had sustained he couldn't or wouldn't talk about. If Alfred was like you then he held things inside just like you."

"I do that?"

She wrinkled her nose and laughed. "Oh, Jake. I don't know anyone like you."

"That a good thing?"

"We'll see."

***

Jake left to check with Cal about the progress of the case against Barb and Warner before bringing in Haller.

Cal wasn't confident. "The prosecutor is hesitant to take this on. She won't proceed until she talks to Haller and Tommy. Barb and Warner are out on bail and walking around. Doc is already primed to fry Terry Bill Pennell and some mystery 'big man' with Pennell for this and Haller for Vernon."

"Kellogg coming up with a phantom co-conspirator to help Pennell makes me think Doc Kellogg is blocking us. Convenient he quickly swallowed that bit of information in order to hold Pennell. You find it odd Kellogg is not out beating the bushes for Haller?"

"In the immortal words of my childhood hero, Randolph Scott. Yep."

Jake absently reached into his shirt pocket forgetting he didn't have cigarettes. He wiped a hand across his mouth. Cal offered Jake one of his cigarettes, Jake shook his head.

"This isn't getting us anywhere, is it, Cal?"

"Tough go but it's a marathon not a sprint."

Running out of time. He'd have to report back to Texas. He wanted this finished and now worried Gage's killers would walk and life would go on in Paradise as it had before, the guilty unpunished. It was a sickening realization.

"I leave they'll get away with this."

Cal sighed, leaned back in his chair, exhaled. "Jake, you could be right. Probably are. You know how these things go. I believe we have a decent case against Barb and Warner for assault and maybe we never know what happened with Gage. I don't know what you'll do with Vernon's murder."

Jake saying now, "That's unacceptable."

"But a possibility you may have to embrace."

"There is no one, except you and Buddy, who will look into this or care about it. Vernon's death is already in Kellogg's hands and he will never allow Pam to take the fall."

"You don't know she did it."

"I feel it."

"That's hardly grounds for an indictment let alone an arrest, and as an investigator you know better. You may have to give up on this unless you produce Haller, and you need to do that right now."

Jake thinking he could not leave Paradise without tying the killings together in some fashion. He didn't report, he was out with the Rangers.

"You're right. I'll bring in Haller."

"And he may still go down for killing Vernon. Turn him over and let it go."

Jake had an idea, but it must've shown on his face because Cal said, "What're you thinking about? Or do I want to know?"

***

Things moving faster now. Harper said something that kicked free a thing gnawing at Jake and it came to him in a revelatory flash. The strength of a father's thoughts.

Sheriff Robert Burnell, Gage's dad.

Gage's dad coming home every night with the weight of the sheriff's office on him, talking about his day at the dinner table. What had Gage heard during those years? Sheriff Burnell handing off to Doc Kellogg. All those files and investigations in sheriff's department now accessible to Kellogg. Kellogg would remember the disappearance of Frank and Caroline Yoder. He would remember the Yoder investigation.

Kellogg and Vernon Mitchell became close after Alex and Pam married. Kellogg knew what Burnell knew about the Yoders. Vernon could've told him that Christine McKee was really his daughter by Caroline Yoder. All these years Kellogg covering for Vernon. Kellogg winning re-election every time.

It was supposition. Occam's razor suggested that the simplest explanation was generally the truth. Despite the complexities the entire scenario may boil down to lust, petty jealousy, and the hidden, never talked about stress of life in a small community where ugly resentments percolated below the surface.

But, if Doc knew, did he say something to his daughter caused her to seek Christine McKee? Blackmail Vernon? Tommy telling him Alex was treated special and Tommy was mom's favorite, defending Tommy against Vernon's favoritism.

Incidents of seemingly little consequence had a way of festering and burning into the wounds of people's psyche.

Kellogg may know about Christine McKee. Pam did.

The question was, did Alex know?

Time to find out.

57

Jake called Alex at the Mitchell Chemical plant and offered to buy him a beer.

"I don't hang out with bastards."

"If you don't like what I tell you or find it interesting
I'll give you a free swing and I'll walk away."

"I'll be at Hank's in twenty minutes," Alex said, jumping on the offer, Jake figuring he liked the idea of getting
a free shot. Couldn't blame him. "And I'm thirsty."

Jake got to Hank's ahead of Alex and told Hank what
he had in mind.

"Are you gonna get in another fight in my place?" said
Hank. "You're as big a pain in the ass as the Mitchells."

"Whatever Alex drinks or eats," Jake said. "When he's
done, I want the glass or the flatware he uses."

"You think I give that stuff away?"

"I'll pay you. Name your price."

Hank shook his head. "There's something wrong with
you, no doubt about it. But I will be more than happy to
gouge you at retail prices plus a surcharge due the fact
they have memorial value."

"Whatever, Hank," Jake said.

Alex arrived, his face set in a scowl, his eyes red from
lack of sleep.

"Have a seat, Alex."

Alex jerked a chair from the table and sat down hard

not moving the chair back to the table.

"What the hell is this about?"

Jake saying now, "What're you drinking?"

"Beer. Sam Adam's."

Jake nodded at Hank who brought over a bottle of beer and a frosted mug. Alex ignored the glass and drank from the bottle. Hank frowned seeing a payday pass away.

Alex downed half the beer in one swallow, set the bottle down and said, "Well?"

"I need honesty here," Jake said.

Alex snorted, looking disgusted. "You need honesty. That's something, isn't it? There's no bottom to you, is there? You are the boldest motherfucker. Your audacity is staggering. You cheat on me with my wife and then ask for honesty."

"Wait. Your terminology is off. I didn't cheat on you. Your wife did. I was wrong and I'm sorry."

"You're sorry. I feel so much fucking better now. Who asked you to come back here and spread your shit? I cannot wait to punch you in the face."

Jake nodded. "Have you talked to Pam about the night of our encounter?"

"I did."

"How did she describe it?"

"Said you talked her into meeting you."

"Where?"

"Out on Puck road." Puck road was a rutted dirt and gravel road no longer in use except for the teens that used it for romantic trysts. "Said you came on to her and she resisted at first, but she was drunk."

"Nothing like that. She snuck into my place at three in the morning, stripped off and got on top of me. Had a key to my place. I didn't give it to her."

"You're lying."

"Want to see the DNA results?"

Alex looked confused and said, "DNA?"

"I have resources others don't. Got a match proves she was at my house. Not the first time she was there, either and not with me. You knew that already."

Alex deflated now, eyes closing briefly, rocking in his chair, nodding slowly. "Gage."

"Did you know about Haller and Tommy taking Gage's dog?"

Alex inhaled and let it out slowly. He stared glassy-eyed at the table, his face reflecting the realization his world was changed forever. His father murdered; his wife unfaithful. "Knew something when I saw them with the dog. Said they were playing a joke."

"You didn't stop them?"

"I was angry with Gage because of the thing with Pam. I hated him for it, I'll admit that, but I would never, well couldn't do that. Gage was a good employee and we were friends, hell, he's a fun guy, always kept things lively, but the thing with, well it was too much so I fired him. He didn't argue. He knew why."

Jake watched as Alex took another long drink, draining the bottle. Jake nodded at Hank who brought another bottle and set it down in front of Alex. Hank took the other bottle and rather than tossing it in the trash, set it behind the bar, looking at Jake afterwards. Good boy, Hank.

"We talked about Pam before," Jake said. "Right here two days ago. You were hammered. You remember any of that?"

"Bits and pieces."

"We both have had experiences with Pam Kellogg." Leaving out her married name for effect. "Neither of us has had an even road with her."

"All right. So?"

"We both have had occasion to regret that experience. And, we both have known her to manipulate, even lie to us."

Alex nodded, listening intently.

Jake saying, "Did you know she bailed out Haller?"

"She wouldn't do that. How do you know she did that? Wait, you know where Fat Boy is, don't you?"

Jake nodded. "I might."

Alex's shoulders sagged. "Why would she do that?"

"Not sure."

Awareness came across Alex's face. "You know, Tommy told me he didn't think Noah killed Dad."

"When did you talk to him?" asked Jake, worried now that the idiot didn't listen to his warning and Jake may have waited too long. This would speed up the countdown.

"He called an hour ago. Hadn't seen him since the funeral and didn't know where he'd gotten off to. I asked him why he thought Noah was innocent, but he wouldn't say."

Jake said nothing. Alex lost in thought.

"Take another drink," Jake said. "In fact, hey Hank, brink a couple of shots of bourbon. And bring me a beer."

Hank brought the beer and whiskey and sat it down on the table.

"What's this about?" Alex said.

Jake lifted the shot glass. "Take a drink, Alex."

Alex picked up the shot glass and threw it back and slammed the shot glass down hard enough Jake was surprised it didn't break. Alex said, "Well. What is it?"

"Did you kill Gage? Or have it done."

"No."

"Okay, but you'd say that regardless. Do you know who did?"

"No."

"I have something else and I don't want you to overreact until I verify it."

"Well, say it. What're you doing to me?"

Jake sipped at his beer, set it down, leaned forward, his arms on the table and said, "I tell you this, you tell no one, especially your wife."

Alex thought about it then nodded his head. "All right. You have my word."

"I think you have a sister, believe I can prove it, and Pam knows about her. So did your Dad."

58

Jake decided it was time to turn over Fat Boy Haller, let him plead his case.

Maybe stir the pot a little before going out to get him. Pam knows Haller's location. How long before she turns him to daddy? Or, if she busted a cap on Vernon, would Sheriff Daddy have Haller 'disappeared'?

Jake called Pam, told her to meet him in the football stadium parking lot. A bit dramatic but hoped the location would draw her. Pam saw herself as the homecoming queen who never turned in her tiara.

She arrived in her Cadillac, top up, the same vehicle he'd seen at the Mitchell lake place, where she'd set up Haller. They got out of their vehicles. Pam started to move close to him but Jake, leaning against the Lincoln, held up a hand to stop her.

"I had a talk with your husband. You didn't shoot him straight about the night you showed up at my place. You told him we met somewhere else but now he knows the truth."

Feigning hurt, Pam said, "I was afraid how he would react. Alex can be – "

"You've never been afraid of Alex or anyone else in your life. I understand why you would change the story but that's a problem for me."

"I care for you," she said, dropping down a notch below

'love'. "And that's the truth. You see it another way. Don't
you realize we could be together and have everything? I
have money put away. We'd have a life and you'd never
have to work again."

"I like working."

"So work. We can leave here. Go to Texas and build a
life together. Leave this place behind. I'm tired and bored
with it."

Leading her on was distasteful, even dishonorable but
if she was the killer? He said, "Can I think about it?"

She hesitated before answering, considering him,
her eyes hooded, thinking about what he said. Then she
smiled. Not a smile like 'for joy, he loves me' more like
hedging on her response. Be careful with this one. Keep
in mind Pam was a very insightful and cautious woman.
A woman who may have killed a man and shot at him.

She said, "Of course you can. How long?"

"I'm leaving in tomorrow. I'll give you an answer before then."

"What about little Harper?"

"She won't leave here. We both know that. Right now,"
he said, changing the subject to get her in the place he
wanted her. "I found Fat Boy Haller and I'm going to go
pick him up and turn him in. Your Dad won't have to
worry about him after that."

Her eyes shifted. "Why not just tell Dad and let him
handle it."

"Not in his jurisdiction and I want to do it. I want to
talk to Haller. He may know who killed Gage and that's
my main objective."

Let her think about that. Maybe force a reaction.

As he drove away, he watched Pam punch numbers in
her cell phone.

Better hurry Jake.

59

Jake set land speed records driving to the lake cabin. He called Haller on a number he had and told him that Pam may call and not to answer the phone and definitely do not do anything until he heard from Jake. He knew it was a possibility Pam would try to beat him there. She could also call Haller and tell him to leave the cabin because Jake was coming to turn him in.

The other possibility, a strong one, was that Pam would call Doc and tell him I knew where Haller was.

If she did, that would affirm a hidden agenda, even that she was framing Haller. If Doc showed up that would release the flying monkeys.

Jake found Haller at the cabin, packing up Gage's Dodge SUV.

"I gotta get outta here," Haller said.

"In a stolen vehicle? How far you think you'll get? Use your head. I'm still your only hope. Where's Tommy?"

"Took off. Said he was going ape shit sitting around. I'm the same. Let me go. You wouldn't tell anybody I'm runnin', wouldja?"

"The very second you start the vehicle. Give me the keys."

Haller looked at the Dodge thinking about it. "Pam said she'd make sure I didn't get convicted of the murder."

"You took her call. After everything I told you," Jake

said. "And that idiot, Tommy, called his brother. Maybe Pam can clear you but will hold it over your head for the rest of your life. You can stay out of jail, not because she says so. I can clear you of everything."

"So, what do we do?"

"I've got to take you in."

A panicked look. "You said that wouldn't work."

"I said wait until you heard from me. I've been working on it since you saw me, and I can prove you didn't shoot Vernon."

Jake told him about the shot trajectory.

"Pam?" Haller said.

"Unless you got someone better."

"I trusted her."

"You're not the first to make that mistake," Jake said.

"You give me to Doc he's going to make sure I get blamed instead of Pam."

"I'm not going to turn you to Doc. I'm going to turn you over to the Highway Patrol. Watch me do it. Give me the key."

Haller handed him the keys to the SUV and Jake called the number Trooper Ridley had given him. Ridley's reaction was not the one hoped for.

"You've got Haller," said Ridley. "Now you want us to come and get him, help you out, right?"

"Sheriff Kellogg could be burning up the asphalt to get here. He does that, Haller won't be able to testify. Haller will kill him."

"You may not believe this, but we actually have things to do besides run your errands. You need to think things through before you launch another one of your Jake Morgan, Texas Ranger, exploits."

"Just get here."

"Soon as I can," said Ridley.

Jake put down his cell phone and said, "The highway patrol will be here, and they'll take you into protective custody."

"That what you think?" Haller said, looking past Jake. Jake could hear the crunch of gravel under tires. Haller pointed at the sheriff's vehicle rolling down the road.

Pam had called Doc.

Show time.

Watching the men get out of the Paradise County Sheriff's SUV, Jake told Haller to get in the Lincoln; he'd take care of this.

"Sure, you will," Haller said, unconvinced. "Give me a gun."

Jake shook his head. "Do what I say. The highway patrol is on the way." But would they get there in time?

Doc Kellogg got out of his sheriff's unit. Steve Barb and Robby Warner were with him. Barb and Warner were armed. Jake could see weapons on hips. No doubt what was happening here. Wrong move, Doc.

"Well," Jake said. "What a nice surprise. The whole gang's here. Just getting ready to bring Haller in to you."

"We'll take him," said Kellogg. "You will turn him over now."

"No, Doc, don't believe I will. He willingly surrendered himself to my custody. He wants to tell his side of the story to the State Troopers. This is not your county. Appears we're on equal footing for a change. "That's how this is going to play out. I'm handing him to the state boys and you're going to allow it. Otherwise, you're complicit."

Barb and Steve walked towards Jake and Jake put up a hand like a crossing guard saying, "Keep back. Need to discuss the ground rules with the Sheriff. Why're you guys with him anyway? Don't see a badge."

"I deputized these men to assist me."

"Interesting choice. Recruiting from the bottom of the gene pool."

"Give him up, Morgan," said Kellogg.

"Don't think so," Jake said. "Way I figure, I get to decide how this goes."

"Get closer so I can hear you better," said Kellogg, taking a step. "Getting older."

Jake holding up a hand, again. "You can hear me fine. Keep your distance."

Barb moved a hand to his sidearm.

Jake pulled his weapon and said, "I see a weapon clear I'll kill that man, then the other two. Don't doubt it."

"What the hell arc you talking about?" The sheriff recognizing the change in Morgan's demeanor and voice. "You're threatening law enforcement officers? Believe I'm going to have to place you under arrest."

"Good luck with that. Wonder how you knew Haller was here? Bet I can guess who told you. No accounting a father's love. Barb, you and Warner are going down for killing Gage. I can prove it."

Nobody moving. Quiet in the air. Warner and Barb edgy. Doc considering his options.

"That fat sonuvabitch Haller," said Barb. "I should – "

"Shut up, Steve," said Kellogg. "Morgan, put your gun away and give us Haller. You walk away clean and that'll be the end of it. You have no choice."

"Believe I do. Fact you brought the idiots tells me Haller was right." Jake waved his weapon in the direction of Barb and Warner. "You boys get on the ground, face in the dirt."

Barb and Warner hesitated, confused by this turn of events. This wasn't the way Kellogg told them it would go. Kellogg shook his head and said, to Jake, "By the time the state boys get here it will look like Haller killed you and then he was killed trying to escape."

As Jake suspected.

"What if I don't die?" Jake's eyes fixed, cold now.

Sheriff Kellogg touched the brim of his hat, moving his free hand closer to his sidearm. Trying to be sneaky.

Jake pointed his weapon at Kellogg's face. "Don't do that, Doc."

Kellogg's hand stopped, then said, "You think you're so damned smart. But this time, you've gone too far. Steve, go get Haller," said Kellogg.

"Barb" Jake said. "You touch that car door, I'll shoot you."

"You'd shoot me in the back?"

"Walk backwards then and I won't."

"Dammit, Steve," said Kellogg. "Go get him. He's not going to shoot."

Barb's mouth working now. Unsure. "You go get him, Doc, you think he won't."

"There's three of us," said Robby Warner.

"You ever shoot anybody, Robby? Somebody looking at you? Not an easy thing to do. You'd better sit this one out." Still watching Kellogg. "Keep your hand away from your sidearm, Doc. Doesn't matter what happens you lose today, don't add to it."

Barb trying to work up the nerve, his pale freckles reddening, going for defiant now. "Handled guns all my life, motherfucker."

"Rabbits don't carry guns. I will for damned sure kill you. Won't even be my first. You? You may hit me, you may not. I won't miss. I believe you killed my best friend. How do you think I feel about that? You touch your weapon and it'll be your last day. That what you want?"

"I don't want to go to jail." Worked up now, chest heaving. Getting ready.

"You're scared thinking about it. Affects your aim."

"Who's going to believe you?" said Kellogg. "I'm the sheriff in pursuit of a fugitive. You were assisting the flight of a fugitive."

Jake's eyes were flat. "Trying to convince yourself this will work? It won't."

Impasse. Nothing else to do but go for all of it.

"Get on the ground," Jake said, "Face down, hands laced behind your neck."

"If we don't?"

Calmly, enunciating every word, Jake saying now, "Do exactly as I say when I say it, or I will kill every man does not."

Barb twitchy now, looking at Kellogg, Kellogg fixed on Jake. Was it going to happen?

Warner was shaken, holding his arms out in front of him. He tossed his weapon. "No, I'm out." He got down on his knees and lay down, his hands behind his neck.

"Last chance," Jake said, to Kellogg and Barb. "Two fingers, left hand, toss your weapons and kiss the planet."

Barb's mouth working, chewing his lip. Barb was almost vibrating with anticipation. It was going to happen. Sometimes you just knew.

"You got three seconds. One. Two...

Barb bellowed, cleared his weapon. Jake shot him twice in the chest. Barb never got off a shot. Jake quickly swung the SIG Sauer in Doc's direction who had his hand on his holster.

"What's it gonna be, Doc? Up to you."

Kellogg dropped his head, removed his sidearm with two fingers, and dropped it in the dirt.

"Step away," Jake said.

Doc did so, haltingly, his head shaking. Jake walked towards Doc, keeping the SIG Sauer levelled. He picked up Doc's pistol, walked over and relieved Robby Warner of his weapon.

"You killed Steve," said Warner.

"Probably," Jake said, kneeling to check Barb's vitals. Barb was still breathing but it was liquid and heavy. "He dealt it."

Jake cuffed Warner, checked Barb and then cuffed Kellogg using the sheriff's own bracelets. Jake called for an ambulance and then called the Highway Patrol dispatch. The dispatcher said there was a unit already en route.

Ridley was coming.

"She's my daughter," said Kellogg, looking for redemption. Had to be a hard thing. "Anyone would've done the same."

"Better Pam hadn't called you. All you would've had was an obstruction charge and maybe not even that."

It was as if the life had drained out of him. "I didn't want this. I had to do it. You have to understand. I had no choice."

"I know," Jake said, nodding. "Doesn't make it right, Doc."

60

Fred Ridley and another trooper showed and took Doc and Warner into custody. An ambulance came with them for Barb.

"You'll have to come with us, make a statement," said Ridley. "You ever go out and not shoot people?"

Jake thanked them, following them to troop HQ and called Cal Bannister to explain the situation.

"Damn, son. What do you need from our end?"

"Give a heads-up to Buddy, Deputy Bailey or anyone trustworthy at the sheriff's department and tell them to keep it on the QT. Kellogg is in custody but I don't want Pam to know about any of this until I talk to her."

"You sure about that?"

"Yes. I'll be tied up with the patrol for some time and need radio silence for as long as possible."

"All right. Buddy may be the best choice to clue in Bailey since she trusts him. What do you have in mind?"

"Tie Pam to Vernon's homicide."

"That's a tough one. The only thing you have is the bullet trajectory."

"Maybe I'll get a confession."

"And maybe I'll run for governor. You're working without a net. I think you like it that way."

***

It was early evening before the patrol investigator, a sharp guy in a suit named Reynolds, released Jake. It helped that both Fat Boy Haller and Robby Warner confirmed Jake's report.

Leaving troop HQ Jake checked with Cal again and asked if anything had leaked yet.

"Pretty quiet here," Cal said. "So far, so good."

That done Jake called Pam Kellogg Mitchell.

"Yes, Jake," Pam said, answering the phone call.

"I've made my decision. About us," Jake said. "Listen, the Highway Patrol has Haller and your dad is with him at Troop A." Not really a lie but not totally true. "Something's come up. Concerns you." Letting it hang in the air.

"What?"

"Well, Haller made accusations against you to the highway patrol. I don't think they believe him but he's saying you framed him, and they will have to follow up. We need to put our heads together and come up with a plan. Meet me at the football stadium again."

"Okay. I'll be there."

"Thirty minutes."

"Okay."

He could almost hear the spinning reel sing its happy song.

***

Jake met Pam once again at the high school football stadium parking lot. They got out of their cars, slipping a compact voice recorder Cal gave him into an inner part of his jacket. He walked Pam to the far end of the West bleachers. Pam was carrying a large handbag. Jake noticed the sagging weight in the bag.

"I believe," Jake said. "We can start with you handing me the handgun in your bag."

She shook her head, exasperated. "It never stops with you, does it?"

"At least put the bag out of reach."

She hesitated before setting the bag on a low bleacher seat. "You said you had information about Noah trying to blame me for something."

Noting she hadn't mentioned her father. She either didn't know the truth or believed Jake's scenario.

"First, let's talk about our future."

Pam crossed her arms and screwed up the corner of her mouth. "I'm listening."

Jake had been formulating his monologue on the drive. Pam was sharp and was not going to fall for an obvious trap. She was here and either she had affection for him, or she wanted to know what was being said; Jake didn't know.

"I'm sorry for the way I've treated you," Jake said. "You're right, I was hurt by the way you dumped me years ago. It stung more than I cared to admit." This was tougher to do than he thought. He wasn't an actor, and her standing there in front of him he still felt the tug of their conflicted memories and the allure that was uniquely Pam Kellogg.

Her face softened. "We both made mistakes, Jake."

Maybe they really could wipe the slate clean.

"Anyway, I'm leaving and wanted you to forgive me and you can go with me."

"What if choose to stay?" she said.

"Then I'll ask to part friends. I want to retain the memories, good memories, of our time together without having to know I damaged you since I returned."

She searched his face. Her arms uncrossed and she tilted her head to one side considering him. She was beautiful. She reached out and touched his arm. "Oh, Jake, it could be so different." Pulling him in. He could feel his throat drying up, his resolve inching away.

She was good, really good. He needed to keep in mind that Pam Kellogg was the Master of social manipulation, could play any part. Remembering that she had shot and killed her father-in-law in cold blood then set up another man to take the weight. Still, a part of him wanted to believe she was sincere, and perhaps she was sincere.

Another possibility was she knew what had transpired with her father at the cabin and was playing Jake.

"Where do we go from here?" she said.

"I go back to Texas. You can go with me or won't see me again. But at least we'll be friends."

"Always."

Jake sighed and said, "One last kiss before we part?"

Eyeing him warily, she said, "Okay."

Jake kissed her, long and deep. Her body relaxed and then pressed against his, giving the kiss back, her lips warm, inviting. He was faltering, felt the stirring of desire. They broke the embrace and Jake smiled at her.

Pam saying now, "What is this about Noah?"

Good. Getting to it. Her broaching the subject was a key.

"I found Haller and turned him over to your Dad. Doc gave me some information I didn't have before. What I can piece together is Haller has been trying to frame you for Vernon's homicide."

"How? He did it."

Bailed Haller out, proclaimed Haller was innocent but ready to quickly assert Haller was the killer, thought Jake. Who was she? Always Pam Kellogg like Leo the Lion said, always the girl-most-likely, the girl who could get away with it.

"Here's the way I understand it," Jake said, looking around as if searching for anyone listening. "Haller's story is you sent him to do a chore, but he didn't go and saw you cross the street with a gun."

"What?" That got her attention and Pam lost her usual unruffled demeanor for a brief moment.

"I interviewed Haller with his attorney present before he skipped, and he mentioned that. I didn't believe him at the time, but the troopers might. I'm afraid the accusations will muddy the waters. Together we can blunt him. I have a decent rapport with the trooper took him into custody. He'll listen to me. But, for your part, Pam, you have to be honest with me. One hundred percent. It's the only way I can protect you."

He could feel her retreating from him. The wall between them back up again. Pam would be tough to break down.

"I know," Jake said, holding up a hand his index finger up. "Hold on. You have no reason to trust me. I broke that trust. I don't like Vernon. I think he had something to do with Dad's death which I'll never be able to prove, and probably had Gage killed. I'm happy the son-of-a-bitch is dead. Don't even want anything else for Christmas. I hope Haller gets away with it and if you had done it, I would do whatever I could to get you free of it."

"What could you do?"

"I have experience as an investigator and could steer things away from you."

She was pondering things again. "What about your mention of that person, McKee?"

"That's what I need to tell you and need honesty from you. Christine McKee is Alex's half-sister. Did you know about that?"

"No."

"Pam?" He leaned into her. "This is what I'm talking about."

She chewed the corner of her lip. "Okay. I knew."

"Does Alex?"

"No."

"Did Vernon know you had this information?"

"I told him."

"What was his reaction?"

"He denied it and was angry. Made threats but knew he couldn't act upon them. Vernon is a controlling bully. Look at his boys. Vernon doesn't like anyone having something over him."

Good stuff so far. Wondering how hard he could push this line.

"Well, he's dead and we don't want Haller accusing you."

"I'll testify against him," Pam said. "I'll say Vernon was going to fire him. That I had just warned Noah about that and Noah said he was going to talk to Vernon about that. He was angry but I told him not to talk to Vernon while he was worked up, but I don't think he listened. Usually, Noah listens to me."

Yes, he does, Pam. He surely does.

"There's a couple of other things Haller is telling that are problematic for us."

"What things? There's nothing he can say. Dad isn't going to listen to that, anyway."

"Well, here's the problem. There is a conflict of interest, since he's your father. Your dad tried to make them understand Haller was blowing smoke, but the state guys said they had to pursue it."

"That fat ass is a liar. He shot at you once."

"Really?" Jake said, giving it a subtle 'you're-kidding' emphasis. "When?"

"Apparently you were out hunting, and he and Tommy followed you. Tommy stole your truck and did something to it. I heard them laughing about it."

"Figured it was Tommy."

So far, what he had was 'he said, she said' hearsay and none of it would stand up in court. But, as an investigator, the more information he could glean from a possible killer the better for the end result.

Go with the rest of it. Do it now.

"Pam," Jake said. "Listen to me now. This is important. I don't like telling you this, but... " He reached out and held her arms in his hands, softly. "It appears they're going to take you into custody."

"Why?"

"First as a material witness and if they're not satisfied, they will charge you with Vernon's homicide." Knowing they might bring her in as a witness, but a charge of homicide was wishful thinking. "They're giving credence to Haller's story. Apparently, there is more forensic evidence that you did it and not Haller. That's why I called before they could find you." Throw it in now. "The bullet trajectory suggests Haller couldn't have been the shooter. It's why I wanted to meet you besides getting things straight between us. You have to trust me."

Pam, usually unflappable, chewed a thumb nail and then rubbed the back of her neck with both hands. "All right."

"Between the three of us, you, me and Doc, we can blunt this. Otherwise this could go south. We need the facts. All of them so we can bend them the way we want. They're going to say they can prove a case against you. If you shot Vernon, I need to know that."

"What?"

"If you shot Vernon, I need to know how you did it so we can cover your tracks."

"I didn't shoot Vernon."

"Pam," Jake said. "Sorry, I've seen the forensics and know you did. They've got you. Maybe you can talk your way out of it, but they'll still run you around. You have to trust me."

She turned away. Jake hoping the microphone would pick up their voices. Had to be now. The next few moments would be crucial. Would she trust him? Would she stonewall him? She was at an impasse. So was Jake.

She turned back in his direction. "How do I know you're being honest with me?"

"Wouldn't blame you if you didn't. But it's time to trust someone and I'm your best bet. Otherwise they're coming for you. If you shot him, I don't care. Going forward we have to trust each other."

Pam looked away, considering the horizon past the football field. Several moments passed. Jake could see the tension in her jawline as she thought. Finally, she traced a lock of hair from her face and said, "Jake, do you love me?"

This wasn't going to sound good on tape.

He didn't want to answer. He didn't want to lie, and he didn't want to undo his investigation. If he lied where did that leave him on the integrity scale? How far was he willing to go as a law enforcement investigator in order to trap his prey? Was professing love, knowing it was a lie and the damage it would do, acceptable.

He thought about it. So, she killed Vernon. He was

truthful when he said he didn't like the man. She didn't kill Gage but perhaps supplied the spark that led to his murder. Still, what was to be gained from destroying this woman, a woman he once loved? More specifically, he had loved a girl named Pam Kellogg, that girl long gone and evolving into the woman in front of him. They were both changed and was a chasm with no bridge strong enough to span that time, their differences. He was a cop and he had responsibilities, taken an oath in front of witnesses, to uphold the law.

"I think I can, again," he said, settling on that compromise. "We can try."

She set her perfect teeth in a straight line. "Okay. Yes," she said. "I shot him. I shot the bastard. He was going to cut me out of the business if I told Alex about his sister."

"Why'd you have to shoot him? Sounds like you had him by the short hairs."

"Threatened me. Offered me a severance package. Told me to divorce Alex and leave town. If I stayed married to Alex, I'd never see another cent. Jake, I made the Mitchell Empire. Without me they wouldn't have what they've accumulated. It ticked me off. He said I couldn't prove anything about the sister, and it had already been tried and that person was gone."

"Gage."

She nodded, which wasn't going to be heard on the cell phone recorder.

"So, what do we do?" she asked.

"Nothing right now," Jake said. "Wish you hadn't dropped the weapon at the scene."

"No problem. I had Noah shoot it before I used it. His fingerprints are on it."

"Smart girl. Pack your things and be ready to go once we get you clear of this. That is if you want to."

He kissed her again and she gave herself to him. He felt the same stirring he had always felt with her. He broke the embrace and hugged her to him. A wave of conflicting emotions broke over him. He felt the urgency of her spinning in his head and the ignominy of his imminent betrayal.

"We shouldn't be seen together anymore until this is over," he said. "Leave here in different directions. Don't let Alex know about this."

They walked back to their vehicles and he kissed her again. He still enjoyed kissing her. Damn, he still liked it, half wishing things could be different.

She turned and smiled at him as she opened her car door before driving away.

For the last time. No more of what they once had, and he felt it in the pit of his stomach but knowing it was nostalgia punching away.

Jake clicked off the recorder, rewound it and listened. It was good. He had her on tape confessing to the murder of Vernon Mitchell.

He felt no joy about it.

Alex was right. You really are a bastard, Morgan.

61

Pam learned of Jake's subterfuge the hard way.

Deputy Sheriff Bailey and Trooper Ridley showed at the bank the next morning with a warrant for her arrest, Jake with them. It would not be fun, but he had to see it through.

By this time Pam had heard her father had been arrested, realizing Jake had conned her into a confession.

Pam stood at her desk as the trio entered her office. All the certificates and photos of movers and shakers stared at her from the wall. Her assistant Naomi was in shock.

"Pam Mitchell, you're under arrest," said Ridley. "For the homicide of Vernon Mitchell. You have the right to remain silent..."

Pam heard the rest of the Miranda warning in a fog of shock.

"Tommy raped me," Pam said, as Bailey cuffed her. "You know that. I've done nothing. This is a joke. I'll walk away from this. Naomi, call Langley. Get him here. Now."

Never gives up, thought Jake. Still commanding even now, with the walls crashing down. One hell of a woman. What a waste.

"You'll get the chance to tell your side," said Ridley.

"Jake," Pam said. "Help me, please."

"Sorry," Jake said, his face hard. "Can't. Won't."

Realization in her face now. "How...how can you let this happen? I thought you cared for me?"

"I cared about Gage. You should have and we wouldn't be here."

Her face a mask of fury now, she spat at him, the spittle striking him on the side of his neck. "Jake Morgan, you total bastard. You fucking snake. You played me. You're scum. I wish I'd never met you."

"Really got a way with women, Tex," said Ridley.

"I guess."

Ridley and Bailey escorted her out in full view of her employees.

Jake wiped the saliva from his neck. He dropped his head and followed them out the door. It was a long walk for such a short distance.

***

Doc Kellogg was indicted for obstruction of justice. Steve Barb was in critical condition at County Memorial.

Robby Warner and his court appointed attorney sat in a large room at the courthouse with Jake, Chief Cal Bannister, Prosecutor Darcy Hillman and Highway Patrol Lt. Sam Browne. Warner sought a plea deal proposed by his attorney to turn state's evidence.

"Mister Warner," said P.A. Hillman. "For me to accept a plea deal I will require a full and truthful allocution."

"What is allocution?"

"You tell everything you know without holding back. You talk now and I believe what you say, or we proceed with the full homicide indictment and I'll go for all of it. Life without parole."

"What are you offering if my client allocutes to your satisfaction?" asked Warner's attorney, a prematurely balding thirtyish man, young but effective. He had maneuvered Warner into a good position not afforded Kellogg and Barb.

"Fifteen to twenty-five with possibility of parole after five," said PA Hillman. "Otherwise, we go for all of it."

Warner's attorney nodded at Warner. "Take it. She's being more than fair."

Warner shared evidence at warp speed. Telling them Steve Barb had lost it at the elevator over Hanna Stanislaus and wouldn't stop even after he, Gage, was unconscious.

"We thought he was dead, so we called Vernon and he said to load him up in Burnell's car and take him out to the old bridge on HH."

"Why call Mister Mitchell?" asked Hillman.

"Vernon was happy he was dead. Been telling us to do it. Steve just went crazy and Mitchell told us how to take care of it, said he'd make sure Tommy and Fat Boy didn't talk."

Vernon hadn't counted on Pam throwing a wrench in his plans.

"Did Vernon meet you at the bridge?" asked Ridley.

"Yes."

"What about Alex?"

"Alex didn't know."

"Tommy?" Jake said.

Warner chewed on that for a moment before saying, "No. He knew what was going down but he didn't help us move Gage. He and Fat Boy just took off. If only that asshole hadn't taken Gage's dog this would never have happened."

"Who drowned Burnell?" asked Lt. Browne.

"Steve did that. We were just going to leave Burnell and make it look like an accident, thinking he was dead, I mean, man, he wasn't moving when we took him out there, but he got out of the car. Barb grabbed him and drug him down to the water and Steve held his head under until he stopped moving. Gage was too beat up to fight it."

"Why did Gage have to be killed?" asked Lt. Browne.

"Vernon didn't say. We figured it was because Burnell was fucking his son's wife."

Jake saying now, "Did this have anything to do with the disappearance of the Yoders forty years ago?"

Warner confused. "Don't know nothing about that." Warner took a deep breath.

"Why did you go along with this?"

"Years ago," said Warner. "Right after high school, Steve and I got froggy and robbed a bank in a little town in Arkansas. That bank's gone now. We didn't get much but nobody came after us. Two young guys liquored up doing stupid things. Vernon learned about it and hired us on. Vernon likes to have shit on people. He kept that over our heads, so we had to do what he said. I never liked it. Steve? Steve liked being a shit kicker. Thought it made him a tough guy. He was my buddy, but man got me in so much shit and now he's dead. Vernon told us Burnell learned about the bank job and was going to the FBI."

"You realize he was lying about that?" Jake said.

"Well," said Warner, shrugging, "now I do."

Pam lawyered up and stuck to her story that Haller killed Vernon and was attempting to frame her. Lawyer Langley disputed the taped confession as 'coerced' and perhaps edited. She tried to drag Jake into it claiming he was trying to cover up his "aiding and abetting a fugitive" as her attorney, Langley, phrased it and only taped her confession at the stadium to clear himself. No matter the odds or the situation, Pam Kellogg never stopped fighting.

Alex grudgingly assisted the investigation, his world irrevocably altered and the woman he loved on trial. He moved like a zombie through the proceedings. His testimony affirmed Vernon suspected Pam of cheating on Alex with Gage and again with Jake and was planning on cutting Pam out of the family business.

County Prosecutor, Darcy Hillman, indicted her cousin, Pam Mitchell, then recused herself and changed the venue to a different county.

Due the turmoil at the county sheriff's office, the judge remanded Pam to Paradise Police lock-up in lieu of bail set at $500,000 prior to transfer to another county.

Jake was drained of emotion. It was finally over, and Jake would make it back to Texas in time to resume his duties. It would be good to have a return to normal.

Jake was wrong again.

62

Jake was back home, suitcase packed and lit a cigarette as he watched the Cadillac drive up his lane, slow to a stop.

Looks like Pam made bail. Jake's cell phone ringing earlier but he hadn't answered because he wanted to sleep longer. Looking at the phone's memory he saw it was Buddy. Probably warning him.

Pam exited the vehicle. She was wearing tennis shoes and Capri's, a duster coat over that, like the old cowboys wore on a cattle drive against the chill evening air.

He took a drag on the first cigarette he'd had in days. The autumn sun was low in the western sky, the trees casting long shadows across his lawn stretching toward where he sat, smoking and thinking. It crossed his mind this scenario was B-movie hokey.

She seemed different, flavored with something. Rage? Vengeance. Looking at him now, as if deciding something.

"Hello, Jake," she said, without warmth. "You always disappoint, Jake. You think of yourself as intelligent when you're only clever. You're just another asshole."

"There," Jake said, stepping off the porch. "Much better. A little honest hostility. I like it."

"You're one to talk about honesty. You betrayed me."

Another car burning up his lane. Alex Mitchell's car. Well, the gang's all here. Alex skidded to a stop.

First thing out of Alex's mouth?

"Did you come back for a farewell fuck, Pam?"

It never stops.

That's when the handgun, a nasty heavily blued revolver, appeared from Pam's duster coat. Heightened emotion setting things on fire. A domestic squabble had brought him here and ironically another would be his end.

A mourning dove moaned in the distance. Haunting.

"You killed dad," Alex said. His chest heaving with anger. "Then you run back here to your boyfriend."

"None of that here, Alex," Jake said. "I think she's here for a different reason. Pretty fatalistic. No way out of this, Pam."

"Open your eyes, Alex," she said. "He's the one set me up. Fat Boy killed your father and this guy framed me out of jealousy for what we have. You know it's true, darling. We've had some bad moments, but we can recover."

Jake watching her work her magic on Alex, a man hopelessly caught in her spell. Jake could see Alex wavering.

"Alex," Jake said. "Ask yourself who has reason to lie."

Alex looked at his wife.

Pam saying now. "Don't let him fool you, darling. He's still angry I dumped him years ago."

"Yeah," Jake said. "That's why she snuck into my house the night we had the scene at Hank's."

Pam raised the revolver, her hand shaking now. "He's a dirty lying bastard and I'll never forget what he done to me. To us."

She'd already killed one man. She had nothing to lose.

"Decide, Alex," she said. "Are you going to believe me or him? He tried to wreck our marriage." Working up the tears now remembering Alex saying she never cried. She pointed the gun at Jake. "Tell him you framed me."

Jake shaking his head. "No. You killed Vernon. That is the truth."

Pam snapped back the hammer on the big revolver.

He looked at the dark hole at the end of the revolver. Rush her, make her miss. Her hand was shaking and that would help.

"Put it down," said a voice sounding like Alex only from somewhere deep inside of him.

Jake looked at Alex, now with a weapon in his hand. Everybody with a gun except him.

"Alex, what are you doing?" Pam said.

"You killed Dad." His teeth gritted.

"Maybe I can help," Jake said. Calm things down. "Put away your weapons and everybody ease back a notch."

"Don't you point a gun at me, Alex," Pam said, meaning it. How many times had she given Alex a command and Alex complied? Not this time. Jake could see it. Jake thinking the best way to get to her.

"Alex, don't listen to this asshole. He wants me to leave you and go back to Texas with him."

Quiet for a moment as Alex looked at his wife. "I knew you were fucking Burnell. I can't trust you. I won't. You followed Morgan to his car that day at Dad's," Alex said. His jaw was tight, and his eyes were heavy-lidded.

"Maybe you had Gage killed, Alex," she said. She was groping for an edge, anything. She was cornered and didn't like it. "You were jealous of him."

Alex closed his eyes and dropped his head. "You're not worth it. I wouldn't kill Gage for that."

"No," Jake said. "You wouldn't. I know you wouldn't."

"Put the gun down, Pam," said Alex. "I won't let you kill anyone else."

"Alex, darling," Pam said, in a soothing voice. "We can make this work. Fix things. We can be together. We both want that. You and me."

Alex was faltering. Jake set himself for his rush. Maybe she would only wound him before he tackled her. Once he knocked her off her feet, he could disarm her. Every time she looked at Alex, Jake moved closer.

Twenty feet between them now. He could do it. Maybe get lucky. Jake thinking he might die on his father's place after the old man had gone to all the trouble of getting it ready to turn over to him. A strange thing to come back home hoping for a little peace, a reconciliation with his past and then maybe dying where he grew up, gunned down by a woman who had once worn his high school ring on a chain around her neck. Stolen kisses behind corners, notes passed from her friends to him. Football nights and school dances. His high school sweetheart killing him.

Get ready. Feint and zigzag. Ignore the impact of the bullet.

"Goodbye, Jake," she said, her voice sounding as if in a dream, detached from reality.

Alex saying, his voice choked, "No."

Move. Now! Feint left then move right. Hitting a moving target with a handgun wasn't easy. Not like the movies. It took training to handle a handgun with accuracy. Running now, straight at her...adrenaline pumping in his temple.

He heard the loud report of a weapon. You never hear the one kills you. She missed.

Then he heard a second report and a cry of pain. A female cry. Everything in slow motion. Pam falling, her hair dancing, gun slipping from her hands. She hit the ground, bounced once and Jake saw the flower of blood on her shoulder.

Alex Mitchell shot her. Alex had saved his life. It had happened quickly but seemed longer. Alex still had the gun pointed at her.

Jake stayed ready watching Alex.

"You shot me, you prick," screamed Pam, in pain, lying on the ground. "You son of a bitch, you shot me."

Jake moved quickly to secure her weapon. She didn't reach for it as he picked it up. Her shoulder was shattered. She was crying in anguish and rage, like a wounded animal, Pam still dangerous.

Alex sagged and he dropped his weapon. His legs buckled and he dropped to his knees, head bowed.

Jake didn't know what to say.

"Hey, Alex," Jake said. He reached down to console the man.

Without looking up, Alex said, "Don't fucking touch me, Morgan."

Jake stopped. No one moved or spoke for several long moments.

Silence screamed in the autumn air. A cold burst of winter whistled down from the north.

A strange moan coming from Alex, and then:

"Why?" Alex said, looking at the ground. His shoulders began to tremble, and his voice cracked. "Why did you have to come back?"

63

Friday morning, Cal, Buddy and Jake drinking coffee at Paradise PD when Alex Mitchell walked in.

"Look at this," Buddy said to Jake, as Alex walked toward them, eyes set on Jake.

What now?

Alex walked closer. Alex was under a cloud of remorse and mourning his losses. Jake set down his coffee and waited.

Alex stopped close to Jake. Cal Bannister saying, "Careful, Alex."

Buddy stepped between Alex and Jake.

Alex held up a hand and said, "It's okay, Buddy. Alex working up to it, as if he had to free the words in his mouth before they suffocated him. Alex's face vacant, drained of emotion, looking at Jake, said. "I still love her."

"I know," Jake said, nodding at Alex. "Sorry about your dad, Alex. Sorry about all of this. None of your doing. Thank you for saving my life."

Alex started to speak, nodded in resignation, then turned and wordlessly walked back out the door.

After Alex left, Cal said, "Never cared much for him but I don't wish this on anyone."

Buddy said, "You think he'll be all right?"

Jake shook his head, then said, "He won't be all right for a long time now. His entire world is shattered. Glad

I'm not him." Thinking, he could've been. "The good thing is Pam's defused."

Buddy gave him a funny look. "Defused?"

"She's dangerous. Gun or no gun."

"You still have feelings for her, don't you?"

Jake shrugged. Who knew? He didn't.

Buddy saying now, "Pam shot at you when you were hunting. Then tried to kill you. Jake, buddy, when you piss a woman off you get the job done."

"Life's seldom clean," Cal said.

***

Steve Barb died of his wound with no one to mourn his passing.

DNA evidence confirmed that Christine McKee was, in fact, the biological daughter of Vernon Mitchell. She could now put in a claim for her share of the Mitchell Empire. However, Alex Mitchell, satisfied by DNA evidence Christine was his half-sister and not wanting a wrongful death suit, was formulating a settlement through the Mitchell family attorneys. Alex stepping up despite all his troubles. Jake gaining a new respect for the man who had long been his rival.

Gage had discovered Christine's possible parentage and had foolishly let Pam know about it. Pam seduced him, gaining the information, playing Lady D'Winter to Gage's trusting nature. Gage's propensity for adventure proved to be his undoing.

Prosecuting Attorney Darcy Hillman granted a search warrant for two locations on Mitchell property, formerly Franklin Yoder property, where the excavation for a new airport was underway. Skeletal remains of two individuals were uncovered. The disappearance of Franklin and Caroline Yoder four decades earlier was no longer a mystery.

Buddy Johnson would now run unopposed for the office of sheriff.

"My first official act will be to run you out of town,"

Buddy told Jake.

"Maybe I won't go."

"That," Buddy said, "is my second greatest fear."

"What's your first?"

"I'm going to offer you a position in the department. Afraid you'll take it."

"Could make things interesting."

"For who?" Buddy said.

Jake thinking about that now.

Things were changing.

64

Still in Paradise County a week later.

Jake's "leave of absence" was over so he was burning vacation days, Captain Parmalee okayed the extended vacation in view of what had transpired. Jake was packing to return to Texas when Harper knocked on his door.

Jake glad to see her. She said she wanted, no "needed", to talk to him. They were awkward at first, neither knowing how to close the emotional space between them created by events. After a few moments Harper spoke.

"I'm glad you weren't hurt. Could've been though. You take too many chances. Frightens me. Looks like everything is going to turn out well," she said.

"Most of it," Jake said. He offered her a seat and she accepted, sitting in a kitchen chair. "It's done but there's not much satisfaction in it."

"Pam was fixated on you, Jake." She smiled coyly before saying, "Hard to understand." Having fun with him.

"Where are we, going forward?"

"We?" Challenge in her voice.

"You and me," Jake said.

She took a breath and set her chin. "I care about you," she said. She stopped and her eyes searched his.

He said nothing.

She said, "You live in a different world. Dad's world is like yours, but he's never shot anyone."

"No choice."

"That part I understand. How do you live with it, killing another person? Seems you're good at it."

"You want me to explain, make you understand." Knowing he couldn't clarify it.

She turned away shaking her head. He watched her shoulders rise and fall as she sighed. She turned back to him.

"I don't want you to go," she said. "Stay."

"My life's in Texas."

She stood, placed hands on her hips, defiant, now. "Is it?"

Something in her voice. Something making him contemplate possibilities. Hope.

"You're feeling bad about your choices," she said, brushing hair from his forehead. "What you did to Pam had to be done. Don't doubt that," she said. "You've done things you regret. Hard things you wish you could take back. You made mistakes and screwed up. Everybody does and you're not the best little boy ever graduated from Paradise High School."

"I'm at least in the top ten."

"Buddy said he offered you a position when he becomes sheriff. Take the job," she said. "I think Buddy and Dad are working out a deal where they share you. Work for both the county and the city."

"Why would I do that?"

"Because," she said, "you want to stay."

"And?"

She cupped his face in her hands and said, "Because you're crazy for me and I love you, stupid."

"I believe you."

Shaking her head now. Being cute. "Haven't learned a thing, have you?"

"A few things."

"Believe you have. Both of us."

He pulled her to him. She smelled of soap and fresh strawberries.

And hope.

Home at last, the fires out.

IF YOU LIKED THIS, CHECK OUT THE COLE SPRINGER TRILOGY

COLE SPRINGER HAS A MUSICAL SOUL, A QUICK WIT AND A CON-MAN'S MIND.

Ex-Secret Service agent, Cole Springer, has exchanged his badge for a piano and the high-altitude life of Aspen, Colorado but has not lost his appetite for danger.

Springer delights in playing button men and gangsters for personal gain and amusement. Springer, while an affable man, is double tough, hard to kill and has an ironic sense of humor. His girlfriend, determined CBI agent Tobi Ryder, doesn't know whether to love him, forget him, or arrest him for his escapades that skirt the edges of law…

The Cole Springer Trilogy includes: Springer's Gambit, Springer's Longshot and Springer's Fortune.

AVILABLE NOW ON AMAZON

About the Author

W.L. Ripley is the author of the critically acclaimed Wyatt Storme and Cole Springer mystery-thriller series' featuring modern knight errant Wyatt Storme, and Maverick ex-secret service agent, Cole Springer.

W.L. Ripley is a lifetime Missouri resident who has been a sportswriter, award-winning career educator and NCAA Div. II basketball coach. Ripley enjoys watching football, golf, and spending time with friends and family. He's a father, grandfather, and unapologetic Schnauzer lover.

In addition to the Storme & Springer series, Ripley has crafted two new series' heroes – Jake Morgan (Home Fires) and Conner McBride (McBride Doubles Down) for Wolfpack Publishing. Wolfpack is reissuing the Cole Springer series and Ripley is developing a new Cole Springer thriller for Wolfpack.

Find more great titles by W.L. Ripley and Wolfpack Publishing, here: https://wolfpackpublishing.com/w-l-ripley/

Made in United States
Orlando, FL
30 December 2023

41905052R00202